Praise for the novels of Brenda Jackson

"Jackson was the first African-American author to make both the *New York Times* and *USA TODAY* romance bestsellers list. And after twenty years in the business, books like *Love in Catalina Cove* prove that she's still a prevailing force in romance."
—*BookPage*

"The only flaw of this first-rate, satisfyingly sexy tale is that it ends."
—*Publishers Weekly*, starred review, on *Forged in Desire*

"[A] heartwarming romance."
—*Library Journal* on *Love in Catalina Cove*

"[Jackson's] signature is to create full-sensory romances that deliver on the heat, and she duly delivers.... Sure to make any reader swoon."
—*RT Book Reviews* on *Forged in Desire*

"Brenda Jackson is the queen of newly discovered love... If there's one thing Jackson knows how to do, it's how to pluck those heartstrings."
—*BookPage* on *Inseparable*

"Jackson's winning formula of heat and heart will draw readers in."
—*Publishers Weekly* on *The Wife He Needs*

T0356465

**Also available from Brenda Jackson
and Canary Street Press**

Catalina Cove

LOVE IN CATALINA COVE
FORGET ME NOT
FINDING HOME AGAIN
FOLLOW YOUR HEART
ONE CHRISTMAS WISH
THE HOUSE ON BLUEBERRY LANE
THE COTTAGE ON PELICAN BAY

The Protectors

FORGED IN DESIRE
SEIZED BY SEDUCTION
LOCKED IN TEMPTATION

The Grangers

A BROTHER'S HONOR
A MAN'S PROMISE
A LOVER'S VOW

For additional books by *New York Times* bestselling author
Brenda Jackson, visit her website, www.brendajackson.net.

BRENDA JACKSON

Spilling the Tea

CANARY STREET PRESS

If you purchased this book without a cover you should be aware that this book is stolen property. It was reported as "unsold and destroyed" to the publisher, and neither the author nor the publisher has received any payment for this "stripped book."

CANARY
STREET
PRESS™

Recycling programs
for this product may
not exist in your area.

ISBN-13: 978-1-335-92665-4

Spilling the Tea

Copyright © 2025 by Brenda Streater Jackson

All rights reserved. No part of this book may be used or reproduced in any manner whatsoever without written permission.

Without limiting the author's and publisher's exclusive rights, any unauthorized use of this publication to train generative artificial intelligence (AI) technologies is expressly prohibited.

This is a work of fiction. Names, characters, places and incidents are either the product of the author's imagination or are used fictitiously. Any resemblance to actual persons, living or dead, businesses, companies, events or locales is entirely coincidental.

For questions and comments about the quality of this book, please contact us at CustomerService@Harlequin.com.

TM is a trademark of Harlequin Enterprises ULC.

Canary Street Press
22 Adelaide St. West, 41st Floor
Toronto, Ontario M5H 4E3, Canada
CanaryStPress.com

Printed in U.S.A.

To my husband, Gerald Jackson Sr. All of me will forever love all of you.

To my sons, Gerald Jr. and Brandon.
Thanks for making your parents proud.

To all my readers. Thank you for motivating me to make this 150th book possible. You allow me to spread love by writing about it.

To my readers who will be cruising with me in May 2025
to celebrate this 150th book and my thirty years as an author.
I appreciate you, and I am ready for the party to begin.

Thanks to BET, Five Alive Films and Passionflix
for transforming my books into movies.

To my Cruise Support Team—Brenda Woodbury, Jackie Johnson,
Tammi Henry and Connie Moore. Thanks for all you do.

To my Promotion Team—Shay Bohannon, Brandon Terry,
Gerald Jackson Jr. and Brandon Jackson. I appreciate all of you.

To Brenda Woodbury, moderator of the Brenda Jackson Book Club
on Facebook. Thanks for motivating my readers and keeping them
informed about everything Brenda Jackson and her books.

To Harlequin/HarperCollins, who has been my publisher
for twenty-five years. Thanks for such a rewarding relationship.

To my classmates at William Raines Senior High School, class of 1971.
Some of you were reading my stories in middle school at Northwestern
Junior High, and I appreciate that you are still reading them now.

Love knows no limits to its endurance, no end to its trust,
no fading of its hope; it can outlast anything.
—*1 Corinthians* 13:7–8

Dear Reader,

It is hard to believe that thirty years after releasing my first book, *Tonight and Forever*, I would release my 150th book. That's an average of five books a year, and I've enjoyed every moment I wrote them. My first book introduced you to the Madaris family, and they became a favorite of my readers.

Over the years, the matriarch of the Madaris family, Mama Felicia Laverne, has taken on the role of matchmaker, determined to marry off those single men and women in the family. Namely, those great-grands who are the offspring of her first four sons. My 150th book, *Spilling the Tea*, is about the unlikely romance between Chance Madaris and Zoey Pritchard. Zoey arrives in Houston to learn about her family history, only to discover that her family, the Satterfields, were once sworn enemies of the Madarises.

I hope you enjoy reading *Spilling the Tea*, where you will learn about those Madaris secrets that have never been told. Mama Felicia Laverne is finally telling it all to help Zoey, who needs to learn about her ancestral past before she can move forward.

I hope this is one novel you will add to your Madaris Family and Friends series collection.

All the best,

Brenda Jackson

THE MADARIS FRIENDS

Maurice and Stella Grant
|
Trevor (Corinthians)⑥,
Regina (Mitch)⑪

Angelique Hamilton Chenault
|
Sterling Hamilton (Colby)⑤,
Nicholas Chenault (Shayla)⑨

Kyle Garwood (Kimara)③

DeAngelo Di Meglio
(Peyton)⑲

Ashton Sinclair   Drake Warren   Trent Jordache   Nedwyn Lansing   Sheikh Rasheed Valdemon
(Netherland)⑩   (Tori)⑫   (Brenna)⑨   (Diana)⑭   (Johari)⑯

KEY:
( ) — denotes a spouse
◯ and number — denotes title of book for that couple's story

① Tonight and Forever
② Whispered Promises
③ Cupid's Bow
④ Eternally Yours
⑤ One Special Moment
⑥ Fire and Desire
⑦ Truly Everlasting

⑧ Secret Love
⑨ True Love
⑩ Surrender
⑪ Strictly Business
⑫ The Midnight Hour
⑬ Unfinished Business
⑭ Slow Burn

⑮ Taste of Passion
⑯ Seduced by a Stranger
⑰ Sensual Confessions
⑱ Inseparable
⑲ Courting Justice

THE MADARIS FAMILY

Milton Madaris, Sr. and Felicia Laverne Lee Madaris

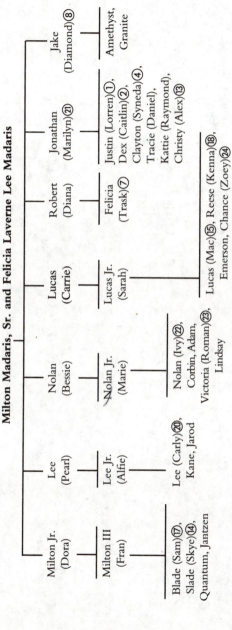

KEY:
( ) — denotes a spouse
u and number — denotes title of book for that couple's story

① Tonight and Forever
② Whispered Promises
③ Cupid's Bow
④ Eternally Yours
⑤ One Special Moment
⑥ Fire and Desire
⑦ Truly Everlasting

⑧ Secret Love
⑨ True Love
⑩ Surrender
⑪ Strictly Business
⑫ The Midnight Hour
⑬ Unfinished Business
⑭ Slow Burn

⑮ Taste of Passion
⑯ Seduced by a Stranger
⑰ Sensual Confessions
⑱ Inseparable
⑲ Courting Justice
⑳ A Madaris Bride for Christmas
㉑ A Very Merry Romance

㉒ Best Laid Plans
㉓ Follow Your Heart
㉔ Spilling the Tea

Prologue

"Chance, are you listening to me?"

Chancellor Madaris tilted his Stetson back off his face. His cousin Corbin had been pacing the living room floor and rambling since arriving nearly thirty minutes ago. Initially, Chance had been listening, but his mind had begun drifting when he remembered all the chores he needed to do that day. When you owned a working ranch, every daylight hour counted, and May was one of his busiest months. When he'd been summoned from the barn, he was told his cousin wanted to see him and said it was urgent. Chance had stopped everything and quickly walked to the ranch house.

His grandfather, Lucas, and Corbin's grandfather, Nolan, were brothers. There had been seven Madaris brothers in all. Milton Jr., Lee, Nolan, Lucas, Robert, Jonathan, and Jacob, who everybody called Jake. All were alive except for Robert, who'd been killed in the Vietnam War. With seven Madaris brothers, there were plenty of cousins to go around, some of whom had been born within days or months of each other. It always amused Chance how the four oldest Madaris brothers made sure they'd had sons named after them, and each of those sons had done the very same thing.

His great-grandmother, Felicia Laverne Madaris, the matriarch of the family, whom they fondly called Mama Laverne, said it seemed that, according to the ages of her great-grands, they formed into groups and ran together around Houston in wolf packs. Her analogy wasn't far from the truth.

And speaking of Mama Laverne, Chance noticed her name being mentioned more than once during Corbin's ramblings, and he could imagine why. Their ninety-something-year-old great-grandmother had stated countless times that she was making it her life's mission to marry off the first sixteen of her great-grands before she took her last breath.

In keeping with that goal, she made a list of all their names, recorded them by age, and was determined to find them suitable spouses. So far, she had a perfect record. Although the males had fought her manipulations tooth and nail, by the time they'd reached the altar, they had been over-the-top in love with the women chosen for them. Chance had to give it to the old gal. She was an ace when it came to matchmaking.

To know Felicia Laverne Madaris was to love her. Her family certainly did, although he would admit there were times you'd want to strangle her. Yet no one would ever harm a single hair on her head. She was too precious to all of them. She was why all seven of her sons had grown up to become God-fearing men…although he'd heard the oldest four had been a bunch of "hell raisers" before settling down, getting married, and starting a family. He figured by then it had been drilled into them, just like they'd drilled it into their offspring, that a Madaris man was expected to keep the family motto of protect, provide, and prosper. Chance knew that to his great-grandmother, to prosper also meant to produce. Specifically, to assure there were plenty of future generations of Madarises. Although that might be the case, he also knew there was never any pressure placed on anyone in the family who didn't agree with her way of thinking.

After losing their great-grandfather, Milton Sr., Chance knew that Mama Laverne was the glue that had held the Madaris family together. She was the backbone of the family, and the woman had a heart of gold. She thought of others before thinking of herself…maybe too much at times. As far as he was concerned, she was the epitome of a strong woman.

"What were you saying about Mama Laverne?" he asked, refusing to admit he had allowed his mind to wander.

Corbin, two years older than Chance's thirty-three years, rubbed a frustrated hand down his face before saying, "It's about that damn hit list of hers. Rumor has it that she will pair me up with Cheryl Carlyle. Can you imagine such a thing?"

Chance leaned back in his chair, stretched his long legs out in front of him, and crossed his booted ankles. Cheryl Carlyle was a looker; there was no denying that. However, he recalled hearing that last year, her father had caught her taking part in a ménage à trois with two ranch hands.

"No, I can't imagine it, and you shouldn't either, Corbin. Don't be another Victoria." Victoria was Corbin's sister and the first girl born in their generation.

Corbin frowned. "What's that supposed to mean?"

Chance responded, "Need I remind you that Victoria assumed Mama Laverne had picked Tanner Jamison for her when that wasn't the case?"

"But I heard Cheryl's father has been privately hanging out after church to meet with Mama Laverne. I bet those meetings are about me," Corbin said vehemently.

"I believe you're way off the mark."

"You think so?" Corbin asked, looking hopeful and putting an end to his pacing to sit down on the sofa.

"Yes. I'm pretty sure I'm right." The one thing Chance knew about his great-grandmother was that she held the Madaris family's reputation as sacred. That meant she would never add anyone to the family who might, in her eyes, one day disgrace it. That would eliminate Cheryl Carlyle. In addition to having an ear for any gossip spread, Mama Laverne read the newspaper daily and was fully aware whenever the Madaris name appeared in print.

Unfortunately, there had been times when not only would a Madaris's name appear in print, but their face as well. Some of his Madaris cousins had been known as notorious womanizers, and the newspaper's social column enjoyed sharing details of their exploits.

"Besides, Corbin, have you forgotten that Mama Laverne modified her list to place those four Bannister brothers ahead of you? Giving you a pass once again."

Everyone knew their great-grandmother's list was being worked with a well-measured timeline. After Nolan had married, Corbin should have been next on the list. However, Mama Laverne had skipped over Corbin and a few of her male great-grands to marry off Victoria, who'd been much younger than all of them. Luckily for Corbin, Mama Laverne had modified the list once again.

The four Bannister brothers they were referring to were Wyatt, Camden, and the twins—Brenton and Branson. Since they were best friends to several of her great-grandsons and were first cousins to six of her grandchildren, she'd had no qualms about adding them to her list.

Corbin's features widened with a grin after being reminded of the reprieve he'd gotten yet again. "Yes, that is true."

"Finding those Bannisters suitable wives might take some time," Chance said. "They deliberately stopped dating to protest what she'd done." No one wanted to fall victim to his great-grandmother's matchmaking schemes.

"Crap, I haven't gone that far," Corbin said. "But I do ask questions first."

Chance lifted his brow. "What sort of questions?"

A smile spread across Corbin's lips. "I want to know if they've ever met Mama Laverne. Who are their parents and grandparents? What schools did those family members attend, and did any attend church summer camps as teens, or do they attend church conventions now? I also want to know if their relatives have gone on cruises out of Galveston within the last twenty years."

Chance shook his head. He figured the latter question had been added because one of his granduncles had been taking Mama Laverne on a three-week cruise annually for the past twenty years. He didn't want to think how many people with eligible daughters, sons, or grandchildren she might have met.

"I've even hired Alex to do background checks on a few of my dates."

Alex Maxwell was married to their cousin Christy and was a well-known private investigator. Chance rolled his eyes. "You're kidding, right?"

"No, I'm not kidding."

Chance stared at his cousin in disbelief. "Do you feel such a thing is necessary?"

Corbin leaned forward in his seat. "Yes, I do. And as far as I'm concerned, you shouldn't have an opinion about it since your name is far down on that blasted list. Quantum's and Kane's names appear on the hit list before yours."

That information about his cousins surprised Chance. "Why would you think that when I'm older than they are?"

"Because you have issues."

There was no comeback he could make because Corbin was right. Chance did have issues. His family members knew he wasn't the easiest person to get along with, and they also knew why.

He joined the military right out of high school with the career goal of being an army ranger. After ten years as a ranger, he returned home after an injury in Iraq left him in a wheelchair with a medical prognosis that he would never walk again.

To make matters worse, the woman he'd loved and planned to marry, Ravena Boyle, broke off their engagement, refusing to be tied down to someone she considered half a man. She had moved from Houston to Nashville and, within less than a year, had married someone else. From what he'd heard, that marriage didn't last long, and she'd gotten a divorce less than two years later.

Her rejection had made him wallow in self-pity, the one thing his great-grandmother wouldn't tolerate when it came to a Madaris. To this day, Chance credited Mama Laverne with giving him the will to live again. She had refused to let him give up on life and gave him the determination to prove Ravena wrong. He wasn't half a man but a whole man.

He recalled those days. They hadn't been easy, and some had been extremely difficult, both physically and emotionally. His great-grandmother had been worse than any drill sergeant he'd encountered, but he had persevered, and she had proved the military doctors wrong. In less than two years, he was out of the wheelchair and back riding a horse again.

Although he had improved physically, mentally was a different matter. The once fun-loving, life-of-the-party guy had become antisocial, a loner, a man who preferred keeping to himself. That was the one thing his great-grandmother hadn't been able to do: make him look at life and love the same way. He was not the same man who'd left home for the military at seventeen and doubted he would ever be that person again. He had seen too much, done too much, and felt too much. As far as he was concerned, heartbreak had been the worst.

His family had been there for him in his darkest times. They were all he needed then and all he needed now. Upon returning home and knowing his career in the military was over, he'd turned to his other love: ranching. He would never forget that day he received a call from his uncle Jake to let him know that a homestead within a few miles of his uncle Jake's Whispering Pines ranch had come up for sale.

Uncle Jake was a dedicated rancher, a highly successful businessman, and a great financial adviser. Over the years, he made many wise investments for the Madaris family. As a result, Chance was able to buy the two-hundred-acre ranch, which he'd named Teakwood Ridge, without a mortgage. That meant he owned his spread free and clear. Like his uncle Jake, Chance raised some of the best cattle in Texas.

As far as women were concerned, whenever he had physical urges that needed to be taken care of, he had no problem doing so. He wasn't into long-term affairs and only engaged in one-night stands. Nothing energized him more than a night of hot, mind-blowing, unemotional sex when needed. Hooking up with a woman who agreed with his terms had never proven difficult.

"I don't envy the woman Mama Laverne picks out for you, Chance."

Corbin's words cut into Chance's thoughts, and he couldn't help but chuckle since he didn't envy the woman either. If what Corbin suspected about his name being further down the list was true, he could see why Mama Laverne had placed it there. She knew the hurt, pain, and bitterness Ravena's rejection had caused him. She was also aware of his vow never to fall in love again.

"I'm not concerned about my placement on her list," Chance said.

His cousin shook his head. "When the time comes, just like Victoria, you'll meekly take whomever she selects for you."

It was a statement, not a question, so Chance addressed it. "And I have no problem doing so. Felicia Laverne Madaris is a miracle worker. For me to be able to walk around is living proof of that."

He paused a moment and then added, "I will never question anything she decides to do regarding me. Who knows?

Maybe by the time she gets to my name on her list, I will be a changed man."

Now it was Corbin who chuckled. "Do you honestly believe that?"

"No."

"Neither do I."

Chance fought back a grin. He wanted to have kids one day. When he was ready to do so, he would marry but would consider such a union as a business arrangement, not a true marriage.

"I'm sure you didn't drive out here to blow off steam about Mama Laverne's matchmaking shenanigans when you aren't next on her list, Corbin. Is there another reason for your visit?"

Chance kept to himself out on his ranch and received very few visitors, so he was usually the last to hear family news or gossip. "Yes, there is another reason I dropped by," Corbin said, sitting up straight in his seat as if remembering.

"Let me guess," Chance said. "Did Mama Laverne dream about fish?" Usually, whenever she did, someone in the family was pregnant.

"No, not that I heard of."

He rubbed his chin and then asked. "Did Tanner call off his wedding?" Tanner Jamison was a family friend whose wedding was scheduled for next month.

Corbin rolled his eyes. "Not hardly. Tanner is so ready for that wedding he's gotten annoying."

Chance sighed as he stood to stretch. "Okay, I give up. What is it?"

Corbin paused a moment, held Chance's gaze, and then said. "Ravena Boyle is back in town."

Dr. Zoey Pritchard placed her mobile phone on speaker while glancing at the document she held. It was a bill of sale of a ranch house in Houston, Texas.

Her paternal grandaunt, Paulina Pritchard, who'd raised her since the age of eight, had died unexpectedly of a heart attack two weeks ago. While going through her aunt's belongings today, she had come across the document in a trunk underneath the bed.

Since the paperwork had been in Zoey's mother's maiden name, she could only assume her mother had inherited the ranch from her parents. The date on the bill of sale, which happened to have been Zoey's ninth birthday, meant Aunt Paulina had sold the property less than a year after Zoey's parents had been killed in a car accident.

That was close to twenty years ago. It was an accident where an eight-year-old Zoey had miraculously survived. The police, paramedics, and fire departments had said it was a miracle. But that miracle hadn't come without a price. In addition to several physical challenges she'd had to overcome, she had lost her memory of the first eight years of her life.

A year ago, Zoey began dreaming of being on a ranch with a couple she knew were her parents from photographs she'd seen of them. As far as she knew, she had been born and raised in Boston. Whenever she mentioned the dreams to Aunt Paulina, she had dismissed such a notion of her parents ever being on a ranch or owning one as ludicrous. Both had been orthopedic surgeons who'd met and married right out of medical school and worked in a hospital in Boston. Why hadn't Aunt Paulina told her about the ranch then? Instead, she'd made it seem like there hadn't been any merit to Zoey's dreams whatsoever.

"I can't believe it, Lucky," she told her best friend. "Why didn't Aunt Paulina tell me about this?"

"I don't have an answer for you, Zoe, but it doesn't surprise me. I always thought your aunt deliberately kept a lot of stuff about your parents from you. Now you have proof that she did."

Yes, she did have proof, Zoey thought, placing the paper in the middle of the kitchen table. She glimpsed out the window and saw how wonderful the weather was outside. San Francisco was always nice during May, with flowers blooming everywhere.

"So, what are you going to do?" Lucky interrupted her thoughts to ask.

She and Lucky Andres-Tankersley had been best friends since junior high school when the Andreses moved into the neighborhood. Zoey had considered Lucky's home to be a fun house. The Andreses were the type of parents she wanted to believe hers would have been had they lived.

After high school, she and Lucky packed their bags and left California for New York to attend NYU. After graduation, Lucky remained at NYU to get an MBA. Meanwhile, Zoey moved to Baltimore to attend Johns Hopkins medical school after deciding to follow in her parents' footsteps and become an orthopedic surgeon, where she remained after completing her internship, while Lucky landed a job with a well-known technology firm in Manhattan.

"I truly don't know what I'm going to do. Now more than ever, I believe those dreams of me on a ranch with my parents might be the start of a break in my memory loss."

"I just don't get it, Zoe. I would think when you told your aunt about those dreams, she would have been happy at the possibility that your memory was returning."

"Yes, I would have thought so too," she said, drawing a deep breath, not fully understanding why her aunt had not.

"Your aunt hadn't been kidding about not approving of your parents' marriage," Lucky said. "It was as if she wanted to wipe your mother's presence from your and your father's lives."

Zoey nodded, sadly thinking the same thing. For the longest time, she'd stopped asking her aunt anything about her parents. Although Aunt Paulina usually had good things to say about Zoey's father, that had not been the case with her mother. She claimed she had no idea where her mother was born or about her family's history. All her aunt would say was that her parents had met in medical school and that Holton Pritchard had lost his ever-loving mind after meeting Michelle Martin. He'd claimed it had been love at first sight. Because Aunt Paulina believed such a thing was complete nonsense, she hadn't approved of the marriage and had seen no reason to attend the wedding.

"I can't help but wonder what else she kept from me other than the document and the necklace," Zoey said.

"What necklace?"

Zoey fingered the beautiful heart-shaped gold pendant necklace with a diamond in the center that she'd placed around her neck earlier. She then told Lucky about finding it in the trunk as well. "It belonged to my mom," she said, trying not to choke on the words.

"How do you know that?"

Zoey swallowed deeply. Her eyes began watering with tears, and she was glad Lucky wasn't there to see them. "Because it's the same necklace she wears in my dreams."

"Oh, Zoe," Lucky said sadly.

Zoey could hear the tears in her best friend's voice. Tears she was shedding for her. For years, Lucky had been the only one to do so. After a few sniffles, Zoey said, "Just think, Lucky. Those dreams are a good sign."

"Yes. I always thought they were a sign your memory was returning. Time for you to hire a hot, hairy, and handsome private investigator to uncover the truth."

Zoey couldn't help but laugh. Lucky always preferred men with a lot of hair on their bodies. With a full beard and hair that went past his shoulders, Lucky's husband, Burke, from Canada, definitely fit her best friend's requirements. "A private investigator, Lucky?"

"Yes. What if your parents hadn't been killed in a car accident? What if you were kidnapped as a child and Paulina

Pritchard wasn't your aunt? What if you have other relatives somewhere?"

Zoey rolled her eyes. Lucky enjoyed watching crime shows. "Although I can't recall what happened when I was a child, I do remember the physical injuries I endured as a result of the accident. Besides, there is no way my aunt would have been given custody of me if she truly wasn't my only living relative."

"I guess you're right." Lucky paused and then asked, "So, when are you leaving for Houston?"

"What makes you think I'm going to Houston?"

"Seriously, Zoe? How can you not? You've found a document that corroborates those dreams you've been having, as well as a necklace. Do you honestly want me to think you aren't going to Texas to check things out for yourself?"

Zoey didn't say anything, and the silence was thick. Lucky knew her like no other and was right. She was going to Houston but still had a few misgivings. "The ranch was sold close to twenty years ago. I'm not sure the people who bought it could tell me anything about my mother's family."

"But what if they can?" Lucky countered. "It would be nice if they let you look around to see if anything about the house is familiar to you."

Zoey knew Lucky was right. There had to be a reason she had been dreaming of spending time with her parents on a ranch. She strongly felt it was the same ranch; if it was, being there could jog her memory even more. "You're right. Maybe I will go."

A short while later, after ending the call with Lucky, Zoey got up from the kitchen table to walk over to the window and gaze again at the flowers. Seeing them reminded her of the beauty in the world. That meant she had to remain positive. After all she'd been through over the past twenty-eight years, wasn't it time for her to experience true happiness?

At least she had the time off work to take that trip to Houston. She'd been selected to teach a medical class at the Johns Hopkins University, and the semester had ended last month. She didn't have to report back to the hospital until September.

She had planned to spend the entire summer touring London, Scotland, and Ireland. Now that wouldn't be happening. In addition to planning to go to Texas, she needed to decide what she would do with her aunt's home. She appreciated Aunt Paulina for taking her in for those ten years before she'd left for college, but she had never truly felt this was her home. Her aunt hadn't mistreated her or anything; she just hadn't experienced that same warm, loving aura she'd felt whenever she visited Lucky's house. Her best friend's parents openly displayed affection for each other, their three children, and their friends. Mrs. Andres seemed to always know whenever she needed a hug.

Zoey reached up and fingered the necklace again, figuring her father had given it to her mother as a gift. It was hard to believe that, after all these years, her memory might be returning. She wouldn't waste time wondering why her aunt had kept information from her. The important thing was that because of that document she'd found, she had a chance to learn more about her history.

It might be a good idea to start in Boston. Surely, her parents had made friends when they'd lived there. Zoey had been born there but had no idea where they'd lived. Her aunt had only told her that her parents had worked at Massachusetts General Hospital.

A smile touched Zoey's lips. Finally, she had a chance to find out about a past she couldn't remember and couldn't wait to discover everything she could.

Part One

"The future belongs to those who believe in the beauty of their dreams."

—Eleanor Roosevelt

Chapter One

Chancellor Madaris left Burney's Feed Store to return to Teakwood Ridge. It had taken him longer than expected because Burney had been more talkative than usual. The older man had heard that a Madaris had married this past weekend.

Chance decided to quash that rumor by letting him know that it hadn't been a Madaris wedding but the wedding of a Madaris family friend. His single Madaris cousins—those who weren't ready to settle down to protect, provide, and prosper—would blow a gasket if they knew gossip was spreading that one of them had tied the knot. For that reason, he'd wanted to ensure Burney had gotten the right information.

As he exited the interstate, he couldn't help but remember the wedding he had attended last weekend. Not in a million years had he figured he would see Tanner Jamison getting married and happily doing so. At the wedding, Mama Laverne had been all smiles while taking credit for bringing Tanner and Lyric together. Everyone was still pretty stunned by that one.

Another thing his family seemed stunned about was that Ravena Boyle was back in Houston. Years ago, when she moved to Houston, it was due to her wanting a fresh start living somewhere different from Colorado. So why had she returned? That question had some of his kinfolk speculating about all sorts of things, but honestly, he couldn't care less. Ravena meant nothing to him, like he'd told Corbin or anyone else who thought he needed to know about her return.

A short while later, he was on the two-lane road that led to Whispering Pines, Teakwood Ridge, and a couple of other huge spreads in the area. Every time he took this road home, he felt extremely grateful. He loved his ranch, and so far, Chance and his older brothers, Luke and Reese, were the only Madaris cousins who'd followed their uncle Jake into ranching.

Glancing up at the sky, Chance saw dark clouds forming. The weather report had warned of a thunderstorm, and he'd meant to get home long before it hit. He had reached toward his car's console to switch radio stations for a weather update when he noticed a car was stalled on the side of the road. He took a quick assessment of the situation. Since a tow truck was already on the scene, there was no reason for him to stop.

At least, he'd thought that until he'd seen her. The woman was standing by the car and talking to the tow truck driver. She'd heard the sound of his truck and had glimpsed quickly at him before resuming her conversation with the man. That had been enough time for his mind to accept that, without a shadow of a doubt, she had to be the most beautiful woman he'd ever seen.

One of Chance's skills as an army ranger was to do a quick and thorough assessment of a given situation or that of another human. For some reason, those skills had homed in on her. Her height was about 5'6". Dark brown eyes. High cheekbones. Cocoa-colored skin. Shoulder-length black hair whose strands curled at the end. She had full lips and dimples on each cheek that showed even when she wasn't smiling. Presently, her expression conveyed her frustration. Then there was her body in jeans and a white shirt. The outfit looked gorgeous on such a curvy body.

Her beauty had clouded his judgment. That had to be why he pulled over to the shoulder of the road, stopped his truck, and got out. There was no other reason for him to do so. With the tow truck here, the situation was clearly under control.

He was not.

His control had been shot to hell the moment he had seen her. Blame it on the fact that he hadn't gotten laid in close to six months, thanks to back-to-back roundups and an unusually cold and harsh Texas winter.

Closing his truck door, he began moving toward the woman. The closer he got, the more he liked. His gaze roamed over her deliberately, liking everything he saw. She was definitely wearing those jeans. He hoped she was into one-night stands like he was.

"Morning, ma'am. Need help?" he asked, smiling while tipping his Stetson in greeting when he approached her. He wasn't sure what cologne she wore, but it was an arousing scent. The tow truck driver had walked off, and Chance had her full attention. If he hadn't been a goner before, he certainly was one now. When her gorgeous lips had curved into a smile, it was as if a fist had suddenly slammed into the middle of his gut. She was more beautiful than he'd thought. And when smiling, her dimples became more profound.

"No, but thanks for asking," she said in what he thought was a nice-sounding voice. "The tow truck will take my car back to the rental agency and me with it, so I can get another one."

Chance nodded. He had a feeling she wasn't from around these parts. This road eventually led to four homesteads. Namely, his place, Whispering Pines, Cole Wells's Shadow Bridge Ranch, and the Hollisters' spread. He recalled the Hollisters had three daughters. The one who'd graduated from college a couple of years ago would be about her age, which he figured was no more than twenty-four.

He was about to ask if she was related to the Hollisters when she opened the trunk of her car to retrieve her items. That's when he saw the camera and the equipment that went along with it. Damn. He quickly concluded that she was a reporter, and there was only one reason a reporter would be this far from Houston and in this area.

He'd bet every Angus cattle he owned that she was here poking around for a story on his uncle Jake and his movie star wife, Diamond. It wouldn't be the first time reporters had shown up for a story, and he doubted it would be the last.

Chance's expression suddenly turned cold, and his instant attraction to the woman fizzled into a quick death. He didn't like reporters. Very few members of the Madaris family did. All he had to do was recall the hatchet job that tabloid had done on his cousin Victoria last year when it was discovered that she and Senator Roman Malone were having an affair.

Their uncle Jake, who was as serious as a heart attack when it came to protecting the Madaris family, had filed a lawsuit against *The Tattler*. The tabloid quickly issued a public apology and retracted the story, and in the end, a huge settlement was reached out of court. The owner of the tabloid had been lucky Jake hadn't bought the whole damn company right from under him. But Chance was certain the millions the owner had paid out in that settlement was a huge financial loss that had taught him a costly lesson. You come after the Madarises, they will go after you.

Chance's thoughts returned to the present when the woman put the camera around her neck, turned to him, and smiled that much brighter before saying, "We haven't been introduced."

They would not be under the circumstances, as far as he was

concerned. "Since you don't need my help, I'll be going," he said in a curt tone.

Turning, he quickly walked to his truck and got in without looking back. When he got home, he would call his uncle and alert him that a snooping reporter was in the area.

Back in her hotel room, Zoey had just finished telling Lucky how her day had been ruined when the serpentine belt on her rental car broke. All Lucky was concerned about was that cowboy who'd stopped to help.

"Was he hot, hairy, and handsome?" Lucky asked excitedly.

Zoey shook her head as she answered the question. "Since he was fully clothed and wearing a Stetson, I don't know how hairy he was, although he did have a mustache. However, I can certainly say he was tall, hot, and handsome." Then she thought about something else. "And when he first approached me and tipped the brim of his hat, smiled, and said hello, I believe my panties got wet then and there."

"Lordy, girl. He was that hot?"

"Even hotter," Zoey said as she sat on the edge of the bed. Although it was storming outside, she had pleasant memories of when she'd seen him. Her hot and handsome cowboy. She was surprised he hadn't kept driving, instead parking his truck and getting out to ask if she needed help. Up close and personal, she was convinced he was the epitome of what she'd always thought a Texas cowboy should be. Looking into such a gorgeous face had caused her pulse to skitter, followed by a shiver that had touched every one of her nerve endings.

Dressed in a pair of well-worn jeans, a Western shirt with the sleeves rolled up to his elbows, cowboy boots, and a Stetson on his head, he'd appeared rugged, all macho, virile, and sexy as hell. Unable to help herself, her gaze had latched onto a pair of well-defined lips that had curved into a smile beneath a neatly trimmed mustache. And Lordy, he had dimples. Dimples that only appeared when he smiled.

Then, there had been his rich copper skin tone that emphasized the beauty of his sexy brown bedroom eyes, and the alluring shape of his Nubian nose. She was convinced everything about his looks had been perfect. Her attraction to him had baffled her. After her relationship with Conrad Johnson ended last year, she'd sworn off men, especially those of the egotistic type. But then she hadn't known what type the stranger was since they'd barely shared a conversation.

The one thing she had noticed was that he had gone from smiling, friendly hottie to a frowning, distant frosty. She wasn't sure what had caused the extreme attitude shift, but he certainly hadn't wasted time leaving in a hurry when she'd suggested an introduction. That episode had truly been weird.

"If I were you, Zoe, I'd make the most of my time in Houston."

Zoey beamed. Of course, Lucky would say that. Her best friend's parents had given her the right name. She'd been lucky to meet and marry the man of her dreams a few years after college. As far as Zoey was concerned, Lucky and Burke were the perfect couple.

Whereas Zoey had been unlucky with love. She should have known Conrad was a piece of work since Aunt Paulina had been the one to introduce them. During the six months of their long-distance relationship, he had spent most of his time trying to get her to move back to San Francisco. For a while, she'd wondered if her aunt was paying him to do so.

"If you recall, girlfriend, I'm here for a purpose," she reminded Lucky.

"That doesn't mean you can't enjoy yourself in the process. Meet someone. Engage in a fling."

Zoey couldn't help but laugh. "A fling? Seriously?"

"Yes, seriously."

She hated admitting it, but that thought had crossed her mind when she'd first seen him. She'd found that odd since meaningless affairs had never been her thing. It was exclusivity or nothing. "I would love to see that cowboy again, but I doubt our paths will cross a second time. It was probably a one-and-done chance meeting."

"You never know."

"I do know that I don't know anything about him. We didn't exchange names. At least he didn't have a ring on his finger." Zoey was convinced his looks and everything sexy about him was emblazoned into her brain. She wouldn't forget him anytime soon.

"If not him, then another tall, hot, handsome cowboy," Lucky suggested. "You're in Texas, filled with plenty of rugged hunks."

True, but she was stuck on the sexy cowboy she had seen today. While walking away, he'd done so with a swagger that had filled her head with all kinds of romantic thoughts—of the hot, steamy, and erotic variety. She stood and began fanning herself. That guy had left too much of a sensual impression on her.

"I know how you feel about exclusivity. Maybe it's time you let your hair down. Live a little. Walk on the wild side. Be daring. So, what are your plans tomorrow?" Lucky asked.

"If the weather clears up, I plan to do what I wanted today. Find that ranch. That shouldn't be hard since I have an address."

"Just be careful. I don't like you being out in rural Texas alone."

"I'll be fine, Lucky. Stop worrying and stop watching so many of those crime shows."

An hour later, Zoey returned to her hotel room after going downstairs to grab something to eat at the hotel's restaurant. The storm outside had gotten worse, and bolts of lightning were crisscrossing the sky. As she prepared for bed, she couldn't help but remember how well her visit to Boston had gone last week.

The moment she'd walked into the orthopedic wing of Massachusetts General Hospital, an older doctor had stared at her as if he was seeing a ghost. His stare was eerie until he approached her and had introduced himself as Dr. Jerome Kemmic, the chief of Orthopedic Surgery. He'd then asked if she was related to the late Dr. Michelle Pritchard. He'd told her the resemblance was uncanny. She had told him that she was Holton and Michelle Pritchard's daughter.

He had worked with them. Of course, he'd known about the tragic accident and how she had been the lone survivor. He'd also remembered the long months she had remained in the hospital and he, and other colleagues of her parents, had come to visit her during that time, before she left for California with no forwarding information.

She had told him about her memory loss and why it was so important for her to find out as much about her childhood as she could. He had been pleased to hear she'd followed in her parents' footsteps and was also an orthopedic surgeon, claiming her parents would be proud of her.

She'd also been told that one person who could help with her memory was Sharon Newberry, a doctor who'd been her mother's close friend. Dr. Newberry had transferred to a Florida hospital after getting married nearly fifteen years ago. He'd felt certain the woman would love to talk to her and had told Zoey how hard the woman had taken her parents' death. After obtaining Zoey's contact information, Dr. Kemmic said he would contact Dr. Newberry on her behalf.

Zoey went to bed that night excited about what the future would bring, and when she finally closed her eyes, the image of the tall, hot, and handsome cowboy she'd met that day filled her mind.

Chapter Two

Chance returned to the house after visiting with his men in the bunkhouse. He had eight men in total. The three who made Teakwood Ridge their home—Purdy, Amos, and Larry—had private sleeping quarters.

Before going into the house, he turned to gaze over his land. It was an awesome view from where he stood on his back porch. He didn't know of anything more spectacular. Suddenly, out of nowhere, the face of the woman from yesterday flashed across his mind.

Chance would admit there had been something about her that was unforgettable, although he was trying hard to forget. Hell, he would admit thoughts of her had consumed his mind when he'd drifted off to sleep last night. Knowing how he felt about reporters, he couldn't understand how such a thing happened.

He couldn't rightly say he disliked all reporters because there were two in the Madaris family. His cousins Victoria and Christy. Because of them, he wouldn't say all reporters were bad.

Chance drew in a deep breath when he realized what he was

doing, namely, trying to find an acceptable excuse for the occupation of the woman he'd seen yesterday. He was well aware that everybody had to work for a living, but when someone's occupation deliberately invaded the privacy of others, he had a problem with that.

It baffled the hell out of him as to why he was still thinking about her. He'd met attractive women before. But there had been something about her that he couldn't explain, although he had been in her presence less than five minutes. However, that's all the time it had taken for him to be captivated. His lips tightened at the thought since he was not a man easily dazzled.

Had it been her smile? Those damn dimples? The way her hair had touched her shoulders at a seemingly perfect angle. The way her jeans had hugged those luscious-looking hips of hers?

He shoved his hands into the pockets of his jeans and squinted in the morning sun. At least the sun was out, which hopefully meant today would be a better day than before. The weekend was three days away, and he would make it a point to visit downtown Houston—specifically, Vance's Tavern. You could usually meet a willing woman there, and it was time to take care of his sexual needs. It had been six months since he'd shared a bed with a woman, and he was horny as hell.

Considering how intense his attraction had been to that woman yesterday, which hadn't been typical for him, it was a good thing he knew nothing about her. Their paths wouldn't likely cross again—end of story.

And speaking of story…he had alerted his uncle she was in the area. Jake thanked him for the information. However, Chance knew Whispering Pines was like a fortress. No one got on its lands unless invited by Jake and Diamond. That meant if the woman was determined enough to tell a story, she might bother the neighbors. If she did so, she would soon discover that, like the men who worked for Jake, his neighbors were just as loyal and kept their mouths shut.

Chance checked his watch. It was close to nine. His house-keeper and cook, Ms. Cate, was a timely person. She would have breakfast ready at nine, and unless it was roundup time or an emergency on the ranch that needed his attention, she expected him to be sitting at the kitchen table and eating by nine-fifteen.

Ms. Cate hadn't just come highly recommended; his great-grandmother practically installed her there. Trying to convince Mama Laverne he didn't need a housekeeper, or a cook had been a waste of time after she'd unexpectedly visited him one day. She hadn't liked his housekeeping, or how his freezers were stocked with microwave dinners. She took offense to the latter since she had required all her grands and great-grands to attend her cooking classes when they'd turned sixteen. She'd felt there was no reason for microwave dinners to be in his freezer when he was a perfectly good cook. She knew because she'd taught him herself.

Cate Neville was an older, grandmotherly woman who had been the childhood best friend of his grandaunt Bessie, who was married to Nolan Sr. She arrived at eight and left at five on Tuesdays and Thursdays. Since he spent most of his time on the range, they didn't get in each other's way. He'd gotten used to having his home nice and neat and a delicious meal prepared for him, with enough leftovers for the days she didn't come.

Drawing in a deep breath, he inhaled the scent of fried bacon and knew there would be mouth-watering pancakes or biscuits to go along with it. Turning, he went inside to wash up for breakfast.

Zoey took a deep breath when she brought her car to a stop at the entrance of the huge wooden marker that read Teakwood Ridge. The address beside the sign indicated this was the place. The home that her mother had once owned. The ranch that her aunt Paulina had sold on Zoey's ninth birthday.

Already, there was a tingling sensation in the bottom of her stomach. Not only had she chased her dream, but she was finally about to face it. Had her parents deliberately led her here for a reason? Was this her mother's way of reaching out to her, allowing her to discover another part of her past? Namely, the one Aunt Paulina refused to tell her anything about?

Lucky had called this morning wanting details of her agenda for today. She'd suggested that Zoey reinstall the tracking app the two of them shared as a security measure while in college, since they were two single women living alone in New York.

It took Zoey a good thirty minutes between brushing her teeth, washing her face, and blow-drying her hair to convince Lucky that such a thing was unnecessary. Best friend or not, she preferred Lucky not know her every single move. When she told Lucky this, her friend had laughingly accused Zoey of living a double life. Zoey had found the accusation hilarious, given she didn't know everything about the one life she had. However, to appease her best friend, she promised Lucky that she would provide periodic updates throughout the day.

Checking her watch, she now saw it was almost ten thirty. Deciding not to waste any more time and hoping that the person who currently owned the house would be kind and understanding, she pulled onto the horseshoe driveway. After driving thirty feet, she saw the enormous ranch-style house in the distance. The tingling sensation in her stomach increased. Bringing the car to a stop, she gazed around.

There was something familiar about that tall oak tree she saw, whose branches seemed to stretch the perimeter of the front yard. Had she tried climbing it once? She beamed broadly, imagining doing so. Just because such a thing hadn't been in her dreams didn't mean it hadn't happened.

Moving the car forward again, she finally stopped in front of the huge house. In addition to the tingling sensation, she felt a shiver begin washing over her as she stared at the wide wraparound porch with a swing. There was no doubt in her mind she had been here before. That swing seemed familiar.

Not far away, she saw a huge red barn, and beside it was another enormous structure. There was so much land, and it amazed her to think that, at one time, her mother owned all of it. She could imagine her mother growing up here as a child. Suddenly, Zoey felt a connection to this place that would have been hers had her aunt not sold it.

As she got out of the car, she wondered if anyone was home. There weren't any cars parked out front, but there was a detached six-car garage. Did that mean a large family lived here? Would they believe her story about why she would show up on their doorstep asking to look around? Well, there was only one way to find out, she thought as she moved up the steps to the door.

It turned out to be a gorgeous day after such a torrential downpour the day before. Texas's weather was different from Maryland's, but she liked it more after two days.

After knocking on the door, she glanced around again. In the distance, she saw a herd of cows being moved toward an open range by several cowboys. That made her remember the cowboy she had seen yesterday. Did he work at one of the ranches in the area? Possibly even here?

"What the hell are you doing here?"

The angry male voice made her jump, and in stunned silence she turned and stared at the person who'd opened the door. The cowboy from yesterday—the same one she'd just been thinking about—was standing before her and looking just as tall, hot, and handsome as he had yesterday. And it was apparent that he was very angry. Why? Since he'd opened the door, she could only assume he lived here. She guessed his age to be in his early thirties. Was he the son of the owners? Why was he frowning at her like that? Surely, he remembered her after he'd stopped and offered help the day prior. What had him so riled today?

"I asked what the hell are you doing here?" he said again in a harsher tone. "If you're here to ask questions, don't bother. I won't be telling you a damn thing."

Zoey swallowed. How had he known she wanted to ask him questions? The only person who knew why she was here was Lucky. Finding her voice, she said, "Surely you can answer a few of my inquiries."

He placed his arms across his chest, and his frown deepened. Why did his menacing stance make him appear even sexier? And why on earth was she noticing that? "I won't answer anything," he snapped. "Nor will any of the other neighbors. So, I guess you'll have to write your article without our input."

Now she was the one frowning while looking up at him. "What article?"

"The kind reporters write. And to give you a warning, the last tabloid that thought of doing so found out the hard way what can happen when they publish lies."

Tabloid? What on earth was this man talking about? "You think I'm a reporter?" she asked incredulously.

"Aren't you?"

"No."

"And you want me to believe that?" he asked, chuckling derisively.

Zoey mimicked his stance and crossed her arms over her chest. "I don't see why not."

She wasn't sure how it was possible, but his frown deepened even more. "Look, lady, I can tell you why I don't believe you. I saw your camera and the equipment you took out of the trunk of your car yesterday. Secondly, you're here to ask questions. That's what reporters do."

She stared at him. Now it all made sense. She recalled that when she'd taken that stuff from her trunk, his entire demeanor had changed, and he'd quickly left like a bunch of hounds were on his heel. That meant his attitude, then and now, was because he assumed she was a reporter. Although she had no idea why a reporter would come here, she could see why he thought she was one.

"Photography is a hobby of mine, and my camera and equipment usually go wherever I do," she said, refusing to be intimidated by the likes of the man standing in front of her. However, she wished that would somehow extend to her attraction to him.

She momentarily broke eye contact with him by glancing down at the doormat beneath her feet. It was either do that or risk a heart rate and blood pressure increase. His sexual magnetism should be outlawed. She met his eyes again when she felt better in control of her senses. "Maybe I should introduce myself," she said in a calmer, less defensive voice.

"Don't bother."

"I honestly think that I should bother under the circumstances. If for no other reason than to prove I am not a reporter," she said, opening her cross-body purse and pulling out her business card. Just in case he assumed it was a phony business card, she also took out her driver's license. She handed both to him, but for a minute, she thought he wouldn't take them.

Then he did.

Chapter Three

Chance glared at the woman who, like yesterday, was gorgeous. And like yesterday, he couldn't help but home in on everything about her, especially the way her wind-blown hair gave her a sexy appeal and how good she looked in a pair of jeans and a yellow shirt. Yes, she was a beauty. And why was her scent more arousing than yesterday?

It was hard to believe their paths had crossed again. He would never have thought that would occur in a million years. Now she was here, on his property, invading his space, and he didn't like it.

Forcing his gaze off her, he studied the business card.

ZOEY MICHELLE PRITCHARD
Orthopedic Surgeon
Johns Hopkins Hospital
(410) 111-1112 (bus.)
(410) 100-1001 (mobile)

Chance blinked several times at the card containing both her business and mobile phone numbers before switching his gaze to her driver's license. There was no doubt she was the same woman in the photo. She was twenty-eight? She didn't look it. Yesterday, he'd thought she was no older than twenty-four. All he had to say was that she wore her age well.

He glanced back at her. She wasn't smiling, but those gorgeous dimples were showing nonetheless, making something rock all through him.

"You're a medical doctor?" he asked, surprised.

She lifted her chin, and he saw a hint of fire flash in the depths of those gorgeous brown eyes. "Yes."

"An orthopedic surgeon?"

"That's what my business card says, doesn't it?"

Chance lifted a brow at her smart response. Apparently, it didn't take much to get her hackles raised. She had a backbone and a part of him liked it. In fact, he liked a lot more than her attitude, he thought, staring at her. His gaze seemed drawn to her like a magnet. Because of his injuries from being in combat, he'd seen numerous orthopedic surgeons in his day, but none were gorgeous like her. Her first name was Zoey. He didn't know another Zoey, but for some reason, he thought the name suited her.

He returned both her driver's license and business card. Okay, she wasn't who he thought she was, but still…

"Why are you here, Doctor Pritchard? You're a long way from Baltimore. The only doctors in these parts who make house calls are veterinarians."

For a minute, Chance saw the semblance of a smile appear with those dimples, and then she frowned again. "Like I said earlier, I'd like to ask a few questions."

Now he was back to crossing his arms over his chest. "Why? Doctors don't normally go around knocking on doors asking questions," he said, his words laced with sarcasm.

He saw the flash of fire in her eyes again. Why did seeing it do things to him? Like making him want to see more fire within her. The kind that naked bodies rolling between sheets could ignite. "There is a reason for me doing so, and I would like to explain it to the ranch owners if I may," she said while glaring at him.

It was on the tip of his tongue to say, no, she may not. He wasn't sociable and rarely got visitors unless they were family members. Some considered him the unfriendly Madaris, and for that reason, most people kept their distance.

Chance studied her again and had to admit she had him curious.

He then recalled what she'd said about wanting to talk to the ranch owners. Well, he had news for her. "I am the owner."

She seemed surprised. "You are?"

"That's what I said, isn't it?"

Okay, he'd deliberately given her a smart-ass response like she'd done to him earlier. Although she tried not to, her lips twitched at the corners in a smile again, and he thought her dimples would be the death of him. He wished he could kiss them right off her face. Of course, such a thing wasn't possible, but he would love to try anyway.

He dropped his hands by his sides, not liking how his thoughts were going. His resolve had never been weakened by an intense attraction to a woman, and he was determined it wouldn't do so now. "Okay, I'll give you five minutes, Doctor Pritchard, and that's all. This is a working ranch, and I'm busy."

"Thanks. I appreciate it."

Chance moved aside, and she entered. He watched her scan his living room intently and wondered why. Although his home was neat and clean, he couldn't see her wanting any decorating ideas.

He was about to tell her she was down to four minutes when he suddenly saw her sway on her feet like she was about to faint. Rushing to her, he ignored the flash of desire he felt the moment he wrapped his arms around her waist to lead her to the sofa. "Are you alright?"

When she didn't answer quickly enough to suit him, he called out frantically. "Ms. Cate, come quick."

His housekeeper rushed into the room. "What's wrong, Chancellor?"

"She almost fainted," he said, easing Zoey down into a sitting position on the sofa.

Cate nearly knocked him out of the way when she reached them. "Miss, are you alright?"

"I felt lightheaded for a second."

Cate nodded and said, "I'll get you a glass of sweet tea." And then she was gone, rushing into the kitchen.

Chance watched Dr. Pritchard and saw how she continued to look around the room as if in a daze. What in the world was wrong with her? He was about to ask when Cate reappeared with the glass of tea and handed it to her. The woman took a large sip, smiled up at Cate and then said in a soft voice, "Thank you."

"You're welcome, Miss…" Cate gazed at Chance for a name. He shrugged and said, "She's Dr. Pritchard."

"Oh," his housekeeper said. Turning back to Zoey, Cate said. "You're welcome, Doctor Pritchard. That sweet tea should relieve the dizziness. I know it happens sometimes."

Chance rolled his eyes as Cate left the room. Knowing Ms. Cate, she probably assumed the woman was a veterinarian. There was no other reason for a doctor to make house calls in the area. And she probably thought the woman had gotten dizzy because of him. Cate would often tease him and his male cousins and say that a Madaris man was known to make women swoon since the beginning of time.

Chance eased down in the chair across from her. He figured it would be rude at this point to let her know she didn't have any more minutes left. Due to what just happened, he would display some degree of empathy.

After she'd taken another sip of her tea and after giving her another few minutes to pull herself together, he felt she had been in his home long enough. "What was it that you wanted to explain, Doctor Pritchard?"

Zoey took another sip of her tea and studied the man who had yet to introduce himself. However, she did recall the lady who'd come into the room had called him Chancellor.

"That was kind of her to bring me a glass of sweet tea."

He said nothing as he extended his long legs out before him without responding to what she'd said. When the silence stretched between them, she then said, "She called you Chancellor."

"That's my name." He'd said the words through clenched teeth. It didn't take much to get him testy, she thought.

She was about to give him a smart comeback and inquire if he didn't have a last name as well when he said, "Doctor Pritchard, I don't have the time to—"

"Zoey," she interrupted. "Please call me Zoey, and I hope I can call you Chancellor."

He didn't say if she could or not. Instead, he said, "I am busy and don't have much time. You were going to explain why you are here."

Yes, she was. He had let her inside his home, and she'd almost fainted in the middle of the floor, so she owed him that much. Besides, she needed to be honest if she wanted to see more of the house and land. The moment she'd entered his home and looked around, she knew. She wasn't sure how long he'd lived here, but he had retained some of the original furniture. She could see why. The oak furnishings added warmth to the huge living room.

Drawing in a deep breath, Zoey said, "It's about this house. I might have spent a lot of time here growing up."

"Don't you know if you did?" he asked, frowning.

She shook her head. "I don't. I have very little memory of my life before I was eight." What she should have said was that she had no memory of it.

Now he appeared perplexed, so she quickly added, "I think I need to start from the beginning."

She began telling him her story, starting with the accident that killed her parents, with her being the lone survivor and the loss of her memory. She watched his eyes go from disbelief to amazement and then to acceptance that she was telling the truth. She felt relief when she'd detected the latter.

"To this day, the doctors don't know how I survived with so many broken bones." She paused, remembering that time. At least her aunt Paulina had made sure she got the best medical care. She'd always been grateful for that.

"For almost a year after the accident, I couldn't walk and I wore braces on both my legs until I was eleven." She paused a minute and then added, "The physical therapy I endured to learn to walk again was painful."

He nodded as if he understood. There was no way that he could. Someone who'd never experienced anything like it really couldn't. That was the only part of her childhood she remembered. Specifically, what she'd gone through medically to have as much of a normal life as she could.

"Is that why you chose to become an orthopedic surgeon? To help others the way your doctors helped you?" he asked her. She'd noticed his tone had lost some of its frostiness.

"That's part of the reason. The main reason was that both my parents had been orthopedic surgeons. They worked at Massachusetts General Hospital in Boston, and I wanted to follow in their footsteps."

"You remember them working there?"

Zoey shook her head. "No. I have no memory of my child-hood before that accident."

He lifted a brow. "None?"

"None."

"But how do you know about this place?" he asked, seem-ingly confused. "Earlier, you said that you thought you'd spent time here. That would have been before the accident, right?"

"Yes." She took another sip of her tea and said, "A little over a year ago, I began having dreams, which were always about the same thing. My parents and I are spending time on a ranch."

Zoey couldn't help the smile that spread across her lips. "I recall there were cows, horses, and the big red barn they were kept in. Other dreams were about picnics we had near a lake on the ranch."

When he didn't confirm whether there was a lake on his property, she pressed on by saying. "There are some nights the dreams appear so vivid and real. Then there are other times when they are like several snapshots focusing only on certain things at the ranch."

He was staring at her with an intense look on his face, one filled with questions, but obviously, he was willing to let her tell her story. She was grateful for that.

"I told my aunt, who raised me after my parents' deaths, about my dreams. I was hoping it was a sign my memory was returning. However, she insisted that my parents never owned or visited a ranch. That left me assuming my mind was just coming up with dreams of my own making. Wishful dreams, you might say."

He nodded. "But that wasn't the case?"

"No, that was not the case." She figured by now he detected the anger in her voice that was at odds with the smile plastered on her lips. "A month ago, my aunt died of a heart attack. Then, while going through her belongings, I found a bill of sale. My mother had inherited a ranch house from her parents—this must have been before she married since the deed was in her maiden name. The date on the sales document indicated my aunt sold the ranch less than a year after I went to live with her, which had to be around twenty years ago."

He didn't say anything, and neither did she. She was letting him draw his conclusions about what she'd said. It didn't take long before he stated them out loud. "That means your aunt lied about your parents owning a ranch. Why?"

She shrugged. "I have no idea." And she honestly didn't.

At first, she'd thought her aunt might have needed the money for Zoey's medical care, which must have been expensive. However, Zoey had discovered that wasn't the case when she'd visited her aunt's attorney a week before she'd left for Boston.

Jed Thornsley had been her aunt's attorney for years. He'd given Zoey papers to a bank account her aunt left for her that represented the proceeds from the sale of her parents' Boston home. There was also a trust her parents had established for her to receive on her thirtieth birthday. Over the years, both had accumulated an extremely high amount of interest.

Mr. Thornsley knew nothing about the sale of a ranch house in Texas. When she'd shown him the documents, he'd seemed as baffled as she'd been. When she'd suggested that perhaps her aunt had sold the ranch to help pay Zoey's medical bills, the older man assured her that was not the case. He stated that all her medical care had been taken care of by her parents' life insurance proceeds, along with a medical policy her parents had on her.

It surprised Zoey that her aunt hadn't used any of her funds. Although Aunt Paulina never said or insinuated that she had, Zoey always assumed she did, and that was the reason Zoey had felt indebted to her aunt all those years and had never made waves about anything.

"Am I to assume this is the house?" Chancellor asked, breaking into her thoughts.

"Yes. It's the same address. Although that huge oak tree has never appeared in my dreams, something about it is familiar. The same thing with the swing on the porch. I doubted my parents lived here permanently since they worked and lived in Boston, but I imagined they came back here often to see my mother's family."

She drank the last of her tea and then said, "I felt lightheaded after entering your home because of this room. Some of the same furniture was in my dreams."

He said nothing momentarily, then noted, "I bought the house already furnished except for new bedroom furniture for the master suite and appliances I had upgraded. The furniture was in good shape, and I saw no reason to replace it. The people who sold me the house felt the same way."

He then asked, "What was your grandparents' surname? The ones you believe left this house to your mother?"

"They were the Martins. I don't remember their first names. The only reason I know that much is because my mother's maiden name was Martin."

"And your aunt never told you anything about your maternal history?"

Zoey paused a moment before answering. "No. She refused to tell me anything about my mother's family. They're deceased since Aunt Paulina was my only living relative."

He became quiet, and she figured he was drawing his conclusions about what she wasn't saying, and he was probably right in his assumptions. Time passed for a minute or two, and then he said, "I bought this property a few years ago from Henry and Rosalie Johnstone. I understand they had lived here for close to fifteen years. Did that bill of sale state who your aunt sold the property to?"

She shook her head. "It didn't show a name—just a bank. The Houston National Bank," she said.

"That would mean it was a private sale. That's not unusual

around these parts. It keeps developers from hounding you about selling your property."

She nodded. "Did you know the Johnstones?"

"No. I never met them. I understand they were an older couple. I can only assume that caring for this spread became too much for them. They moved out months before I bought the place."

She nodded again. "So, as you can see, Chancellor, this entire thing is a big mystery to me. I am not questioning the legitimacy of the sale of the house to you or anyone. The only reason I'm here is that I'm hoping that perhaps I'll see something that will stimulate my memory. Do you know anyone I can speak with, who has lived in this area a long time and might have known my grandparents?"

He hesitated for a moment, and then he said, "Yes, there is someone. My great-grandmother. Our family spread, Whispering Pines, is less than thirty minutes from here and has been in our family for generations. Mama Laverne is in her nineties, but her memory is as sharp as a tack."

"Do you think she'd be willing to talk to me?"

"I don't see why not. Not today, though, since I don't know where she is. She travels around quite a bit."

"In her nineties?"

His lips twitched as if amused, and although it had been rather quick, seeing it had her pulse racing. "Yes. To my great-grandmother, age is nothing but a number. Give me that business card of yours again. I'll contact you when a conversation can be arranged. How long will you be in the area?"

"For however long it takes to piece together my memory. I don't have to return to the hospital I work at until September; I have the entire summer free. I plan to use that time to learn as much about my maternal family as possible."

She took the business card from her purse and presented it to him again. "I would love to speak with your great-grandmother. Here is my business card," she said, giving back the card he'd returned earlier.

It didn't go unnoticed by Zoey that, although he now had her contact information, she didn't have his. He hadn't offered it to her. For all she knew, he might have a jealous girlfriend or something.

He slid her business card in the pocket of his shirt before standing. "Now, I'll show you to the door."

"You want me to leave?"

A scowl appeared on his face. "Any reason you think you should stay?"

"I was hoping I could look around."

He seemed taken aback by her words, and his tone was rather frosty when he said, "I won't have time to give you a tour, Zoey. Neither will Ms. Cate."

In other words, he was letting her know that although he might believe her story, he had no intentions of letting her roam through his house alone. "I don't recall asking you to do so, Chancellor."

"Then what are you asking?"

He was glaring, so she glared back, refusing to let him intimidate her. "I understand that neither you nor your housekeeper have the time to give me a tour of your home. However, I would appreciate it if you allowed me to look outside. I promise not to get in your way, and I will be gone before you know it."

He stared at her, and although his eyes hadn't moved beyond her face, she felt the intensity of his gaze on every part of her body. She thought he would deny her request, but then, in that same frosty tone, he said, "Fine. Follow me."

Chapter Four

Chance watched Zoey out of the corner of his eye while trotting his horse, Ambush, around the corral. The woman was moving around his backyard like one of those insurance inspectors who were there to examine his property before issuing a policy. She wasn't missing a thing.

But then, neither was he.

That was why his attention was focused on her whenever her full attention was on something she'd found of interest. For a while, she seemed fixated on that tree in his backyard. He recalled her saying something was familiar about the big oak in his front yard. Was there something about this one that was familiar as well?

And why did she have to stand there, with her hands positioned on her hips, in a pose that looked way too damn sexy for his peace of mind? If that wasn't bad enough, the wind had risen, causing her hair to whip wildly around her face. In defiance, she had pulled a hair clip from her small purse and used it to secure her hair back. He preferred it flying free in the wind and was tempted to get off his horse, cross the yard, and pull the clip from her hair.

What the hell?! When had he begun caring how a woman wore her hair or what she did with it? Why was this woman getting to him? More importantly, why was he letting her? Where was all that control that he was known to have when he needed it? It had failed him yesterday when he'd first seen her, and it was trying to do the same today. But he refused to let it.

Okay, checking out a good-looking woman was normal. Something he did often. No harm was done, as long as the woman didn't get under his skin, which was the one thing he wouldn't ever let happen again.

Chance forced his gaze from her and tried giving his horse his full attention. Ambush was the first horse he'd ridden after being able to do so again, so they had a special bond. As he trotted the horse around the yard, he couldn't help but recall what Zoey had told him. He wished he could say he hadn't believed a word she'd said and that her story was too far-fetched to be believable. However, he knew that it was.

He'd watched her closely while she'd been talking. Chance had seen the pain in her eyes, the haunted look that had been there while reliving the days of that car accident that had spared her life but taken her parents. She'd been a mere child of eight, but she'd been a fighter, and he would admit he admired her strength. Like him, she'd had to endure both physical and emotional challenges. The likes of which most people would never know or experience. He'd done so as an adult. She'd only been a child—a little girl who'd lost not only her parents but her complete memory of them.

Right at that moment, something about her pulled at him, and it was more intense than just a physical interest. It had been her life's story for the past twenty years. It was so different from his, yet similar. In a way, they were two of a kind. He had felt her pain and understood her need to become whole again regardless of the fight she'd faced after her accident. Just like him, she'd overcome the obstacles and beat the odds.

Who had been her Mama Laverne? The one person who hadn't given up on her? Had encouraged her to keep fighting on those days when she wanted to give up? The one person who'd championed her? Had it been her aunt? He had a feeling it hadn't been. He'd listened to what she'd said and read between the lines. It had been easy to detect there were some things she'd deliberately left out of her narrative. Her aunt hadn't approved of her father marrying her mother for some reason.

Even if that was true, that didn't excuse her aunt for lying to her about this ranch. Why had she done this when the truth might have helped recover her memory? He could only imagine how she felt when she discovered that her only family member had deceived her. If you couldn't trust your family, then who could you trust?

She deserved to have her memory restored, and he hoped that it would eventually happen. Had she seen anything else on his land that may have triggered it? He wished he didn't own the ranch that could be the key to regaining her memory. He didn't like that one damn bit.

He glanced to where Zoey stood before his barn. She tilted her face in his direction, and their gazes connected. For a quick moment, he'd felt something. Some affinity for her was the last thing he wanted to feel toward her or any woman. He was a loner and had chosen that kind of life for a reason. He had his emotional baggage and didn't need to take on anyone else's.

He knew it was time for her to go when their gazes continued to hold. Something was happening and coalescing inside him. Damn, he could feel it right to the bone. Whatever it was, he didn't want it. He would fight it like hell. He was the Chance who refused to take a chance. Never again. He'd tried the love and relationship thing and had nearly been destroyed.

He had her business card and would give Mama Laverne her

contact information. Hopefully, his great-grandmother could provide her with the information she sought. That was the best he could do and the only thing he intended to do.

After tying Ambush to a post, he started walking toward Zoey as their gazes still held. Once again, he got that feeling that he'd seen her before. Why was there something oddly familiar about her? She broke eye contact with him to gaze at the huge red barn she was standing in front of.

When Chance reached her, she turned to him, and he saw a jarred look on her face—like she was shaken up. "What's wrong, Zoey?" he asked in concern.

"I just remembered something, Chancellor," she said almost breathlessly.

Immediately, his pulse raced. "What?"

"This barn. I remembered the day my father put a new coat of red paint on it. He was on a ladder, and I called him and told him my mother had said lunch was ready. He smiled down at me. I saw him. I saw my daddy, and he looked just like he did in the pictures I have of him. That memory only lasted a few seconds, but it has to mean something, right?"

He saw tears in her eyes and knew his brain was scrambling with emotions. He was happy for her. How could he not be? More than anything, he hoped that what she'd just experienced was another missing piece of her childhood. "Yes, I believe it means something," he said.

She swiped at her tears and then said, "You've been more than kind about letting me look around your ranch. I would not have had that experience if you hadn't let me stay. Thank you."

He nodded, feeling like a heel since initially, he hadn't wanted her there. "Are you sure you're okay?"

"Yes. Just a little emotional now."

Chance could see that, understood, and felt she had every right to be. He would never forget the day he took those first steps without his wheelchair. He'd been filled with emotions, too.

He was about to suggest to Zoey that she stay until she felt more composed. But some part of him knew she had to go before he did something he'd later regret, like pulling her into his arms to kiss away those tears still glittering in her eyes.

"I'll be going now."

"And you're sure you're okay?" he asked again, wondering what he would do if she said she wasn't this time.

"Yes, I'm okay. I need time alone for a while."

He should have been relieved by her response, so there was no reason for her words to rub him the wrong way. He, of all people, should understand and respect a person's desire for space. Some needed it more than others, whatever the reason.

"I'll walk you to your car," he offered.

"Alright, thanks."

He walked beside her, and when they reached the car, he opened the door for her to get in. An inner voice told him that he'd said and done enough. If he hadn't allowed her to look around, she would never have had a portion of her memory returned. Besides that, he would be connecting her with his great-grandmother. That was enough. He should wish her well and let her move on.

For some reason, he couldn't do that.

Rubbing his hand down his face, he then said, "This place is huge, and there's a lot more of it you might want to see, Zoey. There's a lake near the south pasture. Can you ride a horse?"

"Yes. After one of my doctors recommended taking horse riding lessons to strengthen my leg muscles, my aunt enrolled me in a horse riding class. I enjoyed it so much that I kept it up for years. I often go to this horse ranch in Virginia to ride on my days off."

"Good." The thought that she enjoyed riding a horse pleased him for some reason. "You might also want to take a tour of my home. Like I told you, many rooms have the original furnishings."

He could tell his offer surprised her. "Thanks, Chancellor. I'd love to return and do that if you're sure I won't keep you from your work."

She didn't have to worry since he didn't intend to be here when she returned. He would spend an entire day on the range and ensure Ms. Cate cared for her. "I'm sure."

"Will tomorrow be too soon?" she asked excitedly.

For him, it would be, since Cate didn't work the next day. "Thursday would be better."

"Then I'll be back Thursday. Is eleven o'clock okay?"

"That time will be fine."

A look of happiness covered her face, and he wished he wasn't affected by the flashing of those dimples. "Thanks again, Chancellor."

"Chance. The only people who call me Chancellor are my great-grandmother and Ms. Cate. To everyone else, I'm Chance." He chuckled and added, "Unless I'm in trouble about something."

"Okay, then. I will call you Chance."

He stood back from the car before he was tempted to reach out and remove that clip from her hair to see it blowing in the wind again. "Take care, Zoey, and I hope more of your memory returns."

Her smile widened even more. "I believe that it will. Goodbye."

He tipped his hat in farewell, then stood there until her car was no longer in sight. At that moment, Chance wondered what he'd gotten himself into.

Zoey had driven several miles before finally reaching a gas station. She began crying, feeling overwhelmed by everything she'd experienced over the past few hours, and needed to talk to Lucky, but not until she got herself together. The last thing she needed was for her best friend to worry about her more than she already did. Pulling into a parking space, she stopped in front of the convenience store. After wiping her eyes and drawing a deep breath with trembling fingers, she tapped the call button on Lucky's contact. Her best friend picked up on the first ring.

"There better be a good reason you're just checking in, Zoe."

For a moment, she couldn't say anything. As if Lucky detected something was wrong, she continued, "Zoe, what's going on? What happened?"

Zoey honestly didn't know where to start. "You won't believe who owns that ranch, Lucky."

"The ranch that would have been yours had your aunt not sold it?"

Lucky's words and tone indicated she was still salty about that. "Yes, that ranch."

"Who owns it?"

"Chancellor."

"Who's Chancellor?"

Now, this was the part that was still hard to believe. She had to convince herself that every aspect of today had happened, especially the part of her memory that had returned.

"Zoe, who's Chancellor?"

Again, tears threatened, but she fought them back. "He's the cowboy I told you about yesterday."

"Tall, hot, and handsome?" Lucky asked in a disbelieving voice.

That made her smile. "Yes, tall, hot, and handsome." She began telling Lucky everything. Of course, her best friend often interrupted with questions, which delayed the telling.

"That's wonderful, Zoe—for you to recapture part of your memory while on that ranch is awesome. I am so happy for you. Now, tell me all about your cowboy."

Her cowboy? Boy, she wished. "Like I told you, at first, he wasn't all that friendly. Because he thought I was a reporter."

"Why would he be worried about a reporter showing up at his place?"

"I have no idea. Once we cleared that up, he invited me inside." Zoey paused a minute and then said, "He's different."

"Different in what way?"

"I think he doesn't like people intruding into his space."

"Yet he invited you back."

"Yes. Probably because I poured out everything to him. I needed him to understand the depth of my situation. No doubt he now considers me pathetic."

"Well, at least you know he has a heart. Some men don't have an empathetic bone in their body."

As far as Zoey was concerned, a heart wasn't all he had. The man was too virile for words. When he'd been on his horse, trotting around the corral, she'd had to fight hard to keep from staring at him when he hadn't known she was doing so. He appeared masculine, rugged, and very much like a cowboy.

"What else do you know about him?"

"Not much. I didn't ask a lot of questions. For all I know, he might have a girlfriend. I'm certain he does."

"Why do you say that?"

"I can't imagine a man who looks like him not having one."

"Well, I'm wondering why he thought you were a reporter. What's Chancellor's last name?"

"I don't know. We never got that far. Like I said, I was busy telling him my story to gain access to his ranch. He only trusted me enough to let me nose around outdoors."

"Yes, but look what you achieved when you saw the barn. But still, when you see him tomorrow, you need to get his last name."

"I won't see him tomorrow. He said Thursday would be a better day for him to give me a tour."

"Well, whenever you see him again, I want a last name, Zoe.

There has to be a reason he's leery of reporters. Take some pictures of your cowboy. I'd like to see him."

"He might not want his photo taken. Like I said, he probably has a girlfriend."

"Where are you now?"

"I'm on my way back to the hotel. I'm excited about the prospect of his great-grandmother talking to me."

"Regardless of what he told you about his great-grandmother's mind being sharp as a tack, you know how it was with my grandmother at eighty. We shouldn't expect her to remember much of anything."

After ending her call with Lucky, Zoey entered the gas station's convenience store for a candy bar and a bag of cookies. Normally, she wasn't into junk food, but today, she felt she needed a sugar kick.

She hadn't mentioned anything to Lucky about how she and Chance had stared at each other across the yard. She'd felt something and wanted to believe he had, too. It was as if a magnetic pull trapped them, and neither could look away.

She had felt the intensity of his gaze touch her everywhere, from the top of her head to the soles of her feet and areas in between. Those areas in between still felt sensitive because it had been a while—years—since she'd made love with a man. Not since she'd first moved to Baltimore and began dating Luther.

Over the years, she'd dated guys she considered nice, but they turned out to be toads. The only thing on their mind was getting her into the nearest bed. Then Dr. Luther Fitzpatrick, a heart specialist, transferred to Johns Hopkins Hospital. He was someone who enjoyed doing a lot of the things she did, like playing tennis, going horseback riding, going to the theater, and attending concerts. They'd dated for almost a year when he got the opportunity to work at a hospital in Wyoming. He hadn't loved her, and she hadn't loved him. His move to Wyoming had officially ended things between them.

Eight months later, when she'd gone back to San Francisco to visit her aunt and tell her about the dreams she'd begun having, Aunt Paulina introduced her to Conrad. He was the son of a friend who'd worked in international banking. He'd warned her up front that he wasn't used to long-distance relationships and would try to persuade her to move back to San Francisco. He certainly had tried. Every chance he got.

She'd gotten that call from a friend in San Francisco that Conrad was seen around town with numerous women. When she questioned him about it, he admitted it and she hadn't wasted time ending things between them. More than anything she was glad they hadn't shared a bed. After nearly two years of not being intimately involved with a man, she'd been convinced she didn't need one…until she'd met Chance.

He reminded her of all the pleasure a woman could share in a man's arms. Just looking at him made her think of hot bodies between silken sheets doing all sorts of naughty things. His walk alone was sensuality in motion, and how he wore those cowboy outfits—from the Stetson on his head to those boots on his feet—was sexiness personified.

For her, just the very thought presented a new set of problems. She knew little about him other than she was fiercely attracted to him. What if he was seriously involved with someone else? Would he have looked at her the way he had today if he was? Lucky was pushing for his last name, but more than anything, Zoey needed to know if there was a woman in his life. Special or otherwise.

She had opened the door to get back inside her car when her cell phone rang from a number she didn't recognize. "Yes?"

"Dr. Pritchard, this is Dr. Kemmic."

Her heart began racing. Had he located Dr. Sharon Newberry? "Yes, Doctor Kemmic?"

"I just wanted to give you an update. I talked to a doctor at the hospital where Dr. Newberry worked and was told she retired last year. She and her husband are traveling abroad for six months and won't return to the States until August. He will try to get word to her to contact me when she gets back."

"That's wonderful. I appreciate it, Doctor Kemmic," she said, trying to keep the disappointment from her voice. She had anticipated talking to Dr. Newberry sooner than that, but she had to believe good things came to those who waited. Look how long it had taken for her to begin getting her memory back. Even her doctor had warned her for years there was a fifty percent chance it might never return.

It was returning, and she was happy about it.

Felicia Laverne Madaris sat on the edge of her bed with her bifocals perched on her nose while knitting a baby cap for her great-great-grandbaby, the one she figured would be born seven months from now. To be on the safe side, she was using yellow yarn instead of pink or blue.

Although the expectant parents hadn't made an official announcement, Felicia had dreamed about fish a couple of weeks ago but decided to keep it to herself. There was no reason for her to tell anyone about her dream. That would only cause a lot of speculation, and this was one time she would let the couple do the honors themselves.

The Madaris family motto, passed down from generation to generation, was "Protect, Provide, and Prosper." Those words summed up the family's beliefs, values, and goals. They protected their own, and often, that protection extended to others. They also provided for each other, growing the family's wealth while at the same time remembering those less fortunate through their numerous charities. And while they were certainly a successful family prospering financially, they were also prospering physically. It always filled her heart with joy when there was a Madaris wedding or birth. That meant the family was growing, and that made her happy. Felicia Laverne knew she wouldn't live forever and intended for her family to continue being prosperous in every aspect of the word while she was here.

She had given birth to seven sons, all of whom were alive except one. She felt that familiar pain in her heart whenever she thought about Robert. The only one she had lost.

Her remaining six sons did just as their father would have wanted by caring for her needs. As she began getting older, they insisted she no longer live alone in her home on Whispering Pines. They wanted her to spend more time with them and their families. They proposed that she stay at Whispering Pines with her youngest son, Jake, and his wife, Diamond, for six months out of the year. She would stay with her oldest son, Milton Jr., and his wife, Dora, two months out of the year, including that three-week cruise she always enjoyed. During the remaining four months, she would rotate between the other sons—Lee and his wife, Pearl; Nolan and his wife, Bessie; Lucas and his wife, Carrie; and Jonathan and his wife, Marilyn. This month, she was with her third-born son, Nolan, and his wife, Bessie.

She loved her family and knew they loved her, although she was well aware they thought she sometimes overstepped her boundaries. That was utter nonsense. As far as she was concerned, she had no boundaries regarding their happiness and well-being. Her family would always come first, and she would do what was best for them, whether they thought it was or not. That was the promise she'd made to her beloved Milton on his deathbed, which she intended to keep.

She heard the knock on the door. "Come in."

Bessie opened the door, and although it was fairly early, Felicia figured she was checking on her for the last time before settling in for the night. Nolan Sr. and Bessie loved playing checkers before going to bed. However, from the look on Bessie's face, she immediately knew something was wrong. "What's the matter, Bessie?"

Bessie came and sat in the chair beside the bed. "Mama La-verne, I just got a call from Cate, and she told me something that I think you should know."

Bessie and Cate had been best friends growing up, and Cate was now her great-grandson Chancellor's housekeeper and cook. If Cate had called, that meant it concerned him. "Has something happened to Chancellor?" she asked, trying to keep the distress out of her voice. "Did he get hurt today on the ranch?"

Bessie reached out and took her hand. "No, Chance is fine, but it does concern him."

"What is it, Bessie?" Felicia Laverne asked, staring into her daughter-in-law's troubled gaze. Lord, she hoped it had nothing to do with Ravena Boyle, whom she heard was back in town. There were family members who were worried about that since they'd known how much Chancellor had loved the girl. However, she, of all people, knew about the Madaris pride. A wounded Madaris didn't forgive easily and could hold a grudge forever. She believed any love Chancellor had for Ravena had turned into loathing.

"He got a visitor today," Bessie said.

"Ravena?" she asked softly. The woman was conceited enough to think after all she'd done, she could recapture Chance's heart.

"No, it wasn't Ravena, thankfully. It was a young woman by the name of Dr. Zoey Pritchard. She's a medical doctor from Baltimore."

Felicia Laverne didn't recognize the name. "Why would his visitor be concerning enough for Cate to call you?"

"Because she came to the ranch asking questions, wanting to know about the people who owned the ranch before. Namely, the Martins."

A knot formed in Felicia Laverne's throat. "Why would this woman want to know anything about the Martins?"

"She's claiming to be their granddaughter."

Felicia Laverne now understood why Bessie was troubled. The last thing the Madaris family needed was someone asking questions about the Martins, which would ultimately lead to questions about the Satterfields. The Satterfields and Madarises had been rural neighbors for several generations. Waylon Satterfield had been her husband Milton's very best friend. His only child, a daughter named Arabella, had married a man whose last name was Martin. Could the woman be Arabella's granddaughter, as she claimed?

"Mama Laverne, you know what that could mean, right?" Bessie asked, intruding into her thoughts.

Mama Laverne nodded, suddenly feeling the weight of the Madaris world on her shoulders. If this woman asked questions, they could reveal scandals, lies, and a cover-up involving the Madaris and Satterfield families. There were secrets her sons knew nothing about. Secrets she had hoped to take to her grave. Bessie didn't know everything. She only knew what she'd overheard as a teenaged girl growing up as a preacher's great-granddaughter.

Lord help her if the cover-up was ever revealed—a murder cover-up that she was the only living soul with any knowledge of.

"Yes, I know what it means," Felicia Laverne said, trying to keep her voice calm, although she felt anything but that.

"There's more," Bessie continued.

Felicia Laverne wasn't sure her heart could take any more. It was already beating faster than it should. "Lordy, what else is there?"

"Cate overheard Chance tell the woman he would be contacting you. That you could tell her all the information she wanted about her family since he was certain you'd remember them."

Yes, she remembered them. She could decline a meeting with

the young woman, but then her family would wonder why. Doing something like that would be so unlike her. They knew how much she liked talking about the past. However, when it came to her family, some things from the past should stay there.

Moments later, after Bessie had left her alone again, Felicia Laverne just sat on the edge of the bed, her mind in turmoil. Unable to finish her knitting since her hands were trembling, she placed the basket aside to look at the framed photograph on the nightstand. She carried it with her whenever she was shifted from son to son. It was the picture of her and Milton on their wedding day, well over seventy-five years ago. She was so much in love then and still was. He was a handsome man who'd passed his looks on to his sons, grandsons, and great-grandsons. Generations of Madarises that he would be proud of.

"My beloved Milton," she whispered in a soft tone. "What am I going to do?"

She lowered her head, and when she did, she swore she heard her husband's voice saying, "You will do what you've always done, Fee. The right thing."

Chance couldn't sleep and knew what was bothering him. Zoey Pritchard. How had he allowed her to get next to him? Today, he had done something he'd never done other than to one of his relatives. Namely, invite a woman to his home. A logical explanation would be because of her circumstances, which were the most bizarre he'd ever heard.

Knowing her situation was true and not a fabrication of her imagination, he pulled himself up in bed. Reaching over, he switched on the lamp on his nightstand, bringing light into the room. Why did a surge of sensations swamp him whenever he thought of her? Like now. Like ever since she'd left his ranch earlier. When his men returned to update him on today's activities, his mind had drifted. It had been years since any woman

had caused that to happen. He'd believed he'd grown way beyond such madness. Obviously not.

He would call her first thing in the morning and renege on
the invitation if he had any sense. He would tell her he would
be busy the remainder of this week and the rest of the next. He
would be amenable to doing that if he didn't remember the last
smile she'd given him. It had been filled with so much appre-
ciation and gratitude; there was no way he could deny her the
one thing she now needed more than anything. A chance to
discover a past she desperately needed to know about.

Chance would try calling his great-grandmother again in
the morning, too. He'd called earlier, and she hadn't picked
up. That was unusual. She loved it when her grands or great-
grands called to check on her. The old gal must have been busy
and gone to bed early. That shouldn't surprise him since today
had been Bingo Day at the senior citizen center. There was no
way she would have missed going to that.

Reaching over to turn off the lamp, he intended to get some
sleep tonight, no matter what. Closing his eyes, he tried to settle
into a comfortable position. Suddenly, his eyes flew open, and
he sat up when he remembered why Zoey's features were familiar. Turning back on the lamp, he got out of bed and slipped
into the pair of pajama bottoms he kept nearby.

Dismissing from his mind that what he was looking for could
wait until morning, he negotiated down the darkened hallway
to the stairs that led to his attic. He muttered a curse when one
of his toes came into contact with the bottom of a broken bal-
uster. He'd forgotten the damn thing needed fixing since he
barely had reason to go into his attic. He was certain he hadn't
been up there more than a few times since buying the house.

Opening the door to the attic, he switched on the light,
knowing exactly what he was looking for. This room contained what he'd considered junk that the previous owners had

left. The stuff he'd intended to get rid of but hadn't found the time to do so.

Moving several items around, he saw the huge portrait in the corner covered in cloth to protect it from dust and other elements. He recalled uncovering it one day, looking at it, re-covering it, and not giving it another thought until tonight.

He quickly uncovered the portrait and stood stunned at what he'd revealed. It was that of a woman who had to have been no more than twenty-one at the time, and she bore a striking resemblance to Zoey. Or, more precisely, Zoey bore a striking resemblance to her. She was standing by that huge tree in his front yard, and the ranch house was captured in the background. He could tell the painting had been commissioned work.

He doubted the woman was Zoey's mother since the painting had to have been done over fifty years ago. This had to be Zoey's grandmother, whose last name was Martin. Something else suddenly caught his eye. The necklace the woman wore was the same one Zoey was wearing.

Chance had to tell Zoey about what he'd discovered. He couldn't wait to see her happiness when he showed it to her on Thursday. It then occurred to him that he wouldn't be show-ing it to her since he'd made plans to be away from the ranch that day. Knowing this might be a missing piece in reclaiming her memory, he didn't want to delay letting her know. That meant he would call and tell her tomorrow.

Tomorrow…

Rubbing a hand down his face, he drew in a deep breath. He would only ask for trouble if he reached out to her tomor-row. She would want to see it immediately. That meant com-ing to his ranch, and they would be alone. The thought of him being close to her curvy body, staring into her beautiful face, and inhaling her arousing scent was way too much to take on.

Why? He'd been attracted to women before, and when the time came, he had no problem backing away. Another question he should ask was why he kept having this same conversation with himself. He should admit that deep down, although he didn't know everything there was to know about her, he had a feeling Dr. Zoey Pritchard was getting under his skin. He would admit it and then come up with a solution to deal with it.

One that readily came to mind was introducing her to one of his cousins. Plenty of single ones would appreciate getting involved with her while she was in town. Corbin readily came to mind. His cousin wouldn't have to worry about Mama Laverne's involvement since Chance would introduce them. Also, he knew for certain she didn't know Mama Laverne. She did not know his last name because he hadn't told her.

Satisfied with his solution, he decided to call Zoey in the morning and suggest she come to the ranch around eleven. Glancing at his watch, he saw it wasn't quite midnight, so he would call Corbin and tell him what he needed to know and make sure he agreed to be here tomorrow before Zoey arrived.

Upon returning to his bedroom, he called Corbin who answered immediately. "What's wrong, Chance? What the hell happened?!"

Chance heard the depth of panic in Corbin's voice. "What makes you think something is wrong?"

After a few expletives that almost burned Chance's ears, Corbin said. "Because you rarely call anyone, especially not at this time of night."

"Nothing is wrong. However, I need a favor."

There was a pause before Corbin asked, "What kind of favor?"

He then spent the next twenty minutes telling Corbin Zoey's story. It would have taken less time if his cousin hadn't interrupted by asking so many questions.

"Wow, that's sad about her parents, and her memory loss sucks," Corbin said between yawns.

"I know," Chance agreed.

"And you swear she's a looker?"

"I wouldn't say she was if she wasn't," was Chance's response.

"I'm taking your word for it, so you better not lie."

"Whatever. You agree to be here no later than eleven in the morning?"

"Yeah, I'll be there, Chance, but I need to say something."

Chance rolled his eyes. "Say what?"

"This Dr. Zoey Pritchard must have really gotten next to you for you to be so eager to turn her over to me. Good night."

Chance frowned when he heard the distinct sound of a click in his ear.

Chapter Five

The next day, Chance dialed his great-grandmother's number. She answered on the first ring. "Good morning, Chancellor."

"Good morning, Mama Laverne. I hope you slept well last night."

"I did. What about you?"

There was no way he would tell her thoughts of a certain woman had invaded his sleep. "Yes, I did. I need to ask you something."

"Alright."

"Did you know the family that used to live at this ranch?"

"Yes, I knew the Johnstones. I didn't get to know them that well since they moved in while I was doing missionary work in Haiti."

Chance nodded. "What about the people who lived here before the Johnstones? The Martins?"

When she didn't answer immediately, he figured she was thinking, trying to recall. "Yes. The Martins owned the ranch but didn't live there except during the summer months. Joshua and Arabella Martin were college professors at Howard University in Washington, DC."

"If they weren't here to run the ranch, why didn't they sell it?"

There was another pause, and he figured Mama Laverne was trying to recollect her thoughts again. After all, that was a long time ago. "I understand that Arabella's grandfather, Kurt Satterfield, stipulated in his will that the property could not be sold until the third generation after his death. When the Martins weren't in residence, they hired good people to run things."

"I see."

"Chancellor, why are you asking me these questions?"

He didn't want to tell Mama Laverne Zoey's story, especially the part about her memory loss. He preferred that she tell that to his great-grandmother herself. "I got a visitor yesterday saying she was the Martins' granddaughter."

"You believe her?"

"Yes, I believe her." He then told Mama Laverne about the framed portrait in his attic. "The resemblance is simply amazing."

"That doesn't surprise me. Arabella favored her mother, and the women had striking features."

"Did you know Arabella?"

"Yes. She was an only child and a very striking woman."

So is her granddaughter, he thought, deciding to keep that opinion to himself. "Arabella's granddaughter's name is Dr. Zoey Pritchard."

"What's her reason for being in Houston?" his great-grandmother asked.

"She is trying to get as much information as possible about her mother's side of the family. She doesn't remember them, and her parents were killed in a car accident almost twenty years ago when she was a child. She was with them and was the lone survivor."

He heard his great-grandmother gasp. "I'm sorry to hear that. I didn't know. I'd heard the ranch had been sold and assumed the daughter, who I recall was named Michelle, no longer wanted to keep it since the three-generation mandate in her great-great-grandfather's will had ended. I wished I had kept up with her. The last time I saw Michelle was at her parents' funeral."

Chancellor lifted a brow. "The Martins died at the same time?"

"Yes, from Legionnaires' disease. There was an outbreak at an educational conference they attended somewhere in the Midwest. They caught it and died within days."

Chance didn't say anything, thinking how sad it was that Zoey had lost her grandparents and then, years later, her parents. Except for that paternal aunt, she had indeed been left alone.

"Michelle and her husband were doctors living in the north," his great-grandmother was now saying. "He was a fine-looking young man. The day I saw them, I also saw their daughter. She was about five or six and was a cute little girl."

Chance thought that cute little girl had become a beautiful woman. A woman who could get under his skin if he allowed it to happen. He was determined that he wouldn't. "Since you recall her grandparents and parents, and Zoey as a little girl, I think conversing with you will be meaningful for her, Mama Laverne. Is it possible for the two of you to talk?"

"Yes."

"May I give her your phone number?"

There was another pause. This one was longer than the last. "I prefer meeting her in person, Chancellor. Can you bring her here on Friday?"

He preferred not to. "I might be tied up at the ranch on Friday. I'll see if Corbin is available to bring her."

"She's met Corbin?"

"He's stopping by this morning and will meet Zoey when

she drops by to see that portrait. Any particular time you want to meet with her on Friday?"

"She can join me for lunch."

"Thank you for agreeing to talk to her."

"You're welcome, Chancellor."

Chance disconnected the call, thinking Mama Laverne didn't sound like herself. That made him wonder if she'd been over-exerting herself lately. He didn't want to alarm his family members, but he would talk to his aunt Bessie to see if she'd noticed anything concerning.

Corbin, who'd arrived an hour earlier than he was supposed to, stood beside Chance as they gazed out the kitchen window and watched Zoey get out of the car.

Chance heard his cousin's sharp intake of breath before saying, "To show my gratitude for turning this gorgeous creature over to me, I apologize for any mean trick I've ever played on you while we were kids." Corbin stared out the window at Zoey as if transfixed.

"I didn't turn Zoey over to you. I merely want the two of you to meet."

Corbin rolled his eyes. "Bullshit. You want me to take her off your hands. And as I alluded to last night, maybe it should concern you why."

Chance had news for Corbin. He knew why, which was why he'd taken such drastic steps. "You better not get out of line with her," he grumbled.

"Now that's something I can't promise I won't do." Corbin then resumed looking out the window. "Damn, Chance. Look at those curves, that stunning face, that mass of hair, and how it blows in the wind."

Corbin's words annoyed Chance because he was also seeing those things. However, he was seeing beyond them to the decent woman he believed her to be. It bothered him that his cousin's main focus was Zoey's physical attributes. "She's a nice person, Corbin."

Corbin laughed. "I believe you, but at the moment, her niceness is being outplayed by all that fineness," he said, playfully slugging Chance in the shoulder with a sexually suggestive grin on his face.

When Zoey's feet touched the steps, Corbin rushed to the door instead of waiting for her to knock.

Chance frowned, already regretting his decision to introduce Zoey to Corbin.

Before Zoey could raise her hand to knock, the front door flew open. There stood a man who resembled Chance. A brother, perhaps? A cheerful expression touched the corners of his lips as he extended his hand out to her. "Zoey Pritchard, it's nice meeting you. I'm Corbin Madaris."

She returned his smile and took the hand he offered. *Madaris.* Where had she heard that name before? If this was Chance's brother, then it stood to reason that his name was Madaris, too. Chancellor Madaris. She liked the sound of it.

"Nice meeting you, too, Corbin." If they were related, this man had a more pleasing personality upon opening a door than Chance.

She switched her gaze to Chance when he came to stand beside Corbin. The two men were identical in height, and she could see how much they favored each other. Upon seeing Chance, her smile automatically widened. "Good morning, Chance."

"Good morning, Zoey. Come in. I hope I didn't call you too early this morning."

"No, you didn't," she said, stepping over the threshold. There was no way she would tell him he'd awakened her from her dream about him. "I've barely been able to contain my excitement since your call. I can't wait to see the portrait you told me about."

She turned to Corbin. "Do you live here, too?" she asked when he closed the door behind her.

Corbin shook his head. "No, I have a place in town. Chance said you're a doctor."

"Yes, I'm an orthopedic surgeon at Johns Hopkins Hospital in Baltimore."

"And I understand you had an aunt who recently passed away. I offer my condolences," Corbin added.

"Thank you."

"Do you know if your aunt ever went on a cruise in the last twenty years?"

Zoey thought the question was odd. Before she could answer, Chance spoke up and said tersely, "Corbin, you don't need to know that."

Corbin shrugged and said to Chance. "Just thought I'd double-check."

Zoey's gaze shifted from one man to the other, sure she was missing something. It was some inside joke between the two brothers. However, she had no problem answering Corbin's question. "My aunt has never gone on a cruise. She hated being out on the water in a boat of any size. Can I see the portrait?" she asked, not caring if she sounded anxious.

"Yes, follow me this way," Chance said, and she didn't miss the glare he gave Corbin. "I brought it down from the attic and placed it in the dining room."

"Okay." She was surprised when Corbin linked his arm with hers—she figured he was being a gentleman. They followed Chance from the living room.

She'd noted his spacious kitchen yesterday when he'd led her to the backyard. Now she saw how massive his entire ranch house was. There was a charming staircase that curved at the top before reaching the landing. She wished she could remember spending time here with her parents and grandparents. Now all she had was just pieces of her dreams.

She stopped and pulled her arm from Corbin to place her hand on her upper chest. Her breath caught when she saw the large portrait Chance had propped in the middle of his dining room table. The wooden frame was sturdy with beautiful decorative edging. But what captured her attention was the woman who'd posed for the artist—her grandmother. Chance was right. The two favored each other. And from the photos she'd seen of her mother, she also looked like them.

"You're wearing that same necklace," Corbin said.

"Yes, I am," she said softly, reaching up to finger the heart pendant necklace. "I found it in my aunt's belongings when I discovered the documents about the sale of this ranch. I figured it had been my dad's gift to my mom since Mom always wore it in my dreams. Now I see it once belonged to my grandmother."

The necklace had become her inner strength from the day Zoey began wearing it. Whenever she felt down in the dumps or sad, just touching it reminded her of the woman who'd worn the necklace before her, whom she'd assumed had only been her mother. Now knowing the necklace had been passed down through generations touched her deeply.

Zoey had told herself she wouldn't get emotional when she saw the portrait, but she couldn't help it. Just knowing this beautiful young woman, smiling with similar dimples, had been her grandmother was affecting her. And she was standing by that huge oak tree in the front yard of this ranch house.

She noticed Chance was staring at her as if he was able to feel her joy and pain. Like yesterday, their gazes locked, and the same intense attraction she'd felt then overwhelmed her. She knew she should pull her gaze from his but couldn't.

He began moving toward her, and her heart kicked up a notch. She wanted him to pull her into his arms because, more than anything, at that moment, she needed to be held by him.

He stopped directly in front of her, and made a move to reach for her when, suddenly, Corbin cleared his throat.

She'd forgotten Corbin was in the room, and from the look on Chance's face, it was obvious that he'd done so as well. He stepped back to put distance between them.

"Your grandmother was beautiful," Corbin said as if to break the awkwardness in the room.

Zoey appreciated his effort. "Yes, she was," she said, looking at the portrait again.

"Just like you," Corbin added.

She gave him a smile. "Thank you." She then studied the painting again. "I have no idea what her name was."

"Arabella," Chance said in what she thought was a deep husky tone. "Your maternal grandmother was Arabella Martin."

Glancing over at him, she asked, "How do you know that?"

"I talked to my great-grandmother this morning. She remembers her."

Zoey couldn't downplay the excitement she felt. "She does?"

"Yes, and she remembers your mother as well."

"Did your great-grandmother agree to talk to me?" she asked hopefully.

"Yes. Are you free to join her for lunch on Friday?"

"Yes, of course," she said, smiling brightly. The most she had imagined had been telephone communication. Sharing lunch with his great-grandmother was more than she had hoped for.

"Since Chance will be tied up at the ranch Friday, I'll take you to meet her," Corbin said. "She's spending this month with my grandparents."

Zoey lifted a confused brow. "Your grandparents? Aren't your grandparents also Chance's grandparents?"

"No. Why would you think that?" Corbin asked.

"I assumed the two of you were brothers."

Corbin grinned. "Our great-grandparents had seven sons.

Chance's father is one, and mine is another. That means plenty of Madaris cousins and some of us favor each other."

"Your last name is Madaris, too?" she asked Chance.

He nodded. "Yes. I'm sure you've heard of my family."

She shook her head. "Not sure. Should I have?"

She saw the exchanged glance between the two men and felt she was missing something. "Should I have?" she asked again.

"Most people have."

"Why?" When neither man said anything, she looked from one to the other and decided to figure things out. She repeated the name out loud. Twice. "Madaris. Madaris." Then she said. "I do recall that, after my accident, one of the nurses would come to my room and read a children's book written by Lorren Madaris to me. The Kente Kids series. That same nurse gave me a collection when I was discharged. That was almost twenty years ago. Is that author related to you?"

"Yes," Chance said. "Lorren is married to our cousin, Justin."

Zoey beamed broadly. "Well, let her know I enjoyed her books growing up and that a number of my teenaged patients are reading her young adult line of books."

"I will let her know that."

She then turned to Corbin. "Where do you want us to meet on Friday?"

"I'll come pick you up," Corbin offered.

"I hate to be a bother."

"No bother. Where are you staying?"

"The Houston Riverfront Hotel."

Corbin grinned and winked at her. "I'll pick you up in the hotel's lobby at eleven. And I have another idea. How about sharing dinner with me on Saturday? Afterward, we can go dancing," Corbin suggested.

"I'm sure Zoey will have other things to do on Saturday," Chance said tersely.

Zoey thought dinner and dancing sounded like fun, although

she wished Chance had been the one to ask her out. But he hadn't and seemed annoyed that Corbin had. More than ever, she suspected he had a girlfriend or was in an exclusive relationship. Heck, for all she knew, he might be engaged to get married. In that case, he had no right to feel any kind of way if she went out with Corbin.

Smiling at Corbin, she said, "I don't have plans for Saturday evening and would love to join you for dinner and dancing."

Chapter Six

"Aren't you going to ask me how things went today, Chancellor?"

Chance paused in removing his boots to glance at Ms. Cate. She had her purse on her arm, which meant she was ready to leave for the day. It was Thursday, the day Zoey was to return. That was why he'd deliberately remained in the north pastures the entire day with his men while rounding up strays.

Of course, he was chomping at the bit, wondering how things had gone, but he refused to let his housekeeper know. It was bad enough that Corbin suspected his interest in Zoey; he didn't need Ms. Cate getting ideas. If she did, his family would soon get wind of it.

That meant he had to continue to downplay his interest. Since entering his home, he'd been trying to act nonchalantly. He figured before Ms. Cate left, she would get around to telling him something. She wouldn't be able to help herself. He'd been right.

"I have no reason to think things didn't go well, Ms. Cate. You gave her the tour like I asked, right?"

"Yes. I think she thought you would be here to show her around."

He didn't have anything to say to that, so he didn't. He hoped Ms. Cate would take his silence for disinterest.

"She likes this place," Ms. Cate then said.

It didn't matter to him if she liked his home or not. "Did she see anything familiar?" he asked.

"Yes, a few things. However, I think the biggest impact was when she rode down to the lake."

He leaned back in the chair. "Why do you say that?"

"When she returned, she seemed shaken up and immediately left."

He wondered what that was about. Had parts of her memory returned as they had the other day? He could call her and find out but knew he shouldn't. He'd decided to put distance between them, and that's what he intended to do. Being around her made him want a woman in a bad way, which was why he decided to go to Vance's Tavern tonight instead of waiting to do so tomorrow night. He'd told his men not to expect him home until midday. While in downtown Houston tomorrow, he would check on his parents. He'd called and told his mother to expect him for breakfast, and he could tell by her voice that she'd been happy about that.

His thoughts shifted back to Zoey and how happy she'd been when he'd given her that portrait yesterday. It had certainly made her day. He'd told her that when she'd returned today, if she saw anything else in the attic that might have belonged to her family, she could have it as well. He wondered if she had.

"Did she see anything else she wanted in the attic?" he asked.

"Yes. That antique jewelry armoire. It was too heavy for us to bring down, so she'll return to get it. If Corbin had arrived an hour earlier, he could have helped."

Chance frowned. "Corbin's been here?"

"Yes. He'd hoped to ride to the south pasture with her."

Chance just bet he had. Why did it bother him that Corbin might be genuinely interested in Zoey? Any able-bodied man with a lick of sense would be, as well. That said a lot about him. Standing, he said, "Have a good weekend, Ms. Cate."

"I hope you do the same, Chancellor. I'll see you Tuesday."

"Are you saying Chancellor's last name is Madaris?" Lucky asked.

She and Lucky hadn't connected yesterday because Lucky and Burke had spent most of their time flying to Calgary to attend Burke's parents' anniversary party. "Yes, and I could tell they figured I should have made some connection to the last name. The only thing I could remember was reading those Lorren Madaris books as a kid. She's married to one of their cousins."

"I read her books as well, but the Madaris name is known for another reason."

"What reason is that?" she asked, looking through her closet for something to wear for tomorrow's lunch with Chance's great-grandmother.

"Diamond Swain."

Zoey lifted a brow. "That name sounds vaguely familiar. Who is she?"

"Honestly, Zoey. It would help if you had stopped exclusively watching those Korean movies years ago. If you had, you would know that Diamond Swain is a well-known American actress."

Rolling her eyes, Zoey reached for a dress from the closet she thought would suit her. Like Lucky loved watching her crime shows, Zoey enjoyed Korean movies. That was the one thing her aunt Paulina had passed on to her.

In her younger days, her aunt worked in Seoul for years as a private English teacher for some of the wealthiest Korean families. As a result, she preferred watching Korean movies to American ones. That meant Zoey didn't have much choice when it came to watching movies and discovered she enjoyed them, too. Since Aunt Paulina taught her to speak Korean, she didn't have to read the subtitles.

"What does Diamond Swain have to do with the Madaris family?" Zoey asked, looking the dress over to see if it needed to be ironed.

"She is married to Jacob Madaris, who I bet is a relative of theirs. If I recall correctly, he also has a ranch in Texas. Probably right there in Houston. I would love for you to get Diamond Swain Madaris's autograph when you meet her."

Zoey rolled her eyes again. "What makes you think I'm going to meet her?"

"Why wouldn't you? Though you bailed on getting any interest from your cowboy, he did introduce you to his cousin, who sounds just as sexy."

Yes, but Chance wasn't her cowboy, Zoey thought despondently. She had hoped to see him again today when she went to his ranch but hadn't. She'd been slightly disappointed, although she should not have been. She could understand him putting distance between them since he was involved with another woman.

"Although Corbin is a very handsome man, I'm not attracted to him like I am to Chance."

"And you're sure Chancellor Madaris has a girlfriend?"

"I'm not sure of anything about him other than our attraction. That can't be denied. I think even Corbin picked up on it. But since Chance is fighting the attraction, so will I."

"How did today go at the ranch?"

"It was nice. Chance was kind enough to have a horse saddled for me, so I could ride to that lake. It was a beautiful place, and I saw several things that I remembered from my dream, but nothing jogged my memory there." She paused momentarily and then said, "Just being there and knowing I shared time there with my parents touched me deeply, and it was hard not to get emotional. I left soon after that."

"Did you see Chancellor again?"

"No. He was busy on another part of the ranch." She then told Lucky how his housekeeper had been the one to give her a tour of his home. She also told her about the jewelry armoire and how charming it was.

"It was nice of Chancellor to give you that portrait of your grandmother and let you have the armoire."

Zoey shrugged. "Yes, it was. They've been in his attic for years. He was planning to toss them out. I'm glad he never got around to it."

"I am, too. I can't wait to see them. Especially the portrait of your grandmother. Are you ready to meet his great-grandmother tomorrow?"

"Yes. Too ready. I doubt I'll be able to sleep tonight."

"Well, go to bed early and get plenty of rest so you don't fall asleep on her tomorrow."

"Good idea. Give Burke my love, and I will talk to you later."

Chapter Seven

Chance entered Vance's Tavern and scanned the establishment. He hadn't been here for a while, but the place was crowded as usual. Vance had expanded the size of the tavern earlier that year to add more space for dancing. Already, several people were out on the floor doing a Texas line dance.

He removed his Stetson and hung it on the rack before crossing the floor to a vacant booth. He had barely sat down when Cheryl Carlyle slid into the seat across from him. The same Cheryl Carlyle who had gotten Corbin in a tizzy last month when he'd heard the rumor Mama Laverne would marry them off. A rumor Chance figured was started by Cheryl herself.

"Hello, Chance."

"Cheryl."

"What is it you want that would bring you off your ranch on a Thursday night?"

One thing for certain, he thought. It wasn't her. He wasn't that desperate. "I thought I'd come here and enjoy a drink or two. Alone." He stressed the latter, hoping she took the hint that he didn't want company.

She ignored it when she said, "Well, I'd rather not be alone tonight. In fact—" she deliberately loosened the top button of her blouse to expose that she wasn't wearing a bra "—I want a drink or two myself. You buying?"

"No," he said flatly, not caring if his response sounded rude.

She frowned. "You're not being friendly."

"Most people don't consider me much of a friendly person. And since I'm on a roll, I might as well take being bad-mannered to another level and say I prefer you vacate that seat."

Her frown deepened. "Why? Are you expecting someone?"

"It doesn't matter if I am or not. I don't want you sitting in it."

"You're worse than bad-mannered, Chance Madaris. You're an ass."

He'd been called worse. "Duly noted. Now I suggest you leave before this ass tells you what he thinks of you. Uncensored."

She stood and huffed off, deliberately swaying her backside when she did so. Seeing her in those jeans did nothing for him. Not like seeing Zoey in hers.

Zoey.

Why had he thought about her during the hour-and-a-half drive from his ranch? Why was he thinking about how things would go with her and Mama Laverne tomorrow? More importantly, between her and Corbin. He would be taking her out on Saturday. His cousin better not get out of line with her or else.

Or else what? He didn't have anything to say about anything when getting Zoey and Corbin together had been a deliberate move on his part. He figured he would have no reason to think about her once he'd done so. Damn, that strategy wasn't working. He was thinking about her even more.

"You want the usual, Chance?"

He met his waitress's gaze. Barbie had been his first one-night stand years ago, and he appreciated she'd understood the rules then and had abided by them since. "Yes, Barbie. The usual."

When she walked off, he scoped the place again. This time focusing on the women. There seemed to be a lot of them. Some were sitting alone. Some in groups. Several had met his gaze and held it, and then he'd broken eye contact. He hadn't felt anything. Not that sensuous connection, magnetic pull, or sizzling chemistry he felt whenever he stared into Zoey's eyes.

Like yesterday. Not only had he dismissed Corbin's presence, but he'd also not given a damn. He only considered pulling her into his arms and kissing her to share her emotions. Lucky for him, Corbin had made a sound to knock some quick sense into him.

"Here you are, Chance," Barbie said, interrupting his thoughts as she placed a beer before him.

"Thanks."

When she walked off, he picked up the bottle and began scanning the place again. Several more women had arrived. Some he'd shared a bed with before. Others he had not. He concentrated on the latter, but still, he felt nothing. Not a single one aroused him to a spark of hunger or enticed him to a boner.

The music had ended, so he shifted his body around to check out the thinning crowd on the dance floor to see if there were any prospects.

"I figured sooner or later you'd come here."

He went still upon recognizing that voice. There once was a time when just hearing it would arouse every male thing in him. Now it did nothing. All he felt was immediate repugnance. He slowly turned to look into the face of the woman sitting in the seat he'd asked Cheryl to vacate earlier. Ravena Boyle.

He met her gaze and felt something—instant repulsion. And while studying her features, he thought she'd undoubtedly had a hard life since he'd last seen her, which was close to five years ago. Her beauty had diminished, and he thought nothing about her remained attractive. Her makeup was heavy. He could remember a time she hadn't worn any at all.

"Ravena. I heard you were back in town."

"And I heard you'd recovered from your injury. I'm happy for you."

He picked up his beer to take another sip. "Are you? During our last conversation, you called me half of a man."

"I want to apologize for that, Chancy."

Hearing her say the pet name she'd always called him sent spikes of chills all through him. "The name is Chance," he said through gritted teeth.

"I prefer Chancy."

"Then don't expect me to answer. And if you don't mind, I need that seat kept vacant."

"Why? Are you waiting for someone?"

"No. I'd rather not have you in it."

She didn't respond for a minute, then said, "Do you remember this is where we met? You were home on leave for a month. I saw you and used one hell of a pickup line to garner your interest. You even complimented me on how original it was. Then we had one hell of a time together. When you returned to Germany, we wrote to each other practically every day, and when you came home that Christmas, you asked me to marry you."

He placed his beer down and stared hard at her. "That was the biggest mistake of my life."

"People said you've changed. You aren't the fun-loving man you used to be, and I regret my part in that."

"No need to have regrets, Ravena. Walking out of my life was the best thing you ever could have done for me."

He could tell she hadn't liked his comment. "Then why are you so miserable?"

"Miserable? You think I'm miserable?"

She lifted a haughty chin. "Aren't you? I hear you rarely come off your ranch. And when you do, it's to visit your folks or to come here. To the very place we met. Why is that?"

He could tell her he came here to get laid but figured that wasn't her business. "You think the reason I come here has something to do with you? To relive memories? Seriously?"

She shrugged. "There are some who think you're pining for me."

"They're thinking wrong."

"Are they? I understand you haven't been seriously involved with another woman since I left. I'm back now. I admit I made a mistake in walking away and leaving town the way I did, and I apologize for hurting you. Regardless of whether you accept my apology, there's something you can't deny. I've always been in your blood, and you've been in mine. That's the reason my marriage didn't last."

Chance stared at her. Did she honestly think he believed any of her bullshit? As he continued to hold her gaze, he hoped she could feel all the intense dislike he was emitting. "There might have been a time when you were in my blood, Ravena, but not anymore. I've had several transfusions since then. I don't have any feelings for you whatsoever. None. What I do feel is disgust with myself for ever getting involved with you."

He could feel her anger. She didn't want to believe his words. Damn. Did she think she could return to Houston, and they would pick up where they'd left off? After what she'd said? After what she had done? Hell would freeze over first.

"You don't mean that. You still love me, Chancy. I can prove it."

Rage boiled inside him, rising to the top, almost reaching an explosive level. "The name is Chance, and I meant everything I said. I think you're pretty damn pathetic if you think I could still love you, so please don't waste your time trying to prove anything. You can't."

Standing, he threw enough bills on the table to pay for his

beer and a tip for Barbie before turning, grabbing his Stetson off the rack, and walking out.

Chance had barely driven five miles when his cell phone rang. He answered it remotely on his steering wheel, not knowing who it was. "What?" he snapped, still steaming over his encounter with Ravena.

"Are you okay?"

He released a deep breath. Clayton, one of his older cousins, had always been protective of his younger Madaris cousins. Chance always appreciated it while growing up. Now, as an adult, not so much.

He didn't have to wonder how Clayton knew. Vance's Tavern was Clayton's old hangout in his womanizing days, and he and the owner were good friends. "I'm fine."

"You sure?"

"I'm positive, Clayton."

There was a pause. "It was bound to happen—you and Ravena running into each other. I hope you were prepared for it."

"There was nothing to prepare myself for. Would you believe she honestly thinks she can return after all this time, say a few apologetic words, and become a part of my life again?"

"Can she?"

Chance frowned. It bothered him that some members of his family thought she could. "Hell to the double digits, no."

"Honestly, I didn't think so, but thought I'd check. Enough about Ravena Boyle. What about that woman I heard showed up at your ranch this week?"

It sure didn't take long for that news to get around. "What of it?"

"How do you feel about it?" Clayton asked.

Chance was glad the question hadn't been, "How do you feel about *her*?" Clayton would be surprised by his answer. "I feel she has a right to want to know about her family, and I'm glad she'll talk to Mama Laverne tomorrow."

"You're not concerned she has ulterior motives? Like thinking she has a right to your ranch?"

Chance rolled his eyes. It shouldn't surprise him that Clayton would think that way. It was the attorney in him to do so. "No, Clayton, I'm not concerned. I know you mean well by asking, but please let me handle my business."

There was a pause and then. "Alright. But if you need us for anything, we're here."

Chance knew he meant the entire Madaris family. "I know that. I've always known that thanks to you, Justin, and Dex," he said, mentioning Clayton's two older brothers. The three— more than ten years older—had always been there for their younger cousins. "And I appreciate it. Thanks."

"No thanks needed. That's how we roll."

After the call ended, Chance exited the interstate for the hotel. He had planned to rumble between the sheets with a woman. One thing was for certain, he wouldn't be getting laid tonight. For some reason, some part of him was glad he wouldn't be.

"For crying out loud, Ravena, will you undress and come to bed?"

Ravena gazed across the hotel room to the naked man in bed as she angrily paced the floor. She and Ken Cox, whose family owned several jewelry stores in Texas, considered themselves sex buddies and nothing more.

She'd known winning Chance over might not be easy, but she never thought it would be impossible. "Will you believe he called me pathetic?"

"Although I don't think you're pathetic, I think you have a lot of nerve to assume you could return to town and expect Chance Madaris to take back up with you after the way you dumped him when he was in that wheelchair."

That's not what she wanted to hear. "He still loves me."

"After what you told me he said tonight, he undoubtedly does not."

Ravena placed her hands on her hips. "What other reason could there be for him not having a life? He's miserable."

Ken laughed. "Looks to me like he's living a damn good life. He has his pick of women for a night whenever he wants one. He owns a nice spread. He has the Madaris name, money, notoriety, and respect. If that's being miserable, then I'll take misery. You should have held on to a good thing when you had it."

"Dammit, Ken, he was in a wheelchair. A cripple. How was I to know he would one day walk again?"

"Well, Ravena, there is that part of the wedding vows that says, 'in sickness and in health.' You failed that part before you could get to the altar."

She glared at him. "I want him back."

"Good luck with that happening. I understand Ms. Felicia Laverne rules that family with an iron fist. She might have accepted you being part of it years ago, but she won't now."

"In that case, I think it's time for me to get on Ms. Felicia Laverne's good side," Ravena said, moving toward the bed.

"You think that's possible?" Ken asked, throwing the covers back for her.

"She's ninety-something, old, senile, and probably easy to manipulate. I have to convince her that I regret what I did in the past, and that I'm the only one capable of getting Chance out of the funk he's been in for the past five years."

"Regardless of the old lady, you must win Chance over. It sounds like he's immune to you," Ken stated.

"I know just the way for him to get un-immune. He could never resist me," Ravena said with much self-assurance.

"I hate to remind you, but he did so tonight."

She stared at Ken, and her confidence dropped a notch. Could he be right about Chance not desiring her anymore? She refused to believe that. Like she'd told him, she was in his blood. Granted, she hadn't expected him to welcome her with open arms when he saw her, but she hadn't expected such bitterness and anger toward her either.

Damn him. Five years had been good to him. He was more handsome and had more muscles on his body than before. But his attitude was atrocious. For him to feel so much hostility toward her meant the hurt she'd caused went deep. For it to have gotten to that depth meant he'd love her with the kind of love that couldn't die, regardless of what he'd said. He might have resisted her tonight but he wouldn't do so for long. She had to believe that.

"Chance is the man I want, and the man I intend to get, Ken. No one will stand in my way of getting him back. Not that old lady or any other member of his family," Ravena said with her complete confidence returning. "And until then…"

She removed her clothes when she reached the bed.

Chapter Eight

"Good morning, Mama."

Felicia Laverne looked up to find her sixth-born son standing in the patio's doorway. A happy expression spread across her features. "Jonathan. Good seeing you. Is Marilyn with you? How's the family?"

Jonathan Madaris crossed the room to give his mother a kiss on the cheek and an affectionate hug. That was the way with all her sons. They'd had a close relationship from the time all seven of them were born. She was proud of every one of them.

"No, Marilyn isn't with me. She and Diana left early to go shopping," he said, easing into the chair across from where she sat on the screened-in patio. "Knowing those two, it will be an all-day thing."

Diana was her daughter-in-law who had been married to Robert. It didn't matter that she was no longer a Madaris since she'd remarried a retired senator a few years ago. Diana, who'd given her a granddaughter named after her, would forever be a part of the Madaris family and a member of the Madaris Wives Club.

"And the family is doing fine, Mama," Jonathan replied.

"That's good. Do you want a cup of tea?" she asked while motioning to the teapot on the table in front of her. As far as she was concerned, there was nothing like a cup of Madaris tea—a secret tea recipe made of special herbs and spices—that had been in the Madaris family for generations.

"No, thanks. I'm fine. Marilyn and I had breakfast together before Diana arrived."

"So, what brings you here this morning?" Although Jonathan visited her often, she knew something else had brought him here. She had a sixth sense where her sons were concerned. Her beloved Milton used to refer to it as "mother's intuition."

"I heard about the young lady who visited Chance the other day. I also heard she's joining you for lunch later."

A knot settled in Felicia Laverne's stomach. "And?"

Jonathan's thick brows drew together, but his expression gave nothing away otherwise. She figured it was something he'd perfected after years of being a teacher; and even more years as a principal and college professor. "And I understand she might be Arabella's granddaughter," he said.

Felicia Laverne nodded. "And what if she is?"

Jonathan didn't say anything for a moment, but then continued. "Arabella Satterfield and I were best friends until she turned fifteen and was sent to that all-girls school in the East."

Felicia Laverne smiled softly. She'd known at the time Jonathan had been sweet on Arabella. "I recall you would walk her home from school every day. She was a couple of years younger than you."

"Yes, and back then, I was only allowed to walk her to the boundary of her family's property. I think her parents would not have minded had I gone beyond that marker. However, her grandmother, Ms. Penny, didn't like our family. Neither I nor Arabella knew why. I asked my older brothers, and they said they'd heard about some feud between the two families that happened before we were born, but they didn't know any specifics about it. So, one day, I asked Dad."

She took a long, deep breath. When it came to her husband, she knew him better than anyone. He'd always been close to his sons. If one of them asked him anything, he would have told them what he felt they needed to know and nothing more. But this particular son would have dug deeper, asked more questions. "And what did he tell you?"

Jonathan paused a moment and then, leaning slightly forward, said, "Dad told me that the two of you postponed your wedding for a while, and why."

Felicia Laverne took a sip of her tea. So, he knew that part of it. The Madaris scandal. "Although our wedding was postponed, Milton and I did marry and had seven handsome sons."

"Meeting with this young lady won't bother you, knowing she is a Satterfield?" he asked.

"No, it won't bother me. Waylon's mother, Penny, deliberately kept the discord between the two families, as if the lies and deceit hadn't started with her daughter."

To this day, Felicia Laverne believed Penny Satterfield had been behind Waylon's decision to send Arabella to that school in Alexandria after his wife, Deedra, died. Penny feared another Satterfield would fall in love with a Madaris.

"And then there was your grandfather Jantzen," Felicia Laverne said, shaking her head. She, of all people, knew Madaris men could be bullheaded, stubborn, and unforgiving, all because of that blasted Madaris pride. "Pa Jantz died before you were born, Jonathan, but he was alive for my first four sons. When it came to protecting his family and the Madaris name, he was a force to be reckoned with."

"Dad said he and Mr. Waylon never stopped being best friends. They just let Ms. Penny and Grampa Jantz think so."

"They only fooled Penny. Pa Jantz knew the truth, and in his own way, I believed that he admired Milton for his loyalty to his best friend. After all, when it counted, Waylon had remained loyal to Milton."

She paused, thinking of the words Pa Jantz had spoken on his deathbed and how, in the end, he had made things right. "Even if Milton and Waylon had become enemies, I would have no ill feelings toward Waylon Satterfield's great-granddaughter. Why would I?"

Jonathan shrugged. "I thought her visit would dredge up unpleasant memories, Mama. I'm sure postponing your wedding was a difficult time for you."

"Yes, but I look back at that period as a test of Milton's and my love, trust, and devotion to each other. We made it through. But like I said, Ms. Penny was determined to keep the feud going. There were days I honestly thought hatred for this family would consume her soul. But then Pa Jantz had a problem with forgiving, forgetting, and moving on, all because of that Madaris pride."

Jonathan stood. "Trust me, I know all about that blasted Madaris pride. I almost lost Marilyn because of it."

Felicia Laverne remembered that time. Jonathan wasn't the only Madaris man who almost lost a good woman because of it. "Did you ever tell your brothers about your conversation with your father regarding the Satterfields?"

"Nope," Jonathan replied. "Like you said, you and Dad did get married in the end, so it was water under the bridge."

He grinned and added, "Besides, my four older brothers would have found any excuse to get rowdy."

"That's the truth," Felicia Laverne agreed. Although her four oldest sons had settled down by then, it would not have taken much to rouse them back into their hell-raising ways. That was the main reason she and Milton had agreed to cover up the full details of his sister Victoria's death. Had her sons known everything about their favorite aunt's death, they would have taken the law into their own hands.

"Alright, Mama," Jonathan said, interrupting her thoughts. Leaning down, he placed another kiss on her cheek. "I'll leave so you can return to your knitting. What are you making, by the way?"

Not wanting to say just yet, she replied. "Umm, just a little something to keep my hands moving so my joints won't get stiff."

Jonathan nodded. "I appreciate how you take care of yourself. We all do, Mama."

Felicia Laverne smiled at her son. "I have no choice. I intend to be around to see my great-grands get married. At least those on my list."

"I understand some of them call it your 'hit' list," Jonathan said, grinning again.

"Nolan the third started that foolishness and Corbin is keeping that nonsense going." She sighed. "Thanks for dropping by and expressing your concerns, Jonathan. I'm fine with Waylon Satterfield's great-granddaughter's visit."

As Felicia Laverne said the words, more than anything, she wished they were true.

Zoey saw Corbin the moment she stepped off the elevator the next morning. He stood by a bevy of flowers and plants in the atrium and smiled when he saw her. She smiled back.

She had chosen to wear a sundress that wasn't too long or too short. Living with Aunt Paulina had taught her that older people would assess your clothing as part of your character. She didn't want to get off on the wrong foot with Corbin and Chance's great-grandmother.

He moved toward her. Whereas Chance was a cowboy through and through, Corbin was the ultimate businessman in expensive suits. He was tall, handsome, and professional. She loved how his thick, neatly coiled dreadlocks flowed around his shoulders. Yesterday, he told her that he was the CEO of the Madaris Foundation and that he enjoyed what he did. She could see him in the boardroom more than on a horse riding the range.

Corbin continued walking toward her, and although he and Chance favored each other, it was Chance's face that had invaded her dreams every night since they'd met. Chance who had that turn-you-on swag in his walk. Chance made her blood hot just by looking at her. Chance could light a fire in every part of her body whenever she saw him.

She knew that she needed to let it go since he belonged to another. Besides, she couldn't forget that her sole purpose for being in Texas was to try to regain her memory, not to cultivate a romance with anyone.

Corbin stopped in front of her. "Zoey," he greeted cheerfully. "You look terrific."

"Thanks. I wanted to look nice. This meeting with your great-grandmother is important to me, and I want to make a good impression."

Placing her arm in the crook of his, he led her out of the hotel. "And you will."

She wasn't surprised to see his car was a two-seater sports car. It suited him. They had driven a few blocks when he said, "I understand you're into photography."

"Yes, and I love it, although I'm sure Chance told you how my camera and equipment made him think I was a reporter."

A wide grin appeared on Corbin's face. "Yes, he told me."

"I didn't understand then, but I do now after talking to my best friend last night. A relative of yours is married to a movie star," she said.

"Yes. My uncle Jake. He's my great-grandmother's youngest son. He and Diamond have been married for over fourteen years. Chance and I were surprised you didn't know that."

"Well, I didn't." She then told him why.

"I dated a couple of women who were hooked on Korean

movies," Corbin said. "What about when you left home for college?" he asked, turning the corner to join bumper-to-bumper traffic. "Your preference for movies didn't change?"

"No. I rarely watched television in college. I was too busy trying to get good grades for medical school. However, since I attended NYU, I took a break from studying once in a while to see a few Broadway plays." She smiled over at him. "So, Corbin Madaris, you can say I led a boring life."

"And now you're trying to find the missing pieces of that life."

She nodded. "Yes, I am. So, tell me about yourself."

He shrugged. "There's not much to tell. Within the Madaris family, I'm part of the Lover Boyz Pack."

"The what?" she asked, amused.

He grinned as well. "Let me explain. My generation of cousins were born close together. At the time, sixteen of us were grandkids from the first four sons my great-grandmother had birthed. Milton Jr., Lee, Nolan, and Lucas. Those four produced fourteen boys and two girls in less than eight years."

"Wow. That's a lot of pregnancies," Zoey said, shaking her head.

Corbin chuckled. "You're right about that. While growing up, we somehow shifted into groups. My great-grandmother likened the groupings to wolf packs. That's how the idea came about. There are four male cousins in my group, and we were born within eighteen months of each other."

"You said there were two girls in your generational group. Tell me about them."

When he stopped at a traffic light, he said, "Both Victoria and Lindsay are my sisters. Victoria is twenty-eight and Lindsay is twenty-three. Vic, as we mostly call her, always did her own thing, and she hung out with Christy, one of our older cousins from the prior generation. Vic considered Christy a big sister instead of an older cousin. However, some figured they bonded so well because of their names and looks."

Zoey lifted a brow. "Names and looks?"

"Yes, both were named after important women in our family. Christy, whose real name is Christina, was named after the first Madaris wife, who settled on our family land in the eighteen hundreds. And Vic was named after our great-grandfather Milton's sister, Victoria Madaris. She was also Mama Laverne's best friend. Aunt Victoria introduced Mama Laverne to her brother, Milton Madaris. Milton married Felicia Laverne, and they had seven sons who produced a slew of kids, grandkids, great-grands, and now even great-great-grands."

He rounded a corner to enter a community of stately-looking Victorian-style homes on massive lots. "Regarding their looks, Christy and Vic also favor each other. They look more like sisters than cousins. If it wasn't for the red hair, it would be hard to tell them apart."

"Red hair?" she asked curiously.

"Yes. The original Christina Madaris had natural red hair, and so does Christy. I'm told my grandaunt Victoria had red hair as well. They claim Christy is the spitting image of Victoria. Vic inherited the looks but not the hair color."

Zoey nodded. "Is your aunt Victoria still living?"

"No, she died before I was born. To my great-grandmother's seven sons, she was their favorite aunt, and I understand that they took her death hard."

"How did she die?"

"A robbery. She lived in town and worked as a nurse at a Houston hospital. She was planning to catch the bus to work one morning because her car was in the shop when she was robbed and killed."

"How tragic and senseless," Zoey said softly.

"Yes, it was."

"Did she have any kids?"

"No. Aunt Victoria never married."

Zoey enjoyed what he shared about his family. It certainly made her feel less nervous. "What about your other sister?"

"Lindsay is attending law school at Harvard with plans to one day become a corporate attorney. She gets annoyed whenever her brothers and cousins remind her that she's the baby in the group and gives us hell about it when we do."

Corbin pulled into the driveway of an attractive home with an immaculately landscaped yard. "We are here," he said, stopping the car.

She scanned her surroundings. "What a nice yard, and those flowers are so pretty."

"They are my grandparents' pride and joy. All their grandsons take turns and keep the grass mowed, but Grampa Nolan and Gramma Bessie won't let you touch their flower gardens."

He exited the car and came around to open the door for her. "I can't wait to introduce you to my great-grandmother, Mama Laverne."

"And I can't wait to meet her."

Felicia Laverne heard the car outside and drew a deep breath to prepare herself for the young woman she was about to meet. Hopefully, Miss Pritchard only wanted to know about her grandmother, Arabella Martin.

"Mama Laverne?"

She turned her face toward the entrance to the screened patio and met the gazes of her great-grandson and the beautiful woman by his side. Chance had been right. She bore a striking resemblance to not only her mother and grandmother, but she also favored her great-grandmother, Deedra. She looked simply beautiful in the sundress she was wearing, a floral dress of giant yellow daffodils.

Holding the woman's arm in the crook of his, Corbin crossed the room to kiss his great-grandmother's cheek before making an introduction. "Mama Laverne, I'd like you to meet Zoey Pritchard. Chance set up a meeting with the two of you."

"He most certainly did," Felicia Laverne said, smiling at the woman and extending her hand. She tried not to show any reaction when she saw the necklace the young woman was wearing. She forced the thoughts from her mind about the importance of that jewelry. "It's nice to meet you, dear."

"And it's nice meeting you as well."

While holding the woman's hand, Felicia Laverne realized she was feeling good and not at all threatened by her presence. At that moment, she knew she could not lose sight of Waylon Satterfield's blood flowing through Zoey Pritchard's veins. And Waylon had been an honorable man.

Releasing Zoey's hand, she said, "I hope you didn't mind my invitation to lunch, but I wanted to meet and speak with you in person. Although I didn't see much of Arabella once she moved away, I remember her well. Chance told me you were in a car accident that killed your parents. I was sorry to hear that. It was a blessing that you survived."

"Yes, but one of the prices I had to pay, in addition to all my physical injuries, was the loss of my memory."

Felicia Laverne raised a brow. "What do you mean?"

"I have no memory of anything or anyone before I woke up in that hospital and was told I had lost my parents. Every single thing before that day has been wiped from my mind."

"You remember nothing?"

"That's right. Other than the few vague flashes of memory at Chance's ranch this week, I remember nothing. Not even my parents or anything about them."

Lordy. Chance hadn't told her that part, Felicia Laverne thought. She couldn't imagine how it would be not to remember things that were precious to you. Shifting her gaze to Corbin, she said, "I'm sure you have other things to do, Corbin. Please leave Zoey with me. We'll enjoy a nice lunch here on the patio while we chat. On your way out, please let your Gramma Bessie know we're ready to eat."

"Will you let me know when I can return for her?" Corbin said, chuckling.

"I'll call you. Now, scat," Felicia Laverne said, shooing him out.

Corbin grinned and gave her another kiss on the cheek. After telling them goodbye, he left.

"Mama didn't tell me you were in town when I talked to her yesterday, Luke," Chance said to his oldest brother.

He had checked out of the hotel and arrived at his parents' home to find his older brother and his family—namely his wife, MacKenzie, and their three kids—were in town for a week. Also joining the family for breakfast had been his second-oldest brother, Reese, his wife, Kenna, and their twins, as well as his brother Emerson, who never missed a free meal, regardless of whether it was breakfast, lunch, or dinner. Just as long as it was cooked by their mother, Sarah Madaris.

He was also glad to see his grandparents were there. That saved him a trip since Chance planned to check on them before returning to Teakwood Ridge. After breakfast, Emerson and Reese left for work. MacKenzie and Kenna had gathered all the kids for a swim in his parents' pool.

"Mom didn't know I was coming," Luke said. "We surprised her, arriving late yesterday evening. Grampa and Gramma were already here since they'd spent the night. Mom loves having all of us together under one roof whenever she can."

His parents' home was on fifteen acres of land, and they had taken a couple of horses to ride out by the huge pond they played around as kids. Chance had always admired his oldest brother, who for years had been a rodeo star. Now he was a family man and rancher living in Oklahoma. Because of that huge rodeo school Luke had opened a few years back, he was teaching young kids, including his own, how to perfect their riding techniques. Also, under Luke's expertise, the older students who had dreams of joining the rodeo circuit as bull or bronco riders, or who were interested in calf roping or barrel racing, were getting Luke's expert training.

They came to a stop by the pond, dismounted, and tied the horses to a nearby post. Chance felt he was being scrutinized by his brother when Luke said, "I was somewhat surprised when Mom mentioned you had planned to drop in for breakfast. I'm glad to see you getting off the ranch more."

Chance shrugged. "I leave my ranch when I need to."

He figured that's all he needed to say. There was no doubt in his mind Luke knew what he meant. And because he knew news traveled fast in the Madaris family, and although no one had brought anything up during breakfast, he added, "I ran into Ravena last night at Vance's Tavern."

"I heard."

Chance nodded as they began walking around the pond. "Then I'm also sure you heard how things went."

"I didn't have to hear that part. There's no doubt that if Ravena's return to Houston is due to her wishful thinking that the two of you will get back together, then that's all it is. Wishful thinking on her part."

He was glad to hear that at least someone in his family thought that, but still… "How can you be so sure?"

"Because I know you, Chance. You've always been easy to get along with, but you've become a lot like Dex over the years."

Dex Madaris was one of their older cousins and Clayton's brother. Dex had always been serious as a heart attack; he said what he meant and meant what he said and could hold a grudge longer than anyone they knew. He took what Mama Laverne referred to as the "Madaris pride" to a different level. If you got on his shit list, chances were you stayed there. However, when it came to the family, he was loyal to a fault.

"Dex was born with his attitude. Yours was acquired," Luke added.

"Whatever."

"And what about this woman I heard about?"

Chance didn't have to ask but did so anyway. "What woman?"

"The one who showed up at your ranch. She must not have gotten the memo that nobody shows up at your ranch uninvited other than family," Luke said, chuckling.

"She had a reason for showing up the way she did."

"Well, you're lucky Clayton didn't have her investigated when he heard about her showing up like that. You recalled what happened with Skye."

Yes, Chance remembered. Skye Barclay had shown up at Clayton's oldest brother Justin's home one day, claiming she was the long-lost sister of their sixteen-year-old adopted son, Vincent. Clayton found her claim farfetched and immediately investigated her, believing Skye had an ulterior motive for wanting to attach herself to Vincent. Not only did the investigation prove Clayton's suspicions wrong, but their cousin Slade fell in love with Skye the moment he saw her, and within a year, he married her.

"Well, when he called last night, I assured Clayton that I could handle my business and would prefer to do so. And, like I said, Zoey had a reason for showing up at my place the way she did. That's why she's having lunch with Mama Laverne as we speak."

"So, I heard. Aunt Bessie didn't waste any time calling Gramma Carrie, giving her the scoop when she arrived at her house. According to Aunt Bessie, Zoey Pritchard is a very striking woman. Aunt Bessie is hoping she catches Corbin's eye."

"Like hell," Chance all but growled. He stopped walking and stared at his brother.

Luke stopped as well, threw up his hands with palms out in

surrender and said, "Hey, don't shoot the messenger. I just told you what she's hoping."

Dropping his hands, Luke folded his arms across his chest and stared at him. "You want me to believe that the thought of Corbin and Zoey Pritchard hooking up doesn't bother you?"

"It doesn't bother me."

"Yes, it does."

Dammit, Luke was right; it did bother him. Chance rubbed a frustrated hand down his face. He shared a close relationship with all three of his brothers. However, since Luke was the oldest and Chance was the youngest, the two of them shared a special bond. He knew he could talk to his older cousins, Justin, Dex, and Clayton, about anything; the same was true with Luke.

"I don't know what's happening to me, Luke."

Luke lowered his hands to his sides with a concerned look. "What do you mean?"

"For the first time since I broke up with Ravena, I'm interested in a woman for more than just a one-night stand."

Luke relaxed his stance. "It was bound to happen, Chance."

"Not to me," he snapped.

"And why not to you?" Luke snapped back. "Because the woman you loved couldn't handle the fact you might not be able to walk again? I'm going to say now what I maybe should have said then: good damn riddance."

Luke leaned over, picked up a stick, and threw it into the pond. Chance could tell his brother was riled and had more to say when he looked back at him. "At some point, Chance, you need to accept that Ravena Boyle wasn't the woman meant for you to marry. If a woman can't stand by her man when the going gets tough, or a man can't stand by his woman for the same reason, they don't deserve each other. Ravena never deserved you."

"I know that, Luke." They began walking around the pond again.

Luke pushed back the Stetson on his head and asked, "You know *what* exactly, Chance?"

"Everything you just said. I've known it for years. That's why I don't understand how any family member could think I would take back up with her when she returned to town."

"I'll tell you why. Because for five years, you've given Ravena power over you, whether you realize it or not."

"Power?"

"Yes, power, by acting like she is the only woman who could mean anything to you. I could understand you not wanting to dive back into a serious relationship with a woman initially, but it's been five years. While living a miserable life on your ranch, you might let the woman who could mean something to you slip away."

Living a miserable life. Last night, Ravena had accused him of that very same thing. He denied it then and would deny it now. "I'm not living a miserable life, Luke."

Luke shrugged. "You sure about that? I think engaging in one-night stands will get old at some point. Especially for you."

Chance lifted a brow. "Why, especially for me?"

"Of Lucas Jr. and Sarah Madaris's four sons, you were the one who wanted it all. You knew exactly what you wanted. You'd clarified that you wanted a career in the army, love, marriage, and children. You always talked about owning a ranch after your career with Uncle Sam ended. You might not have gotten the twenty-year career in the military that you wanted, but you got a college degree while enlisted. And you got your ranch, Chance. Love, marriage, and children are possibilities if you let them be."

Chance's jaw tightened. "I will never fall in love again, Luke. Until you experience the pain of heartbreak, you will never understand. And don't get anything twisted about my interest in Zoey Pritchard. It's nothing more than a strong attraction and intense desire. It's all purely sexual. Love has nothing to do with it."

"So you say, Lil Brother."

"So I know, Luke."

"I thought the same thing about Mac. If you recall, I refused to accept I had fallen in love with her. The same thing with Reese and Kenna."

Chance held his brother's gaze. "That's you and Reese. Neither of you experienced heartbreak before falling in love. It's something you wouldn't risk happening again." He then checked his watch. "It's time for me to get on the road if I want to reach Teakwood Ridge before dark."

"There you have it, Ms. Felicia Laverne. I remember nothing of that time. Not even the accident. I recall waking up in a hospital room in excruciating pain. Although several doctors have told me there's a fifty percent chance I won't ever remember that period of my life again, I want to believe that I will get my memory back."

Felicia Laverne didn't say anything. Hearing what this beautiful woman sitting beside her had gone through as a child nearly broke her heart. And then for her not to recall the years before that car accident that had taken away her parents? That was eight years wiped away from such a precious little mind.

While Zoey was talking, Felicia Laverne remained silent and focused. She had heard her pain and anguish. She couldn't imagine what she'd gone through after waking up in a hospital in critical condition and without her parents. A part of her wished she would have done a better job of keeping up with Arabella's child after Arabella died. When she'd talked to Michelle that day at her parents' funeral, she had told her of her plans to keep the ranch. When she'd heard it had been sold, she assumed Michelle had changed her mind.

Felicia Laverne didn't know it hadn't been Michelle who'd sold the ranch but Zoey's grandaunt. There was something about that entire situation that just didn't sit right with her. Why wouldn't the woman want Zoey to know about her maternal relatives? As far as Felicia Laverne was concerned, that was heartless, especially if confirming the ranch's existence might have helped restore her memory.

Reaching out, she took Zoey's hand in hers. For the second time that day, she felt good and honest vibes. She felt strength in the young woman, yet there was also a vulnerability that touched Felicia Laverne deeply. Zoey had suffered so much sadness and pain in her young life. She had gone through all her trials and tribulations without a family—she still didn't have one.

Suddenly, she heard Milton say, *"Take care of Waylon's great-grandbaby, Fee. She's suffered enough and needs you."*

Her beloved husband's words removed her inhibitions, and although there were some things she could not share with the young woman, Felicia Laverne felt more at ease. "I will tell you everything you need to know, Zoey," she spoke up to say. "However, I can't do it all in one day. How long will you be in Houston?"

"For as long as I need to be here. I told you about how I got flashes of my memory just from standing in front of Chance's barn. I believe it's returning and will do so completely if I hang around here for a while."

After a short silence, she added, "This might sound crazy, Ms. Felicia Laverne, but I feel there is a reason I started having those dreams about the ranch. I want to believe my parents are reaching out to me. They want me to know them and remember them. They want me to know just how much I was loved."

Felicia Laverne felt Zoey's hand tighten in hers and could see tears misting her eyes. A lump formed again deep in Felicia Laverne's throat. Her heart went out to the child who never got the chance to grieve her parents because she didn't remember them. She knew then she would do all she could to help Zoey regain her memory. Instead of only telling Zoey about the Martins, as she'd first intended to do, she would start where it should be. With the Satterfields.

"Your grandmother was born Arabella Satterfield. Her parents were Waylon and Deedra Satterfield. Deedra died when Arabella was twelve. When Arabella turned fifteen, Waylon sent her to an all-girls finishing school in Alexandria, Virginia."

Zoey nodded. "What did my great-grandmother Deedra die of?"

"Pneumonia. I understand Waylon did not want to send Arabella away to school, but Waylon's mother, Penny, felt a ranch wasn't a place for a young girl growing into womanhood. I heard she could ride, shoot, and hunt just as well as any boy her age. She and her father, Waylon, were extremely close."

Felicia Laverne released Zoey's hand to sip her tea and continued, "Arabella would come home for the holidays and the summers when school was out. Whenever I saw her, I thought she was blossoming into a lovely young lady with a heart like her mother. Deedra was a good and godly woman.

"Waylon always anticipated the days Arabella would come back home. Waylon's father, Kurt, died years before Waylon's wife, Deedra, and Ms. Penny died some years later. Waylon lived on the ranch alone after his mother's death, and then he died. It was right after Arabella finished high school at eighteen."

"What happened to my great-grandfather Waylon?"

A knot formed in Felicia Laverne's throat. "One stormy night on his way home from town, he lost control of his truck. It went into a ravine, and he was killed instantly."

"Oh, how sad."

"Yes, it was a sad time. Arabella took her father's death hard. She decided to remain in Virginia to attend college. I understand she met a guy there, and after college, they got married and made their home in Virginia."

"Why didn't she sell the ranch?"

"She couldn't. Waylon's father, Kurt, decreed in his will that the Satterfield ranch, and all the land it sat on, could not be sold for three generations after his death," Felicia Laverne explained.

"That meant the ranch could not be sold until my generation," Zoey said softly. "Since I inherited the ranch from my mother, as my legal guardian, my aunt was able to sell it on my behalf."

It was presented as a statement, and Felicia Laverne took it that way. "Yes. Since Arabella could not sell the ranch, she hired workers to look after it. I doubted Arabella would have ever sold the ranch anyway. She loved it there and said it would always be her happy place. I recall how she would return during the holidays to check on things. During the summer months, she stayed the entire time. After she married, her husband, Joshua, would come with her."

Felicia Laverne had carefully worded everything she'd said, purposely leaving some things out. Like the other stipulation Kurt Satterfield had placed in his will. Zoey didn't need to know about that.

"Was my great-grandfather Waylon an only child?"

Felicia Laverne's hand trembled slightly as she lifted her cup to take another sip of her tea. A part of her wished Zoey hadn't asked that. She didn't want to say the woman's name from her lips, but she had no choice. "No. Waylon had a sister named Charlotte."

"What happened to her?"

Felicia Laverne worded her response carefully again. "She died less than a year before her mother, Ms. Penny." Placing her teacup down, she quickly said, "I've told you all I can for today. It's nap time for me. I would love to visit with you again and tell you more the next time. Will you be available after today?"

Zoey beamed happily. "I will make myself available."

Felicia Laverne nodded. "Good," she said, patting Zoey's hand. "When will you be revisiting Chancellor's ranch?"

Zoey sighed deeply. "I believe I wore out my welcome the last time I was there. I probably won't get another invitation to come back."

"Poppycock. The key to your returning memory is that ranch and all the surrounding land. I recall your mother, Michelle, as a young woman. Like Arabella, she was such a pretty girl. She would join her parents here during the summers while in college. I recall how much she enjoyed riding horses. Your father did as well. Chancellor should give you a tour of his property on horseback."

"I rode on my own to the lake the other day. I was grateful to him for letting me borrow one of his horses. Although I felt something while there, I didn't remember anything, which was frustrating."

"Don't get frustrated, Zoey. Give your memory time. I believe it will return. You should return to the lake since it was in your dreams."

Suddenly, Felicia Laverne remembered something. "Maybe that wasn't the lake. There is another lake with a cabin on the property toward the east side." Forcing to the back of her mind who that cabin had been built for, she added, "I recall it was where your parents often stayed whenever they came to visit Michelle's parents. I guess as a young married couple, they preferred their privacy."

"Chance didn't mention there were two lakes."

"He probably didn't think about it. When the Johnstones bought the ranch, they did not need a cabin that far away from their ranch house. They sold that parcel of land. Since it was sold before Chance purchased the ranch, it's not his property."

"Oh," Zoey said in a disappointed voice.

"But don't worry, dear. I know the person who bought it.

He's a childhood friend of three of my grandsons and is an honorary member of the Madaris family. His name is Trevor Grant. He and his wife, Corinthians, live on the opposite outskirts of the city and use the cabin as a getaway to enjoy the lake."

Felicia Laverne remembered the time Trevor had loaned the cabin to his friend Sir Drake Warren and his now-wife Tori, two former CIA agents, who were hiding out from an assassin. "Um, come to think of it, that cabin might be perfect."

Zoey raised an arched brow. "Perfect?"

"Yes. This is my last week with my son Nolan and his wife, Bessie. I'll return to my son Jake's home at Whispering Pines next week. I'll be there for the next six months. It will be closer for you."

"Closer?" Zoey asked.

"Yes. You don't need to stay in one of those pricey hotels and drive to Whispering Pines to chat with me. That particular property borders Whispering Pines. I can't see why Trevor wouldn't let you use the cabin while you're here."

A huge smile touched Zoey's face. "You think that he would?"

"I don't see why not. I'll call him this weekend."

"Thank you so much for everything. You've been most kind."

At that moment, Corbin entered the patio. Felicia Laverne frowned. "I don't recall sending word for you to come, Corbin."

"You didn't have to. Everybody knows when it's your nap time." He grinned.

Felicia Laverne knew that was true. "Make sure Zoey gets back to her hotel safely. She and I will talk again one day next week." She turned to Zoey, smiled, and said, "I enjoyed our chat, dear, and I can't wait to see you next week. And by the way, the Madaris family will host their annual family reunion in July. I hope you'll attend, so I can introduce you to all my sons and their families."

"Thank you, Ms. Felicia Laverne. It was kind of you to invite me, and I would love to attend."

When Felicia Laverne awakened from her nap, she'd discovered Victoria, her first-born great-granddaughter, and her husband, Senator Roman Malone, had made a surprise visit from Washington, DC.

The couple happily announced to everyone they were expecting. Their news filled the entire house with overwhelming joy. Although Victoria and Roman had been married for only six months, they wanted to start a family immediately.

When Felicia Laverne showed the couple what she'd begun knitting weeks ago, letting them know that she'd known but had kept their secret, Victoria had thrown her head back and laughed before giving her a huge hug.

Later that night, Felicia Laverne placed her knitting aside. Sitting on the side of her bed, she gazed at her wedding picture and thought about that day and how happy she and Milton had been. It was a day some thought would not happen. But she and Milton had loved and trusted each other and had been determined to be together.

She closed her eyes at the thought of being unable to remember precious moments in her life…like Zoey Pritchard was unable to do. Just thinking of such a thing was disheartening. She'd watched Corbin and Zoey and hadn't felt anything there. No chemistry. No attraction. The two had established a relationship built on friendship and nothing more. That made her wonder about Chance, who claimed he'd been too busy to bring Zoey to meet her, which was why Corbin had done so.

Had he been that busy, or was there another, more profound reason for his absence?

She seriously doubted it. Chance had deep-rooted issues that needed to be resolved before he could give his heart to another woman. During breakfast, Bessie shared what she'd heard about last night's encounter between Chance and Ravena at Vance's Tavern. Unlike some family members, Felicia wasn't worried about Ravena getting back with Chance. She was confident he'd come to terms with it and concluded she hadn't been worth his love.

Felicia Laverne then switched her thoughts to the words she believed her beloved Milton had spoken to her regarding Zoey. If it was the last thing she did, she would help the young woman restore as much of her memory as possible.

Pushing back the covers, Felicia Laverne eased between the sheets, shifted into a comfortable sleeping position, and then closed her eyes. Telling Zoey about the past had dredged up memories—memories that were still haunting her, refusing to let her slip into a peaceful sleep.

Memories of how the actions of one woman, who'd wanted something she was never meant to have, had caused a feud between two families, the Madarises and the Satterfields. Families who were destined to be united for life.

Part Two

"There are times when revisiting the past is the key to sustaining the present and solidifying the future."

—Brenda Jackson

Chapter Nine

The early nineteen-fifties…

Jantzen Milton Madaris studied his son Milton when he came from the back of the house, dressed up for a night in town. He would celebrate his twenty-first birthday with his best friend, Waylon Satterfield. Since Milton and Waylon's birthdays were just days apart, tonight's celebration was for them both.

It was hard to believe his first-born was now legally a man and old enough to take his first drink in a bar. There was no doubt in his mind that both Milton and Waylon had good heads on their shoulders regarding the consumption of alcohol, but there was another topic he needed to discuss with his son, and now was the time.

"I'm about to leave, Pa."

Jantz nodded. "We need to talk first," he said, pushing a chair back from the table.

Milton sat down in the chair. "What's wrong? Is Mom okay?" He glanced around the kitchen. "Where is she?"

"Nothing's wrong, and your mama is alright. She and Victoria are out back taking clothes off the line."

Milton leaned back in his chair and took note of his father. He'd always thought his father, who stood almost six-three with a muscular frame, was bigger than life. He still did. "So, what do you want to talk about, Pa?"

Jantz stared at his son. "You know I married your mother when I was your age, right?"

Milton gave his father a wide grin. "Yes. But that was back in your day. I doubt I'll be ready to settle down with a wife before I turn thirty."

Jantz frowned. "Well, you need to be ready sooner than that. The way things are going, Victoria will be getting married before you," he said of his only daughter, who was five years younger than her brother. "Earlier today, Waylon asked for her hand in marriage."

Victoria was barely sixteen and had a lifelong dream to attend nursing school in the East when she graduated next year.

"Waylon has agreed to wait three years. That will give your sister time to finish high school and nursing school before getting married. His father, Kurt, has also given his blessings and has even given Waylon a nice piece of land from his spread near that huge lake. I understand this summer Waylon plans to build a cabin for him and Victoria to live in after they marry."

Milton nodded. Since he was Waylon's best friend, he'd known about Waylon's plan to ask for Victoria's hand in marriage. He also knew Waylon was eager to start building the cabin, although they wouldn't occupy it for three years. Waylon had loved Victoria for years, and Milton knew his sister had also loved his best friend for a long time.

"I'm happy for them, Pa."

His father nodded, eyed him speculatively, and said, "At twenty-one, Waylon has marriage plans. You don't."

Milton was fully aware that his parents were getting older and would expect him to take things over one day at the Whispering Pines cattle ranch...with a wife and family.

"I haven't met a woman I want to be tied down with for the rest of my life, Pa."

"What about Charlotte Satterfield?"

"Whoa," Milton said, sitting up straight in his chair, knowing he probably looked as horrified as he felt. Waylon's sister, Charlotte Satterfield, was a year older than Victoria. Although she was indeed a pretty girl, as far as he was concerned, she was annoying as hell. Her mother, Penny Satterfield, spoiled her rotten and called her Queen Charlotte, sometimes even Queenie. She acted like she thought she was a queen and entitled to anything she wanted.

Charlotte and Victoria were as different as day and night. That was probably why, although their brothers were best friends and had been since birth, the two girls had never been close. Charlotte was snooty, and Victoria didn't do snooty at all. She was down-to-earth and got along with just about everybody. Charlotte did not. Another thing he'd observed over the years was just how unkind she was to people she felt were beneath her. He would never forget the day he was coming out of the feed store and saw Charlotte deliberately knock over Old Lady Mills's homemade pie stand, causing all the pies to fall to the ground. He'd said something to Charlotte about it, and she'd sworn it had been an accident. He'd seen what she'd done and knew it hadn't been. What was even more appalling was when she tried talking him out of reimbursing Mrs. Mills for the pies, saying the woman should not have been selling in front of the feed store anyway. He realized that day just what an unkind person Charlotte was.

"Absolutely not, Pa. I don't like Charlotte Satterfield's attitude about many things."

"A man knows how to be firm with a woman and change her after marriage, Milton," Jantz said.

"That might be true, but I have no plans to marry Charlotte. Ever. I admit she's pretty, but she is also annoying as hell. She gets on her brother's nerves, and I refuse to be shackled with her and let her get on mine. Besides, she's not a nice person. Definitely no one I'd want as a wife."

When his father sat there staring at him, Milton rubbed his hand down his face and said, "Look, Pa, I can understand you and Kurt Satterfield wanting to combine the two most prosperous ranches in Houston. You and Mr. Kurt should be happy that Waylon and Victoria are more than happy to oblige. And the good thing is that they are truly in love. That's what I want for myself. The kind of marriage you and Mom have is one based on love. That means I intend to pick my bride."

Jantz's frown deepened. "And when will that be?"

Milton shrugged. "I have no idea. But I'm convinced I will know her when I meet her." He stood. "Anything else?"

"Yes. Don't forget you'll drop your sister off at that summer camp in Tennessee in two weeks. She's all excited."

"I know. That's all she's been talking about lately." Milton studied his father's gaze. He and Victoria were blessed to have the parents they did. Jantzen Milton Madaris, III, was a fair man. He was a good and honest man, and as far as Milton was concerned, he was the best father in the world. Then there was his mother, Etta Madaris, one of the most warm, loving, and generous women he knew. There had never been any doubt in his mind as to why his pa had married her. Pa would always say that she was the love of his life, and he'd known she was the one he wanted as his wife the moment they'd met.

"Is there anything else you want to discuss with me, Pa?"

"No," Jantz said, standing and placing a hand on his son's

shoulder. "I am proud of the man you've become, Milton. Now you and Waylon go out tonight and enjoy your birthdays."

Milton grinned. "Thanks, Pa."

Victoria Madaris glanced over at the brother she adored. "Will you get me to summer camp on time, Milt?" It seemed they'd been on the roads from Texas headed to Tennessee for months instead of days.

Milton gazed at his sister when he brought the truck to a stop at a railroad crossing. "I told you it would take longer by truck than a bus since we check into a motel every night. Don't worry. I'll have you there a day earlier than you need to be there. What's the rush?"

Victoria smiled brightly. "There are a couple of reasons. First, I'm teaching a history class to ten-year-olds this summer. My first time doing so. I'm excited because I'll get to tell them about my own family history, which I am super proud of."

Milton nodded. He knew their family history had been passed down through generations. The Madaris family had settled in Houston, Texas, in the early 1800s after acquiring a ten-thousand-acre Mexican land grant. At the time, when most newly freed Blacks were still waiting for their forty acres and a mule from the United States government, Milton's great-great-great-grandfather, Carlos Antonio Madaris, half Mexican and half Black, along with his wife, Christina Marie, were shaping their legacy on land they used to raise cattle.

It was a parcel of land they proudly named Whispering Pines. Now Milton and Victoria's father, Jantzen, was determined to keep it in the family for future generations of Madarises to enjoy. Milton had known from the day he was old enough to understand just what the Madaris legacy meant and had always been proud of it. He thought it was nice that Victoria shared their family history with others.

"And what's the other reason?" he asked.

"My new best friend. Her name is Felicia Laverne Lee. We met last summer when we were roommates. She's from Atlanta, Georgia. We've been writing to each other, and I can't wait to see her again."

Milton could hear the excitement in his sister's voice, and for the life of him, he couldn't understand it. He had gone to that same church summer camp years ago and had been bored to tears. For some reason, Victoria loved it and eagerly anticipated attending every summer.

"Tell me about this friend, Felicia Laverne Lee," he said, more for conversation than any real interest.

"Well, Felicia Laverne and I are the same age, her father is a preacher, and…"

For the next hour or so, his sister went on and on about this girl, saying how smart she was, pretty, kind, had a wonderful singing voice, and that everybody liked her. He would admit, after a while, he stopped listening. Deciding to let Victoria chatter away, he thought of other things. At least she was no longer complaining about how long they'd been on the road.

Already, he was missing Whispering Pines. This was branding week, and he enjoyed working with the ranch hands to get things done. He knew Waylon would be just as busy at his family's ranch. He would have loved to come along, but Jantz and Etta Madaris would not allow such a thing without another female present as a chaperone. Victoria might be Waylon's future wife, but when it came to proper behavior, his parents were strict regarding protocol. There had never been a Madaris scandal, and his family was determined there never would be one.

"May I ask you something, Milt?"

Victoria's question cut into his thoughts. He hadn't realized she'd stopped talking about her new best friend. "Yes."

"Do you plan to marry Charlotte someday?"

Milton wondered where in the world that question had come from. "Why do you ask?"

Victoria hesitated, then said, "I overheard her tell a group of girls the last week of school that you were her beau."

Milton frowned. "I'm nobody's beau, Victoria, and the answer is no. I have no intention of ever marrying Charlotte Satterfield."

"Well, Charlotte Satterfield thinks you're hers. I don't like her, which is sad since I am marrying into the family. She can be so mean at times and was such a bully around school. I've seen her in action with my very eyes."

Milton frowned. He'd seen her in action before as well. At the time he thought she'd acted worse than a bully but as a mean-spirited, awful person. "Did she bully you?"

"No. I think she figured I would tell you if she did."

"Have you talked to Waylon about her behavior?"

"Honestly, Milt, when could I do such a thing? Although I'm old enough to take company now that I'm sixteen, Pa hasn't permitted me yet. That means Waylon and I are never alone. And I cannot discuss anything with him in front of our parents or his. Penny Satterfield thinks the sun rises and shines on Charlotte. I've heard Mr. Satterfield chastise her before, but never Mrs. Satterfield. She thinks Charlotte can do no wrong."

"I think it's something you and Waylon need to discuss if you think it will cause problems in your marriage."

Victoria nodded. "I don't think it will since Waylon and I will have our own place. I couldn't imagine living under the same roof as Charlotte."

Although Milton didn't say anything, he thought the same thing. He couldn't imagine living under the same roof as Charlotte either.

Milton glanced at Victoria. "Are you looking forward to nursing school?"

"Yes. Then, as my fiancé, it will be appropriate for Waylon

to visit me in Savannah. I am hoping those two years go by fast. When I return home with my degree there shouldn't be a problem with me being hired at the hospital in Houston after we get married."

She got quiet for a minute and then asked, "How much longer now?"

Milton grinned. The one thing his sister lacked was patience when she was anxious about something. "We'll spend another night at a motel and should reach your summer camp before noon tomorrow."

They reached the camp around ten in the morning the next day. Milton had planned to unpack Victoria and then haul-tail it back to Houston. He'd missed a week on the ranch getting her here and would be missing another getting back.

"Felicia Laverne!"

"Victoria!"

He was busy getting his sister's luggage out the back of the truck and had heard the two females' excited hellos. He didn't bother to glance up. All he wanted to do was help get his sister settled into her cabin and then return to the road.

"Milton, I want you to meet my best friend, Felicia Laverne Lee."

He intended to give the girl a cursory nod, but he suddenly went still when he turned to look at her. Then he drew in a ragged, deep breath. At the same time, he felt like he'd been punched in the gut. Standing before him was the most beautiful female he had ever seen. She was a pinup babe whose picture he wouldn't hesitate to put on his wall.

Milton wasn't sure what was more appealing: the shape of her finely arched eyebrows, the color of her almond-shaped eyes that reminded him of a copper penny, or those cute freckles that were spread across her nose. Her skin was smooth, creamy, light brown, and seemed to glow. But then he couldn't discount her lips, which were tilted in such a stunning smile.

He let go of his sister's luggage, which fell at his feet, while extending his hand to her. "Nice to meet you, Felicia Laverne." The moment their hands touched, he knew just as sure as he was standing beneath the heat of the Tennessee sun that she was affecting him in a way no other girl had before. He could actually feel his body heating up.

"It's nice meeting you, too. Milton. Victoria has told me a lot about you."

He nodded as he continued to hold her hand in his. There was no telling how long he would have continued to do so if Victoria hadn't cleared her throat while pointedly looking at their joined hands. He let go of her hand and then switched his gaze to his sister. "Where do you want this?" he asked, picking up her luggage.

"Just follow me," Felicia Laverne said. "I got here yesterday and claimed our room already. I got us one close to the bathroom."

"That's great!" was his sister's reply.

The two girls were walking ahead of him with their arms entwined and heads together. Both were wearing poodle skirts and short-sleeved blouses with bobby socks and black-and-white saddle oxfords on their feet. Their steps appeared in unison as he followed behind, trying hard to recall everything Victoria had said about her new best friend when he'd been trying not to listen. Now he wished that he had. Milton knew she and Victoria were the same age and that Felicia Laverne's father was a minister. Had Victoria mentioned anything about a boyfriend? College plans? Did she like children?

When they reached the cabin, he entered behind them and gazed around. The room with the two beds wasn't all that big, but he could see them making it work.

"You can set my luggage over there, Milt," Victoria said, claiming his attention.

"Sure."

He crossed the room to the other side, which he figured belonged to Victoria. He made two trips out to the truck before returning and saying, "That's it." Both girls had their heads together, looking at a picture, and he knew it was one of Waylon. He'd seen Victoria slip it inside her satchel before leaving home.

"Do you girls need me to do anything else before I leave?" he asked.

Victoria looked over her shoulder just long enough to say, "No. Have a safe trip back to Whispering Pines. Tell Ma and Pa that I promise to write each week."

He stood there, feeling dismissed, and honestly didn't like it. After a few minutes, he cleared his throat, and both girls gazed at him. "Is something wrong, Milt?" Victoria asked with curious eyes.

He switched his gaze from Victoria to the girl standing by her side. "No, but I was wondering if the two of you would like to join me for lunch at that restaurant we passed down the street?"

Victoria lifted a brow. "I thought you wanted to get back on the road to make it to Arkansas before dark."

He checked his watch and then said, "I still have time. So, what about it?"

Victoria smiled at Felicia Laverne. "That would mean we'll get a good meal before eating the camp's chow for supper."

Felicia Laverne grinned, and Milton felt weak in the knees at how her lips had looked when she'd done so. "That sounds good to me."

He couldn't help but return her smile. "Alright. Lock up the place, and let's go," Milton said.

Felicia Laverne Lee couldn't control the beating of her heart whenever Victoria's brother looked at her. He was so good-looking that she had to tear her gaze away, or else he would detect she liked him. Worse than that, she was totally into him. He was so handsome. The first thing she'd noticed about him had been his smooth caramel skin and eyes the color of midnight. Then his masculine mouth caught her breath in her throat whenever he smiled. He was taller than her father and had such a pleasant, deep-sounding voice. She was convinced nobody pronounced her name the way he did.

"Felicia Laverne?"

She blinked. He was saying it now. "Yes?"

"Tell me about yourself."

It was only then that she realized they were alone. "Where's Victoria?" she asked, looking around.

"She went to the girls' room."

"Oh," Felicia Laverne said softly. "Well, I'm sixteen, attend high school in Atlanta, and will graduate in June next year. I'm part of my church choir and play the piano and clarinet." She paused and then added, "I am the middle child of three sisters. I love to cook. I think my parents are the greatest, and so are my sisters. Also, I love having Victoria as my best friend."

Milton leaned back in his chair, wondering if he made her nervous. "One thing you didn't mention."

She lifted a brow. Confused. "What?"

"You didn't say if you have a boyfriend."

"A boyfriend?"

"Yes, a boyfriend. Do you?"

"No. I just turned sixteen a few months ago, and any guy has to ask my pa's permission to see me. He's a pastor, and that scares them off."

Milton wondered why. He didn't go to church every Sunday, but he went enough and wasn't afraid of Reverend Potts. "Can I ask you something else, Felicia Laverne?"

"Yes."

"I would like to get to know you better. Can I write to you this summer?"

She nibbled on her bottom lip and asked, "Do you have a girlfriend, Milton?"

"No, I don't have a girlfriend."

Felicia was glad to hear that. "Then yes, I would love to get letters from you. May I write to you as well?"

He seemed pleased that she had asked. "Yes, I would love to get letters from you."

"My brother likes you."

Felicia Laverne gazed across the darkened cabin to Victoria's bed. "That's good because I like him, too."

She could hear Victoria pull up in bed. "I knew it! The two of you seemed serious when I came out of the girls' room. What did he say while I was gone?"

Felicia Laverne pulled up in bed as well. Resting her back against the pillow, her knees propped up, she said, "He asked me about myself. He wanted to know if I had a boyfriend, and I told him no and why. He didn't seem bothered that other guys found my dad intimidating just because he's a minister."

She paused and excitedly said, "Milton asked if he could write to me this summer."

"He did?" Victoria asked.

"Yes, and I told him he could. I asked if I could write to him, and he said that I could as well."

"Will you do it, Felicia Laverne?"

"Yes, I'll do, but only if he writes to me first. I really like him a lot, Victoria. He seems so nice."

"He is nice. Just like my Waylon. They are best friends. Wouldn't it be nice if two best friends married two best friends?"

Felicia Laverne chuckled, liking that idea. "I wish that would happen, Victoria, but I'm not sure my father will let me date a guy so much older than I am. He's twenty-one, right?"

"Yes. That's only five years."

"I know, but then there's also the distance of where we live. I'm not sure Dad will allow me to get serious about someone who lives so far away in Texas."

"Well, I think Reverend Lee would love Milton if he were to meet him. I'm not saying that because he's my brother. I'm saying it because he's a man of honor just like my father. They are Madaris men. To them, that means everything. They work hard and believe their words are their bond. The same thing holds true with Waylon, which is why I love him so much. And thanks for helping me hang his picture on the wall by my bed."

"You're welcome, and your Waylon is very handsome."

"Thanks. I'm counting down to when we can become officially engaged. I can accept his engagement ring after graduating high school next year."

When Felicia Laverne said nothing for a long while, Victoria asked softly, "What are you thinking, Felicia Laverne?"

That answer was easy. "I'm giddy at the thought that a twenty-one-year-old man could be interested in me. Do you think he will write me?"

"Yes. If Milt says he will do it, then he will. You can count on it."

Felicia Laverne felt good hearing that. Already, she was envisioning a future with him where she would be his wife, and they would have plenty of babies, both boys and girls. The boys would look after their sisters. She would name their first-born son Milton Jantzen Madaris Jr. after his father.

She and Victoria began talking about other things. Namely, all the fun they would have that summer. Later as she drifted off to sleep, her mind was filled with thoughts of Milton and how he had smiled at her several times that day. She couldn't wait to receive her first letter from him.

Chapter Ten

My Dearest Felicia Laverne,

This is the eighth letter I've written to you this summer; each letter we share means more and more to me. I can't wait to see you again at the end of the summer when I come with my parents to pick up Victoria from camp.

I love you, Felicia Laverne. I knew it the first time we met. I wished I could be there, standing before you, to tell you those words. However, I couldn't pen another letter without making sure you knew how I feel.

I truly hope you feel the same way. Please let me know if you think I am moving too fast, and I will slow down.

Could I talk to your father when he comes to pick you up from camp? I want his permission to visit you in Atlanta in the fall.

Until I see you again, my love,
Milton

★ ★ ★

My Beloved Milton,

I love you, too! I knew when we met that you were special. Getting to know you through your letters has been extra special, and I can't wait to see you again. Victoria is happy for us and thinks it's wonderful that two best friends love two best friends.

Victoria and I have been assigned to supervise two ten-year-olds this month. Yvonne and Isabelle keep us busy and are fun to be around, although they are younger than us. We enjoy our leadership roles and can see bright futures for them.

How is your family? Victoria often gets letters from your parents and a lot of letters from Waylon, too. I love getting all my letters from you and writing you back. I hope you are taking care of yourself.

I think of you all the time, morning, night, and in those hours in between. I will prepare my father for your meeting with him. I am praying it goes well and that he sees you as the wonderful young man that you are.

With all my love,
Felicia Laverne

Chapter Eleven

Waylon Satterfield glanced over at Milton and grinned as they rode their horses along the dusty path to the horseshoe shop. "So, you've fallen in love, Milt?"

Milton chuckled, knowing where he'd gotten his information, but had no problem answering truthfully. "Yes, I have. I guess Victoria told you that in her letters."

"Yep. Are you sure about her? You only saw her that one time?"

"I'm just as certain about my feelings for Felicia Laverne as you are about yours for Victoria."

Waylon threw his head back and laughed. "In that case, you are definitely sure about her. Victoria said she's pretty."

"She certainly is that."

They continued riding for a while, and then Milton said, "I knew the first time I saw her that she was the one. Now I fully understand what you meant when you said Victoria is the only girl who will ever have your heart. I feel the same way about Felicia Laverne."

"I can hear it in your voice just how much you love her."

"We've been sharing letters all summer. Just like you and Victoria have been. I got it so bad that I can't wait to check the mailbox every day. It's a great feeling to care deeply for someone."

Waylon nodded. "So, what are you going to do about it?"

"I don't plan to wait three years to get married like you, that's for sure," Milton said, laughing. "Like Victoria, Felicia Laverne has another year in school. Then I hope we can marry right after that, so she can move here. I'm certain Pa will give me a parcel of land on Whispering Pines to build us a place like your folks did for you and Victoria."

They brought their horses to a stop in front of Mr. Wood's horseshoe shop. Dismounting, they tied them to the hitching post. Waylon then asked, "Are you going to tell your folks about her? What about her father, the preacher? It was hard for me to talk to your father about my feelings for Victoria, and I've known Mr. Jantz all my life. I can't imagine you facing a preacher about his daughter."

"Felicia Laverne is a little worried about it and has said so in her letters. However, I want to believe things will work out, and one day, she will be Felicia Laverne Madaris. I think I'll talk to my parents tonight. They will pick Victoria up from summer camp in two weeks. Usually, I don't go with them, but I want to do so this time. I'm dying to see Felicia Laverne again."

"I know the feeling. I'm dying to see Victoria as well."

Milton studied his best friend and then offered a suggestion. "Why don't you ask Pa if you can ride to Tennessee with us? Don't worry about space because I plan to drive my truck."

"Do you think he'll allow it?"

"I don't see why not. After all, you are Victoria's intended, even if the two of you won't be getting married for another three years."

That evening, at the supper table, Milton decided it was the perfect time to tell his parents about Felicia Laverne. He spoke up when there was a lull in their conversation. "I met this girl, and she's the one."

Jantz's fork froze in midair, giving his son his total attention. "What did you say, Milton?"

Milton didn't have a problem repeating it. "I said I met this girl, and she's the one."

Jantz placed his fork down, deciding what his son had said was more important than the juicy steak on his plate. "Who is she?"

"Not anyone from around here. She's from Atlanta."

"Atlanta?" Jantz asked in surprise. "How the heck did you meet a girl from Atlanta?"

"Through Victoria. It's her roommate at camp. We met when I dropped Victoria off."

Jantz lifted a brow. "Felicia Laverne Lee?"

Milton arched a brow. "You've met her?"

"Of course, we've met her," his mother said, smiling brightly. "We met Felicia Laverne last summer when we picked Victoria up from camp. She introduced her as her new best friend. Felicia Laverne is a lovely girl."

"I agree," Jantz said, smiling broadly. "I guess you know her father is a preacher. Reverend Nolan Lee. We met him, his wife, and their other two daughters. Naomi Lee is Felicia Laverne's first cousin."

"The gospel singer?" Milton asked, surprised. He recognized the name because his mother was a big admirer of the woman and had a couple of her albums. He'd heard Naomi Lee used to be a backup singer for Mahalia Jackson before going solo and establishing a name for herself.

"Yes, the gospel singer," Jantz said, picking up his fork again. "How serious is your interest in Felicia Laverne?"

"We've been exchanging letters all summer. I'd love to accompany you when you pick up Victoria from camp."

His father held his gaze while cutting his steak, not trying to hide his grin. "I just bet you would."

"Will that be a problem, Pa?" Milton asked, hoping it wouldn't be.

Jantz laughed. "Not if it means I might get a daughter-in-law before your thirtieth birthday."

Milton grinned. "It does. I knew the moment I saw her that she was the one. I love her."

Both his parents stared at him for a long moment, and out of the corner of his eyes, he saw his mother dab at hers.

"Then, by all means, yes, you can join us to get your sister," Jantz Madaris said, happily.

"I prefer driving my truck, Pa."

"Why? There's plenty of room in mine."

Milton shrugged. "Not if Way comes, too."

Jantz put his fork down again. "Is Waylon coming?"

"Only if you say it's alright. He intends to ask your permission."

Jantz nodded. "We'll see."

Milton picked up his glass of iced tea to hide his smirk. He knew his father liked Waylon a lot, just like a second son. He wouldn't have a problem with him going to Tennessee with them. Pa just wasn't ready to make things easy on Way. After all, Victoria was his only daughter and his pride and joy.

He wondered if all fathers were hard on any guy who showed interest in their daughter. He hoped that Felicia Laverne's father didn't plan to make things hard on him, too.

"Hello, Milton."

Milton glanced up from repairing the fence and tipped his Stetson to the woman sitting on her horse. "Hello, Charlotte. You're a long way from home, aren't you?"

She gave him that funny little laugh he'd always found annoying. "How can I be far from home when we're neighbors?"

There was no reason to explain that even though their family's spreads bordered, she was on Madaris's land, which covered over ten thousand acres. "If you're looking for Waylon, he left for home about a half hour ago."

"I didn't come here for Waylon. I came here to see you."

He lifted a brow. "Why?"

"The Hollisters are having their annual barn dance next Saturday night, and I'd like you to be my date."

"Date?" He wondered if she knew that a guy was to ask the girl and not vice versa.

"Yes, a date. Although I'm old enough to date—and graduated from high school a few months ago—Pa hadn't permitted me to see anyone yet. I was disappointed that you didn't come to my graduation."

"My parents and Victoria were there."

"But you weren't."

He'd had no reason to go. "Why would I have gone?" he asked.

She lifted her chin. "I bet Waylon goes to Victoria's graduation."

"I would hope so since Victoria is his intended, the woman he plans to marry one day. So, I'll ask you again, Charlotte. Why would I have gone to your graduation?" Recalling what Victoria had told him about the lie Charlotte was spreading, he would set her straight this very day if she hinted that there was something between them.

They both turned at the sound of a horse and he saw Waylon approaching. When he reached them, he gave his sister an angry look. "The folks sent me to find you. They said you told them you would fetch me. Why didn't our paths cross, Charlotte?"

Her chin tightened. "I came another way."

Waylon rolled his eyes. "Well, let's go. You're holding up supper."

She turned to Milton. "You never said if you would be going to the Hollisters' barn dance."

Milton noted she'd been careful not to mention anything about him being her date that night in front of Waylon. "No, I'm not going to that dance. That weekend, I'll be headed with my folks to Tennessee to pick up Victoria from summer camp."

"So will I," Waylon said, grinning broadly, not trying to hide his happiness that Mr. Jantz had given his permission for him to do so. "Let's go, Charlotte, before Mom gets worried. I'll see you tomorrow, Milt."

As they rode off, Milton released a deep breath, glad to see her gone.

Victoria glanced at the clock on the camp's cafeteria's wall. Usually, whenever her parents picked her up from camp, they would do so before lunchtime. That way, they could load her things in the truck and be on the road before dark. She knew from Felicia Laverne that Milt was coming with her parents. She wished Waylon could have asked to come, but she knew her father probably would not allow it. He liked Waylon, but she knew her parents preferred doing things decently and in order.

"You keep looking at the clock, Victoria," Felicia Laverne leaned over and whispered.

Victoria grinned. "So do you, but for different reasons. At least you'll see Milt today, since he'll be with my parents. It will be a few more days before we return to Texas, and I can see Waylon."

"Yes, but you will see him a lot more often than I'll see Milton. After today, I don't know when I'll see him again. He wants to visit me in Atlanta this fall, but I don't know if my dad will allow it."

"Did you get a chance to talk to him about Milt?"

Felicia Laverne's parents had arrived a couple of days ago since her father had preached at last night's ending camp session. "Yes. Pa doesn't have a problem talking to Milton, but I think my father is quick to make judgments sometimes. He said he has a gift in knowing someone's heart and character the first time they meet."

"In that case, you have nothing to worry about. Milt has a good character and heart," Victoria said confidently.

"I know, but what if Dad reads it wrong?" Felicia said in a worried voice.

"Then we will pray he reads it right." A huge grin spread across Victoria's face. "Look! There's Isabelle and Yvonne." They exchanged goodbye waves.

The two ten-year-old girls were best friends from New Orleans. and Victoria and Felicia Laverne had enjoyed supervising them this summer.

When they had finished their lunch, they saw Ms. Dunkins, one of the camp's organizers, head their way.

When the older woman reached their table, she said, "Victoria Madaris, I came to fetch you. Your parents are here to take you home."

Victoria glanced over at Felicia Laverne. "Are you ready to see my parents?" she asked, knowing the main person her best friend wanted to see was her brother.

"Yes," Felicia Laverne said excitedly.

Waylon saw Victoria and another girl when they rounded the corner of some building. She had no idea Mr. Jantz had permitted him to come. He stood on the side, away from the Madaris family, and saw how happy she was to see her parents and brother.

He watched the girl he loved with all his heart. The first thing anyone would notice was her mass of vibrant red hair that flowed down her shoulders. It was an unusual hair color but not for a female-born Madaris. According to her family, she inherited the hair coloring from the first Madaris wife in the early eighteen hundreds. According to Mr. Jantz, there was usually one redheaded female born in every generation.

Then there was her caramel-colored skin that always seemed to glow and the prettiest brown eyes he'd ever seen. He was convinced she was the most gorgeous female ever created. And one day, she would be his wife—with her father's blessings. He anticipated that day and would abide his time by building their home. With Milton's help, he'd framed it already and the walls were up. It would be a spacious single-story dwelling with two bedrooms, each with a private bathroom, plus a vast living room and eat-in kitchen. It would have indoor plumbing for the bathrooms and kitchen, and he'd also designed the cabin so that he could easily add additional bedrooms when their babies were born.

He wasn't sure what gave his position away. Victoria had been quickly walking toward her parents when, suddenly, she turned in his direction. Surprise and happiness spread across her face. That expression touched him deeply. The proper thing was to acknowledge her parents first, so breaking eye contact with him, she resumed walking toward them. Upon reaching them, she gave them both huge hugs. Then she whispered something to her father, who gazed at Waylon before nodding.

That's when she crossed the yard to where he stood and offered him her hand. More than anything, he wanted to pull her into his arms and kiss her. That was something he was anticipating—their first kiss.

Taking her hand, he said, "Good seeing you, Victoria." The warmth he felt holding her hand in his touched him deeply.

"And it's good seeing you, too, Waylon. You look well."

In a low, husky voice, he said, "And you, the love of my life, look beautiful."

Her smile widened, and then she looked over her shoulder. "I'm not sure where Felicia Laverne is," she added, glancing around. "She was here just moments ago. She must have taken

Milt to meet her father in the camp's library. I hope that goes well."

"I'm sure that it will. I better go help your father load your stuff into the car," Waylon said, heading to where her parents stood. She began walking beside him.

"I asked Mr. Jantz if you could ride back in the truck with me and Milt," he added.

"You did?" she asked excitedly. "What did Pa say?"

Waylon chuckled. "He said he would think about it."

"Pa, I would like you to meet Milton Jantzen Madaris," Felicia Laverne said, smiling proudly.

Milton extended his hand to the man who'd eyed him intensely before accepting his handshake. His pa had always taught him that you could tell a lot about a man by his handshake. A firm one denotes strength, fairness, and honesty. Whereas, a weak grip denotes a person who is easily intimidated, insecure, and has low self-esteem.

Milton was a hardworking, able-bodied, confident man who went after what he wanted. And more than anything, he wanted Felicia Laverne Lee. "Reverend Lee, it's nice meeting you, and I hope we can have a conversation."

"About what, young man?"

"About Felicia Laverne."

Reverend Nolan Lee nodded before switching his gaze from Milton to his daughter. "Your mother has volunteered to help break down the classrooms with some other ladies. I'm sure they will be glad to get your help."

"Yes, Pa." Before leaving, she gave Milton a reassuring smile.

Milton returned his gaze to Reverend Lee when Felicia Laverne could no longer be seen. The man was staring at him with an unreadable expression on his face. Then the minister said, "What do you want to talk to me about? Fee?"

Milton raised a brow. "Fee?"

"Yes, that's Felicia Laverne's nickname."

Milton nodded. "Over the summer, Felicia Laverne and I have been exchanging letters."

"So, you're interested in her as a girlfriend?" the older man asked.

"No, sir. I'm not looking for a girlfriend. And to be honest, I want more than a wife. I want someone I believe I can trust and who will be my mate and partner in everything. I want someone who will work by my side to grow the ranch I will inherit one day. I want someone whom I can create a family with, and who I believe would be the best mother any child could ever have. But most of all, I want the person I love: your daughter, Felicia Laverne. I truly do love her."

The minister didn't say anything, and for a moment, Milton wondered if he'd said too much. However, when it came to how he felt about Felicia, he hadn't said enough. He never thought he was the type of man who would wear his heart on his sleeve, but he was doing so for her and had no regrets.

Reverend Lee said, "Fee has another year in school. You're from Texas. How do you intend to make a courtship work when the two of you will be miles apart?"

"With your permission, I'd like to visit her this fall. I understand finishing school is her top priority, but I'd like to marry her next summer."

Now, it was Reverend Lee who lifted a brow. "You've asked her to be your bride."

"No, sir. She knows how I feel about her, but I would never ask her before getting a blessing to do so from you."

Reverend Lee nodded. "I can't give you my marriage blessing yet, young man. However, I will permit you to visit her in the fall. My wife and I want to get to know you better. You also need to meet Fee's sisters."

"Yes, sir, and I look forward to doing that." Milton felt a huge weight had been lifted off his back. This first meeting was an important one. One wrong word, one pompous action, and he could have lost the opportunity to make Felicia Laverne a permanent part of his life.

"I want you to meet Mrs. Lee. And I believe Fee mentioned your parents are here. We met them last year and would love to see them again," Reverend Lee said. "Of course, we've met Victoria. Mrs. Lee and I think she's such a lovely girl. We're glad Fee chose her as a best friend."

Milton was glad, too. Otherwise, he and Felicia Laverne would not have met.

Chapter Twelve

Atlanta. Six months later…

"The flowers were pretty, Milton," Felicia Laverne said as they strolled through her parents' rose garden. "And I know my parents appreciate yet another cooler filled with smoked beef straight from your parents' ranch."

He grinned at her. "I'm glad the flowers lasted as long as it took me to drive here. Mama had assured me they would, but I will admit to getting worried for a minute."

"I would have loved them even if they'd been all wilted because they'd come from you."

She had meant every word. She loved him so much, and over the past six months, her love had grown even more. They continued to write to each other when they were apart, and she was glad to see him whenever he visited Atlanta. More than anything, she appreciated him for making the road trip from Texas to see her. And he would come bearing gifts for her parents and sisters.

Her family had gotten to know Milton, and she truly believed they loved him, too. They saw him as an honest, God-fearing man who stood up for what he believed in. She knew her father had admired his determination to win him over by spending both Thanksgiving and Christmas with them. He'd even attended church with them whenever he visited. News had gotten around the congregation that he was her beau.

When Milton left to return to Texas after spending Christmas with them, he had promised to return to Atlanta to visit her on Valentine's Day. Now he was here, and she was glad to see him. He had asked her father's permission to talk with her privately. Anticipation was rushing through her at what that might mean.

"Let's sit here on the bench," he suggested. After she eased into the seat, he sat down beside her.

She turned to face him, and he said, "On Christmas Day, your father blessed my plan to ask you to marry me, Fee."

She smiled. He'd gotten used to calling her Fee as her family did. "Yes, I know. Pa told me."

Milton stood and knelt on a knee in front of her. He then pulled a ring from his jacket and stared up at her. "I love you, Felicia Laverne Lee. I promise to love you for as long as there is breath in my body. I will continue to love you in death. I will love all the babies you give me, and I will make a home for them and for you. I will take care of you as a husband should and never lose sight of the fact that you are a gift to me from heaven. Will you marry me?"

Felicia Laverne swiped away the tears his words had caused. They had been touching and beautiful. "Yes, Milton Jantzen Madaris. I would be honored to be your wife."

He slid the ring onto her finger and stood while gently pulling her up from her seat. She didn't care if her parents or sisters were peeking out the window. It was not their first kiss. Unlike the others, this one wouldn't be a stolen kiss. It would be one of intense joy.

And it was.

★ ★ ★

Victoria leaned onto her horse as she sprinted across the open plains. She loved it when she could give Magic a good workout. To her, there was nothing more beautiful than Whispering Pines. There was no doubt in her mind that Felicia Laverne would love it here after she and Milton married. To everybody's happiness, the two had gotten engaged last month on Valentine's Day.

Milton wanted a June wedding, but that would barely give Felicia Laverne time to pack up after graduating from high school for her move to Houston. Therefore, they decided on an August wedding at her father's church in Atlanta.

For starters, they would convert a section of the Madaris family home into their private quarters. Within a year, Milton would have finished building their home on Whispering Pines land gifted to them in the south pastures.

Milton had left a few days ago, heading once again to Atlanta. Saturday was Felicia Laverne's parents' twenty-fifth wedding anniversary, and the church would host a special dinner in their honor. Victoria and her parents were also invited. However, she didn't want to miss any days of school to make the road trip. And the thought of being away from Houston, especially away from Waylon, was another reason she wasn't anxious to go. Her mother had gone with Milton to Atlanta, and Victoria and her father had stayed behind.

Things were also progressing well for her and Waylon. Her parents had allowed her to ride home from summer camp with him in Milton's truck. Although they'd given her strict orders to sit in the middle and closer to her brother than Waylon, the two had held hands the entire trip home.

He had told her how the cabin he was building for them was coming along, and when she'd finally arrived home and had gone with him, her parents, and her brother to see it, she'd gotten misty-eyed knowing he had spent his entire summer building it for them. She figured seeing it had affected her father as well. From that day on, he gave her and Waylon more breathing space. Although they hadn't gone out on a date yet, Waylon was allowed to visit her on the weekends so as not to interfere with her schoolwork during the week.

Victoria had been given an engagement ring from Waylon for Christmas. Although she wouldn't get married until finishing nursing school, it was wonderful that she and Felicia Laverne were now engaged young ladies. Their wishes had come true. Best friends would be marrying best friends. Just the thought of it made her feel happy inside.

Ms. Penny's sister, who lived in Denver, got ill and passed away at the end of February. As Waylon's fiancée and best friend, she and Milton traveled to Denver to attend the funeral services. During that time, Waylon mentioned to other family members after the repast that he had given Victoria an engagement ring for Christmas, officially making her his fiancée. He also announced that Milton had gotten engaged to Victoria's best friend from Atlanta on Valentine's Day and would get married over the summer.

Everybody was so busy congratulating Victoria, Waylon, and Milton, that nobody noticed the angry look that appeared on Charlotte's face with the announcement about Milton's engagement.

When they returned home to Houston, Victoria mentioned Charlotte's angry expression to Milton. He'd shrugged it off, saying he'd never given her any reason to think he was interested in her and didn't intend to worry about her foolishness.

Bringing her thoughts back to the present, Victoria slowed down Magic before bringing him to a stop in front of several rows of fruit trees. It had been a while since she'd ridden this far from the main house. She'd forgotten about this particular grove that grew oranges and grapefruit and other kinds of fruit.

After tying her horse to an orange tree branch, she decided

to try one of the oranges. Leaning up on tiptoe, she reached for the one closest to her when she heard a deep, husky voice ask, "You need help getting that, pretty lady?"

She quickly swung around to stare into the most handsome face she'd ever seen—that of her future husband. "Waylon?" she asked in breathless surprise. "What are you doing here?"

Waylon leaned against one of the orange trees as he studied the beautiful girl standing before him, who would one day become his wife. Even in jeans and a Western shirt, she was feminine as hell. Then there was all that red hair flowing wildly around her shoulders, since she hadn't bothered to tie it back.

He was happy to see her. "I could ask you the same thing, Victoria, since you're on Satterfield property," he said.

"Satterfield property?" she asked while glancing around. "But this is a part of Whispering Pines. I distinctly remember this fruit grove over the years."

He grinned. "Yes, Milt and I planted it. The reason I'm here is to check the irrigation system. The grapefruit trees are on Whispering Pines property and the orange trees are on Satterfield's. The property line divides them."

"Oh, I never knew that," she said. "My parents never said."

"Probably being this far from both of the main houses, nobody ever cared. It was my and Milt's decision. I think we were only ten when we planted the trees. Beyond the fruit grove is the lake where the cabin I'm building for us is located. The land for our home borders Madaris property."

"I didn't know that." Taking a few steps back to stand by a grapefruit tree, she grinned before saying, "Now I am back on Whispering Pines land."

The smile that tilted his lips widened. "You could have stayed on Satterfield land since you and I will share it one day." He met her gaze, and that desire he'd always felt for her stirred his insides. "What if I said I prefer you over here with me, the future Mrs. Waylon Satterfield?"

She began nervously gnawing her bottom lip. "I should go. We shouldn't be out here alone. It's not proper to be so."

He knew that was true, but she was the woman he would marry in less than three years. The one who would share his name, his life, and their babies. "I know that's true, Victoria. However, I'm unsure I can let you leave before sharing our first kiss."

"Our first kiss?"

"Yes, and I want to share it on Satterfield land. The same parcel of land you will share with me one day."

She tilted her head and met his gaze. He wondered if she could feel the intense heat flowing between them. He would love more than a kiss but would never compromise her that way. "What do you say about sharing a kiss on our land?"

She held his gaze for a long moment before walking toward him. When they stood in front of each other, he reached out, took her hand in his, and lifted it to his lips to kiss the ring on her finger. Releasing her hand, he placed his arms around her waist before lowering his head to hers.

Never having been kissed before, Victoria didn't know what to expect. She certainly hadn't contemplated the feelings that awaited her when Waylon's mouth touched hers. Nor had she known he would put his tongue in her mouth and take hold of her own. It was as if someone had dropped a bombshell on her very existence.

She continued following his lead and hoped she was doing everything right. When she felt the solid hardness of his chest but also the hardness of him below the waist, that should have frightened her, but it didn't. She felt safe and secure in his arms. His mouth, although applying soft pressure to hers, was thorough yet gentle. Suddenly, she felt his fingers comb through her hair. When had he released her by the waist to do that? He was massaging her scalp in a way it had never gotten rubbed before, and it felt good.

Were his kisses something she could always expect once they got married? Like every single day? She knew there was more to the marriage act than kisses, but his were so good. Suddenly, Waylon ended the kiss and they tried to get their racing hearts under control. When she tried pulling away, he tightened his hold on her and whispered softly in her ear. "Not yet, sweetheart. I need to hold you for a minute. Okay?"

She nodded, and he held her. Moments later, he whispered. "I love you so much, Victoria." Then he released her and took a step back.

She looked at him. "And I love you, Waylon."

He smiled at her, and she couldn't help but smile back. "It's time for you to get home before your father begins worrying about you," he said, grabbing her horse's reins to bring it over to her. "When are Milton and your ma expected back from Atlanta?"

"Not for a few more days."

He nodded. "I suggest you not ride this far out again."

She knew why he was telling her that. Since she wanted to be a nurse, she had read several books about the human body. He desired her, and she desired him. Temptation was a powerful thing.

Drawing in a slow breath, she said. "I enjoyed our first kiss, Waylon, on our land."

"So did I, Victoria," he said, assisting her onto Magic's back.

Just the feel of him touching her in places he'd never done before as he assisted her made intense heat circle around in her stomach. Once seated in the saddle, she stared down at him and said, "So that you know. I'm not sure I'll be able to wait until after we're married to share another kiss with you."

Without waiting for his response, she and her horse took off like the wind.

Chapter Thirteen

Charlotte looked up from reading her book when her mother entered the room. "Yes, Ma?"

Ms. Penny closed the door and approached her daughter who was sitting on the bed. "I think we need to talk, Queenie."

Charlotte nervously placed her book aside. "About what, Ma?"

"Why, you've only received one visitor since we returned from Denver. There should have been two more by now. What's wrong with you, girl?"

Charlotte's breath came out in a whoosh. Her mother had always kept up with her monthly like clockwork, so she shouldn't be surprised that she would notice she'd missed the last two.

"Charlotte, I am waiting for an answer."

Air practically stalled in her lungs. It had been a long time since her mother had called her Charlotte. It was always Queen Charlotte or Queenie unless she was in trouble. Considering her condition, she was definitely in trouble. There was nothing she could do now but give her mother an answer.

"I'm with child, Ma."

"With child!" Penny Satterfield's words echoed through the room like a sonic boom. The look on her face was even worse. "Yes."

Her mother stood there for a full minute and stared at her in disgust before she backed up as if Charlotte's presence sickened her. At that moment, Charlotte's heart slammed against her breastbone. "I'm sorry, Ma."

"Too late to be sorry now. I have to tell your father."

Now she felt her heart missing a few beats. If her aunt Jessie were still alive, she would have asked her mother to send her to Denver before her mother could have detected anything. Her aunt would have known what to do. It was the same thing she had done two years before. But now Aunt Jessie was gone.

"No, Mama, please don't tell Pa. Can't you take me to someone who will know what to do?"

"Know what to do?" her mother asked sharply, thoroughly appalled. "How do you know about such matters?"

"I don't," she said quickly.

"Then why would you mention anything like that? Is there something you're not telling me, Charlotte?"

"No." There was no way she would tell her mother what Aunt Jessie had done two years ago when she'd gone to spend that summer in Denver and met that boy.

Her mother stared at her for another long minute, and Charlotte hoped she hadn't given her mother any ideas about anything. Her mother had adored her younger sister and must never know what secrets Charlotte and Aunt Jessie had shared. "I just heard girls at school talk, Ma. That's all."

"Well, that's nothing decent girls would discuss. Not good Christian girls anyway."

Late afternoon sunshine was coming through the bedroom window, but it could have been storming outside for all the gloom Charlotte felt in the room. "Your father and brother should be coming in for supper soon. I'm going to tell them. I suggest you have the baby's father's name ready to give because there will be a wedding tonight."

Shock covered Charlotte's face. "A wedding?"

"Yes. A wedding. There's no way your father is going to let the man who did this to you turn his back on you. You will be forced into a marriage just because you can't keep your legs closed. I thought we raised you better than this. You have greatly disappointed me, Charlotte. Be prepared for your father's anger."

With those final words, Penny Satterfield walked out of the room.

A full hour later, Charlotte sensed the heavy footsteps of her father and brother, denoting their return home. All this time, she'd been in her bedroom, her thoughts consumed by her mother's words. There would be a wedding. The unexpected news had left her reeling, but she couldn't deny the flicker of hope that her pregnancy brought. She had come up with a plan. Ultimately, she would get the man she desired and was destined to be with.

There would be no way Milton could get out of marrying her. Her father and his pa would see to it just on her word, even if he denied it. It would be the honorable thing to do, and those Madarises were all about honor and maintaining a blemish-free family name. Besides, there was no reason they wouldn't believe her over him. Why would they?

Her father and brother had barely been home for twenty minutes when the tranquility of Charlotte's room was shattered. The door was flung open with such force that it was wrenched off its hinges. Kurt Satterfield, his face contorted with fury, stood in the doorway, his twelve-gauge shotgun clenched in his hand. The sight of it sent Charlotte scrambling back against the wall, her heart pounding.

"Who did this to you?" he all but snarled in a voice that sent chills all through her. Over her father's shoulder, she saw Waylon, who looked just as outraged.

Meeting her father's gaze, she lifted her chin. "He didn't mean for it to happen," she said as if intentionally protecting the person's identity.

"Tell me who did this to you!"

"He didn't mean for it to happen, Pa," she said again, trying to sound even more convincing.

"Tell me, Charlotte!"

She jumped. Her father had never raised his voice to that degree with her. She paused a moment and then: "Milton. Milton Madaris got me this way."

"You're lying. There's no way Milt got you that way," Waylon said, storming from behind his father to face her.

"He did. Why should I lie?" Charlotte asked heatedly.

"That's a good question, so how about giving us an answer," he said, glaring hard at her before turning to his father. "There's no way Milt got Charlotte with child, Pa. You know Milt as well as I do. I don't know who Charlotte is trying to protect by pinning such a thing on Milt, but what she's doing is unforgivable."

His father frowned. "You would place Milton Madaris's character above that of your sister's?"

Instead of answering his father, Waylon stared at Charlotte and said, "You've had a crush on Milt forever. You don't think I know that? Milt is engaged to get married in a few months. Why are you doing this to him?"

"Because he did this to me!" she nearly screamed, knowing they thought she meant he'd gotten her pregnant instead of what she truly meant. Milton had broken her heart by planning to marry someone else. "He told me he would call off his engagement if I was with child. Well, I am with a child. You don't want to admit what he's done to me for fear it will jeopardize your engagement to Victoria. Well, what about me? I am your sister, Waylon. I can't believe you would choose him over me. Blood is thicker than water." Charlotte then turned to her father. "You asked me, and I am telling you, Pa. Milton Madaris fathered my child."

Her father stared at her for a long moment and then asked, "I'm going to ask this once, Charlotte, and you better tell me the truth. Is Milton Madaris the father of the child you carry?"

"Yes, Pa. Milton fathered my child. I would never lie to you or Ma."

Kurt Satterfield then turned to Waylon. "Go get the preacher and bring him here. Then we'll all go to Whispering Pines."

"Pa, I don't believe Milt—"

Kurt Satterfield threw up his hand to stop Waylon from saying anything more. "I don't care what you believe, Waylon," he interrupted to say. "I think it's a disgrace that you don't believe your sister. She would never lie to me or her ma about this." He drew a deep breath as if trying to control his anger before saying, "How dare Milton do this to my daughter while planning to marry someone else? Well, I have news for him. The only wedding that will be taking place is the one we're having tonight. Now, do what I say and fetch the preacher. And don't ever take the side of an outsider against this family again."

"Outsider?" Waylon asked, not believing what he was hearing. "Pa, the Madarises have been our neighbors and good friends for years. Milt is my best friend and the brother of my future wife."

"And Charlotte is your sister. If you don't stand with her, you stand against her, and I won't have it. The Satterfields are a family united. Now go get Reverend Potts like I told you to do."

The Madarises were sitting at the table just finishing supper while Victoria told them how happy she was that she had graduated and would be moving to Savannah to attend nursing school in September, after Milton and Felicia's wedding. Earlier that month, the entire Madaris family and Waylon had traveled by train to Atlanta for Felicia Laverne's graduation. Both Victoria and Fee graduated at the top of their class, and Milton was proud of them.

He was counting the days until he and Felicia Laverne would marry. It would be the weekend before Labor Day, and he couldn't wait. Already, he had begun constructing the house that would be theirs. Waylon had completed the one where he and Victoria would live one day. Since it had been finished ahead of schedule, whenever Waylon had any free time, he would come to help Milton. There were days when Milton had to pinch himself at how well life was going.

The only sad moment was when his pa's younger brother, Quantum Travis Madaris, visited a couple of months ago. He had told everyone that he'd decided to leave the United States to live in Paris. Uncle QT, as they'd fondly called him, was their father's only sibling and Milton and Victoria's favorite uncle. They always enjoyed his visits, and he had taught Milton to play the trumpet over the years.

Quantum was a fun-loving, easygoing uncle who hadn't been cut out for ranching. Instead, he'd chosen the life of his first love, that of a musician. For years, he'd played in Cab Calloway's band. He thought it was time for him to go solo and felt Paris was the place to expand his musical talents. Years ago, he'd been married to a woman named Adaline. From what Milton had heard, she'd been bad news. Thinking she could be trusted, Uncle QT had shared the secret Madaris tea recipe with her. That hadn't turned out well when Adaline schemed to sell the recipe to a major tea company and run off with one of the ranch hands with the proceeds. Luckily, Quantum found out about the plan before she could proceed with it. He hadn't wasted time divorcing Adaline and had been single ever since, swearing never to remarry.

Milton was happy that his uncle was going after his dream but was saddened that he and Victoria wouldn't see him as often. Before leaving for Paris, he had turned his half of Whispering Pines over to his brother Jantzen, saying there was no reason for him to hold on to it when he had no desire ever to be a rancher.

"I hear someone pulling up," Jantz said, interrupting Milton's thoughts. "I wonder who's visiting during our supper time." He then stood when there was a loud knock on the door. "I better see who that is."

Milton stood and followed his father out of the dining room. When his father opened the door, he saw Mr. Kurt with a shotgun.

"Kurt, what's wrong?" Jantz asked in concern, stepping aside. When he did, Kurt entered, followed by Ms. Penny, Charlotte, Reverend Potts, and Waylon.

Milton met Waylon's gaze. Over the years, he and Waylon had mastered the ability to silently communicate with each other, especially when some crazy bullshit was about to go down. The look in his best friend's eyes warned him this would be one of those times.

When everyone was inside, Jantz closed the door. By then, Milton's mother and sister had come out of the dining room. Victoria stood beside Milton, but Etta Madaris went to stand next to her husband when it was apparent the Satterfields were upset about something.

Reverend Potts looked like he'd hastily gotten dressed and preferred being anyplace than here, and probably didn't like the fact he was missing his supper.

"Kurt, I'm going to ask you again, what's wrong? What's this about?" Jantzen asked.

"I'll tell you what's wrong and what this is about," Kurt said in a loud, booming voice that almost shook the rafters. "Your son," he said, pointing at Milton. "Got my daughter in a family way, and there's going to be a wedding tonight or a funeral."

Chapter Fourteen

Milton went completely still, and then, when he realized the impact of Mr. Satterfield's words, he became enraged—fully enraged—especially when everyone, the Satterfields, his parents, and Reverend Potts, were staring at him.

His gaze flew to Charlotte and to his way of thinking, she had some smug look on her face. That enraged him even more. He turned to Mr. Satterfield. "I don't know what your daughter told you, but if she's in a family way, her baby isn't mine. I've never touched her. I'm an engaged man."

"You did touch me!" Charlotte screamed, her eyes flowing with what he knew were fake tears. "I was a virgin, and you told me if I got pregnant, that you would marry me!"

This was damn unbelievable, Milton thought. He couldn't believe this shit. Charlotte was lying, and they both knew it. Turning to his parents, still staring at him, he said furiously, "She's lying, Dad. I would not have touched her that way. I love Felicia and would not have betrayed her."

"I believe my daughter, and there will be a wedding tonight," Kurt snarled.

"Over my dead body," Milton snarled back.

"That is your only other option," Kurt snapped.

"That's enough!" Jantzen bellowed loudly before Milton had a chance to say anything else. "I need to speak with my son alone." His father turned and walked toward his study, and Milton followed.

When the door closed behind them, an angry Jantzen stared long and hard at his son before asking, "Is Charlotte Satterfield pregnant with your child?"

Milton wanted to kick something. Hadn't he just said in front of everyone that she wasn't? Charlotte was putting on a believable act, but his family had to know she was lying through her teeth.

Drawing a deep breath, he knew he had to regain his composure and answer his father. "No, Pa. If she is pregnant, it is not my child."

Seeing the Madaris family Bible on his father's desk, he picked it up and placed his hand, palm down, on top of it. "This is our family Bible, Pa. In it are the names of all the Madarises before me, back to Carlos Madaris. It has been handed down from generation to generation with honor. It is an honor I've never taken lightly. An honor I've always been proud of. On this Bible, I swear to you, as your son, as a Madaris, that I have never touched Charlotte Satterfield. If she is pregnant, her baby isn't mine."

Milton then returned the Bible to the desk. He had no idea what Jantzen Madaris was thinking. Usually, when a woman made such an accusation, her word was to be believed. He hoped, in this case, his father would believe him. He just had to.

Finally, his father said, "I believe you, Milton."

Relief flowed through him. "Thanks, Pa." He paused momentarily and then said, "Even if you had said you didn't believe me, I still would not marry her. Doing so would be a slap to the faces of all the Madarises before me."

He paused before continuing, needing his father to understand what he meant. "Whispering Pines is Madaris land. It is
a Madaris birthright. I would willingly die by Mr. Kurt's shotgun before being forced into a marriage where I knew the next
person to inherit our land was not a true Madaris. If Charlotte
is pregnant, her baby is *not* a Madaris."

He knew his words had hit home when he saw fury in his
father's face. "Why is she lying, Milton? Has Charlotte ever
come on to you before?"

Milton shrugged. "She's been a nuisance all her life, Pa.
However, never in a million years would I have thought she
would stoop so low as to try something like this. I love Felicia.
She is the woman I love and the only woman I've ever loved."

Jantzen nodded. "Alright, let me handle this. Kurt's allegations are an attack on my family and the Madaris name, and I
won't stand for it."

Milton had never seen his father this angry, and considering
the circumstances, he understood. He followed his father from
the study. Everyone was standing in the same spot they had been
in when they'd left them minutes ago. He met his mother's and
sister's gazes and knew, without them saying a word, they believed his denials. He glanced at Waylon. Although to others
he might have had an unreadable expression on his face, Milton understood. His best friend believed him and was taking
his word over that of his own sister.

"What's it going to be, Jantzen?" Kurt Satterfield asked in
an angry tone. "A funeral or a wedding?"

Jantzen frowned. "There won't be a funeral."

Milton's gaze was trained on Charlotte, who, in turn, met
his gaze and had the nerve to smirk.

"So, there will be a wedding," Kurt said, assuming as much.

Jantzen crossed his arms over his chest, met Kurt Satterfield's
gaze, and then, to not be misunderstood, spoke in a loud voice.

"Milton says he is not the father of Charlotte's baby, and I believe him. There won't be a wedding either."

Jantzen Madaris's words were not what Charlotte had expected, and by the shocked look on her parents' faces, it was apparent they weren't what they had expected either. Indeed, they would do the honorable thing and order Milton to marry her. Right away. Tonight.

"What do you mean there won't be a wedding?" Kurt roared, lifting his shotgun as if ready to aim.

"Gentlemen, please," Reverend Potts implored, rushing to stand between the two men and the shotgun. He then turned to Jantzen. "Mr. Madaris, why do you not believe Miss Satterfield?"

Jantzen met the pastor's stare. "Because my son swore upon our family Bible that he's not the father of Charlotte's child. That's good enough for me."

"Well, it's not good enough for me," Kurt Satterfield snapped. "Charlotte has no problem swearing upon our family Bible as well."

All eyes turned to Charlotte. She lifted her chin. "Yes, Pa, I will do that because I am telling the truth. Milton is my baby's father."

All gazes shifted to Jantzen. "It doesn't matter if she does place her hand on the Bible. My boy is not marrying your daughter. If he does, it will be *after* the child is born, and I'm convinced it's a Madaris baby."

"And just how will you know that?" Penny Satterfield asked snappily.

"The child will have a certain birthmark. All Madarises are born with it."

Charlotte swallowed deeply as she tried to retain her composure. Was that true? Were all Madaris babies born with a birthmark? When her father turned to look at her as if allowing her to recant her accusation, she knew there was no way she could. "Then my son or daughter will be born with that birthmark. You'll see."

Emboldened by his daughter's words, Kurt bit out, "You want my daughter to bear her child as an unmarried woman? Just because you refuse to accept her word that Milton fathered her child? Do you not know the shame that will cause her?"

"No more than the scandal it will cause my family when people in these parts accuse my son of not doing the right thing by her."

Charlotte knew she had to make them see reason. She was determined that Milton marry her. "Milton is engaged to marry someone at the end of the summer, Pa. What happens when I give birth to a Madaris baby in seven months, but Milton has married someone else?" Charlotte wailed.

Reverend Potts turned to Jantzen before shifting his gaze to Milton. He refocused on Jantzen. "If your position is that Milton won't marry Charlotte until it's proven the baby is his, Jantzen, then it's only fair that Milton not be allowed to marry anyone until after this issue is resolved."

"Fine," Jantzen snapped.

"No! That's not fine, Pa," Milton said furiously, turning to his father. "You want me to postpone my wedding to Fee because of her lie?" he said, pointing a finger at Charlotte. "I won't do it!"

"Listen, son. Like Reverend Potts said, it's only fair," Jantzen said with regret.

"No, Pa, it's not fair to me or to Felicia."

"What about me?" Charlotte demanded. "You were engaged to her and slept with me. Besides, chances are she won't marry you when she hears you deceived her."

"Is that what you're hoping, Charlotte?" Milton snapped.

She placed her hands on her hips. "I am hoping you do the right thing like you said you would do and not cause me any shame. All you told me were lies." She had to play this farce for all she could. The last thing she wanted was to be exposed.

Reverend Potts felt it was time to intervene again and address Jantzen. "Mr. Madaris, why can't there be a wedding tonight? If it is discovered after the baby is born that it's not your son's child, as the pastor, I will annul the marriage as long as it hasn't been consummated."

Both Jantzen and Milton said simultaneously, "No!"

Kurt then said, "If your son won't marry my daughter, then my son won't marry yours either. I am officially calling off any union between a Satterfield and Madaris. I am taking back my blessing."

"No, Pa!" Waylon, who'd been quiet all this time, said, coming to stand before his father. "Leave me and Victoria out of this."

"Our families are now in a feud with the Madarises since they won't force their son to do the honorable thing. There is no way I will accept one of them as part of our family," Kurt said bitterly.

"I love Victoria, and we will get married as planned," Waylon said forcefully, looking at Victoria, who had tears clouding her eyes. "I won't give her up."

He made a move toward Victoria, but Jantzen blocked his path. "Your father has spoken, Waylon. As such, although it pains me to say this, your engagement to my daughter is officially off. There will not be a Satterfield and Madaris wedding."

Jantzen then turned to his daughter. "Give Waylon back his ring, Victoria."

With tears flowing down her cheeks, Victoria did what she was told. She then rushed from the room with Etta following behind her.

Waylon stared at Charlotte with a furious expression before storming out of the house.

Milton knocked on Victoria's bedroom door.

"Come in."

He braced himself before turning the knob, knowing she was an emotional mess.

Victoria stood at her bedroom window, looking out at the Madaris's land. He figured her gaze was focused toward the east, where a certain cabin sat. The one Waylon had built for them to live in together after they married. Thanks to Charlotte's lies, a marriage that would never take place.

He called out to her softly when she hadn't turned around. "Victoria."

When she did, his heart clenched at the pain he saw in her features. He held out his arms, and his sister quickly crossed the room to him and cried into his chest. Her tears soaked through his shirt. He wanted to give her words of comfort. Instead, he silently cursed Charlotte with Victoria's heart-wrenching sobs. Charlotte hadn't just hurt him with her lie, she had hurt her brother and his sister, and Milton would never forgive her for doing so.

He wasn't sure how long he stood holding Victoria in his arms, but it didn't matter. He would have held her the rest of the evening and the next day if necessary. His sister was hurting, and he was hurting right along with her.

She finally pulled away and swiped at the tears still flowing from her eyes before asking, "When are you leaving for Atlanta?"

He drew in a deep breath. Felicia had to be told, and it would be up to her to decide whether she believed him enough to postpone the wedding and not call it off entirely. He would be asking her to postpone their wedding. Would she willingly postpone their wedding knowing what he'd been accused of? Would her parents even allow her to do such a thing, knowing the embarrassment it would cause their daughter? There was another possibility he had to face: What if Felicia believed Charlotte's lie and ended their engagement altogether?

"I'll start packing tonight and leave first thing in the morning. I called to let her know I'm coming but won't tell her why. Since this visit wasn't planned, I'm sure she knows something is wrong." There was no doubt in his mind that his voice had given something away.

"I am praying things work out for you and Fee."

He nodded. "And I'm hoping things will work out for you and Waylon. I'm sure you know that, regardless of his father's directive, he will not give you up just like he said."

"I hope not."

"He won't." There was no way he would tell her their pa was so mad that Milton was convinced the "unforgiving Madaris pride" he'd always heard about had kicked in with a vengeance. If it had, he had a feeling that regardless of the outcome seven months from now, the feud between the two families would never end. Hopefully, a marriage between Waylon and Victoria would reunite the families again and mend the hard feelings. "I hope you believe me when I say Charlotte's baby isn't mine," he finally said.

"Of course, I believe you." Then she asked, "Is it true that Pa can tell whether it's a Madaris baby when it's born?"

"Yes, but there's no birthmark. Pa is certain he will be able to tell but it doesn't matter."

"Why?"

"He saw the look of fear of being caught in a lie flash in Charlotte's eyes when he mentioned the birthmark. Now he knows for certain she's lying."

Victoria nodded. "Charlotte will be exposed as a liar. I hope things will turn out alright for you and Fee. It's not her that I'm concerned about, Milton. It's her parents. Postponing the wedding because of the accusations against you might not sit well with them."

Milton was afraid of that. "I know, and I'm asking for everyone's prayers. I have to believe things will work out for all of us—me, Fee, you, and Way—in the end."

★ ★ ★

"There you have it," Milton said, not only to Felicia but also to her parents. Over the past months, he had forged a bond with his future in-laws and hoped they believed his innocence in what he had told them.

"My goodness. This Charlotte sounds like such an evil person," Mrs. Lee said with distress in her voice.

Nobody said anything else for a moment. While telling them everything, he had been focused on Felicia's features. They were expressionless, so he had no idea what she was thinking or even if she believed a single word he'd said.

Reverend Lee began speaking, and Milton held his breath. "Those are serious allegations leveled against you, young man. However, just as your parents believe in your innocence, I do as well."

Before Milton could expel a sigh of relief, the minister added. "However, as my wife said, that Charlotte woman is truly evil. I honestly don't like the thought that if you and Fee were to marry, their paths would eventually be crossed. Someone that evil will do anything. If this plan doesn't work, who should say she won't try something else? Something even more devious."

"And if she does, Milton will protect me, Pa."

Felicia's words, the first she'd spoken since he'd begun talking, filled his heart with even more love for her.

"Well," Reverend Lee said, breaking into the quiet stillness of the room. "The final decision will be left up to Fee. I am sure the two of you know all the embarrassment postponing the wedding will cause. Tongues will wag and lies will be told. Some will get the news all the way from Texas. I agree with your father that you and Felicia should not communicate for the next seven months. That might seem like a lot to ask, but something that, under the circumstances, is fair."

The minister then turned his attention to his daughter. "Felicia, your mother and I will abide by your decision."

He stood and extended his hand out to Milton. "If Fee believes you will protect her from that evil woman, I will, too."

After Felicia's father released his hand, Felicia's mom hugged him. They then left the room, giving him and Fee privacy. When the sound of the door clicked behind them, he turned to his beloved. "Like your father said, the decision is yours. So that you know, if you agree to wait, things might get ugly. I have no doubt Mrs. Satterfield will spin her tale, far and wide, to protect her daughter's reputation since I've refused to marry her."

Felicia nodded as she crossed the room to him. "Then let her because I will know the truth, and that's all that matters." She then asked, "What about Waylon? Does he believe you didn't take advantage of his sister?"

Milton rubbed a frustrating hand down his face. "Although he couldn't admit to such, Waylon knows I would never do such a thing. I guess he told his parents as much, and they thought he was being disloyal to his family. That's probably why Mr. Kurt reneged on his blessing for Way to marry Victoria."

"Victoria has to be devastated."

"She and Waylon both are, and it's not fair. He loves Victoria and will allow himself to be disowned by his family before giving her up."

Felicia nodded. "I hope he won't have to do that. I know how much Victoria loves him as well." She paused a moment and then said, "As for us, there will be a Madaris-Lee wedding. I am willing to wait because, in my heart, I know that you, Milton Jantzen Madaris, are a man worth waiting for. Not communicating with you for seven months will be one of the hardest things I've ever had to do. But I will do it because I love you and believe in you. I believe in us and the family we will have one day."

With love flowing through to his heart, even more than before, Milton reached out and gently caressed the side of her face. "And I love you, Fee." Drawing her in his arms, he lowered his mouth to hers.

Chapter Fifteen

Seven months later

"**P**ush, child. It won't be much longer now."

Charlotte pushed and released a scream. Then another one. She'd been screaming at the top of her lungs since the first labor pain ripped into her more than five hours ago. Was Hattie Duncan, the area's midwife, standing over her and hollering orders as crazy as she looked? She was tired of pushing and was in too much pain to do anything but scream.

"For God's sake, stop howling like a banshee and push. This baby won't be coming out until you do your part." Just the thought of that made Charlotte push while screaming again.

The moment she'd gone into labor, her father had sent for the midwife, Milton, and his parents. He'd also sent for Reverend Potts, certain there would be a wedding once her baby was born and it was proven to be a Madaris. What if Jantzen Madaris had told the truth, and there was a birthmark on every Madaris baby born? It would be something her child would not have. She was counting on her father to force Milton to marry her regardless.

The last seven months hadn't gone at all like she'd hoped. Definitely not like she'd planned. She figured with the threat of a scandal, the Madarises would back down, and Milton would marry her. That hadn't happened. Nor had he taken pity on her when people began shaming her by calling her loose, wanton, and a tramp. Milton's attitude made her parents even more determined to prove to everyone how the Madaris family had deliberately embarrassed the Satterfields. Thanks to those who had believed her story, the Madaris name had gotten drug through the mud. They accepted as true that she'd been a virgin before Milton had seduced her, and he was refusing to marry her because he wanted to marry someone else.

Tonight, it all ended. She would claim it was Milton's baby regardless of what Milton's father said. She refused to believe Jantzen Madaris could prove otherwise. But what if he could? Those thoughts were interrupted by another sharp pain, this one sharper than before, and she screamed at the top of her lungs.

"Push, gal. This wouldn't be so hard on you if you hadn't gone and messed yourself up down there," Ms. Hattie said sharply. "Now push."

What on earth was the old woman talking about? Saying this wouldn't have been so hard on her if she hadn't gone and messed herself up down there? She heard Ms. Hattie would not allow anyone else in the room to get in her way. Charlotte wished her mother had been allowed to stay with her, but once the labor pains became more frequent, she'd been asked to leave.

Mrs. Hattie was rambling even more now. Not loud enough to be heard and too fast to be understood. Before she could fully comprehend the older woman's words, another pain ripped through her.

"Push!"

She pushed while screaming so loud her throat felt raw. Suddenly, she heard a baby crying and Mrs. Hattie saying, "It's a boy, missy."

The last thing she remembered before exhaustion knocked her into much-needed sleep was the sound of Hattie Duncan saying in a surprised tone. "Well, I'll be."

Milton sat on the steps of the Satterfields' porch. He didn't want to be here, but his parents had insisted he come when they'd gotten the call from Ms. Penny that Charlotte was in labor.

They were sitting on the porch since the Satterfields hadn't the decency to invite them inside their home. Not that he or his parents would have entered anyway. Over the past seven months, Mr. Kurt and Ms. Penny let it be known how much they despised the Madarises for the shame Milton had caused their daughter. Milton wasn't concerned for himself since he refused to claim Charlotte's baby. However, the intense animosity between the two families didn't help the situation between Waylon and Victoria.

The last seven months had been hard on him and his family. What had kept Milton going was Felicia. Although the two of them hadn't communicated, they had stayed connected through Victoria, who'd been going through her own hurt and pain with her broken engagement. Way and Victoria hoped that once Charlotte's baby was born and Mr. Kurt saw it wasn't Milton's baby, he would take back what he'd said about not wanting a union between the Satterfields and Madarises. However, Milton felt that even if the Satterfields made such a move, his pa would not accept it. The Madaris name had been unfairly damaged, and its honor and integrity questioned. He honestly couldn't see the friendship between the families ever being repaired.

Unknown to their parents, he and Waylon had continued to meet at what had been their secret meeting place since they were kids. There was no way they could become enemies when their friendship went so deep. Waylon had told him Charlotte had their parents thoroughly convinced Milton was the father, but Waylon himself did not believe his sister's lies.

Charlotte let out one hell of another scream. Then suddenly, there was the sound of a baby crying, and moments later, Kurt Satterfield opened his front door, stepped onto the porch, pointed to him, and said, "I suggest you come take a look at your son."

Like hell he would, Milton thought. He was about to say those words when the midwife, Hattie Duncan, appeared in the doorway holding a baby wrapped in a yellow blanket. Reverend Potts followed her.

"There's no need for him to look at this baby," Hattie said loud enough for everyone to hear. "It's not his."

Milton exhaled a relieved breath, wondering how the woman would know such a thing. Kurt Satterfield undoubtedly wondered the same thing and stared at Hattie with intense anger. "What are you talking about, old woman? Jantz hasn't even checked for a mark on that baby."

Hattie lifted her chin. "Doesn't matter. Look at this baby and tell me who he looks like."

She uncovered the child, and Kurt stared at the baby. Reverent Potts took a look at him as well. Penny Satterfield stepped onto the porch to join them. Since she didn't look at the baby, Milton figured she'd seen it already, and from the look in Ms. Penny's features, she knew what Hattie Duncan was pointing out to the others. Charlotte's mother appeared too ashamed to even meet Milton or his parents' gazes.

Who on earth did the baby look like? Milton figured his parents were as curious as he was but refused to move an inch to see for themselves.

The front door opened again, and Waylon came out, stared at the baby, looked angrily at his father, and was about to return inside when Ms. Hattie's words stopped him. "And another thing," she said. "Charlotte lied about being a virgin since this wasn't her first pregnancy."

Penny gasped loudly. Milton wasn't sure if she hadn't known that or if she was shocked Ms. Hattie had announced such a thing to everyone. "The reason Charlotte had a difficult labor," Ms. Hattie continued, "was because whoever helped her get rid of the last one botched her up."

Waylon went back inside, slamming the door behind him. Kurt turned to his wife and pinned her with an accusing stare. "You knew about this?"

Penny quickly backed up, bumping into Reverent Potts in the process. "No, Kurt. I swear I didn't."

In a deceptively calm voice, Jantzen Madaris then said, "We're leaving." He headed for the truck. Milton and his mother followed.

"Jantz," Kurt called after him. "I apologize to you and your family."

Jantzen turned and gave him a steely glare. "The embarrassment your family has caused mine these past seven months is unforgivable, Kurt. If Reverend Potts weren't standing on that porch, I'd tell you just what you can do with your apology."

The Madarises then got in their truck and drove off.

A furious Kurt kicked in the door to the bunkhouse. Aiming at the ceiling, he released a blast from his shotgun. Five men wearing just their skivvies jumped out of bed, nearly tumbling to the floor as plaster fell from the ceiling, leaving a huge gaping hole. Kurt's gaze was on one particular man. Levon Turban. Everybody living in these parts knew about those Turbans. They all looked alike. From their broad forehead and distinctive nose down to their wide lips.

"What's wrong, Mr. Satterfield?" one of his ranch hands, Stan Anderson, asked in a shaking voice. They were all staring at him like he'd gone plum loco.

"I want all of you to stand on the other side of the room. All but Levon." Four men were quick to do what he'd asked. That left one man defenseless against a shotgun aimed right at him.

Levon backed up with his hands in the air. "What's wrong, Mr. Satterfield? I didn't do anything."

"You slept with my daughter and then stood by while she accused another man of getting her with child."

Levon opened his mouth, then closed it as if he thought better of it. When he saw Kurt's fingers twitch near the trigger, he quickly said, "She never said the child was mine."

"The boy looks just like you. Get dressed. There's going to be a wedding tonight."

"Wedding?" Levon asked, startled.

"Yes, wedding. You either marry Charlotte or die here and now," Kurt said.

Levon swallowed deeply and then said. "Okay, I'll marry her."

Kurt's frown deepened. "You don't have a choice."

Chapter Sixteen

While Charlotte sat up in bed with Levon standing beside it, the two were married by Reverend Potts. Hattie Duncan was a witness. From the look on Levon's face, it was apparent he hadn't wanted to marry her any more than she wanted to marry him.

Nothing she said would change her father's mind about the wedding. He hadn't even given Levon time to dress decently. She had a feeling he was wearing the same buckskin pants and Western shirt he'd worn to work the ranch that day.

After they were declared husband and wife, Hattie and Reverend Potts left. Her pa told Levon to leave the room as well. Her husband of less than five minutes hadn't wasted any time getting out from under the barrel of her father's shotgun. Her mother had cried throughout the ceremony and was still wiping tears from her eyes.

"You brought shame to this family, Charlotte," her father snarled. "Not only did you lie to us, but you swore on the Satterfield family Bible!" he said, raising his voice. "I won't ever forgive you for doing that. Your lie started a feud between two families and neighbors who took sides."

Charlotte figured it would be best to remain silent and let her pa have his say. He seemed determined to have it anyway. He would be mad with her for a while, but eventually, he'd come around and forgive her. She was his daughter. His Queenie.

"What you did to this family is a sin and a shame, and it will be years before your ma, brother, and I live it down. We repeatedly asked you to be truthful, and you claimed you were. And the very thought you were pregnant before, and your aunt Jessie helped you end your pregnancy, is another thing I can't stomach. Thanks to Hattie's wagging tongue, everybody around these parts will know what you did and that you even lied about being a virgin."

He paused as if to let his words sink in before adding, "I'm sending you away, Charlotte. After your six weeks of recovery from childbirth, I want you gone from this house."

"How long will I need to be gone?"

Her father moved closer to the bed to ensure she heard his next words. "You are never to come back, not even to visit."

His words were like a slap to her face, and the loud gasp she heard from her mother was a strong indication that she hadn't known of her father's decision. "What do you mean I can't come back, Pa?"

"Just what I said. I am giving you and Levon your aunt's house in Denver. That's where you will stay the rest of your days with your husband and child."

"You can't mean that, Pa."

"I do mean it. After all the shame you brought to this family and all your lies, we are disowning you as our child. Tomorrow, my attorney will remove your name from the family roll as a Satterfield. When we die, I don't want you to attend our funerals. And you will never be able to inherit anything owned by a Satterfield. Nothing. Not this house, land, or anything else.

You, your husband, nor your offspring—present and future. I will make sure my attorney files the necessary paperwork and sees to it. You are as much as dead to me, Charlotte."

"Kurt, you can't mean that," Penny Satterfield said with tears gathering in her eyes.

"I do mean it, and you will abide by my decision, Penny. It is final."

Charlotte glanced at her mother with pleading eyes. "Ma, surely you won't let him do this to me. What about your first grandchild? Are you willing to never see him again? Turn your back on him, too?" Instead of answering, her mother began crying.

"Lies have consequences," her father said sternly. "You should have thought about that before lying on an innocent man."

"Pa, when I'm well, I'll visit the Madarises and—"

"Do you not fully understand the magnitude of what you've done?" her father yelled, interrupting what she was saying. "The Madarises don't want a Satterfield to set foot on their property. The only thing you'll do is leave here when you can travel and never come back. I'm being gracious by giving you your aunt's home. Free and clear. That is the last thing you'll get from us, Charlotte. If you ever try to return here again, I will have you arrested for trespassing."

Her mother began crying harder but her father ignored his wife.

"You're doing this because of Waylon, aren't you? I'm being punished because of his broken engagement to Victoria."

Her father stared at her for a long moment and said, "I'm doing this because of lies you told not only to me and your mother but to anyone who cared to listen—shaming a decent family in the worst possible way. Penny and I thought we raised a decent human being. Tonight, you proved us wrong. And don't bother writing. We don't want to see or hear from you ever again."

Her pa then left the room, and her mother followed.

★ ★ ★

"In a way, I feel sorry for Charlotte Satterfield, Milton," Felicia said as they held hands while walking through her parents' rose garden.

He had arrived that morning, sharing the news that they could reschedule their wedding. Not only had it been proved that Charlotte's baby wasn't his, but according to the midwife, she hadn't been a virgin either. She had gotten pregnant before, and that had resulted in a botched-up abortion nobody had known about. She'd confessed to her parents that her aunt Jessie had taken her to some woman in Denver while she'd visited over the summer two years ago.

"Well, I don't feel sorry for her," Milton replied. "Pa is still upset about the scandal and won't let Waylon come to our home to see Victoria. She delayed leaving in September for nursing school in Savannah, hoping that her engagement to Way would be back on, but Pa refuses to talk about it.

"To be honest, Fee, I doubt things will ever get back right between the Madarises and Satterfields. Charlotte's lies caused irreparable damage. That's sad because Victoria and Way love each other so much."

"Have you tried talking to your father on their behalf?" Felicia asked.

Milton released a deep breath and said, "Yes. I tried talking to Pa. Mama has, too. However, he is full of what Mom calls Madaris pride and is unforgiving of all the Satterfields, and that includes Way."

"Well, we hope that changes over the next few months, Milton. Every time I talk to Victoria, she starts crying. Can't your father see what it's doing to her and Way? What happened wasn't their fault."

"I know. I even told Pa that Way never believed I was guilty of what Charlotte had accused me of doing. But he doesn't care. The Madaris name has always meant integrity and honor in Houston, but because of a Satterfield it was nearly ruined."

Deciding to change the subject, she turned toward him beaming broadly. "So, what date do you want to reschedule our wedding for?"

He reached out and tucked a strand of hair that had fallen in her face behind her ear. "As soon as possible."

Her smile widened. "Let's talk to my parents to see how that can be arranged."

Three months later

At the Emmanuel Baptist Church in Atlanta, Georgia, Milton Madaris wedded Felicia Lee. Although Jantzen was totally against it, Milton refused to back down from Waylon standing beside him as his best man. Victoria was Felicia's maid of honor, and her sisters were her bridesmaids.

Charlotte, in shame, left Houston for Denver with her husband and newborn child. Even though her lies resulted in Waylon's broken engagement with Victoria, he tried talking his father out of disowning his sister. However, no matter what he said, Kurt Satterfield would not change his mind. It was as if Waylon's words fell flat.

As a wedding gift, their uncle QT sent tickets to Milton and Felicia to join him for a month in Paris. Milton and Felicia would leave within a week after their wedding. He also sent a ticket to Victoria to use whenever she felt the need to get away from Houston for a while. She would have to reapply to nursing school since she hadn't started last year in September as planned.

Milton had made plans for him and Felicia to spend their wedding night in a hotel in Augusta. They would remain there for two days. Then they would travel back home to Texas to catch the steamship to Paris. It would be the first international trip for both of them.

"Happy?" Milton asked her as they danced together.

"Very. I thought this day would never come."

"But it has. Thanks for believing in me, Fee."

"And thanks for giving me a reason to believe in you." She looked across the room. "Victoria and Waylon look so sad and miserable."

"I know. He probably wants to ask her to dance but knows doing so might cause a scene with my father. They aren't allowed to talk to each other. You saw how upset Pa was when he saw Waylon was my best man."

"I'm glad you stood your ground. He is your best friend and was supposed to be the one to stand beside you today. I can't imagine anyone else doing so. I hope Pa Jantz comes around. Victoria loves Waylon."

"And he loves her."

Later that night, in a darkened hotel room in Augusta, with the sultry voice of Billie Holiday flowing in the background, Milton made love to the woman who would always have his heart. His Fee.

Four months later…

Victoria raced Magic across the open plains. Her destination was to meet Waylon in the fruit grove, which had become their secret meeting place over the past few months. They loved each other, and their families' positions in this feud were unfair to them.

Her parents left for Dallas yesterday and would be gone for a few days to visit her mother's brother, who was under the weather. Milton and Fee had returned from Paris and were taking another trip. This was to New Orleans to see Fee's cousin Naomi perform in a gospel concert. Victoria was to have gone with them but encouraged them to go without her because she wasn't feeling well.

She doubted either of them had believed her claim, but neither had said anything. Over the past few months, Milton had given her several warnings that if their pa found out that she was disobeying him and sneaking around and seeing Waylon, it would make things harder for her.

Considering her and Waylon's circumstances now, Victoria didn't know how that was possible. Once Charlotte's lie had been exposed, Kurt Satterfield had given back his blessing for her and Waylon to marry. When she'd run into him one day at the feed store, he had personally apologized for being the one to end their engagement.

On the other hand, her pa refused to discuss the possibility of her and Waylon resuming their engagement. Slandering the Madaris name had been like a personal affront to him. Her mother tried explaining that for a Madaris man, a hit to their pride was hard to overcome. Etta Madaris had asked her to be patient; hopefully, her pa would come around.

What if he didn't? Did Pa honestly expect her to live the rest of her life without Waylon? Granted, they hadn't planned to marry until she'd finished nursing school, but what if he still refused to give his blessings after that time? It just wasn't fair. For the past year, she worked three days a week at the hospital, while hoping her father would change his mind about her and Waylon's engagement.

She and Waylon had developed a way of secretly communicating using the postal box he rented in Hall General Store. She would write a letter one day, and he would get it within two days. Only once did she not show up for their meeting because her parents had unexpectedly changed their routine and hadn't gone to visit the sick church members as they usually would do on Thursday evenings.

When she reached the fruit grove, she saw Waylon waiting.

After bringing her horse to a stop, he helped her dismount. Once her feet touched the ground, he drew her into his arms and kissed her.

She loved it whenever he did. A degree of warmth would flow through her veins, eventually heating her blood, leaving her with a level of yearning that he'd initiated over the past year.

"You look mighty pretty today, Victoria," he said when he finally released her mouth.

That's another thing she liked. The gruff timbre of his voice whenever he finished kissing her. "And you look mighty handsome today, Waylon."

He threw his head back and laughed. The sound was husky and rich, and she couldn't help but laugh with him. It had been a while since they'd shared a laugh. When their laughter ceased, his features turned serious. Using his fingertips, he reached out and tilted her face so his gaze could linger on it for a moment. It was as if he were branding it to memory.

"Waylon?"

Instead of answering, he slowly lowered his head to hers and kissed the unspoken question from her lips. Like all his kisses, this one was filled with passion, the kind he'd introduced her to, which never went beyond kissing. The kind that always made her moan.

When the kiss ended, he pressed his forehead against hers, sighed deeply, and said, "I can't imagine us not marrying one day, Victoria."

His words stoked something within her. Something she refused to acknowledge. Even the possibility of that happening. "Then don't imagine it, Waylon. We will get married one day."

"Your pa has pretty much said he doesn't want me in your family," he said, releasing his hold and taking a step back.

"And your ma has pretty much let it be known that she doesn't want me in yours," she countered. In Victoria's way of thinking, Ms. Penny's hatred of her was unwarranted. She blamed the Madarises for Mr. Kurt banishing Charlotte when Charlotte's lie had started it all.

"Ma is not herself and is directing her anger at the wrong people, Victoria. She will eventually come around. She's always put Charlotte on a pedestal and thought she could do no wrong."

"That's no excuse, Waylon, because what your sister did was wrong. At least your father apologized to me, but your mother has let it be known she will never welcome me into your family." Maybe she should tell him what his mother had said to her a few weeks ago when she'd been leaving the grocery store. She hadn't known Penny Satterfield could be so mean and hateful.

He nodded. "You're right. That's no excuse. Once we're married, we won't live with my parents or yours. We'll have our own place."

"Yes, a place of our own," she said, thinking of the cabin that Waylon had built for them.

"I'm thinking of asking your pa for your hand again."

A lump settled in Victoria's throat. All it took was for her to remember how upset her father had gotten when Milton had told him Waylon would be his best man. "Not sure that's a good idea right now. We have time."

He arched a brow. "How do you figure that?"

"We hadn't planned to get married until I finished nursing school anyway. I'm thinking of reapplying, so that would still be three years away."

"Yes, but I never intended for you to leave for Savannah without wearing my engagement ring."

"And I can still wear it, Waylon."

"But you'd be doing so behind your parents' backs, Victoria, and that won't sit well with me."

It didn't sit well with her either. "So, what do you suggest?"

His features were dead serious when he said, "Elope."

Part Three

"Nothing can bring you peace but yourself."

—Ralph Waldo Emerson

Chapter Seventeen

The present…

Felicia Laverne awoke when the sun seeped through the curtains, revealing the dawn of a new day. Last night, she remembered a period known as the Madaris Scandal. Ultimately, the Madaris family's good reputation was restored.

Although she and Milton had married, things hadn't gone well for Waylon and Victoria. Just thinking about what they went through broke her heart. Victoria had been her best friend, and for years, Felicia Laverne had felt her pain.

Even though the Madaris name was cleared, the Satterfield name was left in shambles. News of what Charlotte had done spread far and wide. Few found fault with Kurt for disowning his daughter, considering the feud she'd started between the Madarises and Satterfields and the disgrace she had caused her family.

According to gossip spread by the Turbans, Levon divorced Charlotte within a couple of years, saying she was an unfit wife. A few years later, more gossip spread when Charlotte took up with some man and got pregnant without the benefit of marriage. That only boosted the Turbans' claim that Charlotte Satterfield was spoiled, self-centered, rotten to the core, and nothing but trash. When the Turbans moved from the Houston area to Mississippi, the gossip about Charlotte faded, and the Satterfields were finally able to put the scandal behind them.

Felicia Laverne heard the knock on her bedroom door. "Come in."

A smiling Bessie entered. "Happy Saturday, Mama Laverne. Are you ready for breakfast?"

"Yes, Bessie. I'll be up in a minute. I overslept this morning."

"No harm in that. Do you need my help with anything?"

"No. I can manage. Thanks for checking on me."

"Of course, you are welcome. I'm going to miss having you with us."

"I'm going to miss being here, but it's time for me to go home." Home for her was Whispering Pines. The place her beloved Milton had taken her to after their marriage. She might live under a different roof with Jake and Diamond, but the land was the same. Land she loved.

When Bessie left, Felicia Laverne reached for her cell phone. A deep masculine voice answered, clearly surprised. "Mama Laverne?"

It had been years since she'd had a reason to call him. "Yes, Trevor Maurice. How are you and the family?"

Trevor Maurice Grant was a childhood friend to her grandsons Justin, Dex, and Clayton—Jonathan's sons.

"We're all good, Mama Laverne. What about you?"

"I'm well. I was calling to ask a favor."

"And what's the favor?" he asked, and she thought she heard amusement in his voice.

"That cabin you own by the lake. The one you bought from the Johnstones years ago. Were you and your family planning on using it this summer?"

"No. Corinthians, the kids, and I plan to spend this summer near Sir Drake and his family in a cabin we built on Warren Mountains."

Drake Warren, a former marine and CIA agent, owned mountains in Tennessee that had been in his family for generations. She'd heard Trevor and Ashton Sinclair, another close friend of theirs, had built spacious cabins there. "That sounds nice."

"Why do you want to know about the cabin, Mama Laverne?"

"A young lady needs a place to stay near Whispering Pines. I was hoping she could stay there. Let me know the cost so I can tell her."

"There won't be a charge. She'll be doing us a favor by keeping it occupied this summer. We haven't been there in a couple of years. Corinthians and I even discussed selling it."

"Well, if you do, please make the offer to Chancellor first. That land was originally part of the spread he purchased after the Johnstones sold it."

"I had forgotten about that. I'll make sure I let him know if we decide to sell. Do you have a pen? I'll give you the four-digit security code for the cabin."

"I don't need a pen. I'll remember it."

He chuckled before rattling off the number.

"And Trevor Maurice?"

"Yes, Mama Laverne?"

"I prefer you not mention any of this to my family. They will find out soon enough."

"Yes, ma'am. I won't say anything about it."

A short while later, Mama Laverne felt good and ready to start her day. She couldn't wait to resume her meetings with Zoey. There was no reason for the feud between the Madarises and Satterfields to come up. If it did, at least one of her sons already knew about the Madaris Scandal. If the others heard about it from her meetings with Zoey, she felt certain their thoughts would be similar to Jonathan's. Since it happened years ago, and she and Milton eventually married, it was water under the bridge.

However, the one thing she couldn't share with Zoey, and especially not her sons, was the incident that took place years later, the one only she, Milton, and Waylon knew about.

Namely, the cover-up of a murder.

Sleeping late in the mornings was something Chance rarely did unless there was a good reason for it. This morning, he thought he had one. He had been enjoying his fantasy dream so much that he hadn't wanted to wake up. Now he was awake and already missing the imagery of making love to a woman. However, it hadn't been just any woman. She had been Zoey.

Even now, he could barely open his eyes for wanting to remember every luscious detail. It had been one of the most passionate nights of his life, even though it had only been a dream. He could only assume the reason was that she had been on his mind most of yesterday. Damn, who was he kidding? Zoey Pritchard had been on his mind the day before that. If he were honest with himself, he would admit to thinking of her a lot since that day he'd first seen her by the side of the road.

After returning home from visiting his folks yesterday, he had been tempted to call Mama Laverne to see how the lunch meeting with Zoey had gone, but then he'd thought better of it. His great-grandmother might have put too much stock in his interest.

He'd thought about calling Corbin but dismissed the thought. His cousin assumed he had things all figured out as Zoey was concerned. But, like he'd told Luke yesterday, what he felt toward Zoey was nothing more than a strong attraction and intense desire. That's why his fantasy dream of sex with her had seemed so real.

Another option would have been to call Zoey since he had her number. Given he'd been the one to set up the meeting between Mama Laverne and Zoey, his interest in its outcome would be understandable. Using that logic, he reached for the cell phone on his nightstand but pulled his hand back. That logic was BS, and he knew it.

Pushing the covers aside, he eased out of bed, and like most mornings, he gazed out the window at his land. It always made him feel good inside to realize that he owned all of it—every valley, plain, and stream. And, like always, he thought it was a beautiful sight.

By the time he had returned to the ranch from visiting his folks yesterday, the place was empty. The ranch hands had left for town to enjoy the weekend and women. Lucky bastards. Thursday night had been a real disappointment for him. However, that fantasy dream last night had made up for it.

He headed for the bathroom. Usually, Saturdays were when he returned to the ranch after spending Friday night in a woman's arms. Going to Vance's Tavern a day earlier than usual had been a mistake. On top of it, he'd run into Ravena.

The nerve of her thinking they could get back together. He'd meant just what he'd said when he told her that walking out of his life was the best thing she ever could have done. He hadn't seen it at the time, but he damn sure did now.

Then why were Ravena's words nagging at him? Maybe because she'd said the same thing his cousins had told him over the years. In the five years since she'd left, he hadn't gotten serious about a woman, making it look like he was still pining for Ravena. At the time, he had not given a royal damn what anyone thought, but for Ravena to think such a thing did not sit well with him. At least he had gotten her straight about that.

A short while later, he was dressed to ride his land, something he enjoyed doing. He had placed his Stetson on his head and stepped onto his porch when his cell phone rang. It was Corbin. "Yes, Corbin?"

"I heard you went to Vance's Tavern Thursday night and ran into Ravena."

"What of it?" he asked, not surprised he'd heard about it.

"Nothing, I guess."

"You're right. Seeing her meant nothing."

"Good. I always told you she was bad news."

Yes, he had. Although many of his cousins hadn't liked Ravena, most had kept their thoughts to themselves. Corbin hadn't. He wished like hell he'd listened to his cousin.

"Is there a reason for your call, Corbin?"

"I'm surprised you hadn't called me to see how things went with Mama Laverne and Zoey."

There was no reason to tell him he had thought about doing that. Instead, he decided to act nonchalant. "No reason to think things wouldn't go well. Zoey certainly makes an impression, and Mama Laverne likes meeting people."

"I agree, and they hit it off well."

"Did Zoey get all the information she needed to know?"

"Evidently not since more meetings have been arranged. I believe Mama Laverne has taken a liking to her, to the point where she'll take it upon herself to help Zoey regain her memory."

"It wouldn't surprise me if she succeeded in doing so. Like I've always said, Felicia Laverne Madaris is a miracle worker."

"Well, I prefer she performs her miracles on someone else. Especially when it comes to my love life or lack of one. And just so you know, Mama Laverne invited Zoey to the family reunion. I guess she wants to introduce her to everyone."

"Evidently," he said, annoyed at the thought of his single cousins checking her out.

"Well, I'll talk to you later. I'm going to bed."

"Bed?" Chance asked, heading down the steps toward the stable. "It's ten in the morning."

"I know what time it is. Since Luke was in town, the cousins played poker last night, and I'm just getting in. I need to rest up for later."

"What's happening later?"

"Have you forgotten I'm taking Zoey to dinner and dancing? I need my energy for the latter."

Chance had forgotten all about Corbin's date with Zoey. He hoped that his cousin's energy wasn't being replenished to do more than dance. "I had forgotten," he said. A part of him wished he hadn't been reminded.

"So, what are your plans for today?" Corbin asked.

"The usual for a Saturday. I'm on my way to ride the range. Then I plan to go fishing and return here to enjoy a beer and chill."

"Okay, I'll talk with you later."

"Will do."

A short while later, while riding the range on Ambush, Chance tried to put out of his mind that Zoey would join Corbin for dinner and dancing. Like planned, after riding the range, he'd gone fishing and then cooked what he'd caught for dinner. It was late afternoon when he decided to relax on his porch with a beer.

Sitting there, he couldn't help but think about his fantasy dream, which had drifted across his mind several times today. He couldn't recall the last time he'd had one, but since meeting Zoey, they'd come pretty damn regularly, almost nightly, and it was always her. In bed, she was just like he imagined she would be. Filled with passion and fire.

He gazed at his property while taking the last sip of beer from the can. Instead of seeing his land, he imagined Zoey dancing to a slow song on the dance floor in Corbin's arms. The thought made him crush the empty beer can in his hands.

What in the hell was wrong with him? Jealousy was beneath him. When had his attraction to Zoey become an obsession? That had never been the case with him and any woman before. He wasn't looking to get involved with anyone and preferred being the loner that he was. Yet, something about Zoey had gotten to him.

It was dark before he finally got up and went inside the house. Instead of moving toward his television, he began pacing. Every ounce of good sense told him to let it go.

He had deliberately introduced Corbin to Zoey for a reason. Namely to get her out of sight and out of mind. Well, the latter definitely wasn't working. She might have been out of his sight for the last few days, but she was so embedded in his mind that he wasn't thinking straight.

He'd never been this taken with a woman. Not even with Ravena. He had loved her true enough and anticipated seeing her whenever he came home. But she had never been his only focus. Being an army ranger had also been high on the list.

Chance recalled most of their arguments had been about him making a career in the army. Ravena hadn't particularly liked him placing his life in danger for his country. More than once, he reminded her that he had decided on a career in the military before meeting her, and that wouldn't change.

Ultimately, she said if the military was his career choice, she would stick by his side, no matter what. So much for keeping her word. She hadn't wasted any time hauling ass when he returned home in a wheelchair.

Chance stopped pacing and headed up the stairs. Less than an hour later, after showering and getting dressed, he grabbed his Stetson off the hat rack and walked out the door. Pulling his keys from his pocket, he opened the door to his truck and slid inside.

As he backed out of his driveway, he figured he would call himself all kinds of fools in the morning, but at the moment, he didn't care. He had a good idea where Corbin would take Zoey for a night of dancing, and more than anything, he wanted to see her again.

Chapter Eighteen

A grin tugged at the corner of Zoey's mouth. She was enjoying herself and especially liked the company she was with. After a delicious meal at Clem's, a restaurant known for their delicious BBQ ribs, Corbin took her to Vance's Tavern, a place known for dancing.

Within minutes, they were joined by some of Corbin's cousins—Luke, Blade, Slade, and Reese—and their wives, MacKenzie, Samari, Skye, and Kenna. Getting to know everyone was fun. The group had already taught her a few of the popular Texas line dances and complimented her on being a quick learner.

She enjoyed listening to the couples tell how they'd met. They had joked about how much Kenna liked to dance, and told her that, before the night was over, she would have partnered with every male sitting at their table. They shared photos of their kids on their phones, and it was obvious they were proud parents.

Zoey immediately knew that Luke, a former championship rodeo rider, was Chance's oldest brother. Although Corbin and

Chance favored each other, Luke reminded her of a slightly older Chance. He had the same dimples and eye coloring, and except for the shape of their noses, their features were nearly identical. Luke said Chance had their mother's nose, whereas he had their father's. Reese, who was also Chance's brother, favored them as well. All the Madaris men were handsome.

Zoey accepted the women's invitation to lunch next week and looked forward to joining them.

"Well, damn. I don't believe it. Look who just walked in," Blade said. "I wonder what he's doing here on a Saturday night."

All eyes went to the entrance of Vance's Tavern, and Zoey was convinced her heart skipped a beat. It was Chance. She couldn't stop the emotions filling her chest upon seeing him. "Maybe he has a date," she heard Mac whisper to Luke.

"Baby, nothing has changed. Chance doesn't date," Luke whispered back.

Chance didn't date? What did Luke mean by that? And he'd said it as if he hadn't done so in a while. Could she have been wrong in assuming he was involved in a serious relationship with someone? If that was the case, why had he fought the attraction between them?

Chance scoped the place, saw them, and headed toward their table. He looked good in his Stetson, shiny belt buckle, and Western shirt. And then there were his jeans. She was trying really hard not to notice how good his firm, tight thighs were in motion as he walked toward them. As always, she thought he was the epitome of a sexy cowboy, all the way down to his boots. Was she mistaken, or was his gaze trained on her?

Her heart skipped a beat with every step he took, and she could feel a degree of heat curling inside of her. There was just something about his walk. It wasn't a stroll but a sensuous swag. Yes, he was definitely tall, hot, and handsome.

"Evening, folks," he greeted, stopping at their table and tipping his Stetson. He was standing right next to where she sat, and she could inhale the manly scent of his cologne.

"Well, aren't you a sight for sore eyes. What brought you off the ranch on a Saturday night?" Reese asked his brother.

"A better question is, what brought you off your ranch, period?" Slade then asked.

Zoey was confused by their questions. Did Chance rarely leave his home?

"Thought I'd come here and dance a bit tonight," Chance answered.

"Dance? You?" Blade asked, surprised.

Chance looked at Blade with an unreadable expression on his face. "Yes, dance. Me."

The entire table got quiet, and Zoey didn't miss the look of disbelief on most faces. However, she noted that neither Luke nor Corbin seemed stunned by what Chance had said. When she shifted her gaze back to Chance, she saw how his dark, mesmerizing eyes had zeroed in on her.

"Will you dance with me, Zoey?" he asked, extending his hand to her.

Zoey's breath caught in her throat. All she could do was nod. Standing, she took his outstretched hand. The moment she did, a sensuous shiver flowed down her spine. Her pulse quickened, and she hoped the loud music had drowned out the moan she was certain she'd just made.

"We'll be back," Chance said to those sitting at the table.

"I should hope so. Need I remind you that Zoey is *my* date, Chance?" Corbin asked, placing emphasis on the word *my*.

Zoey glanced at Corbin. Was he trying to shield amusement behind his frown?

Chance didn't respond to his cousin's question. Instead, he led her toward the dance floor. As if on cue, a slow song began playing. He pulled her into his arms, and when he did, she felt her senses aligned with everything about him. That made her intensely aware of him even more.

Gazing into his eyes, she studied his features: the dark, penetrating eyes staring at her beneath his Stetson, his chiseled jaw, nostrils that seemed to flare with every breath he took, and lips that could be her downfall if she were to let them.

"How have you been, Zoey?"

Her gaze moved from his lips back to his eyes. "Other than being annoyed there's still strong sexual chemistry between us, I've been doing fine."

If her honesty surprised him, he didn't show it. "Why are you annoyed?"

"Because it's a first for me."

He lifted a brow. "You've never been attracted to a man before?"

"Not of this intensity and not when the man seemed to be on the same giving and receiving end as I am." Even now, her body was heating something fierce under his concentrated stare. From the moment he'd entered the establishment and captured her gaze, he had focused on her like she was the only woman in the room.

"I must admit such a thing hasn't happened to me before either. However, unlike you, I'm not annoyed by it. I will accept it as just one of those wonders of the universe. By the way, how did your meeting with Mama Laverne go?" he asked.

He had smoothly changed the subject, which was okay with her. "I thought it went well. I wanted to call to thank you for setting it up and to tell you how things had gone."

"Why didn't you call?"

Was she imagining things, or did he sound salty that she hadn't contacted him? "You never gave me your number, Chance."

He held her gaze and didn't say anything. Then he said, "You will have it before tonight ends."

She frowned at him. "Why now? Have you broken up with your girlfriend?"

"My girlfriend? Was I supposed to have a girlfriend?"

"I assumed you did," was her comeback.

"Well, I don't."

She'd overheard the whisper about him not dating but wanted to hear it from him. "You might not be in an exclusive relationship, but you do date, don't you?"

He focused on her for a long moment and then said, "No, Zoey. I don't date."

"Why not?" she asked as if she had every right to know. In a way, she did. The same intense sexual attraction they were experiencing now had emitted between them from the first. They had both put a lid on it—or at least, they had tried—for various reasons. She'd known her reason for doing so. Now she wanted to know his.

"My life is complicated, Zoey."

She tilted her head back to study his gaze, then said, "Your life can't be any more complicated than mine, Chance."

Chance stared at Zoey. She was so damn right it wasn't funny. So why did he choose that moment to grin? From the frown on her face, she undoubtedly was wondering the same thing.

"You find what I said amusing, Chance?"

"No. I found what you said so brutally correct that I could kick myself in the ass for what I said. What I found amusing was the fact you are one of the few women gutsy enough to call me out on my foolishness."

"I don't consider what you said as foolish since I know nothing about your complicated life. However, I did find your statement insensitive."

"I apologize, Zoey. That wasn't my intent. What I said was both insensitive and thoughtless."

She didn't say anything for a minute, but he could see it in her eyes. Those alluring brown eyes that were staring back at him. The same ones that had been inflamed with passion while he'd made love to her in his fantasy dream last night. Only now, what he saw was a curiosity she couldn't hide. For that reason, he wasn't surprised by her next question.

"You already know about my complicated life, Chance. So, what's yours?"

At first thought, it was on the tip of his tongue to say his complicated life wasn't any of her business. But then, hadn't he just admitted to being thoughtless where she was concerned? "Some might not see it as a complicated life, per se. My family sees it as issues."

She shrugged her attractive shoulders—shoulders that had been naked in his fantasy dream. Tonight, she was wearing jeans with one of those off-the-shoulder tops. It was blue. Why did that particular shade of blue do something to those brown eyes? It made them look more sensual than usual.

She looked hot. Desirably so. When he'd led her to the dance floor, he'd seen how men stared at them. Mainly her. She fit in his arms. She felt good in them. He wasn't surprised. Sexual chemistry had been there between them from the first. Tonight, it was obvious that nothing had changed. Although he'd done his best to suppress his desire for her when he'd reached the table where she'd sat, he'd failed miserably. There was no way his perceptive relatives hadn't picked up on all that heat emitting between them.

"A complicated life or issues that need dealing with all mean the same. So, what are yours?" she asked again.

Again, he thought about telling her what she was asking was none of her business. But for some reason, he couldn't do that. He realized for the first time in years he felt comfortable enough with a woman to be forthcoming and not a total ass when it came to his business.

"It would take me longer than this dance to define them," he heard himself saying.

She nodded. "Any reason you can't invite me to dinner tomorrow to discuss them?"

He nearly missed his step. Invite her to dinner? Hell, he could think of several reasons. He didn't even invite members of his family to dinner. "Yes, there's a reason I can't invite you to dinner."

That curious look in her eyes was back. "What's the reason?"

"I don't do that."

"You don't to what?" she asked.

"Invite women to my place for dinner."

"Why? Can't you cook?"

He frowned. "I can cook very well. I don't like people in my space. I'm a loner."

She studied him for a moment before asking. "Why are you a loner, Chance?"

He sighed profoundly, thinking he had it bad when following the movement of her tongue while she talked was a total turn-on. Then there was her scent. A luscious aroma that was Zoey. His focus was on her. All of her. She felt good in his arms, and the slow dance made him ache each time her thighs brushed against his.

Chance knew at that moment he'd made a mistake coming here tonight, dancing with her, letting her get all inside his head. He much preferred her in his bed. Even if it had been nothing more than a fantasy dream. After drawing in a deep breath, instead of answering her question, he said, "I think I should leave."

"Why did you even come?"

If he told her the truth, she would really think he was an ass. But then maybe that was good. Letting her know the real him, issues and all. "I'm into one-night stands."

She tilted her head. "And?"

"And the one-and-done kind. I make it my business to never sleep with the same woman twice. I came here tonight thinking I'd hook up with someone."

She nodded, staring at him. Was that disappointment that flashed in her eyes? "Some woman you've never slept with before?"

"Yes."

"Oh, I see."

"No, I don't think that you do, Zoey. The woman I wanted to hook up with tonight was you."

He saw the heat in her eyes, and then he watched the heat turn into a glare. "You honestly thought I'd be your one-night stand? Your one and done?" she asked. "Why would you assume such a thing?"

"Because we're intensely attracted to each other."

"No matter how attracted I am to you, Chance, I don't sleep with anyone to relieve sexual urges. For me, it has to mean more than a tumble between the sheets. You would have known that if you had gotten to know me instead of passing me off to Corbin."

He shouldn't be surprised she had figured that out. The music ended, and she walked off without waiting for him to escort her back to the table.

Damn. He'd messed that up big-time and knew he owed her an apology. The second one that night. He followed her back to the table, and when his relatives began shifting in their chairs to make room for him to sit down, he said, "Don't bother."

He turned to Zoey. "May I speak with you privately for a minute?" It would have served him right if she'd refused in front of everyone.

She pushed her chair back and stood, and Chance released the breath he'd been holding. He was tempted to take her hand but figured it was best not to press his luck. Instead, they walked outside to an area away from prying eyes and nosy ears.

"What do you want to talk to me about, Chance?" The glare was back in her eyes.

"I want to apologize."

"Again? Why? Obviously, you were being you. A person I'm beginning not to like."

Her words were like a kick in the gut. Over the years, he'd prided himself on not caring what anyone thought about him or his attitude. However, now it mattered. "We need to talk, Zoey."

"No, we don't."

"Yes, we do, and here is not the place. Will you join me for dinner tomorrow at my ranch?"

She crossed her arms over her chest. "Did you not tell me earlier that you don't invite women to your place for dinner?"

"Yes, but I want to share a few things about myself. Then you'll understand why I am the way I am."

She didn't say anything for a long moment, then uncrossed her arms and said, "Okay, Chance. I will join you for dinner tomorrow. But like I said before, I'm not into meaningless sex."

He nodded. "I got that. Now, may I give you my phone number?" he asked.

She pulled her cell phone out of the back pocket of her jeans. He did the same, and he called her. It then occurred to him this wasn't the first time he'd called her from his cell phone. However, this was the first time he'd invited her to use it to call him. Any other woman would have done so regardless. That once again proved how different she was from other women. He appreciated she didn't make a pest of herself.

A short while later, while walking Zoey back to her table, he noticed Ravena sitting at the bar, staring at him. When he and Zoey reached the table, he was about to bid everyone good night, but impulsively, he reached for her hand before she could take a seat. "Another dance? Okay?"

"It's a Texas line dance, Chance. It's been a long time. You think you're up to it?" Blade asked jokingly.

"I'm a Texan. I'm also a Madaris. Watch me." He led Zoey to the dance floor, and the line dancing began. A full hour of it.

His family joined in with the line dancing, and he figured they were surprised he knew the steps. There was no need to mention dancing was a great form of leg exercise. Therefore, for years he'd subscribed to one of those line dance channels.

When the line dance marathon was over, it was followed by several slow dances. He danced every one with Zoey. If his cousins found it odd that although Zoey was Corbin's date, Chance was dominating her time, they didn't show it.

When the DJ took a break, and everyone returned to the table, he knew it was time to leave. It had not been his intent to stay. Nor had he assumed he would have such fun. He came close to offering to drive Zoey home but knew that wouldn't be a good idea. Not when every slow dance with her had stoked his desire for her even more. Besides, he would see her tomorrow and was looking forward to doing so.

"Good night, everyone." He smiled over at Zoey. "And I'll see you tomorrow for dinner."

"Dinner?" several voices asked in shock, nearly sounding like an echo. Then Reese, who still seemed stunned, said. "I can't believe you're inviting someone to your ranch for dinner."

Instead of commenting on his brother's statement, Chance turned and walked away. Although he was tempted to look back at Zoey, he didn't.

"Did you see how Chance held that woman while they slow danced, Ken?"

Ken Cox eased off Ravena while rolling his eyes. "Why do I get the feeling there's another man in this bed. Namely, Chance Madaris. When will you get it through your head that he doesn't want you?"

"Just answer the question," she said, glaring at him.

He let out a frustrated breath. "Not only did I see how he was holding her while they danced, Ravena. I also noticed how taken he was with her when they weren't dancing. He's smitten as hell and probably doesn't even know it. Happy now?"

"No, I am not happy. I'm angry as hell," she said, exiting the bed to begin pacing the room. "I want to know who she is and where she came from."

Ken rested his hands behind his head and watched Ravena angrily pace the room naked. "Someone that gorgeous would be known if she was from around here, so she must be new to the area," he said. Shifting in bed, he then added, "I did find something odd, though."

She stopped pacing. "What?"

"I arrived a good hour before you. She came with Corbin Madaris and left with him, but Chance, not Corbin, was the one who claimed all of her time tonight. The one thing I do know about those Madaris cousins is that they don't share women. So, I wondered which of the cousins she's really interested in."

"I need your help to find out everything I can about her."

"You can count me out on that, sweetheart. The Madarises obviously like her, and I don't intend to get on that family's bad side. They're our best customers since the men in that family love buying jewelry for their wives. Especially the expensive pieces."

Ravena knew that to be true. She hadn't given Chance back her engagement ring. Instead she had sold it back to Cox Jewelers the day before leaving Houston. That's when she met Ken. She'd discovered that day just how valuable her engagement ring had been.

"There was something I did find interesting other than the woman's beauty," he interrupted her thoughts to say.

"What was that?"

"That necklace she was wearing. I got a good look at it during one of the line dances. It's one of ours from many years ago, a good sixty or so. I recall seeing a sketch of it in one of our old binders a while back. Since vintage jewelry pieces are making a comeback, I thought it would be a good one to re-make and sell."

"And?"

"And Dad said since it had been custom-made for someone, with the understanding that it would be the only one of its kind, it couldn't be duplicated. It's an heirloom handed down for at least four generations. Pure gold, and that diamond is of the highest quality. I can imagine how much it's worth now."

Ravena came back to bed. "That means if she's not from here, some past family member was. Since your great-grandfather ran the business when that necklace was made, he probably designed the necklace himself, right?"

"Yes, why?"

"The woman is my competition, and I want to know everything about her."

"Chance Madaris proved tonight he is definitely over you, Ravena. You need to leave well enough alone and move on."

"I can't, and I won't."

"Well, count me out of any of your shenanigans. You're only headed for trouble if you mess with those Madarises. Why are you so obsessed with trying to get him back? You had your chance and blew it. Chance doesn't like you."

Ravena refused to answer She didn't say anything for a moment and then said, "At least your great-grandfather likes me."

She watched Ken roll his eyes and knew he assumed she was trying to change the subject. "Gramps likes anyone who sneaks anything sweet into his room at that senior living facility," he said, glancing over her naked body. "I'm tired of talking. Come back to bed and leave Chance Madaris out of it this time."

Ravena eased back in bed between the sheets, feeling much better now that she'd devised a plan to visit his great-grandfather.

Chapter Nineteen

Felicia Laverne stared at Bessie. "What are you saying?" Her daughter-in-law had come into her bedroom to see if she intended to go to church today and, if so, see if she needed help getting dressed.

"I'm saying that Carrie called this morning with great news. It seems that Chance has finally decided to live again, and we might owe it all to Zoey Pritchard."

Felicia Laverne eased down in the chair near her bed. "What do you mean?"

Bessie's smile widened. "Luke and Mac went out with Slade, Blade, Reese, and their wives last night. They met up with Corbin and Zoey Pritchard at Vance's Tavern. Well, Chance showed up, and according to Carrie, her youngest grandson not only hung out with everybody dancing way after midnight, but he also shocked everyone when he invited Zoey to dinner at his ranch today. It seems he's sweet on her. Can you believe that?"

No, she couldn't. "That is hard to believe."

"Well, honestly, I was hoping that something would develop between Zoey and Corbin, especially after meeting her and seeing how nice she was, and noting that you liked her, too. But Chance did meet her first, so I can see him being smitten. She's such a pretty girl. And another thing: Ravena was at Vance's Tavern last night as well."

"She was?"

"Yes, and she saw Chance and Zoey dancing together. Luke told Carrie that he kept an eye on Ravena. Although the look on her face was furious and, at times, even enraged, she didn't make a scene or anything. Probably because there were so many Madarises there who she knows don't like her. The nerve of her getting jealous after how she treated Chance…"

Felicia Laverne didn't say anything for a long moment. Her mind was consuming everything her daughter-in-law had said. She agreed that Ravena had no right to get jealous seeing Chancellor with someone else. Obviously, she believed that foolishness that Chancellor had been pining for her all those years since he hadn't been seriously involved with anyone. Seeing him with Zoey had undoubtedly painted a different picture.

She couldn't help but wonder if perhaps that had been an intentional move on Chancellor's part. She knew that great-grandson better than anyone, and she wasn't buying Bessie's take on things that Chance had decided to "live again."

When Bessie left the room, Felicia Laverne picked up her cell phone to make a call. It didn't matter to her that it wasn't yet seven in the morning.

"Mama Laverne?" a groggy voice said. "Is everything okay?"

"I'm not sure, Chancellor. I need to talk to you."

"You need to talk to me? Now? It's not even seven in the morning."

"I know what time it is. And yes, I need to talk to you. In person. This morning."

"This morning? Aren't you going to church?"

She had planned on going, but meeting with him was more important. "Not today. I will expect you at ten. Goodbye."

★ ★ ★

"Hello?" Zoey asked drowsily, not bothering to open her eyes after grabbing her cell phone off the nightstand. Who would be calling her at this hour?

"Zoey? Zoey Pritchard?" a feminine voice asked.

She forced open her eyes, not recognizing the caller's voice. "Yes, this is Zoey Pritchard. Who is this?" The clock on the nightstand indicated it wasn't even seven in the morning.

"Oh my God! I can't believe it! I truly can't believe it!" the feminine voice said.

Zoey asked again. "Who is this?"

"This is Sharon Newberry. I was your mother's best friend."

The woman's words had Zoey quickly sitting up in bed. "Doctor Newberry?"

"Yes, and I apologize for calling so early. I'm presently in New Zealand, and was told one of my former colleagues, Dr. Kemmic, was trying to contact me. We finally connected and he told me everything. I can't believe it. I'd tried reaching out to you for years. Your aunt Paulina refused to let me connect with you."

"What! Why?"

"I was your mother's best friend, and she knew it. All I wanted was to keep in touch with you. To make sure you were okay. That's something I knew Micky would have wanted me to do."

"Micky?"

"Yes. That was your mother's nickname in college."

Suddenly, a fuzzy scene flashed before Zoey. A man, who she knew was her father, answered a telephone and then called out saying, *"The phone is for you, Micky."*

"Zoey are you still there?"

A lump formed in Zoey's throat. "Did my dad call my mom Micky, too?"

"Yes. Micky met Holt while we were in med school, so he

also called her by her nickname. Dr. Kemmic told me your aunt had passed. I want to extend my condolences. He also mentioned that you still had memory loss. I ran into your aunt a few years ago, and she said the doctor told her there was less than a twenty-five percent chance your memory would ever return."

"That's what my aunt told me as well. However, when I began having dreams with images of me and my parents, I sought the help of a doctor without my aunt's knowledge. According to Dr. Wheeler, what I was led to believe for all those years was not true. There's a fifty-fifty chance of my memory returning, Doctor Newberry."

"Please call me Sharon. *Doctor Newberry* sounds so formal. Especially for a woman who was your godmother."

"My godmother?"

"Yes. I'm the one who named you. I wanted to keep in touch with you, but your aunt said seeing me would force you to remember the past, and the doctor said that would not be in your best interest."

Zoey recalled she'd been told something similar. Her aunt had led her to believe that if she tried piecing together her memory on her own, instead of letting it return naturally, there was a strong chance it would never return. For that reason, she'd never researched anything about her parents.

She felt a deep sadness at her aunt's lies. She would have loved having Sharon be part of her life while growing up. "Thanks for sharing that with me, Sharon. There is something I want to ask you."

"Ask me anything."

"Did you know my parents owned a ranch in Texas?"

"Yes, the Satterfield Ranch. It was such a beautiful spread—big and spacious. I spent a lot of time there with your mom during the summer breaks from college. Your grandparents, the Martins, were the best. They were college professors and mostly lived on the ranch during the summertime."

That's the same thing Ms. Felicia Laverne had told her. "I'm in Texas now."

"At the ranch? That's wonderful! Micky and Holt enjoyed going there to relax and unwind."

"No, I'm not at the ranch. My aunt sold it."

"What?! Micky wanted to keep the ranch to give you one day because you always liked visiting there. You learned to ride a horse before you were two."

"Unfortunately, I don't have any memory of that." She told Sharon about finding the deed to the ranch—a ranch her aunt claimed her parents didn't have. She also told her that she had met the person who now owned the ranch, and after looking around, parts of her memory had returned.

"I don't know why your aunt would say she knew nothing about the ranch when she did. If telling you might have been a key component in your memory returning, that should have been a good enough reason to do so."

"I wish I could remember my grandparents and parents," Zoey said, despondently.

"I have some things that belonged to your mother, grand-mother, and great-grandmother."

That cheered her up somewhat. "You do? What?"

"Their diaries and photo albums. I had a key to your par-ents' home to check on things whenever they stayed at the ranch for extended periods. When I heard your aunt was sell-ing the house, I gathered everything I figured Micky would want you to have. I've kept them for you all this time, hop-ing you would reach out to me one day, and when you did, I would have them for you."

Knowing Sharon Newberry had done that touched Zoey deeply. "Thank you."

"No need to thank me. Micky was my best friend. I under-stand you followed in your parents' footsteps and are an ortho-pedic surgeon."

"Yes, I am."

"That's wonderful. Holt and Micky would be proud of you. They loved you a lot, Zoey." There was a pause, and then Sharon said, "I'm not sure if your aunt ever told you this, but at the time of your parents' accident, your family was driving home from the hospital—after the birth of your baby brother."

Zoey gasped. "Baby brother? I didn't know that." Tears Zoey couldn't hold back flowed down her cheeks. She had lost a brother in that accident. A brother she'd never been told about.

"Do you know why Aunt Paulina disliked my mother so much?"

"Holt told Micky there was another woman that Paulina wanted him to marry. The daughter of someone she knew. She'd even told him she would not accept any other woman as his wife."

"That's crazy."

"I agree."

"When will you be returning to the States?" Zoey asked, wiping tears from her eyes.

"Not for another month. However, my niece is house-sitting for us. I will tell her where the items are and have her ship them to you. How much longer will you be in Texas?"

"I plan to be here the entire summer."

"I will text you my niece's phone number. Her name is Kourtney. Call her to let her know where you want the items sent. I plan to fly to Texas to see you as soon as I return to the States. Dr. Kemmic says you look just like Micky. That means you are an attractive young woman, and I can't wait to see you again."

"Thanks, Sharon, and I'm looking forward to seeing you, too." Before ending the call, she thought of a question she needed to ask. "My baby brother...what was his name?"

"Holton Pritchard Jr."

"Thanks."

After Zoey ended the call, she eased between the covers and clutched her necklace while crying. Not only had she lost her parents that fateful day, but she'd also lost a baby brother, and she couldn't remember any of them.

After parking his truck, Chance strolled up the walkway and knocked on the door. His granduncle Nolan answered with a grin. "I'd heard you'd been summoned. What have you gotten yourself into, son?"

"Heck, if I know, Uncle Nolan," he said after giving his uncle a huge bear hug. "I got a call before seven from Mama Laverne, who ordered me to be here by ten. Is Aunt Bessie at church?"

"Yes. You know she still likes getting there by nine for Sunday school. I volunteered to stay with Mama since Reverend Hill's sermons put me to sleep anyway. She's sitting on the patio."

He reached the patio and saw his great-grandmother sitting there with her glasses perched on her nose while knitting something yellow. Mama Laverne looked pretty, but then she always did. She was wearing a light pink dress with her signature pearls. Her beloved Milton had given her the pearls on one of their wedding anniversaries.

"Good morning, Mama Laverne."

"Chancellor."

"You want to talk to me?"

"Yes. Please have a seat," she said, putting her knitting aside. "I understand you enjoyed yourself last night."

"I did," he said, not surprised that she heard about it.

"Glad to hear it. I'm sure you heard that Zoey Pritchard and I had a nice meeting on Friday. She's a nice young woman. You didn't tell me about her memory loss."

He shrugged. "I figured that was something she should tell you yourself."

"I see. Her story of being in that car accident that killed her parents and not remembering them touched my heart."

"Yes, that was sad."

"I will do all I can to help her by providing as much information about her family as possible. Hopefully, doing so will trigger her memory. Both my beloved Milton and Waylon would want me to do that."

"Waylon?" he asked, stretching his legs out and leaning back in his chair.

"Yes, Waylon Satterfield, Zoey's great-grandfather. He was Milton's best friend."

"He was Arabella Martin's father?"

"Yes. Now that I've met Zoey, I feel protective of her since she has no one. More than anything, she needs her full concentration to get her memory back. That's one of the reasons I've arranged for her to spend the summer in Trevor's cabin."

Chance sat up straight in his chair. "Trevor's cabin?"

"Yes. I talked to Trevor yesterday, and since he and his family are spending the summer on Warren Mountains, he's given permission for Zoey to stay there. I plan to tell her about it later today."

"Why does she need to stay at that cabin? What's wrong with the hotel?"

His great-grandmother leaned forward. "I'll be returning to Whispering Pines this week. Since Zoey and I will continue our meetings, staying at the cabin will be more convenient. Definitely a closer drive than coming from town."

He nodded. "Is that why you summoned me here? To tell me that you've made arrangements for Zoey to stay in a cabin that borders my property?" he asked, unsure how he felt about that, although her staying there made sense.

"That property was an original part of the Satterfield land before the Johnstones sold it to Trevor. While talking with Zoey, I realized that the lake in her dreams is not the lake on your property, as she assumed. It's the lake on Trevor's property. I am hoping that being in that cabin will increase the chances of her memory returning. She's been told there's a fifty percent chance her memory might never return, but I'm of the mind that it will."

He recalled she'd said something similar when he returned home in a wheelchair… *"Those doctors claim you will never walk again, but I'm of the mind that you will."* And with her help, he had.

His great-grandmother stared at him intently through her glasses. "The reason I wanted to meet with you today is to tell you to stop whatever foolishness you've cooked up involving Zoey just to score a point with Ravena."

He frowned. "What are you talking about?"

"I'm talking about your need to prove to Ravena that you haven't been pining for her like she assumes and using Zoey for that purpose."

"You think I would do that?"

"Didn't you do that very thing last night, Chancellor?"

Chance eased out the chair and shoved his hands into the pockets of his jeans. "Okay, I'll admit the thought entered my mind and would even say that's why I'd decided to stay at Vance's Tavern longer than planned. However, when I got on that dance floor with Zoey, thoughts of Ravena and proving anything to her never crossed my mind again."

"For you to even think you needed to prove anything to that woman means you still have issues where she is concerned," Mama Laverne said before taking another sip of her tea.

"Zoey came to Texas to try remembering her past," she said. "Namely to get her life together. I don't intend for you to mess hers up just because your life is a mess. I know what you think of women since Ravena, Chancellor. Not one is good enough beyond a night spent in bed. Just the thought of you flaunting Zoey in front of Ravena last night to prove a point is unacceptable and unfair to her."

Chance knew his great-grandmother was on a roll, and the best thing to do was to let her keep talking and not interrupt until she was finished.

"Unlike other members of the family," she continued, "I don't think your issues have anything to do with you carrying a torch for Ravena. Your problems have everything to do with Madaris pride, which I know all about.

"What Ravena did not only broke your heart but damaged your pride. Your heart might have healed, but not your pride. That's what your issues are about—and a man with issues is the last thing Zoey needs in her life."

Feeling it was okay to speak now, he said. "Again, Mama Laverne, I forgot all about Ravena when I danced with Zoey. I honestly enjoyed being out last night with her and the family." There was no need to add he'd gotten a taste of what he'd been missing the past five years.

He met his grandmother's gaze. She stared at him like she could decipher everything going through his mind. He eased back down in his chair. "Are we having this conversation because you've selected someone for Zoey? Corbin? Adam? One of the Bannisters? Emerson?" Why was he feeling anger at the thought that she had? He had learned a long time ago not to let his emotions get the best of him when it involved a woman.

Mama Laverne leaned closer to him to ensure he heard her following words. "To be honest, neither you, nor any of those that you named, nor any great-grandson you didn't name, would I consider as a match for her. All of you have whorish ways, and after all she's been through, that's not the type of man she needs in her life. Zoey needs someone who will want to give her the type of love she's lacked for the past twenty years."

Mama Laverne shook her head sadly as she settled back in her chair. "Poor child didn't even get the love she deserved from that aunt who raised her. The woman might have treated her decently, but considering what Zoey had gone through, she needed more than that. She needed unconditional love."

Chance watched his great-grandmother pause and figured it was highly likely that her Christian side was warring with the side that wanted to say how she truly felt about Zoey's aunt Paulina.

"Whether Zoey gets her memory back or not," Mama Laverne continued, "at least she will leave Texas knowing more about her family than when she arrived. I will see to it. She's a good person. She can't help but be one with Deedra as a great-grandmother and Arabella as a grandmother. Both were kindhearted and decent women. And then she had Waylon as a great-grandfather. He was a good man."

Mama Laverne then said in a softer tone, "From just that one meeting with Zoey, I felt a kindred connection to her, Chancellor. One just as strong as I do to my biological granddaughters and great-granddaughters. It might be because of my and Milton's love and respect for Waylon."

"I like Zoey, too, Mama Laverne," Chance said. "Just in the short time I've gotten to know her, I picked up on those same qualities in her that you did." There was no need to add how intensely attracted they were to each other. Chance also knew there was no way he would tell Mama Laverne what he'd told Luke. Namely, any feelings he had for Zoey were purely sexual.

He would, however, tell her this much to put her mind at ease, hopefully. "The only relationship I want with Zoey, and the only kind we both agreed to share, is one of friendship," he said. "I had invited her to dinner before I saw Ravena last night. I did so to explain why I've been a loner for so long. She asked me about it, and I wanted to be up-front with her. I would never deliberately hurt her."

Mama Laverne stared at him for a long moment before nodding. "I'm taking you at your word, Chancellor. As I said, a romantic involvement is not what Zoey needs right now, not with you or anyone with the last name of Madaris. Or Bannister. However, there is nothing wrong with being her friend, and I'm glad the two of you agreed to only be friends. Everyone could use a friend. Even you." After taking another sip of her tea, she added, "Besides, I believe she already has a boyfriend back in Baltimore."

Did she? He'd had no reason to ask her anything about a boyfriend and assumed she didn't because of the intense sexual chemistry between them. And then she had agreed to go out with Corbin. However, last night, she had asked him about a girlfriend, and he'd made sure she knew he didn't have one. He'd been clear about just the type of affairs he preferred. "Why would you think she was involved with some guy? Did she mention that she was?"

"No, but I can't imagine a young woman as beautiful as Zoey unattached."

After his talk with Mama Laverne, Chance remained at his granduncle Nolan's house when his grandfather Lucas unexpectedly dropped by. After hearing that his brother Nolan was not attending church, Grampa Lucas decided to do the same. It wasn't long before two other brothers, Milton and Lee, came knocking. It seemed they'd decided to play hooky from church as well.

Chance had stayed for breakfast, knowing the four hoped he would enlighten them about why their mother had summoned him that morning. However, he decided it would be best not to tell them anything since they tended to talk just as much as their wives.

When he was headed back to his ranch and had driven a few miles, his phone rang. It was Zoey. Last night, he'd given her a particular ringtone. "Good morning, Zoey."

"Hello, Chance. I'm calling to cancel dinner."

"Cancel dinner?"

"Yes."

He hadn't talked to her since last night and hoped that none of his cousins had put the same idea into her head that Mama Laverne had in hers. Specifically, that he'd used her last night to prove a point with Ravena. He doubted they would have, but still… "Would you mind telling me why?"

She didn't say anything, but he could hear her sniffling. Was she crying? "Zoey, what's wrong?"

"I don't want to talk about it now, Chance. I can't."

He pulled to the side of the road. "Tell me what's wrong. Why are you crying? Is it about last night and Ravena?"

"I don't know anything about a Ravena, and it has nothing to do with last night. It's about a call I got this morning from a woman who was my mother's best friend. And she told me that…"

He strained to hear, but she stopped talking and started crying again. "What did she tell you?"

"I—I can't talk about it now," she said between sobs. "I just can't. It makes my heart hurt. I just wanted you to know I won't be coming to dinner. I wouldn't be much company. Bye, Chance." She then hung up.

Chance sat there, knowing that whatever was wrong with her didn't concern him; it was her problem to deal with. But then another part of him knew that wasn't true. Not when the sound of her crying had torn deep into him. He rubbed a frustrated hand down his face. After Ravena, he'd established a rule not to make any woman a central component of his life again. Then why was he breaking that rule for Zoey? Why was he making her problems his? Was it because she'd unloaded her issues on him and, in doing so, had broken through a barrier he'd so firmly erected? Or was it because like he'd told Mama Laverne, he considered her a friend?

Hell, he wasn't sure of the reason. However, he did know he wanted to get to her and find out what was wrong. He recalled her telling Corbin the name of her hotel. The Houston Riverfront. He had no idea of her room number but would worry about that when he got there.

Chapter Twenty

Zoey heard her phone ringing and refused to answer it. She regretted calling Lucky before pulling herself together because now her best friend was as upset as she was. The phone stopped ringing, and when it started again, she knew that Lucky would be on the next plane to Houston if she didn't answer.

Swiping tears from her eyes, she picked up the phone. "I'm fine, Lucky."

"No, you're not. You sound terrible, and I'm going to start packing. I don't want you in Texas alone."

"Please don't start packing. I'll be fine. What Sharon revealed just came as a shock. Why wouldn't Aunt Paulina tell me about my baby brother? Did she hate my mom that much just because she wasn't the woman Aunt Paulina had wanted my dad to marry? That doesn't make sense."

"None of what your aunt did ever made sense, Zoe. Your heart is hurting, and I can feel it."

"I'll be fine. I just need time to pull myself together. Honest."

At that moment, she heard a knock on her hotel door. "I'll call you back. Someone is at the door," Zoey said, getting up off the sofa with her box of tissues in hand. "It's probably housekeeping."

"Okay. Call me back."

"I will. Promise."

Tightening her robe around her, she walked to the door to look out the peephole and almost dropped her tissue box. It was Chance. She had talked to him less than thirty minutes ago. Driving from his ranch into town would have taken him an hour. How did he get here so fast, and why had he come? She'd only canceled a dinner he probably didn't want to have with her anyway.

She opened the door, not surprised he stared at her since she surely looked a mess. No doubt it was apparent she'd been crying. "Chance, what are you doing—"

Before she could finish, he swooped her into his arms and slammed the door shut with the heel of his boot. "What do you think you're doing? Put me down."

He walked to the sofa in the sitting area and sat down with her in his lap. When she tried scrambling away, he tightened his hold on her and twisted her around to face him. She couldn't hold back the tears still falling from her eyes.

"What's wrong, Zoey? What did your mother's friend tell you that has your heart breaking?"

She swiped the tears away. He took a few tissues out of the box to wipe her eyes, and in a softer tone, he said, "Tell me, sweetheart."

Why on earth did he call her that? Although it was a term of endearment, she knew he hadn't meant it as such. She met his gaze, and the genuine concern and tenderness she saw in the dark pupils staring back at her made her catch her breath on a sob before lowering her head to his chest to cry openly.

She felt the warmth in the arms that wrapped around her and took comfort in the hands that began to stroke her back gently. Then there was the calm, soothing, masculine voice telling her everything would be alright. She wished she could believe him. More than anything, she wanted to believe him.

"Tell me what's the matter, Zoey. There's no way I can make things better if you don't tell me."

She lifted her face from his chest. "Not sure you can make things better, Chance."

"I plan to try."

She heard both sincerity and determination in his voice and appreciated both. Although she still didn't know his issues, he had no problem going full speed into hers. Drawing in a deep breath, she said, "Dr. Sharon Newberry was to my mom what Lucky is to me."

"Lucky?"

"Yes, whereas Dr. Newberry was Mom's best friend since college, Lucky Andres-Tankersley has been my best friend since middle school. While talking to Sharon, I discovered something else regarding the car accident that I didn't know."

"What?"

"She told me where my parents and I were going that day."

He nodded. "And where did she say you and your parents were going?"

"Home. Mom had just gotten out of the hospital."

"Had she been ill?"

"No," Zoey said, unable to keep her lips from trembling and new tears from falling. "My parents weren't the only ones killed in that car accident, Chance. I also lost my newborn baby brother."

She then lowered her head to his chest and began crying again.

Chance stood at the window in Zoey's hotel room and gazed at downtown Houston. Once she'd calmed down, he made her some Madaris tea, after which, he persuaded her to lie down for a while. He had checked on her a few moments ago, and she was still sleeping.

He didn't know Paulina Pritchard since he had never met the woman. But at that moment, he didn't think a lot of her for the pain she'd caused Zoey. He could understand her not telling Zoey about her baby brother as a child, but there was no reason not to tell her when she'd gotten older.

At that moment, Zoey's phone, which was on the table next to the sofa, began ringing. He decided to ignore it. It stopped, and when it started ringing again, the last thing he wanted was for the sound to wake up Zoey. Crossing the room, he picked it up and was about to switch it to message mode when he saw the caller was Lucky. The woman Zoey had referred to as her best friend. He decided to answer.

"Hello."

There was a pause, and then the caller asked. "Who is this?"

"Chance Madaris."

"Tall, hot, and handsome?"

He lifted a brow. "Excuse me?"

"Nothing. Where is Zoey?"

Not sure what, if anything, Zoey had told her, he said, "She's unavailable at the moment."

"Does that mean you got her to lie down? Lord, I hope so. The only thing that can calm her from a crying spell is sleep. I can't stand Ms. Paulina for all those secrets she kept."

Her words let Chance know that Lucky knew what was going on. From the sound of it, she knew much more than he did about the situation, which made sense if they'd been best friends since middle school.

"Let me give you fair warning, Chance. When Zoey wakes up, she will be calm. Too calm. She will try to convince you that she's okay when she really won't be. She will attempt to distance the two of you. Don't let her. That's when you must put your foot down and let her know she isn't alone."

Not sure what he should say to all of that, he didn't say any-thing. But it soon became obvious Lucky had no intentions of letting him remain quiet. "Chance? You still there?"

"Yes, I'm still here."

"And you got what I said?"

"Yes, I got it."

"Good. Now I won't have to pack and fly to Texas after all. I know she's in good hands, and she won't be alone."

Immediately, Chance felt something he hadn't felt in a long time—a sense of purpose. Zoey Pritchard had a way of grow-ing on you. Hadn't Mama Laverne said that very morning that she felt a kindred connection to Zoey? A part of him didn't want Zoey to grow on him. Nor did he want any connection. Yet he was feeling those things, regardless.

"Zoey is in good hands, and she won't be alone," he as-sured her.

"Thanks, Chance. Zoey is a special person. After all she's gone through in life, it didn't make her mean and bitter. She is a loving individual with a heart of gold. I will call back later to check on her. Goodbye."

It was two hours later before he heard movement in the bed-room. Then he heard the shower start. Thirty minutes passed before the bedroom door opened. Zoey appeared and blinked as if surprised he was still there. Her next words confirmed it: "I thought you had left."

He stood and shoved his hands into the pockets of his jeans. It was either that or he cross the room to pull her into his arms and kiss her. The mass of hair he liked seeing flying in the wind was now soft waves framing her face. A very gorgeous face.

Seeing her standing in her bedroom doorway made him remember all those fantasy dreams he'd had of her. One had been just like this, with them standing across a room, staring at each other while sexual chemistry simmered between them. In that particular dream, they'd given in to the most passionate of temptations, and they had met in the middle of the room and begun ripping each other's clothes off.

And speaking of clothes… He loved the way she looked. She wore a pretty sundress, and those cute sandals from last night were on her feet. A camera was around her neck.

He finally spoke against the hard lump in his throat. "Going someplace, Zoey?"

"I thought I'd go to the park and take pictures."

"You were supposed to have dinner with me," he said, trying to focus on her face and not her legs—a very shapely pair.

"Like I said earlier, I wouldn't be good company."

"How about letting me be the judge of that," was his response.

She didn't say anything, so he decided to press on. "Besides, if you want to take nice photos, my ranch will provide better landscape shots than a park."

"You think so?"

"I know so. The one thing Teakwood Ridge is known for is its beauty. I consider some parts of it to be nature's paradise. We can go riding after dinner, and you can see for yourself. The last time you went to the south. The east is a lot prettier."

"Your great-grandmother said there's another lake with a cabin east of your property."

He wouldn't tell her that Mama Laverne had gotten approval for her to stay there. It would be for his great-grandmother to tell her that. "Yes, there's a cabin on a lake. We can ride to see it if you'd like."

He saw happiness enter her eyes before spreading to her lips. "We can do that?"

"Of course. And I'll return you here later."

"Okay," she said eagerly. "Let me change into a pair of jeans and a top. I'll be back in a few minutes." She slowed before reaching the bedroom, turned around, and asked, "How did you get here so fast? When I drove from here to your property, it took me over an hour."

Deciding not to mention anything about the meeting he had that morning with his great-grandmother, he said, "I was already in town. I joined my granduncles and my grandfather, for breakfast," he said. That wasn't a lie.

"Oh."

She then turned to hurry off to her bedroom.

Chapter Twenty-One

Zoey glanced out the truck's window at the scenery they passed. It was obvious Chance was taking her a different way than the GPS had instructed her to go when she visited his ranch. Shifting her eyes to him, she said.

"I recall mentioning the name of my hotel to Corbin in front of you. But how did you know my room number?"

"I didn't. At least, I didn't until I got here. The woman at the check-in desk happens to be someone my brother Emerson dates on occasion."

"I see."

She decided to keep the conversation going, especially when their silence seemed to stir the attraction they were trying to downplay. "So, what's for dinner?"

"I thought I'd throw a couple of steaks on the grill. I left them marinating this morning. It won't take long to put the baked beans in the oven and prepare my slaw. Corn on the cob is also on the menu."

She licked her lips. "Sounds delicious and since I skipped breakfast, I'm starving."

He smiled at her. "Glad to hear that since I look forward to feeding you."

Today, she was thinking she liked him too much. Probably because of how kind and thoughtful he was being. He didn't have to come to the hotel to check on her, but he had. She was also noticing things about him that she would rather not notice. Such as those dimples that were usually kept hidden until he smiled. She had seen them for the first time that day they'd met on the side of the road. She hadn't seen them again until last night when they'd danced. Then there was Chance's scent. Whatever cologne he was wearing should be personalized and called *Chance*.

He was also a man full of compliments. More than once today he'd told her how nice she looked. She thought the same about him. From the moment she'd opened her bedroom door to find him still there, she couldn't stop her gaze from roaming over him from head to toe. Once they left her hotel room, she still couldn't keep her eyes off him. She hadn't been the only one. Numerous females had turned to stare. But then the same thing had happened last night while they'd been dancing.

She had to remember he was a man who preferred one-night stands. That meant he didn't want an emotional involvement with a woman—just a physical one. On top of that, he was a self-declared loner. Something they would talk about over dinner.

Why wait until then? Besides, there was one thing she needed to know. "Chance?"

"Yes?"

"Who is Ravena?"

Chance could only blame himself for having brought up Ravena's name in their conversation earlier that day. When he brought his truck to a four-way stop sign, he shifted his gaze to Zoey and saw her intently staring at him.

Their gazes held, and he felt it and was certain she did, too. It was more than a flutter in the tummy; it was more than an increase in heart rate. It was sexual chemistry so powerful he was convinced it had more nuclear energy than an atomic bomb. And that wasn't good.

Hadn't he told Zoey last night that he fully understood she wasn't into meaningless sex? And just that morning, he'd told Mama Laverne that friendship was the only relationship he wanted with Zoey. He'd known they were sexually attracted to each other, but when had it become so volatile?

"Ravena was the woman I was engaged to marry five years ago," he said.

He figured she was letting that sink in because she said nothing. Then she asked, "What happened?"

It wasn't until a car blasted its horn behind them that he realized they were still sitting at the stop sign. "She ended our engagement."

"Oh."

When she said nothing else, he glanced at her as he turned a corner. "You have nothing to ask?"

She met his gaze, and a smooth smile touched her lips and extended to her eyes. That made her features different from when she'd opened her hotel room door. Both her eyes and lips had been swollen from crying. She was still sad. There was no way she wasn't. But at least now she was smiling, putting her complicated life on hold to concentrate on his.

"Only if you wish for me to know, Chance."

He had planned to tell her everything over dinner but wasn't sure he was ready to do it now. Did it matter? Maybe telling her now would be for the best.

He refocused on the road again. "After high school, I chose a career in the military. After being an army ranger for eight years, I came home on leave and met Ravena." There was no reason to tell her he and Ravena had met at Vance's Tavern, the very place they were last night.

"We began dating exclusively, and eighteen months later, I asked her to marry me."

"And?" she asked when he paused, obviously a little too long for her liking.

"And I got injured and was sent home in a wheelchair after being told I would never walk again."

Her gasp sounded so deep he actually felt it. "You?" she asked as if she found such a thing unbelievable.

"Yes, me. When I told my fiancée the doctor's prognosis, she told me there was no way she could ever marry half a man."

Another gasp. "She…this Ravena…actually told you that?"

"Yes. That was her reason for breaking our engagement. So now you know why I prefer one-night-stands to long-term relationships."

He noticed she didn't respond right away. The silence was so thick, he glanced over at her to see why. She was angry. He could tell from the narrowed look in the eyes staring at him. From the tightness of her lips. The tilt of her chin.

"Could you please pull this truck over to the shoulder of the road for a minute?" Zoey asked. "I have something I want to say and need your complete attention."

He pulled to the side, turned off the ignition, and turned in his seat to look at her. She was staring at him in a way he'd never seen before. He could feel her anger even more now.

"Let me get this straight. Your girlfriend, your fiancée, the woman you loved, broke off your engagement because she thought you might never walk again."

"That's right."

"And you're a loner who's not into serious relationships because of her?" Before he could respond one way or the other, she continued, her voice raised. "Did it ever occur to you during those five years that you were better off without her? That she didn't deserve you? That she never knew the true meaning of love? You must have loved her a lot to allow her to do that to you."

He'd heard it from various family members before, of course. However, for some reason, it sounded harsher coming from her. "Of course I loved her a lot. I would not have asked her to be my wife if I hadn't." He rubbed a frustrated hand down his face. "Has a man ever broken your heart, Zoey?"

"No."

"Then you have no right to judge or tell me how to handle a destruction to mine. The pain of losing my ability to walk and the woman I loved was too much. I began wallowing in self-pity and pushed everyone away. Including my family."

He paused, remembering that time. "Mama Laverne gave me hell for feeling sorry for myself and convinced me the doctor's prognosis wasn't final. She actually made me believe that I could walk again."

"And you did."

"Yes, I did. It was hard. Some days were tormenting as hell. Even when I heard Ravena had moved away and married someone less than a year later, I refused to give up. Mama Laverne wouldn't let me. She ended up moving in with me. Can you imagine having both her and a physical therapist from hell to deal with? I was back in the saddle riding my horse in less than two years."

"You might have won the fight to walk again, Chance, but you lost the battle to get on with your life. You lost the ability to love again."

He frowned. "I did get on with my life. I bought the spread and made it into a working ranch. Teakwood Ridge became my life. And as far I'm concerned, love is something I can do without."

"And because of a woman named Ravena. She really did

a number on you, and one day, I hope you realize she wasn't worth it."

She paused for a minute and then asked, "Why would anything about Ravena have had me upset this morning?"

He would be frank with her. "Ravena, recently divorced from her husband, returned to town a couple of months ago. She was at Vance's Tavern last night. She thinks I'm carrying a torch for her since I haven't been involved with anyone since our breakup."

"I'd probably assume that same thing, Chance. Are you still in love with her after all she did?"

"No. Ravena means nothing to me. However, some members of my family assume I was all into you last night as a show to make Ravena jealous."

She stared at him. "Was it a show to make her jealous, Chance?"

"No. I was all into you because I'm attracted to you. I told you the main reason for coming there last night. I've been honest and up-front with you about everything, Zoey."

She nodded. "Thanks for sharing that part of your complicated life with me, Chance."

Chapter Twenty-Two

Chance had been right, Zoey thought. His land was beautiful. After exploring the south end previously, he took her riding on the north and west ends, and now they were headed toward the east as well. The property was vast, and she tried more than once to push it to the back of her mind that her ancestors, the Satterfields, had once owned all of it. This land should have been her legacy. Now Chance was making it his.

"You're okay?"

She looked over at him. "Yes. I'm okay." There was no way she would tell him what she'd been thinking.

They had brought their horses to a stop at the top of a valley as their gazes roamed the richness of the plains before them. He had been right about the landscape photo shots. She had taken plenty. She had captured the beauty of the plush greenery, grasslands, and valleys stretching for miles under a captivating Texas sky. Chance had been patient and hadn't rushed her, and she appreciated that.

A few times, she'd been tempted to ask him to pose for her, but after their exchange during the ride to his ranch, she didn't want to press her luck. She would even admit that she'd feared he might turn his truck around and take her back to the hotel. He hadn't. Other than her commenting on the scenery outside the truck window, little conversation had been exchanged between them. She figured he hadn't appreciated her speaking her mind; maybe she should not have. However, she would not apologize, because she'd meant everything she'd said.

His attitude had improved when they'd reached his ranch house. He'd become more talkative. He seemed to be in his element in his kitchen, and as he prepared their dinner, he moved around it like a pro chef. He'd even impressed her outside on the grill. She wanted her steak well done and it was cooked perfectly.

He had explained that Mama Laverne required each of her great-grands to enroll in her cooking school when they turned sixteen. They'd complained for a while, but she had taught them a lot. And he knew as they aged, all his brothers and cousins had appreciated learning how to cook.

One of the first things he'd done once they began riding was to show her his herds of cattle roaming the plains. Before leaving the ranch to go riding, she had met three of his ranch hands who lived in the bunkhouse and thought they were nice guys. Chance told her he got up before sunrise each weekday morning to begin his full day of work on his ranch, so he eagerly anticipated the weekends. He also managed his books.

"Dinner was delicious, Chance."

He gazed at her from beneath the tilt of his Stetson. "Glad you enjoyed it," he said, smiling. "By the way, you're an excellent rider. If I didn't know better, I'd say you've been riding all your life."

"I might have. According to Sharon, I learned to ride here on this ranch when I was two."

He nodded and tilted his Stetson back from his eyes. A gorgeous pair of eyes. "I'm glad you were able to connect with her, Zoey. It sounds like she has a wealth of information to share with you about your parents and your childhood."

Zoey smiled. "I believe she does, and I'm looking forward to meeting her."

She then shared what Sharon had told her about her mother, grandmother, and great-grandmother's diaries and the photo albums. "I can't wait to see them. I'm finally learning about my mother's family history with Ms. Felicia Laverne's help, along with the diaries and photo albums."

He nodded. "Come on. Let's start riding again. In another mile, we'll cross land that was originally part of the Satterfield spread. However, it was sold before I purchased mine."

"That's what Mama Laverne said. You don't think the owner will mind us trespassing, do you?"

"Trevor is a long-time friend and like a member of the family. I figured you might want to look inside the cabin, so I called him earlier, and he gave me the code to unlock the door."

She couldn't stop the huge grin that spread across her face. "That was kind of him. Thanks, Chance."

It didn't take them long to reach the east side, and just like he said, it was more beautiful than the others, mainly because of the fruit grove. There appeared to be acres and acres of fruit trees of all kinds. The scent of citrus filled the air.

"What kind of fruit trees are those?" she asked.

"Peach, orange, grapefruit, fig, and pomegranate. There's even a small vineyard filled with grapes. The property line dividing Whispering Pines and the Satterfield land runs through the middle of the grove."

She lifted a brow. "I wonder how that happened."

"Not sure, but I imagine Mama Laverne does. You might want to ask her."

"I'll be sure to do that."

"She might even tell you about the tomb."

"The tomb?"

"Yes, it is a beautiful tomb built in the fruit grove. Its placement in the middle of the grove, nearly at the beginning, gives the impression that the person inside is watching over the grove."

"Who's buried there?"

"My great-grandaunt Victoria. I understand the fruit grove was her favorite place on Whispering Pines, and she requested to be buried there instead of the family cemetery."

They continued riding. Finally, in the distance, she saw a cabin on a vast lake. Suddenly, there was a memory flash. "That's the lake, Chance," she said excitedly.

He gazed over at her. "You remembered something?"

"I just got a flashback from one of my dreams. My mom, dad, and I enjoying a picnic by that lake."

"Let's get closer and check it out. Hopefully, you'll remember more," he said.

They galloped their horses and slowed when they neared the cabin. They dismounted and tied the horses to a nearby tree.

"That's a rather huge barn," she said, motioning to the barn that was not far from the cabin.

"Trevor built it a few years ago. He made sure it was large enough to store, in addition to his horses, his kids' Jet Skis, a couple of canoes, and trail bikes."

"Horses are kept here?" she asked, glancing around.

"Yes, whenever he and his family are occupying the cabin. Otherwise, his horses are boarded at Whispering Pines. Are you ready to go inside?" he asked her.

She thought the cabin on the massive lake was beautiful, with picturesque flowering trees providing a peaceful setting. On the opposite side of the lake, more trees and high plains appeared as if they were touching the sky.

"Yes, I'm ready."

Taking her hand, they walked up the steps.

★ ★ ★

Chance stood aside as Zoey entered the cabin. He watched her closely, leaning against the door as she moved around the living room, taking in the furnishings, decor, and layout. He was taking in her. Every inch. Every curve. She looked so damn good in those jeans. With every move she made, he could feel it in his lower extremities. He was definitely in need of a sexual fix and wished like hell his horniness wasn't kicking in something fierce.

"Anything look familiar?" he asked after a while, trying to fight his intense attraction to her.

When she met his gaze, more heat flared through his body. That happened whenever her gaze would roam over him as if she was fully aware of him. But then, he did the same with her whenever she was within his focus.

"No, nothing. I guess I should not have expected anything to remain the same. I like the decor, though. Do you mind if I take a look around?"

"Help yourself. It's spacious with two bedrooms, two baths, this living room, and an eat-in kitchen. I understand this is the original layout, except for that uncovered patio that faces the lake."

"Nice pool table," she said, noting the huge pool table in the spacious living room.

"It is nice. I've played pool with Trevor on that table a few times."

"I always wanted to learn to play pool, but Aunt Paulina wouldn't allow such a thing."

"I'd be glad to teach you," he said, quickly regretting the offer. He could just imagine the torture he would endure standing behind her, close enough to show her the proper way to hold a cue stick or make a shot. Then there would be her scent. It was a scent that even now was reaching him across the room and sending his hormones into overdrive.

"I'll look around," she said, interrupting his thoughts.

"Take your time."

He went to the window. The lake was just as large as the one on his property and was a beautiful blue. He recalled swimming in it when Trevor threw a party after buying the place. He had been in his last year of high school then.

"I'm ready to walk around the lake now, Chance."

He slowly turned around. Their gazes met, held. The dark look in her eyes made his entire body ache. He wondered if she knew what it did to him whenever she stared at him like that. And when she moistened her lips, he felt his gut tighten.

"You're ready?" he asked as if she hadn't just said that very thing.

"Yes," she said softly.

Of their own accord, his feet began to move toward her. When he stopped in front of her, all the reasons why he shouldn't kiss her dissolved in his mind. At that moment, knowing her taste was elemental to him. With all his willpower gone, he lowered his head to her.

For a heartbeat, their lips were mere inches apart. He paused, giving her time to step back, but she didn't, so he leaned in and captured her mouth with his. He heard her moan the moment their mouths touched. Or was it him moaning? It didn't matter when their tongues began tangling and dueling in one sensuous dance of desire. Just knowing he was claiming her mouth the way he had in his dreams made him hungrily deepen the kiss.

There had been an intense attraction between them from the first, and they were finally acting on it. He was convinced he'd never tasted a more sensual and passionate woman. It was there in the way she was kissing him back. The way her tongue was mating with his and the way her arms were wrapped around his neck.

It seemed like forever before they ended the kiss. Neither said anything as they continued to stare at each other. When she licked her lips as if recapturing the last of his taste, he struggled to regain his composure. Unable to stop himself, he leaned down and kissed her again. This one was just as hot and passionate as the last.

He lifted his head from the kiss and rested his forehead against hers while breathing deeply. Finally, he pulled back to stare into her eyes. Her passion was just as heated as his own. Unable to resist, he leaned in and lightly kissed her lips. He loved the taste of her. Too much. At the same time, thinking neither kiss was enough.

"I guess we need to talk about what's happening here, Zoey," he said in a throaty voice. "Especially when we agreed there would be nothing between us but friendship."

He watched her take a deep breath before she replied. "Considering our strong attraction to each other, we could say the kisses were inevitable, Chance."

"Yes, we could say that," he agreed.

"And we could say we kissed out of curiosity." Her voice sounded raspy, and she stoked everything below his waist.

"Yes, we could say that, too."

"What do you think?" she asked him, still holding his gaze.

"I think that, right now, we need to do what you suggested and walk around the lake. Otherwise, we might…"

"We might what?" she asked.

"We might end up doing something we'll later regret."

Chapter Twenty-Three

While holding hands, Zoey and Chance walked around the lake. When she'd first seen it while on her horse, she'd had a flash of a dream. However, since then, nothing. But that wasn't what was on her mind right now. Her thoughts dwelled on what had happened before they'd left the cabin. Never had she been kissed like that before. It was as if both her lips and tongue had become his, and he was capable of managing and pleasuring both. He'd done so in such a way that had her questioning the very fundamental values she strongly believed in. She never had a man make her do that.

"It's beautiful here, isn't it?" he said, capturing her attention.

She switched her gaze from the lake to him and thought he was beautiful, although typically, a man wasn't defined that way. She'd already decided he was tall, hot, and handsome. Nothing had changed. "Yes, it is. If this is where my parents spent most of their time when they came to visit my grandparents, I can see why." He was still holding her hand, and she felt comfortable with him doing so.

They stopped walking when they came back to the boat

dock. The wind had risen, and her heart skipped when he reached down and brushed a few strands of hair from her face. "I was wrong. You did understand," she said.

He lifted a brow. "I understood what?"

"That day when I first came to your ranch and explained what I'd gone through to learn to walk again. I told you how painful my physical therapy was. You nodded as if you understood, but I figured there was no way you could have. I was wrong. You did understand because you'd gone through similar challenges."

He stared out at the lake before returning his gaze to her. "Yes, I understood, and I admired you for it. You went through it as a child. I was a grown-ass man, yet there were days I didn't think I could take it. I was in so much pain, I wanted to give up."

"But you didn't give up."

"Like I told you, Mama Laverne wouldn't let me."

"You and your family are blessed to have her, Chance."

"Trust me, although she likes to get in our business more than we like, we know she's a jewel."

They began walking again. Silence lingered between them. "There's something I'd like to know," he said.

Zoey glanced over at him. "What?"

"Are you involved with some guy back in Baltimore?"

She wondered why he wanted to know that. "No. I haven't been involved with anyone in well over a year. Conrad and I were together for less than six months when I found out he was cheating on me."

"For real?" He seemed surprised.

"Yes, for real. He thought he was in his right to do so since we were engaged in a long-distance affair."

"This Conrad sounds like an ass."

"He was."

Chance nodded. "It's time we head back."

"Alright."

He tightened her hand in his. "About that kiss, Zoey. Do we need to talk about it?"

"We already have, Chance."

"Friends don't normally kiss," he said, staring at her.

She felt an influx of feelings from the way he looked at her. "I think today we discovered we have a unique friendship."

He lifted a brow. "What's unique about it?"

"At a vulnerable point in our lives, we beat the odds regarding our physical health and well-being. When faced with a challenge, we don't give up easily."

He didn't say anything as if he was giving a lot of thought to what she'd said. Still holding her hand, they walked over to the horses.

"It's about time you called me back, Zoe."

After taking a shower and slipping into her nightgown, Zoey sat on the edge of her bed, using the remote to find something interesting on the television. Chance had driven her back to town and walked her to her hotel room. After placing a quick peck on her forehead, he'd left.

"I'm surprised you hadn't blown up my phone since I hadn't returned your call before now."

"I didn't have to worry since Chance assured me you were in good hands and wouldn't be alone."

Zoey's hand went still on the remote. "You spoke to Chance?"

"I sure did. I called, and tall, hot, and handsome answered your phone while you were sleeping. Didn't he tell you?"

"No, he didn't mention it."

"Well, no biggie. He has such a nice-sounding voice. I can only assume he was the one knocking on your hotel room door."

"Yes, it was him."

"Had you called him?"

"I had earlier, to cancel dinner plans. He had invited me to his place for dinner today."

"What! You didn't tell me anything about that, Zoe."

Knowing she would not be watching television as planned, Zoey placed the remote aside and eased back on the bed. "I had planned to. It was after midnight when I got home from my date with Corbin, and this morning, I got that call from Sharon."

"So, tell me everything now."

She started with the dinner she and Corbin had shared and ended with her and Chance riding horses to that cabin by the lake. Surprisingly, Lucky didn't ask questions every mid-sentence. She listened to the point where, for a while, Zoey thought her silence was eerie. When she finished, Zoey asked, "Well, Lucky, you don't have anything to say?"

"Why do I feel you're leaving a few things out, Zoe?"

Probably because she wasn't ready to share anything about the kiss she and Chance had shared yet. A kiss that still had parts of her body feeling hot. Nor was she prepared to tell Lucky how it felt being held in his arms while they danced.

"I don't know why you have such a feeling, Lucky."

"Probably because I know you. I won't bug you about anything now since you've been through enough for one day. However, you know what I think?"

"No, Lucky. What do you think?"

"I think tall, hot, and handsome has grown on you, and you've grown on him. You may be engaging in your first fling after all."

An hour after her call with Lucky had ended, Zoey was in bed staring at the ceiling. Unlike what Lucky assumed, she wouldn't be engaging in a fling with Chance, the only man she'd ever been tempted to have one with. He was only into meaningless sex—one-night stands and one and done, something she was not.

She was about to grab the remote to resume searching for something to watch on television when her cell phone rang. She picked it up and recognized the caller's name. "Ms. Felicia Laverne, this is a pleasant surprise. How are you?"

"I'm doing fine, dear. What about you?"

"I'm doing alright." She was tempted to tell her about the phone call she'd gotten from Sharon Newberry but decided she would wait to do so when she saw Ms. Felicia Laverne again. To tell anyone else about it today would be too draining.

"I got some good news for you."

Zoey pulled up in bed. "What is it?"

"That cabin I told you about. The owner permitted you to stay there over the summer."

She smiled. "That's great."

"And he's not charging you anything to do so. He and his family are going away for the summer and appreciate the cabin being occupied."

"That's very generous of him. It's a nice cabin. I had dinner with Chance, and afterward, we went riding and he took me there. He got the owner's permission to look inside."

"How did it go? Did being there spark any of your memory?"

"Not inside the cabin, but when I first saw the lake, I got a quick memory flash of my parents and me having a picnic by the lake. Just like in one of my dreams, so you were correct. That was the lake."

"Glad to hear it. I'm leaving tomorrow to return home to Whispering Pines. Will you join me for lunch on Thursday?"

"I'd love to. How soon can I move into the cabin?" Zoey asked.

"As soon as you'd like. The security code is 5109. Let me know if you need help moving from the hotel, and I'll get one of my great-grandsons to help."

"I don't need any help, and I appreciate everything you've done," she said, unable to hide the excitement in her voice.

"You don't have to thank me, and I look forward to seeing you Thursday. I will text you the address. Whispering Pines is like a fortress, so I'll let my son Jake know I'm expecting you."

She took a deep breath after she and Ms. Felicia Laverne said their goodbyes. Her day might not have started well, but it definitely was ending better.

Before popping open the can of beer, Chance leaned against the refrigerator. Zoey's scent was still there; he figured it would be for a while. Moving over to the table, he sat down in the chair. Instead of taking a sip, he took a huge gulp. He needed it.

He needed *her*.

That kiss should not have happened. But it had, and the memory would live amid his brain cells for a while. He took another gulp of beer, putting that theory to work when he thought of how she'd tasted. Sensuously delicious. He could have stood there and sucked on her tongue until the cows came home. The more he would have done so, the more he would have craved her, hungered for and desired her.

A heated rush of need was pushing through all parts of him in a way that even this cold beer couldn't abate. He wondered how the rest of her would taste if her mouth tasted that good. He would love to find out.

Taking another gulp, he thought about their conversation about the kiss. Their logic. Their decision for it not to happen again. He shook his head, thinking, *good luck with that one*. He was convinced it would happen again. It had taken all the self-control he possessed not to kiss her good night when he had walked her to her hotel room.

He then remembered his conversation with his great-grandmother that morning. She had made it clear she didn't think that he, nor any other single Madaris, not to mention those Bannister brothers were who Zoey needed. At the time, he agreed with Mama Laverne's way of thinking. But that was before he kissed Zoey. Tasted her.

Before she'd wet his shirt with her tears.

He finished off the last of his beer and checked his watch. Starting tomorrow, he and his men would move the herd to a pasture on Whispering Pines; a process that usually took three to four days to complete. That meant he needed to go to bed earlier than usual. He stood and, after disposing of his beer can, moved toward the stairs, thinking there was a good chance Zoey Pritchard would find her way into his dreams that night.

Chapter Twenty-Four

"Thanks for inviting me to lunch, Ms. Felicia Laverne."

"I'm glad you came, Zoey."

"Jake and Diamond are a striking couple, and their kids, Granite and Amethyst, are so nice. It was kind of Diamond to invite me to stay for dinner."

"I'm glad you accepted her invitation. Have you gotten settled in the cabin?"

"Yes, and I love waking up each morning to a fantastic view of the lake." She'd texted Chance to tell him where she was; however, he hadn't bothered to respond. That had been three days ago.

"I know how much you like riding. Did Chance bring one of his horses for you to use?" Felicia Laverne asked.

"No. I texted to let him know I was staying at the cabin but haven't heard from him."

"Probably because he left Monday to move a portion of his herd to parts of Whispering Pines. Doing so requires him and his men to sleep on the range where phone reception isn't good."

"Oh." Chance hadn't mentioned that when they were together on Sunday. Did he forget, or had it been intentional?

Felicia Laverne took a sip of her tea and then said, "I understand you've had a busy week, Zoey."

A smile curved Zoey's lips. "Yes, I have. In addition to moving into the cabin on Tuesday, I met Kenna, Skye, Mac, and Sam for lunch on Wednesday. I like them."

"And from what I hear, they like you. Did you see the Madaris Building that Blade and Slade's construction company built?"

"Yes, I did and thought they did a wonderful job. I love the architecture. It's very impressive. I also saw Laverne Park, which I understand was named after you. It's gorgeous."

"Thanks, and I think so, too."

Zoey sat down her glass of iced tea on the table. "There's something I wanted to tell you about that occurred this week."

Felicia Laverne lifted a brow. "Oh? What?"

"On Sunday, I connected with a woman who was my mother's best friend. They went to college and medical school together." She then told Felicia Laverne what she'd been told about her newborn baby brother also dying in the car accident, and her aunt lying about Zoey's memory.

"I wonder why your aunt would keep something as important as that from you, and why would she lie about the chances of your memory returning?" Felicia Laverne asked, frowning.

"I wish I knew." After taking a deep breath, she asked. "I'd like to ask you a couple of questions."

"And what do you want to know, dear?"

"On Sunday, Chance took me riding, and one of the places we rode to was the fruit grove. It is beautiful. He said it runs straight through the middle of what used to be Satterfield property and Whispering Pines. How had that happened?"

Felicia Laverne leaned back in her chair. "It happened because of two ten-year-old boys who were best friends—my husband, Milton Madaris, and your great-grandfather, Waylon Satterfield. Milton told me that planting those fruit trees to encompass both properties was their way of solidifying their friendship. They knew that one day they would be the heads of each of their lands."

Zoey's lips widened in a smile. "That was a smart idea."

Felicia Laverne nodded. "At the time, they thought so. I doubt when they planted those first fruit trees, they had any idea how big the grove would one day become."

"Tell me about him. My great-grandfather Waylon."

A thoughtful expression appeared on Felicia Laverne's features. "Waylon was a very handsome man who was liked and respected by many. He was best man to Milton at our wedding."

"What about my great-grandmother Deedra? Did she attend your wedding, too?"

"No. Waylon hadn't met Deedra yet. They didn't marry until five years later."

Zoey lifted a brow. "Why? Was my great-grandfather Waylon a ladies' man who wasn't ready to settle down?"

Before Felicia Laverne could answer, there was the sound of a loud bell ringing. "That's the lunch bell letting the ranch hands know it's time to eat at the bunkhouse."

"This ranch is magnificent," Zoey said.

"It is. I will never forget my first day arriving here after marrying Milton. I thought I was in heaven."

"I can understand why."

"Before that bell rang, I was about to tell you about Deedra. She was a beautiful woman with a heart of gold."

Chance saw the lights on in the cabin. He hadn't seen Zoey's text until he'd returned to Teakwood Ridge. She had sent it three days ago. She'd had no way of knowing he'd been out on the range all that time. Did she think he had ignored her message?

He could hear music the moment his feet touched the steps. There were motion lights surrounding the property and a generator in case of a power outage. Although Chance didn't like the idea of Zoey being out this far from civilization alone, at least he was closer to her than when she was at her hotel.

Her text said she'd moved into the cabin on Tuesday. What had she been doing with herself since then? Had she met with his great-grandmother this week? Had she kept her lunch date with Kenna, Sam, Mac, and Skye? It was still fairly early, barely nine o'clock. He hoped she wasn't a person who went to bed early.

Chance had thought about her a lot since he'd last seen her on Sunday.

He knocked on the door.

"Who is it?"

The sound of her voice had his heart thumping erratically in his chest. He'd never braced himself for his reaction to a woman but was doing so now. He needed to pull himself together. "Chance."

When the door opened and she stood there, he thought being interested in her was an understatement. It was more than that. He needed to understand why now and, more importantly, why her? Mama Laverne had said a romantic involvement was the last thing Zoey needed while trying to regain her memory. As far as he was concerned, Zoey was old enough to make her own decisions and didn't need anyone, not even his great-grandmother, making them for her.

"Zoey. I should have called first before dropping by. I hope I'm not interrupting you."

She moved aside to let him inside. "I thought it might be you. It's not like I have a lot of neighbors around here, and no, you're not interrupting anything."

He followed her into the living room and tried not to notice how well her jeans fit her backside. But then they always did. "I saw your text when I returned home today. I've been out on the range a few days."

"Ms. Felicia Laverne told me. I met with her again today. Would you like anything to drink? My refrigerator is stocked with wine coolers, beer, and water."

"No, I'm good."

She nodded as she sat down on the sofa, and he sat beside her but placed what he considered a decent distance between them. "So, how did your meeting with Mama Laverne go?"

"Great. I learned a lot about my great-grandmother Deedra. She was a twenty-two-year-old widow from Laredo."

"Widow? How did her husband die?"

"He was struck by lightning. A bad thunderstorm came up while he was out riding. A bolt of lightning killed him and his horse. According to Ms. Felicia Laverne, she was in town visiting, and she and my great-grandfather Waylon met at church and were married close to fourteen years before she got sick and died. Gramma Arabella was twelve at the time."

"Arabella was their only child?"

"Yes. After Deedra's death, my great-great-grandmother Penny assisted Waylon in raising her. When Arabella became more of a tomboy in Penny's eyes, she persuaded Waylon to send her granddaughter to an all-girls school in the East at fifteen. Ms. Felicia and I will meet again next week, and I can't wait."

"I'm glad you're learning about your ancestors," he said.

"I'm glad, too. Diamond invited me to stay for dinner, and your cousin Clayton and his wife, Syneda, were there. Syneda invited me to lunch with her and the other cousins' wives in the next couple of weeks."

"That was nice of her, but then Syneda is a kind and thoughtful person. Have you recovered any memories since you moved in here?"

"No, and I spent most of yesterday by the lake."

"What about dreams?"

★ ★ ★

Zoey shifted in her seat, thinking she'd had dreams. Plenty of them. However, all of them had been of him. Of course, she wouldn't tell him that. "No, not a one. I checked in with my therapist on Monday and told her about the flashback I experienced on Sunday. She thinks that's progress, but not to force my mind to recall anything. She wants me to unwind and relax and feels that when I do, the flashbacks will come naturally."

"I believe that, too."

Zoey couldn't help but grin. "You're a therapist now, Chance?"

He chuckled. "I've been known to dabble occasionally. But seriously, I've heard the benefits of relaxing and unwinding are that they relieve stress and are good for your memory."

"I hope so."

He pulled up on his knees in his seat. "Come closer with your back to me." When she did, he whispered. "Now close your eyes, Zoey."

She closed her eyes and felt his fingertips gently stroke her temples. While doing so, he began humming softly. He had a sexy voice, and the pitch carried a smooth vibration that had parts of her body vibrating as well.

"How does that feel?" he asked, leaning close to her ear. It was so close she felt the heat of his breath on her neck.

"It feels good."

"And what is going through your mind, Zoey?"

I'll never tell, she thought. Everything going through her mind was about him. Instead, she said. "I was thinking how excitedly I'm looking forward to tomorrow."

He stopped stroking her temples. "What happens tomorrow?"

"That box with the diaries and photo albums will arrive."

He began gently stroking her temples again. "Do you feel you might invade their privacy by reading their diaries?"

"I want to think they would want me to read them. To know

about the men they loved, understand any unfavorable decisions they'd ever had to make, and embrace their happiness."

"You can open your eyes now," he said, standing. "Come walk me to the door."

"You're leaving?" She hadn't meant to ask in a disappointed voice.

"Yes, I'm leaving. I don't want to wear out my welcome," he said, extending his hand to help her off the sofa.

"You could never do that, Chance." The warmth of her hand in his almost made her moan. It felt good, and it felt right. It was getting harder and harder to hide how she felt whenever he touched her. From how his pupils had darkened, she knew he'd felt something, too.

"When do you meet with Mama Laverne again?" he asked when they reached the door.

"Next Thursday."

"How was lunch with the Madaris ladies?"

"I had a lovely time getting to know them better. You have such a wonderful family, Chance."

"I guess I'll keep them around."

"They told me how your great-grandmother likes playing matchmaker of her great-grands and has a one hundred percent success record."

"Yes, she does—it's only the great-grands of her oldest four sons that are on her notorious hit list.

"Well, at least you don't have to worry about her matching any of us with you. Mama Laverne thinks her last remaining single great-grandsons in that category have too many whorish ways and have let it be known that none of us are deserving of your time or attention other than for friendship. Especially me."

"Why, especially you?"

"Because in addition to what she sees as my whorish ways, Mama Laverne has taken into consideration what she knows to be my issues. But guess what she doesn't know?"

She remained silent, waiting for him to continue.

"I'm working on both my whorish ways and those issues."

A lump formed in her throat. Was there a meaning to his words? "Are you?"

He inched a little closer. "Yes, ma'am, I am."

Zoey expected him to brush a light kiss on her forehead like he'd done when he'd returned her to the hotel Sunday night. Instead, he used the tip of his finger to lift her chin for a kiss. It wasn't a light brush across the lips. It was a tongue-tingling kiss that spoke of need, hunger, and a degree of desire she could tell he was fighting hard to control. Then he deepened the pressure of the kiss in a way she felt in every bone in her body. He'd taken control of her mouth for the longest time, as if he couldn't get enough. By the time he broke off the kiss, she felt weak in the knees.

"How about we do something this weekend?" he asked in that low, husky, and sexy voice she loved hearing.

She licked her lips, loving his taste still there, while trying to get her thoughts and body back under control. "Something like what?"

"A picnic at this lake? Around noon on Saturday."

"That sounds nice."

He smiled. "I'll see you then. I'll also bring an extra horse to ride to the fruit grove, so we can pick some fruit. The muscadine grapes should be ripe now. Maybe I'll show you how to make them into wine while you're here."

"I'd like that."

"Good night, Zoey."

Feeling bold, she leaned up on tiptoes and brushed a kiss across his lips. "Good night, Chance."

That night, Felicia Laverne lay in bed and stared at the ceiling, unable to sleep. Dinner was outstanding. It was always good when members of her family dropped by.

Thanks to the ringing of the lunch bell, she'd avoided talking about Waylon's relationship with Victoria. When their talks resumed, she only spoke about his marriage to Deedra. Zoey had no reason to know Victoria had been the love of her great-grandfather's life. Nor did she need to know Waylon had built the cabin she was staying in for Victoria as a wedding gift, and it was to be their home.

Zoey had mentioned that Deedra, Arabella, and Michelle's diaries, along with photo albums would be shipped to her. When she began reading the diaries, there was no doubt Zoey would learn a lot of things; especially the true nature of Waylon and Deedra's marriage. Felicia Laverne needed to prepare herself for Zoey's questions, which meant—reliving many sad memories.

Remembering everything Victoria and Waylon had gone through always brought tears to her eyes. She could recall that night that they had made plans to elope.

Felicia was glad Victoria had not confided her elopement plans with her. Doing so would have made her an accessory to their plans. She and Milton were still newlyweds, and such a thing would have strained their marriage and her relationship with her in-laws.

Although the elopement plans had been kept secret, Penny Satterfield managed to find out and ruin everything. The woman's spitefulness had ended up costing Waylon and Victoria the happiness they had been willing to give up everything to have. As Felicia Laverne closed her eyes, seeking sleep, she couldn't help but remember that night so many years ago.

Part Four

"When a person has been your greatest treasure and the love of your life, the parting will never end with a goodbye."

—Brenda Jackson

Chapter Twenty-Five

Back to the past…

Victoria checked the clock on the wall before easing out of bed. Time was of the essence. She had made sure her window would not make a sound when it was time to climb out of it. Waylon would be there waiting for her. They'd met at the fruit grove two days ago and reviewed their plans. Her father's heart hadn't softened regarding the Satterfields, and she and Waylon refused to live apart any longer. Penny Satterfield wouldn't welcome her to her family, and Pa wouldn't welcome Waylon to theirs. For those reasons, they decided to defy both parents and marry anyway. Life was too short not to be happy.

Waylon had made all the arrangements. Tonight, they would catch a train to Austin, where they would marry. They would remain there for a week before returning to Houston. Since Mr. Kurt had given Waylon back the cabin and land meant to be theirs, that would be where they would live. They hoped that eventually, in time, their parents would accept their marriage and be happy for them.

She quickly began dressing in the dark. Clothes she had laid out and hidden under the chair in her room. Her suitcase was under the bed, packed and ready to go. A short while later, she was tiptoeing toward the window with her suitcase in hand when the light in her room suddenly came on. Her father was standing there, nearly taking up the doorway. She gasped when she saw him.

"I just got a call from Penny Satterfield, and she was right," he said, entering her bedroom. "You and Waylon plan to elope tonight. How could you even consider such a thing, Victoria? After all that family has done to ours?"

Penny Satterfield? How on earth had Waylon's mother found out about their plans? Waylon would know something was wrong when he saw the light in her room. The look on her father's face almost broke her heart. It showed both anger and disappointment.

Lifting her chin, she said, "Waylon and I love each other, Pa. It's not fair that we're being punished because of Charlotte's lies. You and Ms. Penny leave us no choice. We want to be together as husband and wife."

"As your father, I must protect you, Victoria."

"Protect me? Waylon would never hurt me."

At that moment, both her mother and brother appeared in the doorway. "What's going on?" Milton asked, wiping sleep from his eyes. As far as Victoria was concerned, it should have been obvious what was wrong since she had her suitcase in her hand.

"Your sister had planned to elope with Waylon tonight. I can't believe she would do such a thing."

Before she could say anything, there was a loud knock on the door. She knew it was Waylon, and Milton said as much. "A Satterfield is not welcome in my home," her father said in a loud, angry voice. "Then I will go to him, Pa, since I plan to marry him tonight."

"Don't do this, Victoria."

"Pa, please understand," she pleaded, placing her suitcase by her feet.

"If you only knew the threats Penny Satterfield made against you tonight if you married Waylon. For that reason, I would never permit you to be a part of that family."

"Pa, please don't say that," Victoria said, tears forming in her eyes.

The knock on the door got louder, and then Milton spoke up and said, "Pa, please let Waylon in so you can talk to him and Victoria. Tell him about his mother's threats and why you don't want a union between them. Let Way and Mr. Kurt deal with Ms. Penny."

Victoria swiped at her tears, unsure her father would take Milton's advice. She let out a sigh of relief when he nodded. "Fine, let him in."

Her mother approached, giving her a handkerchief for her tears, and Milton went to open the door. After wiping her eyes, she glanced at her father and suddenly realized something was wrong. He reached up and touched his forehead as if he had a headache. Then she saw his lips twitch a few times as he swayed on his feet, just seconds before he crumbled to the floor.

"Pa!"

She and her mother rushed to her father. "Milton! Waylon!" Victoria screamed at the top of her voice.

Both men appeared and immediately rushed to pick him up. "We need to get Pa to the hospital immediately," Victoria said, checking his pulse. Over the summer, while working in the hospital, the nurses showed her how to do it.

"Ma, call Dr. Hargrove," Milton said. "Way, help me get Pa out to the truck."

Everyone went into action. After making a call to Dr. Hargrove, Etta Madaris dashed to her bedroom to change.

Waylon caught Victoria's arm when she was about to go get inside the truck. "Milton told me that Ma called your pa and ruined our plans. He also told me about Ma's threats. I will get to the bottom of it, sweetheart, I swear."

Trying not to feel a sense of anguish and despair, Victoria nodded. She then quickly got inside the truck with her mother and Milton to rush her father to the hospital.

An angry Waylon stormed into his home to find his parents sitting at the kitchen table. Since it was almost midnight, he knew they were waiting for him. That meant they'd figured his elopement with Victoria had failed. "You had no right to call Mr. Jantz, Ma."

"Don't raise your voice to me—I had every right. How dare you elope with that Madaris girl? It's a good thing I found those train tickets in your bedroom drawer. I knew what you were up to."

"You had no right to snoop around in my things." He shifted his gaze to his pa. "You knew about this?"

Mr. Kurt shook his head. "No, I didn't know anything until your ma woke me up and told me what you planned to do."

"You and Ma left me no choice. I love Victoria, and this family has made it known that she's not welcome in it."

"That's not true, Waylon. I've given you back my blessing for a marriage between you and Victoria. It's Jantz who's keeping this feud going."

"Mainly because of Ma's threats."

Kurt frowned at his wife. "What threats are you making, Penny?"

"I'm not making threats but speaking the truth. If Victoria and Waylon marry, she's not welcome in our family."

"Why?" Kurt asked his wife, seemingly shocked at the venom he heard in her voice.

"Because that family is why Charlotte had to leave her home, and you won't let her return."

Kurt shook his head. "No, they are not, Penny," he said

firmly. "How often do I have to say that Charlotte was sent away for her own doing? Our daughter lied to us. She put her hand on the family Bible and lied. She got pregnant by one man and accused another of the deed, and she hadn't been a virgin as she'd claimed, and that hadn't been her first pregnancy. It wasn't the Madarises who brought shame to this family, Penny. It was our daughter."

"She would not have done that if Milton had taken her seriously. She'd been sweet on him for years, but he ignored her. Our Charlotte was beautiful, happy, and liked by all. There was no reason he couldn't find favor with her."

"Ma, Milt never gave Charlotte any reason to think she had a chance with him. Besides, none of what you said is excusable behavior for what Charlotte did. And not all of what you said just now is true. Charlotte was beautiful, and I'm sure she was happy most days, but she was not well-liked. She was mean, hateful, and a bully, and most people around here knew it."

"How dare you say that about your sister? She was well-liked except by those girls who were jealous of her. She told me about them and how mean they were to her."

"You still haven't said what threats you made against Victoria, Penny," Kurt said.

Penny gave Waylon and Kurt a defiant expression. "I told Jantz that if she ever married Waylon, I would do everything in my power to make sure she's miserable every day of her life. She is not worthy to have the Satterfield name, and as long as I live, she won't." She rushed from the room in tears.

Kurt rubbed a frustrated hand down his face. "I realize banishing Charlotte was hard on your mother, Waylon, but I don't understand why she refuses to accept Charlotte was to blame and not the Madarises. Hopefully, one day she will."

"And what if she doesn't, Pa? Ma has made her dislike for Victoria known, and whatever threats she made upset Mr. Jantzen. And just so you know, he collapsed and had to be rushed to the hospital tonight."

"My god, is he alright?"

"I don't know. I'm leaving to go there now. Victoria needs me whether Mr. Jantz wants me there or not. I only came here to confront Ma about what she did."

"Let me know how Jantz is doing, Waylon."

He heard his father's genuine concern. "I will, Pa." He then turned to leave.

"How is my husband?" Etta asked, rushing over to Dr. Hargrove when he entered the waiting room. It was apparent she was trying to keep her voice from breaking.

"Mr. Madaris suffered a stroke."

The doctor's words nearly brought Etta to her knees. Milton was there by his mother's side to keep her standing. Victoria sank in a chair close by, and Felicia wrapped her arms around her best friend's shoulders.

"He was lucky it was a mild one," Dr. Hargrove added. "Since Mr. Madaris is pretty much in good health, I can only assume it was brought on by stress that's been building up for a while that he hasn't released."

The doctor gazed from one to the other. "Has he mentioned anything about having headaches lately?"

"No," Etta said. Milton and Victoria concurred.

"I intend to keep him here for a while. Hopefully, he will recover completely over time if he doesn't experience any more tension and stress."

"Is he awake? May I see him?" Etta asked anxiously.

"Not tonight, Mrs. Madaris. The best thing that can be done is to keep him calm, so he won't have another stroke. He needs to let go of whatever is stressing him out. Otherwise, he might not be so lucky the next time. Since he will be sleeping most of the night, I suggest you all go home and return in the morning."

"No," Etta said firmly. "I want to be close in case he wakes up."

"And I'll stay with you, Ma," Victoria added.

"We'll all stay," Milton said, getting his mother to sit in the chair.

Etta glanced at Milton. "Your Pa would want you to run things for a while. This is the week he was to move the herd to the south pasture."

"And we'll still do so, Ma. Don't worry," Milton said, placing a comforting hand on her shoulder. "I'll call Rafe and let him know what's happening." Rafe Adams was the foreman at Whispering Pines.

"And another thing," Dr. Hargrove said. "When Mr. Madaris wakes up, he will have difficulty talking since his mouth is slightly twisted, and his words may sound slurred. His inability to speak might frustrate him. Be patient, and don't get him anxious."

Etta wiped tears from her eyes. "Alright." The others agreed as well. Milton walked out with Dr. Hargrove to make the call to Rafe.

"It's all my fault," Victoria said.

"No, it's not," Etta said to her daughter. "You heard what Dr. Hargrove said. Your father has been under a lot of stress for over a year. Ever since that day the Satterfields showed up at our house with their accusations. I tried getting Jantz to talk about it, but he wouldn't—he kept it all locked inside. Even after it was proven that Charlotte was a liar and the Madaris named was cleared, it bothered him that we had to go through it."

"This wouldn't have happened if I hadn't planned to elope tonight."

"Your mother is right, Victoria," Felicia said, pulling up another chair. "According to Dr. Hargrove, it wasn't tonight that did it, but a buildup of other times."

The three women held hands and prayed that the doctor was right and that Jantz would fully recover.

★ ★ ★

"Milton, wait up."

Recognizing the voice, Milton turned to Waylon. Frowning, he said. "You know you should not be here, Way."

"How could I not be? If you were in my place and faced with the same circumstances, you would be, too." Waylon could tell by his best friend's features that eased from a frown that he would. "How is Mr. Jantz?"

Milton rubbed a hand down his face. "Pa suffered a stroke. The good news is that it was mild, and the doctor thinks he will fully recover in time."

"Thank God for that," Waylon said.

"I agree, and just so you know, Victoria is blaming herself."

"I know the feeling," was Waylon's response.

"Look Way, you and Victoria have nothing to blame yourselves for. Granted, I'm sure discovering the two of you planned to elope pissed Pa off, but my take from Dr. Hargrove is that what happened to Pa was a buildup of everything from the beginning. He's been carrying a lot on his shoulders during the past year, and he never released his anger and frustration. Stress is what brought it on tonight."

"Stress caused by the Satterfields," Waylon said in disgust.

"Just one Satterfield. We're not holding your entire family responsible for what Charlotte did. I think over time, Pa will come around. If it wasn't for your ma's threats, he would have done so sooner. Ma confided in me tonight that this wasn't the first time Ms. Penny has made them. However, tonight she warned Pa that if you and Victoria marry, she better not ever eat anything she cooked or he and Ma would have a dead daughter. Can you imagine such a vile threat? Victoria is a daddy's girl, and Pa feels he has to protect her. He won't agree to a marriage between the two of you until he believes she'll be in a safe environment."

"How dare Ma say something like that, and that's not what

she told me and Pa she said," he said, furious. "I won't let anyone hurt Victoria, not even my ma. If we have to move away, I have no problem doing so."

"You would leave here and start a new life elsewhere?"

"If it means Victoria's peace of mind and safety, then yes, I would."

Victoria knew when Milton sent her out to his truck for a jacket he hadn't worn, he had an ulterior motive for doing so. Therefore, she wasn't surprised to find Waylon leaning against the truck. She barely held back her tears as she raced across the yard to his opened arms.

He held her while she cried. She wasn't sure how much time had passed before she pulled away and said, "Pa had a stroke."

He nodded as he gently stroked her back. "Milton told me."

"I'm trying not to feel responsible, but I do, Waylon."

"You shouldn't. We shouldn't. Milton told me what the doctor said," he said, using his handkerchief to wipe away more tears from her eyes.

"I know, but what we did only added to his stress."

"So, what are we going to do now, Victoria? I love you and want to marry you."

"And I want to marry you. But…"

"But what?"

"Your mom. Whatever she said to Pa tonight made him think he must protect me from her. Did you find out what she said to him?"

"Yes, and it's too awful to repeat. Pa thinks Ma is going through something because of losing Charlotte and will eventually snap out of it."

"What if she doesn't?"

"Then we'll move away."

"Move away and go where?"

"Dallas, Austin. Beaumont… I'd even be open to leaving

Texas entirely. My cousin left and found work in the steel mills in Chicago. He likes it there."

"You're a rancher, Waylon, not a steel mill worker."

"But I could be one just as long as you're with me."

"Oh, Waylon, what are we going to do?" She asked him the same question he had asked her earlier.

He caressed her cheek with his palm. "We will continue to love each other and believe there is a way. Mr. Jantz will get better, and I hope he will approve of our marriage."

"I hope so. I had better get back or Ma will wonder what's taking me so long. We're staying here tonight."

"So am I. I'll be in my truck over there."

"All night?"

"Yes, all night. I'll be closer to you here than I would be if I were to go home. Besides, I'm too upset with Ma to go back there tonight."

Feeling so much love for him, she leaned on tiptoe to slant her mouth over his. He didn't waste time taking her mouth hungrily. It was a long, drugging kiss that ignited her taste buds with the manly taste of him.

He broke off the kiss, drew in a ragged breath, before saying, "I love you, Victoria."

"And I love you, too, Waylon." Then, without saying anything else, she turned to rush back inside the hospital.

Chapter Twenty-Six

A week later…

Victoria placed a kiss on her father's forehead. He'd been drifting in and out of consciousness for the past few days. Yesterday, he stayed awake for around four hours, which had pleased her mother tremendously. She'd known how much her parents had loved each other, but that had been more apparent by the smile on his face when he'd first awakened and seen her mother. Although it had been difficult for him to do so, he had told her mother that he loved her.

After a good cry, her mother was happy, convinced that Pa was on the road to recovery. Dr. Hargrove said as much but cautioned that he still had a long way to go.

Thanks to Felicia, a pot of coffee was set up in the hospital room, and Victoria walked across the room to a small table to pour a cup. She, her mom, and Felicia were taking shifts, so Pa was never alone. Milton came at the end of the workday. Jantz Madaris had big boots to fill, but her brother was doing a great job.

Although Waylon would also come in the afternoons, he wouldn't come until later tonight since it was branding day on his ranch. To keep down any disturbance, he never came inside the hospital. Instead, he would spend the night in his truck whenever she was there. During the afternoon, he would pick her up a meal from one of the restaurants, and they would eat together in his truck while Milton and Fee watched over their pa.

Fee hadn't been feeling well lately, and Etta Madaris was convinced she was with child. Milton was trying not to get his hopes up, but Victoria thought a niece or nephew would be wonderful.

"Victoria."

She quickly turned toward the bed and saw her father was awake and had called out to her. Placing her coffee cup down, she quickly moved toward the bed. "Yes, Pa? Dr. Hargrove doesn't want you to talk much."

"Promise me."

Speech for him was still rather difficult so she leaned closer to make sure she heard him better. "Promise you what, Pa?"

"That you will not marry into that family. That you won't marry Waylon. I can't let you after what Penny said."

"What did she say?"

He stared at her with stark fear in his eyes, similar to what had been there the night she and Waylon were to elope. She then saw how a mistiness appeared in those same eyes. "Please tell me what she said, Pa."

"Penny said since our family was responsible for her daughter being all but dead to them, she would let me know how that felt if you married her son by poisoning you."

Victoria's breath caught. She could see how saying such a thing would make her father want to protect her.

"Pa, surely Ms. Penny didn't mean that. Waylon and Mr.

Kurt think sending Charlotte away affected her deeply and eventually she will get better."

"What if she doesn't?"

"Waylon will protect me."

"I can't take that chance. You are my beloved daughter. Promise me you won't marry Waylon. Promise me."

Tears Victoria couldn't hold back flowed down her cheeks. "I love Waylon. I've always loved him."

"I know," Jantz said softly. "But Penny has evil in her heart. I heard it in her voice. She will harm you if you marry him. Promise me that you won't."

"Pa, please don't ask this of me."

"Promise me." He grabbed hold of her hand. Although she felt his weakness, she felt his determination to get that promise from her. Her father had grown up on that Madaris motto— Protect. Provide. Prosper.—and would die trying to protect his family. Victoria recalled the warning Dr. Hargrove had given them. Her father had been under a lot of stress. Stress he hadn't let go of. Worrying about her was just another layer he didn't need. Another layer that could cause him to have a relapse. Mainly, another stroke. One that he might not recover from. She met his gaze and said, "If I promise, is there a chance that one day you will change your mind and—"

"No," he interrupted her words. "After what Penny said, I will never change my mind as long as that evil woman is alive. Promise me."

With tears streaming down her face, she said, "I promise I won't marry Waylon, Pa."

It was only then that her father closed his eyes and drifted off to sleep.

Milton knew something was wrong when he arrived at the hospital entrance and saw Victoria outside on the breezeway. It was obvious she was crying. Rushing over to her, he pulled her to him. "Victoria? What's wrong? Did Pa's condition worsen? Is he—"

"Pa is okay, Milton," she said quickly through broken sobs.

"Then what's wrong?" he asked, staring at her while handing her a handkerchief.

"My heart is breaking, Milt."

"Why?"

"Pa made me promise him something."

"Promise him what?"

"That I won't marry Waylon."

He couldn't hide the shocked look on his face. "And you promised him that?"

"There was no way I could not. He was adamant that I make him that promise, Milt. I didn't want to do anything to upset him. Ms. Penny threatened me harm if I married Waylon." She then told Milton what their Pa had told her.

Seeing his lack of surprise, she said, "You already knew, didn't you?"

"Yes. Ma told me the night we brought Pa here. I didn't tell you since you were already upset," he said gently. Soothingly.

She wiped away more tears. "Now I understand why Pa was so upset and he kept saying he had to protect me. I told Pa that regardless of Ms. Penny's threats, I believed Waylon could protect me, but Pa wasn't convinced. Oh, Milt, what am I going to do? I love Waylon. How on earth can I tell him I can't marry him?"

"Is there a chance Dad might change his mind at some point?"

"Not as long as Ms. Penny is alive, and I can see her living to be one hundred years old. How am I supposed to stop loving Waylon when my heart is his? He believes that one day we will marry. I believed that, too."

Milton drew a deep breath. "You have to tell Waylon about your promise to Pa, Victoria. He needs to know."

"She doesn't have to tell me. I heard everything the two of you said," a deep, husky voice said behind them.

Milton and Victoria turned around. Waylon was holding a container of food in his hand. "I knew you hadn't eaten, Victoria, so I took time away from branding to bring you this. Here you are. I need to get back."

The look she saw on Waylon's face nearly broke her heart. "Waylon, I—"

"No, I heard, Victoria. You promised your pa that you won't be marrying me. Although you might not want to keep that promise, you will. It's not within you to break it."

Milton cleared his throat. "I'll let the two of you talk while I go inside to check on Pa."

"No, Milt, you don't have to leave, but I do," Waylon said. "I need to get back to my men. There's no reason for me to be here now anyway. Here, take this," he said, placing the food box in her hand. "And take care of yourself, Victoria."

He moved to go down the steps but stopped and turned back to them. "Mr. Jantz was wrong. I would have protected you with my life if I had to."

While tears streamed down Victoria's face, she watched Waylon cross the parking lot, get in his truck, and drive off. She wept in her brother's arms when his truck could no longer be seen.

Chapter Twenty-Seven

Victoria raced Magic across the open plain toward the fruit grove. This was the fourth time she'd done so over the past two months, hoping Waylon would finally agree to meet with her. She had sent word to him using the postal box he'd set up for them a while back, but he'd ignored her messages. From what she'd heard from Milton, Waylon was having a rough time with their breakup. So was she. Although she no longer cried herself to sleep and was eating better, she was falling into a state of depression.

Her mother was concerned about her. Fee and Milton, too. She figured that was one of the reasons her father's only brother, Quantum Madaris—Uncle QT—had arrived a few weeks ago, three days before Thanksgiving. Granted, she believed he had come to check on Pa, but when he'd made her an offer she couldn't refuse, she'd been convinced there had been an ulterior motive.

After reminding her that he'd sent her a ticket to Paris months ago that she hadn't used, he'd sweetened the pie by offering to send her to nursing school in Paris while she worked for him part-time assisting his booking agent. She'd heard from Milton and Fee that their uncle was doing well, and his house was spacious with four bedrooms. After days of deciding what to do, she knew the best thing was to leave Texas. Her life would be miserable if she remained here, unable to be with the man she loved. She wanted to be the one to tell Waylon of her decision.

Milton had told her that Waylon had confronted his mother after overhearing their conversation that night. When Ms. Penny hadn't denied a thing, he had moved out of his family home to stay in the cabin. The one he'd built for them. The one they would never share together.

Her father was finally home. Although he still wasn't at one hundred percent, he was getting there, under her mother's watchful, loving, and caring eyes. Pa was glad to see his brother.

Like Ma suspected, Fee was pregnant, and everyone was happy, especially Milton. Fee's morning sickness didn't last long, and now she practically glowed. The baby would be born in late spring. It was hard to believe they would celebrate Christmas in a few weeks. Fee's family would travel to Whispering Pines for the holidays, and everyone was excited about it. Victoria tried being excited, but very little thrilled her anymore.

She tightened her coat around her as she rounded the bend, not knowing what she would do if Waylon refused to meet with her yet again. Milton and Fee had gone into town to do some Christmas shopping, and her parents and Uncle QT had driven to the neighboring city of Sugar Land. Uncle QT had promised an old childhood friend that he would perform at one of the civic centers there. She'd been invited to go with them but declined the offer. She was hoping to get the chance to talk to Waylon tonight.

When she reached the fruit grove, she saw Waylon. Her heart raced knowing he'd come. He looked just as handsome as always but as she got closer, she saw the signs of strain under his eyes. A mirror of her own. When she reached him and brought Magic to a stop, he helped her dismount. Once her feet touched the ground, he drew back. "Why did you want us to meet, Victoria?"

His words sounded so distant. "I wanted you to know of a decision I made."

"And what decision is that?"

"I'm leaving Texas for a while. Uncle QT told me about this nursing school in Paris. He offered to pay my tuition if I studied there. To earn extra money, I'll assist his booking agent with the books. The good thing is that my degree will be good to use in this country, too."

He nodded and then said, "I'm happy for you. Nursing school has always been your dream."

It was on the tip of her tongue to say that becoming his wife had also been her dream. "That was all I had to tell you, Waylon. I wanted you to hear it from me."

He paused, then asked. "When are you leaving?"

"Three days after New Year's. We're taking one of those steamboats out of the Houston port." When he didn't say anything, she added, "I didn't want to leave before saying goodbye."

She moved toward Magic and stopped when Waylon touched her arm. "Take care of yourself, Victoria."

She fought the tears threatening to fall. "And you do the same, Waylon."

Their gazes held, and then, like magnets, they were pulled toward each other. She was suddenly engulfed in his strong arms.

Waylon knew they shouldn't be doing this. After all, that promise she'd made to her father had ended things between them. They weren't engaged, and she was no longer "his girl," however, he knew he still loved her and that she still loved him. She had decided to move to Paris to get on with her life, and he should do the same. How could he when the woman he was holding in his arms and kissing was his life?

He broke off the kiss when breathing became a necessity, and then they stood there, staring at each other. He knew this was to be their goodbye. She would leave Texas and possibly meet someone in Paris. A man with whom she could ultimately share his name, his babies, his life. The mere thought of such a thing was breaking his heart.

"Waylon?"

"Yes."

He saw the tears welled up in her eyes. "I always wanted you to be my first and figured as my husband you would be. Although that won't happen, I need to know how it feels to be made love to by a man who loves me and a man I love. Fee said it was the most wonderful experience, and I want to do so with you. Will you give that to me, Waylon?"

Waylon felt his eyes get misty. He didn't want to think ill of those who'd brought them to this point. Charlotte, his parents, and Mr. Jantzen. Did they not understand what their decisions had done? Had brought them to this? "Are you sure, Victoria?"

She swiped at her tears. "Yes, I'm sure."

He studied their surroundings. Although the fruit grove had always been a special place for them, there was no way he would make love to her on the cold ground. He stared at her and asked. "Will you go to the cabin with me? *Our* cabin?" He knew for as long as he lived, no other woman would ever share that cabin with him. He had built it for her. For them.

She nodded. "Yes, I'll go."

Chapter Twenty-Eight

"All aboard!"

The steamship conductor's voice increased Victoria's heart rate when she realized that she was really doing this. She was leaving Texas for Paris. She wished she could think of this as an exciting new adventure, but there was no way she could when she was leaving her heart in Houston.

Victoria would forever have memories of the day she and Waylon spent together at their cabin. She got goose bumps whenever she thought about how she'd given herself to him, totally and completely, and how he'd done the same for her, knowing it would be their first and last time. Their lovemaking had been beautiful, passionate, and special—just as she'd always dreamed.

Afterward, they held each other, not saying anything. There was nothing left to be said. However, he had made her promise that if their time together resulted in a pregnancy, to write and let him know. Promise or no promise, they would marry.

Later that day, when they re-dressed, she began crying. He'd drawn her into his arms and, with misty eyes, told her that he loved her and would always love her. His heartfelt words made her cry even more.

In consideration of her soreness, he hitched his horse trailer to the back of his truck and returned to the fruit grove for Magic. Hoping Milton and Fee had not returned from shopping, he had driven her home.

"Last call. All aboard!" the conductor's second warning sounded, interrupting her thoughts. Scanning the crowd gathered on the dock to see the passengers off, she saw her entire family was there. Uncle QT's visit had greatly helped with her father's rehabilitation. He was no longer using a cane, and his facial features showed no sign he'd had a stroke.

When the steamship whistle sounded, Uncle QT, who'd gone below to check out their cabins, returned by her side. "You're okay, Victoria?" he asked her with concern.

She forced a smile. "Yes, Uncle QT, I'm okay."

When she felt the ship beginning to move, she waved goodbye to her family, blowing kisses to them. Suddenly, she felt an intense stirring in the pit of her stomach. Shifting her eyes from her family, she searched the crowd and saw him.

Waylon.

He was standing on a section of the dock—alone. Seeing him and the mistiness in his eyes and the look in his features, displaying all the love he had in his heart for her, nearly brought her to her knees. She also saw his pain. The same pain she felt in every part of her body. Not bothering to fight back her tears and not caring if any of her family members were watching, she raised her hand in a final wave to him, and knowing he could read her lips, she mouthed the words, "I will always love you."

She watched him raise two fingertips to his lips to blow her a kiss. She read his lips. "And I will love you forever, Victoria."

Their gazes held until they could no longer see each other.

Part Five

"Love recognizes no barriers. It jumps hurdles, leap fences, penetrates walls to arrive at its destination full of hope."

—Maya Angelou

Chapter Twenty-Nine

Present day…

When Zoey returned to the cabin from the post office, she tried to stop her heart from racing while opening the box. Placing the three diaries aside, she immediately opened the first of four photo albums, deciding to start with the oldest and work her way through.

There weren't many pictures of her great-grandparents, Waylon and Deedra. The ones taken were in black-and-white and, in some instances, grainy. But still, she could tell Waylon Satterfield had been a very handsome man. In one photo, he appeared to be in his thirties, tall and muscular, with a pair of dark, friendly eyes. Deedra Satterfield stood around five-six and had beautiful features. They wore their Sunday best, indicating they'd probably gone to church that day.

There was also their wedding picture. Waylon was dressed in a dark suit, and she was in a pretty blue dress and holding a lovely bouquet. Zoey recalled Ms. Felicia saying Deedra had been a widow, which was probably why she hadn't worn a gown. She looked young, no more than eighteen, although Ms. Felicia Laverne said she'd been twenty-two when they'd married.

There were also photos of Arabella as a little girl with her parents. They projected the perfect family.

An hour later, she placed the photo albums aside, filled with emotions after viewing numerous snapshots of her ancestors. The photos that had touched her emotionally more than the others were the ones in the album her parents had kept. It contained their wedding pictures, vacations they had taken together, her baby pictures, and pictures of various stages of her life while growing up under her parents' loving, watchful, and protective eyes.

Numerous pictures included not only her and her parents together but also her grandparents. One such photo showed her fifth birthday being celebrated on the ranch. A table had been set up on the lawn, right in front of that giant oak tree. Was that why she remembered that tree that day she'd driven onto Chance's property?

Zoey hoped seeing those photos of her childhood would trigger her memory. So far, they hadn't. She was trying not to feel frustrated and not force her mind to recall anything like her therapist said. Instead, she would unwind and relax, believing the memories would come naturally. Still, she couldn't wait for Lucky to see the albums and for Chance to see them, too.

Chance.

A shiver of excitement raced through her at the thought she would be seeing him tomorrow for their picnic.

She had considered that Chance Madaris might be the one man she couldn't handle when it came to controlling her sexual urges. She certainly thought of jumping his bones whenever they were together. For a woman who didn't do flings, she was having second thoughts when it came to him.

She would return to Baltimore at the end of the summer.

Why did the thought of parting ways with Chance set her on edge? She usually had more control of her emotions than that, especially when it involved matters of her heart.

Her heart? *Honestly, Zoey.* Her heart had nothing to do with it. It was about an increase in her hormones and nothing else.

Putting the photo albums aside, she went into the kitchen to pour a glass of wine. She loved this place and wondered since it was located so far from the main house, had it been Waylon and Deedra's first home?

Anxious to read the diaries, she returned to the living room and reached for the one with a moss green cover and a beautiful large scripted letter *D* on the front. She figured *D* stood for Deedra. Goose bumps appeared on her arm as she eased onto the sofa and curled her legs beneath her. After taking a sip of wine, she opened the diary and began reading.

Dear Diary,

Today, I met Waylon Satterfield. Reverend Potts, a child-hood friend of my late father, invited me to Houston to meet him, and I'm glad he did. Mr. Satterfield is my last hope. Otherwise, I will be forced to marry Forest, Dale's brother, who always gave me the creeps. I was still griev-ing my beloved Dale's death when his family showed up on the ranch and took everything. They said as a widow, I could not own anything, and if I wanted to continue to live there, I would have to marry Forest. Dale had once confided in me just how abusive his brother could be to women.

Waylon seems like a nice man. He understands I could never love him like a woman or wife should love a man or her husband. My heart will forever belong to Dale. However, I told him that if we married, I would perform all my wifely duties and care for his household. He was okay with my position and explained that just like my heart would forever belong to Dale, his heart would forever belong to a woman named Victoria Madaris.

What?! Zoey recalled Corbin had told her Victoria Madaris had been their great-grandaunt—and Ms. Felicia's best friend. She also recalled Chance saying that same aunt was buried in a tomb in the fruit grove. Zoey continued reading after taking another sip of wine.

Zoey read twenty more entries and, upon finishing, knew why Waylon and Victoria had broken off their engagement, and the cause of the Satterfield and Madaris feud. Fighting back tears, her heart couldn't help but go out to the couple who'd been so much in love but could not marry. She also knew why Waylon and Deedra had agreed to a loveless marriage. She checked her watch and saw it was time to prepare something for dinner. But she was so into Deedra's diary that she didn't want to stop reading.

Chapter Thirty

Zoey sat down at her kitchen table to enjoy her morning cup of coffee. She had awakened later than she had planned, blaming it on staying up reading her great-grandmother's diary. Although she had a lot more to read, she understood her great-grandparents' marriage well. She'd even gotten to know her great-great-grandmother Penny, a woman who wanted her son to marry Deedra for all the wrong reasons. She also knew of Penny's intense dislike for the Madarises and the reason for the Satterfield and Madaris feud.

Ms. Felicia was right; her great-grandmother had been a God-fearing woman with a heart of gold who was loved and respected by all who knew her. Deedra and Waylon's marriage was based on a strong friendship and not love, and both had kept their vows to each other. Zoey needed to talk to Ms. Felicia, and it couldn't wait until their next planned meeting on Thursday. She would call her later to see if she could meet with her sooner.

One of the first things she'd noticed was that it had rained overnight, and the forecast today indicated it would rain again later today. Would Chance cancel their plans ? No sooner had that thought entered her mind than her phone rang. It was Chance.

Placing her coffee cup aside, she picked up her phone. "Good morning, Chance."

"Good morning, Zoey. Did you sleep well?"

"Yes. I hadn't known it had rained until I woke this morning."

"That's the reason I was calling," he said. "The ground will be too wet for a traditional picnic, so I thought we could enjoy lunch on your patio since it has a good view of the lake. Then, afterward, we can go canoeing. I'm sure Trevor wouldn't mind if we used one of his."

"That's a wonderful idea, Chance."

"Great. I'll be there around noon."

Since he didn't mention the ride to the fruit grove, she figured he would see how the weather held out before canceling that. After finishing her coffee, she placed a call to Mama Laverne who agreed to meet with her Tuesday. After the call, she went upstairs to shower and dress.

She was headed toward her bedroom when suddenly, she had a flashback of doing the same thing as a little girl. She'd been happy that day because she and her parents would go to Gramma Bella and Grampa Josh's big house for dinner.

She wanted to believe that being here was what she needed and that before leaving, she would get her memory back.

Chance's gaze traveled the length of Zoey when she opened the door. She was wearing a cute pair of denim shorts and an off-the-shoulder blouse. She had a broad smile on her face. As much as he wanted to think it was for him, he figured it was for something else. "You had another flashback?"

"Yes!" she said excitedly, moving aside for him to enter. "I remembered being here, inside this house with my parents.

Later that day we joined my grandparents at the big house for dinner. That's what we called your house. The big house."

He followed her into the kitchen and placed the huge picnic basket on the table. "Come here, sweetheart," he said, opening his arms to her. She came to him, and he held her in a tight embrace. "I'm happy for you. That's great news, baby," he said, liking how the terms of endearment had easily rolled off his lips.

She pulled back and gave him a cheerful grin. "Thanks, and I feel it will all come back before I leave, Chance. I really believe that."

"Then it will happen. Just continue to believe. As I told you, Mama Laverne convinced me I would walk again. I believed it, and it happened."

She nodded, looked over at the basket, and laughed. "What all do you have in there?"

He laughed. "Just a few things I threw together."

She grinned. "That looks like a lot, Chancellor Madaris."

He had told her to call him Chance instead of Chancellor, but he would admit hearing her say his proper name just now sounded damn good. "Go check it out for yourself."

She did, and he couldn't stop his gaze from roaming all over her while she did so. "Barbecue ribs and chicken, mac and cheese, potato salad, and chips. You've been busy, Mr. Madaris."

"I got up early. With Cate fixing many of my meals, I'd forgotten how much I'd enjoyed cooking."

She nodded and walked back to him. "I'll get the table on the patio ready."

"I'll help, but first, I need this," he said, pulling her into his arms.

The instant their lips touched, he felt something he hadn't felt in years—at peace. As if holding her in his arms was what he should be doing. Not just today but every day. The thought of that should have given him pause, but it didn't. Instead, he concentrated on her taste—sweet, delicious, and so damn hot.

He desired her and felt it in every part of his body, a need he was fighting to control but was finding it hard to do so. He was losing it in one delectable way. She moaned softly, and when she did, he lowered his hands to cup her bottom, gently squeezed it, and eased her more firmly to his middle. She responded, rising up on her tiptoes so he could deepen the kiss.

Chance did. Never had he kissed a woman with such intensity and passion. Those other times they'd kissed didn't count. This was the real deal, as real as it could get. He wondered if she remembered their agreement. She didn't engage in meaningless affairs, but he did. At least, he used to. He hadn't done so in seven months, and the idea of doing so again didn't appeal to him. And all because of her.

He finally ended their kiss and she smiled at him before he grabbed the basket and followed her to the patio.

Chapter Thirty-One

Zoey glanced across the table at Chance. Seeing him eat ribs was total arousal. He would hold the rib with his fingers while his mouth went to work, biting, chewing, licking, and then swallowing. Lordy, she was getting hot just watching him.

"Is something wrong, Zoey?"

Her gaze moved from his mouth to his eyes. "What makes you think that?"

"You're watching me eat."

She could tell him the truth but decided not to do so. "I can tell you're hungry."

"Am I eating too fast?"

Lordy, if he ate any slower, she would become a sensual basket case. "No. And there's nothing wrong with enjoying your food. I guess I'm not equipped to eat as much as you." Thinking of all the other things she figured he was equipped to do, certain parts of her got heated.

"The food is delicious, by the way."

"Thanks."

To get her mind off him and onto something she wanted to

talk to him about, she said. "I picked up the box from the post office yesterday."

He nodded, pushed his plate aside and wiped his fingers and mouth with a napkin. "Have you opened it yet?"

"Heavens yes. As soon as I got back here. I browsed the photo albums first. The one belonging to my parents was the most emotional. There were pictures of them on their wedding day, on vacations, and pictures of me when I was a baby, as well as numerous photos of the three of us and some with my grandparents."

She paused a moment and asked, "Do you know what saddens me more than anything, Chance? Knowing what might have happened to these albums and diaries had Sharon not gotten them for me."

He reached across the table and captured her hand in his. "But your mother's best friend did get them for you."

"Yes, she did and I will be forever thankful. I finished looking through the albums and I'm almost at the end of my great-grandmother's diary."

"Any revelations there?"

"Yes. Did you know there was a Satterfield and Madaris feud?"

"No, I didn't know that. Does that mean we're supposed to be enemies?" he asked grinning.

"Hmm, what do you think?" she asked, chuckling as well.

"I think they obviously got over it. If they didn't, that's too bad."

She nodded. "I have another question. Did you know that, before the feud, my great-grandfather Waylon had been engaged to your great-grandaunt Victoria Madaris?"

He lifted a brow. "No, I didn't know that either."

"Ms. Felicia told me about my great-grandparents but never mentioned anything about my great-grandfather Waylon having been engaged to her best friend."

"Why would she? If he fell in love and married someone else, there was no reason to mention it."

"But that's the thing, Chance. Waylon didn't fall in love with anyone else. He and my great-grandmother Deedra had a marriage of convenience."

His features showed his surprise. "Are you sure?"

"Yes. Deedra says so in her diary. She needed a husband so she wouldn't be pressured into marrying her deceased husband's brother, who was a real ass, and Waylon wanted to get married to move on with his life after Victoria ended their engagement. Waylon and Deedra were up-front and honest with each other. She told him she would always love her deceased husband and didn't have room in her heart for another man, and he told her he would always love Victoria. Deedra even made him promise that when she died, her remains would be returned to Laredo to be buried beside her first husband."

"And he agreed to do that?"

"In her diary, she wrote that he did and believed he would. He didn't marry Deedra for five years after Victoria left for Paris to attend nursing school. He hoped she would return and they would get back together, but that didn't happen."

Chance nodded. "I wonder what caused the feud in the first place." When she didn't say anything, he stared at her for a long time and added, "You know, don't you?"

There was a lot she knew about the Satterfield and Madaris feud, thanks to what Deedra had written in her diary. She also knew why Victoria and Waylon hadn't married. "Yes, I know, but if you want the full details, I suggest you talk to Ms. Felicia." Deciding to change the subject, she asked, "Are you ready to go canoeing after we clear off the table?"

He smiled at her, and she knew he was aware of what she'd done. "Yes, I'm ready."

Chance couldn't recall the last time he'd had so much fun with a woman. Granted, he had enjoyed himself that night dancing with Zoey, but today was different. The activities in-

cluded conversations on various topics. She told him about
Lucky and the Andres family and how they'd been there for
her while growing up in San Francisco. They talked about her
and Lucky's days in college, attending NYC, and her time in
medical school.

She also told him about her work as an orthopedic surgeon,
and he told her about his time in the military and the challenges of running a ranch. He'd even expounded on his part-
nership with his uncle Jake, which was one of the reasons his
ranch was so successful.

After a couple of hours canoeing on the lake, she changed
into jeans, and they rode the horses to the fruit grove. They
had gotten halfway there when it began raining and turned
back. After making sure the horses were okay in the barn, they
raced to the cabin.

Following her to the mudroom, she handed him some tow-
els. "Dry off well. I don't want you to catch pneumonia."

"Would it be okay to take these wet clothes off and toss them
in the dryer?" he asked, grinning.

She lifted her brow in a way he thought was cute. "And just
what will you wear while waiting for your clothes to dry?"

"I'll keep on my briefs. You're a doctor, so I'm sure you're
used to seeing half-naked male patients. And if you are inclined
to do so, you can strip down to your panties."

She grinned and said, "Maybe another time."

"Is that something I can look forward to, Zoey?" he asked,
easing closer to her.

He wasn't prepared when she eased closer as well. "You can
only look forward to us removing our clothes if you accept my
conditions, Chance."

He wasn't someone who easily accepted conditions; however, he was discovering he could be flexible when it came to
Zoey. "What are your conditions?"

"That your one-night-stand and one-and-done policy won't

apply to me. If we become involved, it has to be a summer fling."

His mind wasn't the only thing absorbing what she'd said, his entire body was—a spike of heat that had caught him low in the gut just now. "I thought you weren't into meaningless relationships."

"There won't be anything meaningless about it, trust me. What I said was that I don't sleep with men just to relieve sexual urges. It has to mean more than a tumble between the sheets."

"And you think a fling with me would mean more than a tumble between the sheets, Zoey?"

"Wouldn't it?"

He was smart enough to know one night with her would not be enough. But then he wasn't sure a short-term fling would either. He thought of how much he enjoyed being with her today, so he knew it wouldn't be all sex. He could see them doing fun things together. Things he hadn't allowed himself to do in years. "Yes. It would," he said.

"I'll be back in a minute."

He caught hold of her hand and immediately felt an awareness of her in every pore of his body. Deep in his gut he knew she'd felt it, too, the intense heat of attraction they shared.

"Where are you going?" he asked in a voice that he thought sounded deep and husky.

"To my bedroom to get out of these wet clothes."

"May I come with you?" he asked, still holding her hand and feeling the currents flowing between them.

"What about my conditions?"

"I accept them." He inched closer still, needing to feel her and wanting her to feel him. He reached up and raked his fingers through her wet hair. She was concerned about him catching pneumonia, and he was concerned about her catching it, too. He could feel her heat through her wet clothing, and a primitive force compelled him to want more.

Leaning in, he took her mouth with greed and hunger that rocked his bones, and she was returning his kiss as if she was all in, stroke for stroke. Following his lead, her tongue was showing just what it could do. It seemed he was tapping a hunger inside of her that had been dormant for a while. He had no problem unleashing it.

Her taste was delicious and unique. It made every part of him crackle with a need he hadn't felt before. He desperately tried to stay in control but felt his resolve weaken to a point he hadn't counted on. He deepened the kiss, and in a surprise move, she jumped his bones—literally.

Zoey wrapped her legs around him and clung to him like her life depended on it. He supported her hips, loving the feel of her breasts pressing into his chest. A rush of adrenaline with a huge dose of anticipation was driving him, and when he heard her moan his name, he nearly lost it.

He broke off the kiss and stared at her, staring into the most captivating pair of dark eyes he'd ever seen. And those curvy, full lips that were so damn desirable.

"Are you going to stand here and hold me like this, or will you take me where we both want to go, Chance?" she asked.

"I'm going to take you where we both want to go." He began moving, holding her tight while carrying her to the bedroom. When they reached their destination, he eased her to her feet, and they began quickly removing each other's clothing. When she was completely naked, his gaze roamed all over her. "You're beautiful, Zoey."

"So are you," she said, as her eyes scanned over him before leaning in for another kiss.

Chapter Thirty-Two

Zoey wasn't sure just what was happening to her. Never had she felt this electrified, emboldened, and out of control. Her brain was filling with all sorts of intimate, passionate, and arousing thoughts. Whenever he kissed her, it was as if he'd lit a powder keg between her legs. If he continued to take her mouth this way, she would incinerate. She knew the moment he'd eased her onto the bed and when his warm, hot, muscular body covered hers. Sensations swamped her body while, at the same time, sexual excitement curled in her stomach.

Suddenly, he broke off the kiss, leaned back, and stared at her as if seeing her for the first time. "Chance, is anything wrong?"

He reached out and cupped her face in his hands. "No, baby. Nothing is wrong." He kissed her again, taking her mouth like his need for survival depended on it. He released his hands from her face and began caressing every inch of her body. She particularly liked how he was fondling her breasts, making the nipples harden against his hand and mouth.

She couldn't stop her moans when he shifted his body to begin kissing a path down her stomach, and then his face was right there between her legs. She almost screamed at the first intimate touch of his tongue inside of her. She heard a clap of thunder, and rain was still coming down hard, but nothing could take her mind away from the way Chance was making love to her with his tongue. She fought back another scream when he clutched her hips to bring her more firmly against his mouth.

Her body came apart from top to bottom. Screaming his name, she surrendered her mind, body, and soul to the sensations that ripped through her almost nonstop. Never had she shared an orgasm this intense, one of this magnitude, that shook the very foundation this cabin was sitting on. It took a moment for her to breathe again. When she felt Chance ease from the bed, she opened her eyes and watched him get a condom from his wallet and sheath himself.

She'd never seen a man do that before and thought it was the most erotic thing to watch. His body was manly, and he was so muscular and well-endowed. She noticed a battle scar on his right hip and knew he had gotten it protecting his country. That made her proud of him.

Returning to bed, he drew her into his arms and kissed her in a way that had her panting. When he eased her back against the pillows, she reached out and rubbed her hands through the thick hair on his chest, loving the way it felt against her fingers. He leaned in and kissed her.

When he released her mouth, she said, "Your mouth is dangerous."

"Sweetheart, you haven't experienced anything yet. Like this, for instance."

He eased his body over hers and while staring deep into her eyes, he began entering her. She felt it, all of him—every swollen inch. When he began riding her easy at first, and then hard and fast, she wrapped her arms around him and hung on. She moaned his name when he leaned in and whispered words in her ear—words no man had ever said to her while making love. Hot words, sexy words, and naughty words.

She began losing herself in his words and his husky voice while saying them. Never had a man given her this much pleasure, where every hormone in her body, every cell, every pulse felt alive in a way they never had. She was filled with so much heat, so much desire, so much of Chance.

She couldn't help the way her hands glided up and down his masculine back while feeling every time he thrust hard, convinced she was about to draw her last breath. Then it happened, and she couldn't stop the scream that flowed from her lungs when so many sensations were shooting all through her womanly core.

"I need you to look at me, baby."

When her gaze locked on his, something happened. She wasn't sure exactly what. All she knew was she felt the connection and knew he did, too. Then she felt his muscles tighten, and his erection seemed to expand even more inside of her when he threw his head back and yelled her name. Not once, but twice. The nerves in her body sizzled, her brain raced, and her inner muscles continued to contract, trying to pull everything he had to give, and she willingly took.

As the storm raged outside, inside her bedroom, locked in each other's arms, they were determined to take each other to a place of excruciating pleasure. And they did. Over and over again.

The sun's rays slipped through the window blinds, and Chance came awake and immediately knew something was different. He was in bed with a woman curled in his arms. He'd awakened in such a position plenty of times, but never had doing so felt so right—like this was where he belonged.

The scent of their lovemaking lingered in the air, and he inhaled its essence. Last night had been wild...and it had touched him in a way no other lovemaking session had. This was the first time he'd thought of it as making love and not having sex. She wasn't a woman to just take to bed; she was a woman he could share a beer with, go dancing with, and have deep discussions with. She was also a great equestrian, making him believe the claim she'd learned to ride as a child. She was also a woman who wouldn't hesitate to give him hell if she felt it was warranted. She'd done it once, and there was no doubt she could and would do so again. He was all for it.

Zoey stirred in his arms, and he glanced down at her, wanting her to see him when she opened her eyes. She did, and the way her lips curved in a smile nearly took his breath away. He was no longer swamped with conflicting emotions and knew exactly what he wanted. When she eased up to offer her lips to him, he took her mouth with a pang of hunger and urgency he doubted he would ever get used to. Zoey Pritchard could rock his world. Instead of letting it be a turnoff, it was a turn-on.

Chance released her mouth, lay there, and held her because he thought the moment had called for him to do so. He wanted to do so. They had shared an extraordinary night, and he intended for them to have a similar day. "Hungry?"

She chuckled. "Why? Are you going to feed me?"

"Yes, at my place. The weather has cleared, and the sun is out. Maybe we can try our luck riding to the fruit grove, and you can spend the day with me. This is the third Sunday of the month, so Mom expects me to show up for dinner. I'd like you to come with me."

She pulled back. "Are you sure?"

"Positive."

She nibbled on her bottom lip. "What will they think?"

He reached out and caressed her cheek. "They will think I've come to my senses. They're already crediting you for making me want to live again."

"I can't take credit for that."

"Yes, you can." And he meant that more than she would ever know.

★ ★ ★

Later that night, when Zoey slid between the covers alone, she couldn't help but recall how her day had gone. They had made love again while their clothes were drying. Then they showered, got dressed, and rode the horses to his ranch. After feeding the horses, they went into his ranch house and prepared breakfast together. For a man who'd just told her last week that he didn't invite women to his home for a meal, he definitely didn't mind having her there a second time.

After breakfast, they saddled the horses and rode to the fruit grove. After picking plenty of grapes and other fruits, they returned to the cabin for lunch. He'd left and told her he would return in a few hours to take her to dinner. It was nice meeting his parents and grandparents.

It had been good seeing Reese and Kenna again, and she got to meet their adorable twins, Landon and London. She also met his brother Emerson and liked him immediately.

It was apparent his family was surprised when she walked in with him, but they'd made her feel right at home, and before long, she felt like part of the family. Chance would be leaving tomorrow to attend a special three-day meeting with the Texas Cattlemen's Club in Austin with his uncle Jake and brother Reese, and wouldn't be back until Thursday.

Keeping true to his word not to make their relationship just about sex, Chance had helped her wash the fruit and packaged it up. He would show her how to make wine from grapes next weekend. When she had walked him to the door, he had kissed her goodbye and left. And boy, what a kiss it had been.

Now she was in bed and ready to read the rest of her great-grandmother's diary. She anticipated meeting with Ms. Felicia on Tuesday. She had a lot of questions to ask; specifically, why she hadn't told her about Waylon's engagement to Victoria Madaris.

Chapter Thirty-Three

"I appreciate you taking me to the mall to pick up my knitting supplies, Zoey."

"I'm happy to do so. Thank you for agreeing to talk to me today instead of Thursday. I read my great-grandmother Deedra's diary, and I have some questions I need to ask."

When she arrived at Whispering Pines, Ms. Felicia said she needed to go into town and asked if Zoey would take her. Her son Jake was in Austin, and Diamond had left to take the kids to Jonathan and Marilyn's house to visit Justin and Lorren's kids, who were in town.

"Go ahead and ask your questions, dear."

"Thank you. Why didn't you tell me my great-grandfather Waylon had been engaged to Victoria Madaris? It was in Deedra's diary, along with why they married."

Ms. Felicia didn't say anything for a minute, and then she said. "I didn't think sharing that information with you was important. He and Deedra were married for fourteen years before she died."

"I know, but it was a sad situation for the both of them.

She never stopped loving her deceased husband, and he never stopped loving Victoria. Although Waylon and Victoria's story was told through Deedra, it was based on what he'd shared with her, and I could still feel the love he had for Victoria."

Ms. Felicia didn't respond for a moment, and then she said, "Yes, Waylon and Victoria loved each other very much, and the reason that caused their breakup was a tragedy. Victoria was my best friend since we were teens. I knew how much she loved Waylon, and keeping her father's promise, breaking up with Waylon, and leaving the country to get over him was hard on her. It nearly destroyed them both."

"Did she ever get over him?"

"No. Victoria lived in Paris for eight years, only coming home on occasion to see her parents and meet my babies. It seemed like I was having one every year. I think she would have made Paris her home if her uncle Quantum hadn't died. She brought his body home and decided to stay. However, instead of remaining in Houston, she left to work at a hospital in Ohio."

"My great-grandmother wrote about a time Waylon and Victoria saw each other when she returned home."

"Yes, I remember that day. It was at Ma Etta's funeral. Deedra attended the services with Waylon. Victoria, Milton, and I were standing together and talking when Waylon and Deedra approached us to offer their condolences. I believe Waylon wanted to talk to Victoria alone, but would not have disrespected his wife to do so. Deedra, being the kindhearted, loving, and understanding person she was, knew and understood her husband's heart. She surprised us all when she suggested to Waylon that he and Victoria probably had a lot to talk about as old friends. She gave them that time by holding a conversation with Milton and me while Victoria and Waylon stood under a huge tree in front of the church."

Zoey nodded. "She wrote in her diary that she did it because she understood true love, since she had experienced it herself.

And she also believed that no matter what, Waylon would honor his wedding vows."

"Like I said, your great-grandmother Deedra was a special woman and a good wife to Waylon, and he was a good husband to her. They were good for each other."

"My great-grandmother also wrote why they didn't live in the cabin he built—the same one I'm staying in now. He had built it with his own hands for him and Victoria, and he refused to share it with any other woman."

"Yes, Waylon was adamant about that. When he and Deedra married, they moved into the family house," Felicia said. "It worked out well since Mr. Kurt had taken ill. Penny was happy that Waylon was married to anyone other than Victoria."

"That is so sad, and it all started because of Charlotte Satterfield's lie. She was a mean and hateful person. I hope her sons and daughter didn't turn out like her."

"I know she had two sons, one from her husband and another from some man she took up with years later. What makes you think she had a daughter?"

"It was written in Deedra's diary. After Kurt Satterfield died, Penny felt emboldened to reach out to Charlotte without Waylon knowing it, although Deedra didn't think he would have cared one way or the other. He'd even tried reaching out to Charlotte himself, but she cursed him and said he hadn't stood for her with their father. He told Deedra that he had but it hadn't done any good. She didn't believe him."

Zoey continued after bringing the car to a stop at a traffic light. "Deedra further wrote that Penny had confided in her about Charlotte's daughter that she had from a man she met after her second divorce. She didn't want the baby and gave it to a couple who couldn't have children."

"I didn't know that," Ms. Felicia said in a low voice.

"I finished Deedra's diary yesterday and will start reading Arabella's tonight. It's almost three times the size of Deedra's."

She turned the car into the shopping center's parking lot. "That's the store over there, right?" she asked Ms. Felicia.

"Yes, dear. That's it. There's a nice café next door to the knit shop. They make the best sandwiches, if I must say so myself. If you're not in a hurry, maybe we can go there for lunch to finish our talk."

Zoey beamed. "I'd love to."

"Ms. Felicia. It's been a while."

Felicia Laverne gazed up from her meal. "Ravena. I heard you were back in Houston. Let me introduce my lunch companion, Dr. Zoey Pritchard." To Zoey she said, "This is Ravena Boyle. She used to be Chance's friend."

"I was more than a friend. I was Chance's fiancée," Ravena replied, narrowing her eyes and turning them to Zoey.

"Nice to meet you, Ravena," Zoey said, extending her hand.

Ravena did not accept Zoey's hand, saying, "I recall seeing you at Vance's Tavern a couple of weekends ago."

"Yes, you did," Zoey said, pulling back her hand since it was obvious Ravena wouldn't shake it.

"That's a lovely necklace you're wearing," Ravena said, sounding more like a sneer than a compliment.

"Thank you," was Zoey's cool response.

"I think I've seen that necklace before."

"Have you?" Zoey asked, looking back at her. Ravena was attractive, and she could see how Chance could fall in love with her. But the woman's attitude was deplorable.

"I doubt you've seen that necklace before, Ravena. It's a family heirloom. Now, if you don't mind, Zoey and I would like to finish our lunch."

"It might be some family heirloom, but I know who it originally belonged to. I understand it's one of Cox Jewelers custom design pieces."

"Is it?" Felicia Laverne asked, trying to sound uninterested.

"You know it is. Maybe I need to visit you, Ms. Felicia and refresh your memory. Which of your sons are you freeloading off this month?"

Zoey was out of her seat in a flash. "You are out of line and showing a lack of respect."

Felicia Laverne reached out and patted Zoey's hand. "Don't get upset on my behalf, dear. Ravena has never displayed any manners, which is why it was meant for her to never be a part of my family."

"I would have been if I hadn't left Chance. Now I am back, and he and I will get back together, regardless of whether you want me in your family or not." She shifted her gaze to Zoey. "Don't waste your time trying to get him interested in you because it won't happen." Ravena then turned and walked out of the café.

Zoey stared at the door the woman had walked out of before glancing at Ms. Felicia. "What was all that she was saying about my necklace?"

"She's just spouting off about stuff she knows nothing about. I never knew what Chance saw in that girl."

Zoey did. "He fell in love with her. When you truly love someone, you don't always see their faults."

Ms. Felicia stared at her for a moment, nodded and said, "You're probably right, dear."

"Mama Laverne?"

Felicia Laverne looked up from her knitting. "Yes, Diamond?"

"Alex is here to see you."

"Please send him in." Alexander Maxwell, a top-notch private detective, was married to her granddaughter, Christy.

"Mama Laverne, I got your voice mail message."

She placed her knitting aside. "Alexander, please have a seat."

The grin on his face meant he found her order amusing. "What can I do for you, Mama Laverne?"

"I'm sure you've heard about the young woman I'm meeting with to help restore her memory."

Alex grinned. "The one who's caught Chance's eye?"

She rolled her eyes. "Chance needs to keep his eyes to himself. The last thing Zoey needs is to involve herself with Chance's issues. Her focus should be on regaining her memory."

Alex leaned back in his chair and stretched his long legs before him. "If you called for me to do a background check on Dr. Zoey Pritchard, it's been done."

Felicia Laverne frowned. "Who asked you to do such a thing? Clayton?"

"No one asked me to do it. I hadn't met her and was curious. I haven't mentioned the report to anyone, not even Christy."

Felicia Laverne nodded. "That's not why I asked you here. There was nothing about Zoey I felt wasn't trustworthy. From your report, you know she was raised by her aunt after her parents' death."

"Yes, Paulina Pritchard."

"I want to know everything there is to know about the woman. For some reason, she didn't treat Zoey the way I think she should have, withholding information that might help her regain her memory. I have a gut feeling there was more to it than her not liking Zoey's mother."

"Anything else?"

"Yes, I ran into Ravena Boyle today, and she wasn't at all nice."

Alex sat up in his chair. "What do you mean she wasn't nice?"

Felicia told him about the incident with Zoey at the café.

"I take it you didn't tell your family about it?" Alex asked.

"No, and I asked Zoey not to mention anything about what Ravena said to Chance. Now I'm asking you not to mention anything to anyone either. You know how overprotective my family can be. Ravena's lack of manners doesn't concern me. What does concern me is the idea that she knows something about that necklace, Alexander. The one Zoey wears."

Alex appeared confused. "Is there something about the necklace I need to know?"

Felicia Laverne took a deep breath and said softly, "Spilling the tea about the family is difficult, Alexander. However, chances are you'll find out everything during your investigation since you're known to be thorough. I'm the only living soul who knows what I'm about to tell you, and depending on what you find out, I will decide what I need to tell the family."

Zoey placed the diary aside when her phone rang. It was Chance. She was hoping he would call. "Hello."

"I miss you."

Chance's words gave her pause. She doubted he knew how much they meant to her, especially after meeting his ex-girlfriend today, who'd let it be known she wanted him back and planned to get him. "I missed you, too."

"That's good to hear, baby. How did your meeting with Mama Laverne go today?"

"Fine. I took her to the knit shop for yarn and supplies. Then we had lunch at the café next door. It was nice spending time with her." Should she mention anything about meeting Ravena? She'd promised his great-grandmother she wouldn't tell him what was said but there was no reason not to mention meeting his ex-fiancée.

"I met Ravena Boyle today."

He didn't say anything and she wondered if he'd heard her. She was about to repeat her words when he asked, "Where did the two of you meet?"

"At the café where Ms. Felicia Laverne and I had lunch. She came to our table, and your great-grandmother introduced us."

"I see. Did Mama Laverne answer all your questions about your great-grandfather Waylon and my great-grandaunt Victoria?"

He'd deliberately moved their discussion from Ravena. Why? "Yes, and it was like you said. She hadn't mentioned it because she hadn't felt it was necessary to do so. It was before my great-grandparents had married, and although Waylon and Deedra didn't love each other, they made their marriage work."

"Did you finish reading Deedra's diary?"

"Yes, and tonight I started on Arabella's. Already I see she was a daddy's girl. The two of them were extremely close. So, how is your meeting going?"

"It's going well. Uncle Jake will be the keynote speaker tomorrow."

They talked for a few minutes longer and ended the call with him—in his sexiest voice—telling her to dream about him. She replied in kind. "Trust me, Chance, I will."

Chapter Thirty-Four

"I am glad you're having more flashbacks, Zoey. Hopefully, in time, your entire memory will return."

"I'm hoping that, too, Lucky." She eased from the sofa and gazed out the window. There was a splendid view of the lake to her left and a wide-open plain to her right. "I love this cabin. And knowing my great-grandfather built it with his own hands for Victoria, the woman he loved, makes it special."

"So, what do you have planned, Zoey?"

Zoey lifted a brow as she walked to the kitchen to check on dinner. "Planned for what?"

"Chance's homecoming. You did say he would be back to-morrow, right?"

"Yes. Am I supposed to have something planned?"

"Men like welcome-home sex. Just ask Burke."

Zoey laughed. "I won't ask Burke any such thing. I'll take your word for it."

"So, are you going to do it, Zoe?"

"Of course not. What you're suggesting is totally not me."

★ ★ ★

The next morning, upon waking, Zoey lay there and thought about the parts of Arabella's book she'd read last night before dozing off to sleep. Her first week at the all-girls school had been difficult. Some girls were mean to her and made fun of her Southern accent. She'd called her father and threatened to run away if he didn't come and take her home.

Waylon came but did not take her home. He took her to dinner instead and they talked for a long time. He assured her that going to this school was good for her to become the lady her mother would have wanted her to be and that he would never desert her. He looked forward to those times when she would come home, and he would come to see her when he could get away from the ranch. On that day, he told her how important she was to him and that she was the pride of his life. Arabella said she had cried that night because she'd gone to bed knowing how much her father loved her.

Zoey cried reading it. She wanted to believe that she and her father also had a special relationship, that she'd been important to him, and that she'd been the pride of Holton Prichard's life. It was those times she wished she could remember her parents and the good times she believed they had together.

Pulling herself up in bed, she looked out the window, and suddenly she had another flashback. This one was her parents taking her for a walk around the lake.

The flashbacks were becoming more frequent now and always something different. She was happy about that and would be happier seeing Chance today. He'd called last night to say he would be returning home around six.

Before leaving for Austin, he had surprised her when he'd given her the key to his home. That was a giant step for a man who didn't typically invite women to his house.

"What do you have planned, Zoey?"

Lucky's question from yesterday came back to her. Just like Chance had done something that was not the norm for him, maybe she should do the same. She smiled, deciding that yes, she would. Her smile deepened when she thought of a plan. One she would execute with plenty of love. *Love?* Yes, love. She knew at that very moment that she had fallen in love with Chancellor Madaris.

Chance entered his home and immediately knew Zoey had been there. Her scent lingered in the air, and he enjoyed inhaling it. Suddenly, he heard a sound and turned around.

"Welcome home, Chance."

A degree of joy that he felt curved his lips, and he immediately became aroused. This was his home, his sanctuary, his private space. And he couldn't be happier that she was here sharing it with him, and damn, she looked good. She was wearing a cute short red dress that stopped midthigh with spaghetti straps that tied at the shoulders. The cut of the cleavage showed what some might consider an indecent amount of breast.

And he loved it.

"Doctor Prichard, are you making house calls now?" he asked, dropping his duffel bag and placing his Stetson on the rack before slowly walking toward her.

"Only for you, Rancher Madaris."

He threw his head back and laughed when he stopped before her. "The doctor and the rancher has a nice ring to it," he said.

Needing to touch her, he reached out and cupped her face. Then he leaned in and kissed her. Heat curled inside him when their lips touched, and he removed his hands from her face and wrapped them around her waist. He'd been hungry for the taste of her for days. He had missed her every minute of that time.

This was definitely a homecoming kind of kiss, and he relished it as a rush of desire clawed away at his insides. And the way her tongue was dueling with his was as raw as it was seductive. He was making love to her mouth in a way he intended to do with her body later, but for now, he needed this. The very essence of what was truly Zoey.

Breaking off the kiss, he drew a ragged breath and rested his forehead against hers. "Baby, you're almost too much."

"No, Chance. You are. Are you ready for dinner? I prepared a casserole."

"Dinner can wait. I am ready for you."

He swept her off her feet, into his arms, and headed up the stairs.

The last time, they had undressed each other in a heated rush. This time, Zoey was determined to take things slow and make it a night they would both remember. That was the plan. "I want to undress you, Chance."

"Will I get to undress you?" he asked in that deep, husky voice that she loved hearing.

"Of course."

"Then have at it, sweetheart."

While standing there in his Western attire, looking sexier than any cowboy had a right to look, she could feel sensual vibes pouring off him. She was being consumed, drowning in all that was him.

Now to start removing his clothes. She went first for his shirt and began unbuttoning it. Her heart skipped a beat with every button she unfastened. He leaned in and whispered something in her ear, and his seductive words nearly made her lose it.

After tossing aside his shirt, she eased the belt from the loops of his jeans. "Have I ever told you how much I like your chest?"

Chance grinned. "No, but I'm sure I've *shown* you how much I like yours."

He had, and she doubted her breasts would ever be the same. He had branded them with both his hands and his mouth. "I need you to take off your boots."

"No problem," he said, easing down on the edge of the bed to do so. When he stood, she immediately went to the zipper of his jeans and eased it down. With a couple of tugs and a little help from him, she finally got everything off, and he stood naked. On impulse, she moved closer and slid her arms around him, loving the feel of his muscled back.

"Now I do you, Zoey."

His throaty words caused a slow roll in her stomach, and she thought he could do her anytime and anywhere. With the expertise he seemed to own, he untied the straps at her shoulders before she caught her next breath, and her dress fell at her feet, leaving her in a strapless bra and barely-there panties—a matching red set. From the hot look in his eyes, he obviously liked what he saw.

Holding her gaze, he unhooked the front clasp of her bra, setting her breasts free. His gaze latched on to the twin mounds before leaning in to capture a swollen nipple in his mouth. She got weak in the knees and appreciated the strong arms he wrapped around her.

"Chance…" She moaned his name when he went to the other nipple, and she could feel her panties wet.

He released her nipple to stare at her. "Tell me what you want, Doctor."

"I want you, rancher."

He grinned. "Baby, you are about to get me."

Chance knelt to remove her panties, licking his way down as he went. He leaned back on his haunches and roamed her body from head to toe, becoming more aroused. She was beautiful. His gaze returned to her center, and he wanted to taste her but wanted to connect their bodies more.

Sweeping her in his arms, he placed her on the bed and then grabbed a condom from his wallet, knowing she watched his every move as he rolled it on. She extended her arms when he returned to the bed, and he went into them without pause.

She smiled when he straddled her and leaned in for another kiss, crushing his mouth to hers. He liked how she clung to him as if he was the only man she wanted. When she arched her hips, he knew what she needed, which was the same thing he did.

Spreading her legs with his knees without disjoining their mouths, he entered her. Immediately, he felt the pull of her feminine muscles to his engorged shaft, and it was sending him over the edge. The intensity of how he felt while making love to her should have given him pause. Instead, he began stroking her in and out while she lifted her hips in sync with his movements. Chance shivered at the sensations he was feeling. His body felt on fire as she clung to his shoulders, arching eagerly to meet his next thrust. She was pure energy in his arms, and he loved it.

He broke off the kiss, immediately caught between a sigh and a moan. The way she was moving with him was filling him with all kinds of emotions. He felt her climax building, and so was his. When he felt her tremors at the same time that she screamed his name, he met her gaze and a bolt of ecstasy lanced through him. Throwing his head back, he hollered her name while his body exploded and shook from the magnitude of his release. He trailed kisses along the side of her neck as shudders of the most intense kind wracked his body, leaving him unable to do anything but succumb to the earth-shattering pleasures she had given him.

Chapter Thirty-Five

The following three weeks seemed to fly by for Chance and Zoey. Chance spent days on the range and Zoey spent her days doing a multitude of things. In addition to her meetings with Ms. Felicia, Zoey had been invited to lunch with Syneda, where she met several wives of Ms. Felicia's sons and grandsons.

Zoey also met all of Ms. Felicia's sons when she attended the Madaris Family Reunion held on Whispering Pines at the end of July. It was good seeing Corbin again and meeting some of the other cousins. He'd been right. They all favored one another. All handsome. She'd also met Victoria and Lindsay and both were extremely friendly.

Zoey spent a lot of time riding around the property to get more pictures. She especially liked spending time in the fruit grove. There was something peaceful and tranquil about it. Chance had shown her how to make wine and had set up a place for her inside the barn. One day, while in the fruit grove picking more grapes, she'd come across the tomb Chance had told her about—where Victoria Madaris had been laid to rest.

It was a beautifully structured building of high-quality white stone with a French design. It was larger than she expected, with a dome at the top. The grounds it sat on were immaculate with a lovely mixture of flowers. Chance had been right; the tomb's location gave it the appearance of looking out over the entire fruit grove.

She and Chance had been spending a lot of time together. They dined together in the evenings and, at night, shared the same bed, whether it was at the cabin or his ranch house. He had taught her how to play pool. He'd also taught her how to fish and operate a Jet Ski. Due to all her activities, she hadn't spent as much time reading Arabella's diary as she'd have liked. When she and Chance were together, she preferred giving him most of her attention.

She checked her watch. Tonight they would enjoy dancing at Vance's Tavern. This would be the first time they went out as a couple. Her memories were returning more frequently, and her therapist thought that was a good thing. Dr. Cosby suggested whatever she was doing to unwind and relax, to continue to do so since it was working. Of course, she didn't tell him that she was doing Chance and had no plans to stop.

It was close to eight when they entered Vance's Tavern, and it seemed all eyes were on them. He had warned her they would be since it had been years since he'd come there with a woman instead of coming to seek one out. The dance floor was full, but that hadn't stopped Chance from finding a spot to hold her in his arms to a slow song. They joined in several of the line dances, and Chance commented on how well she danced for an Easterner. She reminded him that Texas blood did run in her veins, and tonight, she felt like a true Texas cowgirl.

She was enjoying herself and anticipated tonight when they would sleep in her bed or his. They had made plans for the weekend. He would help her make more wine tomorrow, and then they would take the canoe out on the lake. On Sunday, she was invited to Whispering Pines to celebrate Jake and Diamond's daughter Amethyst's birthday with the Madaris family.

She had excused herself to go to the restroom. When she came out of the stall, the woman she remembered as Chance's ex-fiancée, Ravena, was leaning about the bathroom door as if she'd been waiting on her.

"Hello, Ravena," Zoey said, washing her hands at the sink. She felt unfriendly vibes radiating from the woman.

"You honestly think Chance wants you?"

Drying her hands with a paper towel, Zoey decided Ravena's question didn't warrant a response. "I refuse to discuss my and Chance's relationship with you."

"I don't care if you do or not. I find it funny that you're getting played by the entire Madaris family, especially that old biddy, Felicia."

Zoey crossed her arms over her chest. "And just how am I getting played?" Since the woman was blocking the door and seemed intent not to move, Zoey figured she'd let her have her say.

"That necklace you're wearing. I bet you don't know who it originally belonged to."

She recalled Ravena making a similar assertion a few weeks ago when Zoey was having lunch with Ms. Felicia. "Yes, I do. It once belonged to my grandmother Arabella."

Ravena laughed. When her laughter subsided, she said, "It originally belonged to your great-grandfather Waylon Satterfield's lover, who was none other than Victoria Madaris. He bought it for her while he was still married to your great-grandmother."

"That's not true."

"It is true."

"I know all about Waylon's engagement to Victoria Madaris *before* he married my great-grandmother, Deedra. However, once they married, he was faithful to her."

A sneer appeared on the woman's face. "Are you sure of that? I got it on good account—namely the jeweler who handcrafted the necklace years ago for Waylon Satterfield. Granted, he's an old man now, but he recalled it was years after Waylon Satterfield got married. That meant that Waylon and Victoria were having an affair—behind Deedra's back, and Felicia Madaris knew about it. I bet the old biddy was the one who made all the secret arrangements for them to be together. Just imagine her smiling in your great-grandmother's face while betraying her behind her back."

"I don't believe you."

"If you don't believe me then ask that old biddy, Felicia." Ravena then opened the door and left.

Zoey leaned against the sink. Was any of what Ravena had said true? The necklace belonged to Arabella, and she'd been wearing it in that portrait. How would Arabella have gotten it if it had once belonged to Victoria Madaris? Had Waylon broken the promise that he and Deedra had made to each other about keeping their marriage vows sacred despite not being in love?

Zoey took a deep breath, knowing she needed time to think and couldn't do it here. Leaving the lady's room, she went to where Chance was waiting for her. He frowned when he saw the look on her face. "Zoey, what's wrong?"

"Please take me home, Chance. I need to go back to the cabin?"

"Why?" he asked, standing. "What's wrong?"

Instead of answering, Zoey turned and walked out of the tavern.

"Will you tell me why you're upset, Zoey? What happened in that bathroom?" Chance asked, pulling his truck out of the parking space.

"Ravena happened."

He put on the brakes. He hadn't known Ravena was there. "What the hell did she say to you?"

"It's a matter of what she told me. She claims my great-grandfather and your great-grandaunt were having an affair while he was married to Deedra. She also said Ms. Felicia befriended my great-grandmother while covering for them."

"That's bullshit, and you know it."

"Do I, Chance? Do you? Ravena says she has proof that the necklace I'm wearing was a gift Waylon gave Victoria while married to Deedra."

"Then how did your grandmother Arabella get it? She's wearing it in that picture."

"I don't know, Chance."

"The one thing I know about Mama Laverne is that she is a God-fearing woman who strives only to do good and will help those she can. You're proof of that. She's not perfect, but she would never do what Ravena has accused her of doing."

"Right now, I'm confused. When Ms. Felicia and I ran into Ravena at that café, she mentioned something about my necklace. Although she tried not to show it, I could tell your great-grandmother had been rattled by the comment. I have a gut feeling that your great-grandmother is keeping something about this necklace from me, Chance, and I don't know what it is."

Chance felt himself getting angry. "Mama Laverne has only been kind and open with you, Zoey. This is how you repay her? By believing Ravena's lies?"

"I didn't say I believed her. I need to think about what she said."

"You wouldn't have anything to think about unless you believe it's true."

"That's not fair, Chance."

"It's a fair assessment to me, and until you can wrap your head around what's true and what's not, I suggest you separate yourself from me and my family."

"What do you mean?"

"Just what I said. Ravena is trying to place a wedge in the relationship you've developed with my family. It's the kind of relationship that, even as my fiancée, she never had. I don't know what's happened to her over the years, but now she's vindictive and manipulating. Maybe she was that way all along, but because I was away in the military, I didn't see it. Nevertheless, it sounds like you've chosen your side and I'd prefer not discussing the issue any longer."

"Chance, I—"

"No, Zoey. I don't want to hear anything else about it."

He was glad she didn't say anything during the remainder of the ride. When they got to the cabin, he walked her to the door, made sure she was safe inside, and left. He didn't kiss her goodbye, or mention their plans for tomorrow. As far as he was concerned, they didn't have plans for tomorrow or any days after that.

When Chance left, Zoey immediately felt a deep sense of loss. He was right to be upset and protective of his great-grandmother, but like she told him, she had a gut feeling there was something about her necklace that Ms. Felicia was deliberately keeping from her.

After dressing for bed, Zoey picked up Arabella's diary from the nightstand.

Needing answers and hoping Arabella's diary gave them to her, she skipped the pages to when Arabella was seventeen. That would have been five years after Deedra's death. As Zoey settled in bed, she read the entry written on Arabella's seventeenth birthday.

Pa came to celebrate my birthday with me today. I knew he would since he's never missed doing so. I could tell there was something on his mind, but I wanted him to tell me what it was when he was ready. Today, he seemed to be in a much happier mood. I want so much happiness for my pa. A part of him always seemed sad, and I know why.

He doesn't know that I read Ma's diary. I remember as a little girl, she would often write in it. I knew where she kept it, and the last time I went home, I took it back to Virginia with me and began reading it. It was a shocker to discover my parents never loved each other. However, over the years, they developed a true friendship.

That's probably why it was no surprise when Pa finally got around to telling me what he wanted me to know. A woman he was once engaged to marry, Victoria Madaris, had moved back to Houston to help care for her ailing father. He said he hadn't seen her in years since she had lived in Ohio. Pa wanted me to know he'd begun seeing her again.

Since I've never been able to keep anything from Pa, including my crush on Jonathan, I told him about Ma's diary and that I understood and would be happy if he and Victoria Madaris rekindled their love. She never married, and he'd been a widower for five years, so there should not be a big deal about it.

He told me there would be a big deal with Gramma Penny, who despised the Madarises. Currently, he and Victoria saw each other in private so as not to upset his ma. It was Victoria's idea that they do things that way, not his. As far as he was concerned, they were adults, and after all this time, he didn't care who knew. I told him to do whatever made him happy since Gramma Penny would never change. She had grown into a bitter old woman and should not dictate his happiness. We hugged, and I told Pa if being with Victoria Madaris made him happy, then I was happy for the both of them.

Zoey wiped tears from her eyes. Like her mother Deedra, Arabella possessed a heart full of love. Waylon and Victoria hadn't been involved in an affair and only began seeing each other *after* Deedra's death. Five years after, in fact. Ravena had lied. Chance was right. There had been no reason to consider that Ravena had been telling the truth.

Zoey rubbed her hand down her face knowing she had screwed up big-time. Not only had she lost Chance but probably the entire Madaris family.

Chapter Thirty-Six

Felicia Laverne awakened to a new day. After getting dressed she would see if Diamond needed help with Amethyst's birthday party tomorrow.

She was about to grab her robe off the chair when her cell phone rang. Each of her grands and great-grands had their own special ringtone. "Good morning, Chancellor."

"Mama Laverne, you need to stop meeting with Zoey."

She raised a brow. "Why?"

"We went dancing last night and Ravena waited for her in the bathroom and told her lies. Lies that upset Zoey so much, she asked me to take her home to think about whether there was any merit to what Ravena had said."

Felicia Laverne didn't say anything for a minute, then she asked, "And just what were these lies?"

"She told Zoey that her great-grandfather Waylon and my great-grandaunt Victoria were involved in an affair while he was married to Deedra, and you covered for them. Not only that, but he gave Aunt Victoria that necklace while still married to Deedra."

Felicia Laverne felt a slight kick in her gut. "None of that is true."

"That's what I told Zoey, but she said she needed to think about it. There's nothing to think about, and she should know that."

"And why should she know that, Chancellor?"

"She knows you."

Felicia Laverne shook her head. "She is *getting* to know me. Put that Madaris pride aside a moment and think about it. Zoey had an aunt she trusted for twenty years, and in the end, she found out how that aunt had deceived her. Trusting someone and taking things at face value won't be easy for Zoey. I understand that, and considering all she's been through, I'd think you, a man who loves her, would do that, too."

"I don't love her."

"Poppycock. The reason why I haven't taken you to task for doing something I explicitly told you not to do—mainly to not get involved with Zoey—is because I realized you had fallen for her. And she's right. There is something about that necklace that I should have told her. I'm getting dressed. Come pick me up."

"And take you where?"

"To the cabin to meet with her."

Alex Maxwell read the last of his final report. One thing he knew never to do was second-guess Mama Laverne's gut instincts about anything. He couldn't believe everything he had uncovered. There was one more piece of the puzzle he needed solved, and was waiting for a call from a friend he'd worked with years ago as an FBI agent, Joe Alum.

His phone rang and he quickly picked it up. "What do you have for me, Joe?"

Zoey awakened early that morning and went to the barn to make wine, intent on staying busy. She had tried calling

Chance, but he wasn't taking her calls, and she couldn't blame him for not doing so. She had read a lot of Arabella's diary, which revealed a number of things, including how her grandmother Arabella became the owner of the necklace Waylon had given Victoria.

Zoey had just finished weighing the grapes when she heard a truck pull up and knew it was Chance. Placing the grapes aside, she walked to the open barn door to see Chance and Ms. Felicia. The smile on the older woman's face gave Zoey hope. The deep frown on Chance's did not.

"Good morning," she greeted both.

"Good morning," Felicia Laverne said, reaching out to hug her. A scowling Chance said nothing. He stood with his legs braced apart, and arms folded over his chest.

"I think we should talk, dear," Ms. Felicia said. She then turned to Chance. "Leave us, Chancellor. Come back in an hour."

Zoey watched as Chance hesitated momentarily, and his scowl deepened before getting into his truck to leave.

"We can go inside the cabin to talk," Zoey suggested.

"No, I don't want to interrupt whatever you were doing in the barn."

"I was making wine. Chance showed me how and set up a small area with the equipment for me."

"That was kind of him."

"Yes, it was." She offered Ms. Felicia her arm and they walked to the barn and went inside. Zoey offered her a seat at one of the portable tables, then she asked, "Do you want anything to drink? I have bottled water in that mini fridge."

"Yes, bottled water would be nice," Felicia Laverne said.

Zoey got one for her and grabbed one for herself. After taking a swallow, Felicia Laverne said, "You are right, dear. There is something about your necklace that I should have told you. I spent a lot of time wondering how and when I would. There was a time I thought I wouldn't have to, but I've discovered I was wrong, and I hope you will forgive me for that." She paused for a moment and then said, "The most important thing you should know is that Waylon Satterfield was honorable. At no time was he unfaithful to Deedra, although he did love Victoria until the day he died."

Zoey reached across the table and took Ms. Felicia's hand in hers. "I know that now. I read Arabella's diary last night and—"

Suddenly, the barn door slammed shut. Zoey stood, certain it couldn't have been the wind. "That's odd." Walking to the door to reopen it, she discovered it was locked from the other side. "What in the world?"

"What is it, dear?" Ms. Felicia asked.

"Someone locked us in here." Sniffing the air, she said, "And I smell kerosene."

Jake Madaris picked up on the second ring. "Hello, Alex? What's going on?"

"I was trying to reach Mama Laverne, but she's not answering her phone."

"She isn't here. Chance dropped her off at Trevor's cabin to meet with Zoey. You know how bad the reception is out there at times."

"Jake, listen carefully. There's a chance your mother's and Zoey's lives might be in danger."

"What the hell?!" Jake said loudly.

"Uncle Jake? What's wrong?" a number of male voices asked simultaneously.

"Alex, I'm putting you on speaker phone. Several nephews are here helping me put up this bounce house for Amethyst's party. Why do you think Mama and Zoey's lives might be in danger?" he asked as his long strides took him to his truck with his nephews on his heels.

"It's something I came across in an investigation Mama Laverne asked me to do."

"An investigation on who?"

"I can't say right now, Jake. Just get to the cabin to make
sure they're alright."

Jake disconnected the call as they crowded into his truck.
"Corbin, call Chance. He's a lot closer to the cabin than we are."

Corbin nodded. "I already have."

"Unlock this door!" Zoey yelled at the top of her voice.

"I won't unlock it!" a feminine voice called back. "This is
my lucky day. I'll get rid of two birds with one stone."

Zoey recognized the voice. *Ravena.* "Ravena, you have no
right to be on this property."

"I have every right. This land should have been mine, and
it will be mine once I get rid of the two of you."

Zoey frowned. "What are you talking about?"

"I'm talking about how Waylon Satterfield let his parents
banish his sister from this land. I promised my grandmother
before she died that I would seek revenge."

Zoey's gaze slid to Ms. Felicia, who seemed just as confused by Ravena's statement as she was. "Who was your grandmother?" Zoey then asked Ravena.

"My grandmother was Wanda Hagan, the daughter of Charlotte Satterfield. Gramma Wanda raised me when my mother
died of a drug overdose. Charlotte told my grandmother everything. Namely, what the Satterfields and the Madarises had
done to her."

A shocked Zoey looked at Ms. Felicia and asked in a low
voice. "Is Ravena insinuating we're cousins?"

Before Ms. Felicia could respond, Ravena began speaking
again. "I thought I had everything worked out when I got engaged to Chance according to plan. My first goal—to seek revenge for what the Satterfield and Madaris family did to my

great-grandmother Charlotte when they ran her out of Texas. Once Chance and I got married and while he was away in the military, I was to get rid of his great-grandmother Felicia Laverne by making it look like an accident. But when Chance nearly got himself blown up playing soldier and returned home in a wheelchair, I decided I wasn't so desperate for revenge that I'd marry an invalid."

Ravena began laughing and the sound grated on Zoey's nerves. Pulling her phone from her jeans, Zoey tried calling the police but couldn't get a connection. Turning to Ms. Felicia, she said in a low voice, "I can't call out on my phone. See if you can." Zoey intended to keep Ravena talking until help arrived.

"Then, before my Gramma Wanda died last year, she found out Chance could walk again and that he had bought the Satterfield land," Ravena said. "Can you believe that? That's when I promised Gramma Wanda on her deathbed that I would return to Texas and rekindle my romance with Chance, get rid of both him and his great-grandmother, and as his widow, reclaim the Satterfield land. What I hadn't counted on Zoey, was you getting in the way. When I discovered your identity and that we were related and could stand in the way of me not only getting the land but getting Chance back, I placed you at the top of my kill list."

Ms. Felicia got Zoey's attention to indicate that her phone wasn't connecting either. Trying not to panic, Zoey quickly walked to the table and said, "Chance should be on his way back."

Ms. Felicia gently patted her hand. "No worries, dear," she said calmly. "I have this." She showed Zoey her medical alert necklace before pressing it.

Chance had parked his truck a half mile from the cabin and walked while texting Corbin. When he told them of the strong smell of kerosene in the air and what he figured Ravena intended to do, Jake devised a plan. Since Ravena had been yelling at Zoey through the barn door, Chance had heard everything. All the details of her sordid plans, including the reason she'd wanted to marry him in the first place.

When he heard her say to Zoey, "I'm through talking," and she pulled a book of matches from her shirt pocket, he knew that he had to make his presence known. He texted Corbin. **Moving in.**

"Ravena! What are you doing here?" he asked.

She snatched her head around. "Chance, I didn't hear your truck."

"I rode my horse," he lied, approaching her slowly. "I wanted to see if Mama Laverne and Zoey wanted lunch."

A smirk appeared on her face. "They won't be needing lunch where they are going."

"What do you mean?" he asked, knowing he needed to keep her talking to give Jake time to put his plan into action. "And you didn't answer my question about why you're here."

"I came to take care of business," she said.

"And what business could you possibly have here?"

"Don't come any closer, Chance. Just so you know, I've doused kerosene all around this barn, and I plan to burn it down with them in it."

He crossed his arms over his chest. "Why would you want to do something like that?"

She threw her head back and laughed. "You're a fool, Chance. I never loved you. Marrying you was all a part of the plan." And then he stood there while she gleefully told him the same things she'd told Zoey earlier. He listened, hoping Jake, his brothers, and cousins were getting Zoey and Mama Laverne out of the barn.

"Chance is here," Zoey whispered to Mama Laverne after placing her ear to the barn door. "Ravena is telling him what she said earlier about why she planned to marry him, and why she came back. That has to be hard for him to hear."

Felicia Laverne stood. "Chancellor can handle it." Checking her watch, she then said, "Jake should have arrived by now."

No sooner had she said that, a portion of the barn's back wall was removed, and Jake Madaris, bigger than life, stood there. Without saying anything, he rushed in with seven of his nephews. He swept his mother into his arms and instructed his nephews to bring out the Jet Skis, dirt bikes and anything else that might be filled with fuel.

Corbin took hold of Zoey's hand. "Come on. I'm not sure how long Chance can keep Ravena talking before she torches this place."

Everyone was a safe distance from the barn when the sound of sirens could be heard.

Ravena heard the sirens and glared at Chance. "You're going to wish you hadn't done that." Before he could rush over to stop her, she lit a match and tossed it on the rags she had put near the barn's entrance. Because of the amount of kerosene she had used, the structure quickly went up in flames. He grabbed for Ravena when she stumbled back too close to the fire and part of her shirt caught fire. Chance rolled her to the ground to keep her from burning. He was glad when the police officers arrived, along with the fire truck and paramedics.

While the officers handcuffed Ravena, Chance stood and searched the crowd for Zoey and his great-grandmother. Seeing his brother Emerson, he asked, "Where are they?"

"They're near Jake's truck, which is parked not far from yours."

Chance took off running. His great-grandmother was sitting in Jake's truck and Zoey was standing in a group surrounded by his cousins. Coming up behind her, he swept her off her feet and into his arms. "Excuse us for a minute," he said to his cousins. Then, with her in his arms, he walked over to his un-cle's truck. "You're okay, Mama Laverne?" he asked.

"Yes, Chancellor, I'm fine. Glad to be alive."

His gaze shifted to his uncle. "Thanks, Uncle Jake."

"No thanks needed, Chance."

He nodded, shifted his gaze back to Mama Laverne and said, "You were right." He figured she knew what he was talking about. Mainly his true feelings for Zoey.

He carried Zoey a distance away from the crime scene before placing her on her feet. Before she could say anything, his mouth came down on hers.

Chance was kissing her hard, and Zoey kissed him back when it hit her just how close she'd come to dying—the second time in twenty years.

When Chance finally released her mouth, he wrapped his arms around her and whispered, "I thought I was going to lose you both."

Zoey had thought the same and was grateful that she and Ms. Felicia Laverne had been rescued in the nick of time. Once the entire building had quickly gone up in flames, there was no way they would have survived.

She reached up and cupped Chance's face. "And I thought I had lost you after last night. I'm so sorry for jumping to the wrong conclusions, Chance. I'm also sorry Ravena wasn't who you thought she was. I can't believe she and I are related."

"I can't believe what happened all those years ago…caused so much hate to fester. That is truly sad," he said.

He leaned in and kissed her again until the sound of some-one clearing their throat intruded. They broke off the kiss and saw Corbin. He was grinning. "The police want the two of you for statements. They are talking to Mama Laverne now. Dex called Trevor to tell him about the barn and that we got most of the stuff out in time. Did you know Trev intended to sell the cabin, and Mama Laverne told him to make sure you had first dibs?"

Chance chuckled. "No, I didn't know. But then it makes sense for me to own it since it was originally a part of the Satterfield homestead. Where's Ravena?"

"Being checked by the paramedics for her burns, and then she's going to jail."

"Good."

"And before you two get lost," Corbin said, "Mama Laverne has called a special family meeting at Whispering Pines in an hour—as she put it—to start spilling the Madaris tea."

"That ought to be interesting," Chance said.

"It's not as interesting as Jake and Uncle Jonathan trying to talk their oldest four brothers to turn over their shotguns to them. They just arrived ready to kick ass at the thought of anyone messing with their mama."

Chance rolled his eyes. "They shouldn't be running around with loaded shotguns."

"If you ask me," Corbin said, "those four will seize any opportunity to revert back to their hell-raising ways."

Knowing his grandfather Lucas was in the mix, Chance had to agree.

Chapter Thirty-Seven

Felicia Laverne took a sip of her tea while glancing around the living room. Her sons, grands, great-grands, and their spouses were all present to hear what she had to say. The murder attempt on her and Zoey's lives had them demanding to know why Chance's ex-fiancée had tried killing them.

She saw Zoey was sitting close to Chance. His arms were wrapped protectively around her shoulders. Felicia Laverne suspected there would be another Madaris wedding soon. This would be one love match she hadn't orchestrated. However, she was convinced her beloved Milton, Waylon, and Victoria had. Undoubtedly, the three felt it was time to end the Satterfield and Madaris feud once and for all.

"What I'm about to tell you are things that happened in this family years ago, and how that history has become tied to the present," she said, getting everyone's attention. "I had assumed I would take this story to the grave with me, but that won't be the case." After taking another sip of her tea, she said, "First, I must tell you about the Madaris Scandal."

Milton Madaris Jr., her firstborn, who felt he had a right to know everything about the family said, "I never knew about any Madaris Scandal."

"It was before you were born, Milton," she said.

"Oh."

Felicia Laverne then told everyone about Milton Sr.'s close friendship with Waylon Satterfield. Everybody listened, and no one asked questions. She told them of Charlotte's lie and how it tore the two families apart. She shared Charlotte's banishment and the terms Kurt Satterfield had in his will that neither Charlotte nor any of her offspring could inherit Satterfield land. She also explained how Kurt had ended Waylon and Victoria's engagement.

After taking another sip of tea, she resumed her story, bringing them to when Victoria and Waylon attempted to elope, Pa Jantzen's stroke, and why he made Victoria promise never to marry Waylon.

Felicia Laverne wasn't surprised when several women dabbed tears from their eyes. She then apprised them of Victoria's decision to remain in Paris after attending nursing school, and working at a hospital there. After five years, Waylon married a woman named Deedra and moved on with his life. When their uncle Quantum died, Victoria returned to the States and took a job at a hospital in Ohio. Felicia Laverne realized her sons knew that much, since they'd always looked forward to their aunt's visits.

"Then she died in a senseless robbery," Jonathan said with both anger and pain in his voice.

"Yes, but several things happened a few years before that. When her pa, Jantzen, became ill, Victoria returned home to help care for him. Before dying, he released Victoria from that promise to never marry Waylon. His wife Deedra had died of pneumonia five years earlier."

"Did Victoria and Waylon reconnect?" Justin's wife, Lorren, asked, with hopefulness in her voice.

"Yes, they began seeing each other in private."

"Why in private?" her son Lee asked. "They were both single."

"Yes," Felicia Laverne confirmed. "However, Penny Satterfield still had a grudge against the Madaris family."

"Who cared how that old woman felt?" Milton Jr. asked, frowning.

"Your aunt Victoria cared. She didn't want to do anything to upset Waylon's mother in her old age. However, Waylon was past caring."

"Good for him," Clayton said.

"Waylon wanted more than to date in secret. He wanted marriage and felt they owed that to each other."

Felicia Laverne gazed at Jake who was sitting with his wife, Diamond. "So, Jake, you and Diamond didn't have the first secret marriage in the Madaris family."

"Wait a minute," her son Nolan said, standing. "Are you saying Aunt Victoria got married without any of us knowing about it?"

She saw the shocked look on all her sons' faces. "Yes. The only people who knew were me, Milton, and Waylon's daughter, Arabella. They got married in Virginia, so Arabella could be present."

"I never saw Aunt Victoria wearing a wedding ring," her son Lucas said.

"She had one, but since their marriage was a secret, she didn't wear it in public. Waylon had a lovely gold necklace with a diamond designed for her and presented it to her as a wedding gift, to symbolize their union. She wore that necklace every day. It's the necklace Zoey is wearing."

Everyone stared at Zoey. Most had seen her wearing the necklace, but none had known its history.

"Keeping their marriage a secret worked well for them," Felicia Laverne continued. "Victoria moved into the cabin Waylon had built for her years before. Although Waylon spent more time at the cabin than he did at home, his mother never suspected a thing. They also spent a lot of time away in Virginia visiting Arabella. They decided to announce their marriage to Ms. Penny on their second anniversary."

"Wait a minute," Jonathan said, as if he'd just remembered something vital. "The night Aunt Victoria was robbed, her killer took that necklace. The police captured him after he'd pawned it."

"Yes. Milton returned the necklace to Waylon, who gave it to Arabella."

"I knew that necklace was familiar when I saw you wearing it at the family reunion," Jonathan said to Zoey.

"My grandmother Arabella wrote in her diary how honored she felt to wear it because she knew how much her father had loved Victoria," Zoey said sadly.

"Legally, Victoria Madaris was Victoria Satterfield when she died," Clayton said. "That meant Waylon Satterfield should have handled everything as her next of kin."

"True," Felicia Laverne agreed. "However, Waylon took Victoria's death extremely hard. They had been married a month shy of two years. He and Milton knew revealing their secret marriage would cause unnecessary gossip. That was the last thing Milton, as her brother, and Waylon, as her husband, wanted. They also knew it would not have been what Victoria would have wanted. So, Waylon asked Milton to handle the arrangements. However, an agreement was made between the best friends that when Waylon died, he would be buried with Victoria."

The room became silent as what she said sank in. Of course, it was Milton Jr. who asked, "Are you saying Waylon Satterfield is buried with Aunt Victoria in that tomb?"

Felicia Laverne nodded. "Yes, that's what I'm saying. He'd also told Arabella what he wanted, and when he died, the burial arrangements were made in accordance with his wishes."

"I recall going to his funeral and saw his casket lowered to the ground," her son Lee said.

"That night, your father, along with a couple of his trusted ranch hands, dug it back up, re-covered the grave, and placed Waylon's coffin where Milton had promised it would be. Right beside his wife's. Inside the tomb is a beautiful bronze plaque Arabella had made, with the words, *Waylon and Victoria Satterfield. Together forever.*"

"How touching," Sam, Blade's wife, said. "I'm glad that after all they went through, they spent at least two years happily married."

"Is that why the tomb was sealed shut?"

"Yes," Felicia Laverne answered her son Nolan. "Milton knew the secret would one day be revealed if it wasn't. He sealed it shut before he died."

Felicia Laverne paused, then said, "There is something else all of you need to know. Penny Satterfield had been carrying around hate for our family for so long, she hadn't realized what travesty it had caused Waylon. When Victoria died, that's when he told his mother that he and Victoria had been married for almost two years, noting why they had kept it from her. She saw how hard he was taking his wife's death. I understand his revelation made her feel bad because Waylon had been a good son who had taken care of her after Mr. Kurt's death. She felt worse when she learned the name of the young man who'd been arrested for killing Victoria."

"Why?" Jonathan asked. "If I recall, he wasn't from around these parts, but someone passing through. He committed suicide just days after being arrested."

"Did Penny Satterfield know the man?" Jake then asked.

"Yes," Felicia replied. "Although the name meant nothing to Waylon, Penny recognized it as the son Charlotte had from her second husband."

"What?!" Several voices said simultaneously before pandemonium broke out among her sons.

"Are you saying Aunt Victoria's death was not a random robbery but was intentional?" Jonathan asked in a steely voice.

"Yes, but we didn't discover this until months later," Felicia Laverne said. "Although Kurt Satterfield had forbidden Penny to have contact with Charlotte, she did so anyway behind his back. That's how she knew Charlotte's oldest son, the one she'd claimed was Milton's, had gotten killed in a card game at twenty-one. Her second son, I understand, was always in and out of trouble with the law and had been in jail a few times. Charlotte had corrupted his mind against the Madaris family. Doing what he thought would please his mother, he traveled to Houston, stalked Victoria, and took her life when he had the opportunity to do so."

Pandemonium broke out again, her sons all speaking at once.

"Why wasn't Charlotte arrested?"

"Why weren't we told of this?"

Felicia Laverne waited for her sons to rein in their anger before answering. "No one made the connection since the man had a different last name. Ms. Penny only confessed all this to Waylon on her deathbed almost a year later. And there was something else she confessed to Waylon at that time."

"What?" Jake asked when his other brothers seemed too upset to do so.

"When Waylon left town to visit Arabella in Virginia to give her the necklace, Penny Satterfield caught a train to Denver without letting him know she was doing so." Felicia Laverne took a sip of her tea, then added, "She confronted Charlotte about what her son had done and broke the news to her that he'd died by suicide in jail. It seems that particular son had been Charlotte's favorite, and she took the news of his death hard. I'm told she lashed out at her mother, slapped her, and blamed her for letting Kurt banish her. She further stated she was glad Waylon was hurting because of Victoria's death."

She shook her head. "Penny finally saw what a spoiled, selfish, and hateful ingrate her daughter was, unlike Waylon, who'd been a kind and loving son. Before leaving Denver, Penny took her daughter's life."

Sharp gasps sounded around the room. "She killed her daughter?" Nolan the third asked, incredulously. Like the shocked faces of the others, he found such a thing unbelievable.

"Yes. Penny confessed to putting a poisonous drug in the glass of whiskey Charlotte was drinking."

"The police didn't detect foul play?" Emerson asked.

Felicia Laverne turned to her great-grandson, a state prosecutor. Of course, he would find that question of significant importance since he firmly believed in law and order. "No. Penny returned home and told no one what she'd done or that she'd even left Houston. Charlotte's death was ruled as an overdose of liquor. When she was found, it was discovered she'd drunk not only that glass, but several bottles. She had a history of heart problems and had been warned to stop drinking, so it was ruled an overdose. Like I said, Penny didn't tell Waylon what she'd done until she was on her deathbed and apologized for being the cause of his unhappiness for so many years."

"I guess Ms. Penny took the phrase, 'I brought you into this world, and I'll take you out,' literally," Blade said, shaking his head.

"Waylon was shaken by his mother's confession and told me and Milton about it. Since Penny was gone, there was no reason to go to the police with anything. The case was already closed."

"So, how is Ravena Boyle involved in this?" Reese asked.

After releasing a deep breath, Felicia Laverne said, "Ravena is Charlotte's great-granddaughter. All you need to know right now is that Charlotte's hatred for the Madaris family was passed down from generation to generation. Ravena tried killing me for revenge since Milton married me instead of Charlotte. It was only recently Ravena discovered Zoey was also a Satterfield."

Felicia Laverne leaned back in her chair. "So, there you have it. Secrets never told. Hopefully, now we can get on with our lives and finally move on."

An hour later, Felicia Laverne called a private meeting at Jake's study with Alex and Zoey. She wasn't surprised when Chance attended as well.

"Before I let Alexander speak, dear," she told Zoey. "I want to say the reason I asked him to investigate a few things had nothing to do with me suspecting you of anything. It had to do with your aunt. Even if Paulina Pritchard disliked your mother, I found it hard to believe she would go to the extent that she did to try to keep your memory from returning. I wanted Alexander to find out all he could. In investigating her, he discovered a connection to Ravena. I'll let him take over from here and explain."

Alex leaned forward, holding everyone's attention. "According to my investigation, ten years after leaving Houston, Charlotte gave birth to a daughter who she named Wanda. By then, she'd been divorced twice, was unmarried and had fallen on hard times. When she saw she wasn't able to care for both Wanda and her two sons, she gave her two-year-old daughter to a childless older couple she'd met.

"When Wanda Hagans discovered she was adopted, at sixteen, she dropped out of school, abandoned the parents who'd raised her and set off to locate her biological mother. She found her." Alex paused before continuing. "Charlotte made it her life's mission to poison her offspring's minds against her parents, brother, and the Madaris family. When Charlotte died of what everyone assumed was an overdose of alcohol, Wanda was living in Tennessee with her boyfriend and newborn child. A daughter. Upon hearing about her mother's death, Wanda vowed to get revenge against those she felt were responsible for her mother's banishment from Houston, Texas.

"Wanda's daughter, Samantha, got pregnant at eighteen. A few years later, Samantha died of a drug overdose. Wanda raised Samantha's child, and it wasn't long before she began corrupting Samantha's daughter's mind against the Satterfields and Madarises. Samantha's daughter is Ravena Boyle."

Chance shook his head. "When we met, Ravena told me all her relatives were deceased."

"When she told you that, Wanda was very much alive and helping Ravena plan Mama Laverne's death. She only died a year ago."

He then turned to Zoey. "From my report, I discovered Wanda found out about the death of your parents, which made you the heir to the Satterfield estate. After the courts awarded custody of you to Paulina Pritchard, Wanda and her boyfriend showed up in San Francisco and threatened to petition the courts for custody of you, Zoey. Wanda told Paulina that the only way she would agree to leave you alone was if Paulina sold the Satterfield ranch and gave her the proceeds. She also told your aunt to make sure you didn't regain your memory and one day demand the money be repaid."

"That's why the deed indicated the Satterfield Ranch had been sold to a bank," Zoey said.

"Yes, that's why. So, Zoey, it seemed that the reason your aunt never shared anything about your mother's past with you and tried to keep you from regaining your memory was because she was trying to protect you. I don't want to imagine how your life might have turned out if custody had been given to Wanda."

Zoey didn't want to imagine that either. "How did you find out about Ravena and her sinister plan?"

Alex leaned back in his chair. "Ravena's ex-husband. She married him a couple of years after ending her engagement with Chance. The man provided the names of some of Ravena's closest friends he felt I should talk to. One such friend was a woman living in Atlanta named Tanya Goodman. Fearful of becoming an accessory to anything Ravena might do, she spilled her guts. She had just spoken to Ravena a few days ago, and Ravena had outlined her plans on how she intended to get rid of Mama Laverne and later get rid of you, Zoey. Catching the two of you together today gave her the perfect opportunity. She'd only discovered a couple of weeks ago that you were Waylon Satterfield's great-granddaughter."

The room got quiet, and then Felicia Laverne spoke. "As you can see, dear, although I still think your aunt could have done a better job in giving you the love you needed, at least now you know her reasons for doing some of the things she did. She might not have liked your mother very much, but I want to believe she did love you and did what she could to protect you from Wanda Hagans. For that, I'm grateful to her."

Zoey wiped the tears from her eyes. "I am grateful to her, too. I am also grateful to you, Ms. Felicia, for caring enough to want me to know the truth." She loved Ms. Felicia and felt she was everything she believed her great-grandmother Deedra would have been.

Later that night, after making love, Chance held Zoey in his arms. His great-grandmother had unloaded a lot of family secrets on them. He wouldn't lie and say finding out about the depth of Ravena's duplicity hadn't bothered him because it had.

He was about to shift in bed when Zoey suddenly jerked up and began screaming, breaking free of his hold and tossing around in bed. "Zoey, baby, it's okay. You're having a nightmare. Wake up, baby. You're with me. Wake up," he whispered soothingly. He assumed she was having nightmares of the barn burning that day, and thoughts of what could have happened if help hadn't arrived in time.

Her eyes flew open, and she threw herself into his arms and began crying in earnest. He gently stroked her back while continuing to speak soothingly to her. Moments later, when her crying had subsided, she pulled back while wiping away her tears. "I remember, Chance. I remember everything about my childhood. My mom, dad, and grandparents. I remember Sharon. I was to stay with her that day but begged Daddy to take me with him when he went to the hospital to get Mommy and my baby brother. I remember the day I saw him."

More tears fell, and she held tight to his arms as she stared into his eyes. "I remember we were on our way home, singing a happy song—my parents and I—then suddenly a truck appeared out of nowhere. I remember the crash and screaming for my daddy and mommy. Then I recall nothing else until I woke up in the hospital in excruciating pain."

He held her as she cried. He loved her so much that his heart ached at the sound of her crying. So much that he wasn't sure how he would let her leave him to return to Baltimore. With her memory returning, there was no reason for her to stay in Texas. Pushing that thought to the back of his mind, he continued to hold her as she soaked his bare chest with her tears.

"Stop crying, baby. You're breaking my heart—the one that belongs to you."

She lifted her face from his chest. "What do you mean?" she asked softly.

He took his fingertips and gently wiped away her tears. "I love you, Zoey, and when you hurt, I hurt."

She reached out and cupped his face in her hands. "I love you, too, Chance. I believe I fell in love with you that day my car broke down on the side of the road."

He leaned in and kissed her in a full-contact, passion-driven, head-reeling kiss, hungrily devouring her mouth for what it was worth. As far as he was concerned, it was worth a lot. When he finally dragged his mouth away to drop featherlight kisses over her face, he said, "Do you want to know what I've come to realize?"

He heard her moan before she replied, "Tell me what you've come to realize, Chance."

"That letting you leave me at the end of the summer will be hard."

"You got a reason for me to stay?" she asked, kissing his chin.

"I think I do. Will you marry me?"

She went still. Chance knew why. He was asking something of her he'd sworn never to ask another woman, and she knew it. Holding his gaze, she asked, "Are you sure that's what you want?"

"Yes. More than anything, I want you as my wife. Someone I can build a life with. Have babies with. Grow old with. Someone who will wear the Madaris name with honor. After all, you are Waylon Satterfield's great-granddaughter, and if nothing else, today I learned what an honorable man he was. And just like he loved his Victoria beyond the grave, I will do the same for you. Live with me on Teakwood Ridge, Satterfield land that's a part of your legacy. Together, we can make it ours the way Waylon and Victoria would have wanted. Will you marry me, Zoey?"

Chance's words had Zoey's eyes tearing up again. Unable to speak, she reached out and took Chance's hand in hers. This man. This tall, hot, and handsome man had suffered disappointments in life. She wanted to be the one to bring him happiness.

"Yes, Chance, I will marry you." The happiness that spread across his features nearly took her breath away. "You've given me the one thing I've always wanted," she said.

"What's that, sweetheart?" he asked, reaching out and softly brushing his knuckles against her cheek.

"A man who truly loves me."

"And I do, sweetheart," he said, pulling her into his arms. "I truly love you and will do so forever and always."

Epilogue

"I now pronounce you husband and wife. Chancellor, you may kiss your bride."

Chance pulled Zoey into his arms and kissed her, nearly leaving her breathless. Then, he swung her up into his arms and carried her down the aisle. The rest of the wedding party followed. All with huge smiles on their faces.

It was a beautiful day in October on the grounds of Teakwood Ridge. Several people were present, including some of Zoey's co-workers and college friends. Lucky was her matron of honor, and Sharon stood in for her mother. Lucky's father, Mr. Andres, gave her away.

Zoey knew she was marrying into a wonderful family and looked forward to living on the ranch with the man she loved. Their marriage was a continuation of the love that had begun with Waylon and Victoria. After their honeymoon in Italy, she would start work at Houston General Hospital.

She and Chance had their first dance as husband and wife, a slow dance, then they had surprised their guests by breaking into a dance they had choreographed together. It was their own version of a Texas line dance they called the Teakwood Ridge.

Before going inside to dress to leave for their honeymoon, she noticed Mama Laverne sitting by herself and decided to go to her and thank her for everything.

"Mama Laverne, I could never thank you enough for all you've done."

The older woman smiled. "Poppycock. You did it all yourself. You're a fighter and Chance is lucky to have you. We are lucky to have you in our family. Another Satterfield marries a Madaris."

Zoey slid into the chair beside her, which wasn't an easy feat in her wedding gown. "I'm going to love living here."

The older woman nodded. "You will get to do something Victoria never did. Waylon built the cabin as their home. Now you will have both."

Yes, she would. Chance had bought the cabin from Trevor Grant, and a new barn had already been built. She and Chance would use the cabin by the lake as their "getaway" place. She and Chance had gone to the tomb twice now to put more flowers there for Waylon's and Victoria's graves. They'd even traveled to Laredo to place flowers on Deedra's grave.

When she saw Chance walking toward them, she eased out of the chair, kissed Mama Laverne on her cheek, and said, "Again, thanks for everything."

"No thanks needed. It was meant for the two of you to be together. Just like it's meant for those two," she said, pointing to the two kids running around the yard playing together.

Zoey recognized the little girl with red hair as the daughter of Alex and Christy Maxwell; and the little boy as one of the triplet sons of a couple she'd met a few weeks ago—retired Colonel Ashton Sinclair and his wife, Netherland.

"I won't be alive when it happens, but mark my word that one day it will," Mama Laverne added.

Zoey smiled. There was no doubt in her mind that one day it would happen since Mama Laverne had declared it would. Walking down the steps to meet her husband, Zoey was swept into Chance's strong arms.

★ ★ ★ ★ ★